Tom Bradby has been a senior correspondent for ITN for more than a decade. As Ireland Correspondent, he covered the unfolding peace process before going on to become Political Correspondent. He then spent three years based in Hong Kong as Asia Correspondent, during which time he was shot and seriously wounded whilst covering a riot in Jakarta. After a period as Royal Correspondent he has since become the Home Affairs Editor. He is the acclaimed author of *Shadow Dancer*, *The Sleep of the Dead* and *The Master of Rain*, which was shortlisted for the Crime Writers' Association Steel Dagger for Best Thriller of the Year 2002. *The White Russian* was shortlisted for the Crime Writers' Association Ellis Peters Award for Best Historical Crime Novel of 2003.

Acclaim for

The White Russian

'Sad, atmospheric and richly entertaining, *The White Russian* is the kind of historical fiction that may send you back to the real history books to learn more' *Washington Post*

'Unfailingly evocative . . . reminiscent of *Gorky Park*' *The Times*

'This is a beautifully written novel, full of historical detail . . . A good old-fashioned mystery with a shock finale' *Scotsman*

www

'A tumbling pace, emotionally torn and credible characters ... and twists and dubious allegiances enough to leave readers wondering until the closing pages ... A chilling crime yarn and a cautionary tale about the sometimes painful exigencies of love, *The White Russian* is a literary cocktail with a decided kick' *amazon.com*

'Bradby is a quality storyteller' *Bookseller*

'An intriguing blend of detective novel, historical romance and political thriller. The plot is beautifully paced leading to a startling conclusion' *Historical Novels Review*

'A fusion between the traditional detective novel, historical novel and political thriller. Bradby has constructed a gripping and well-thought out plot full of unexpected twists with a startling conclusion. He captures the atmosphere and tension of pre-revolution St Petersburg brilliantly through the use of authentic documents and careful research ... Will delight many fans and new readers alike' *Waterstone's Books Quarterly*

'The idea of setting a murder mystery on the eve of the Russian revolution is terrific, and Bradby ably captures the urban lawlessness, food shortages, unrest and Imperial decadence that characterize the period' *Publishers Weekly*

The Master of Rain

'Tom Bradby's expert evocation of the hothouse atmosphere of Twenties Shanghai makes an exotic backdrop to a cracking murder mystery ... An immensely atmospheric, gripping detective story with just the right mixture of exoticism, violence and romance. Bradby has used his years as a foreign correspondent to imagine splendidly the opulence, corruption, debauchery, violence and mutual racism of a city that fused some of the worst of Asian and European values' *The Times*

'Rich, dark, atmospheric, this fine novel captures time and place perfectly ... it's a great crime story that ends up in a place you won't predict ... and a great love story that you desperately hope will end up in the place you predict'   Lee Child

'Bradby has done for Shanghai what Raymond Chandler did for Los Angeles – created a stylish and cool genre-fiction tapestry ... he weaves together a vivid portrait of the times and a ripping good yarn as he slowly unravels the characters' secrets ... Debauchery at its most elegant'   *TIME magazine*

'Every once in a while a book comes along that combines larger-than-life epic adventure; idiomatic, pungent historical detail and genuine storytelling panache. Tom Bradby's *The Master of Rain* is such a book. This is splendidly evocative writing. Masterly in its depiction of a beautiful, dirty and corrupt city' *amazon.co.uk*

'A gritty thriller ... The atmosphere and menace of Twenties Shanghai is brought to vivid life as the backdrop to a gripping tale'   *Daily Mail*

'Beneath the surface of this clever book, a thrilling yarn of murder and mayhem, we find a wise, richly layered and utterly convincing portrait of what was the most evil and fatally fascinating of all the modern world's cities. No one has managed to bring Shanghai so alive, in all its ghastly splendour'
Simon Winchester

'A brilliant evocation of one of the world's most fascinating cities, which uses the classic thriller genre to draw the reader into this hypnotising milieu. Bradby creates colourful three dimensional scenes which are real and meaningful ... *The Master of Rain* also works as a wonderful travelogue. It will make you yearn to go in search of the old Shanghai'   *South China Morning Post*

'Tightly controlled thriller ... His knowledge and first-hand experience reporting the Troubles give the setting and characters a gripping authenticity'
Good Housekeeping

'Remarkable first novel ... Bradby handles the tension with skill to produce a gripping tale that is at the same time a compelling argument against allowing the culture of killing to take over any cause, however just' Peter Millar, *Times Metro*

'This is the best book on the northern conflict since *Harry's Game* ... *Shadow Dancer* is an excellent read on any level. It scores heavily both as a thriller and an accurate, unblinking look at what is happening right now just a few miles up the road' *Irish Independent*

'Bradby's chilling and compelling thriller unravels the webs of intrigue that criss-cross Northern Ireland's political underworld ... riveting' *Belfast Telegraph*

'An exceptional first novel. On the surface yet another thriller about the murky world of the intelligence war in Northern Ireland, it is also a compelling, incestuous story of love and torn loyalty in a community and family ravaged by hate and betrayal. There are no cardboard cut-outs here. Tom Bradby succeeds in creating real characters. Far too many novels on this subject take refuge in cliché and caricature – Bradby refuses to. Detail is piled on detail until you find yourself immersed in the Republican ghetto of West Belfast ... The book's accuracy makes it stand out from almost any other that I have read on the subject. The language, the tension, the funerals, the fear – all are portrayed vividly and correctly'
Sean O'Callaghan, *Daily Telegraph*

Also by Tom Bradby

SHADOW DANCER
THE SLEEP OF THE DEAD
THE MASTER OF RAIN

and published by Corgi Books

THE WHITE RUSSIAN

Tom Bradby

CORGI BOOKS

THE WHITE RUSSIAN
A CORGI BOOK: 0 552 14900 4

Originally published in Great Britain by Bantam Press,
a division of Transworld Publishers

PRINTING HISTORY
Bantam Press edition published 2003
Corgi edition published 2004

1 3 5 7 9 10 8 6 4 2

Set in 10/12pt Palatino by
Falcon Oast Graphic Art Ltd.

Corgi Books are published by Transworld Publishers,
61–63 Uxbridge Road, London W5 5SA,
a division of The Random House Group Ltd,
in Australia by Random House Australia (Pty) Ltd,
20 Alfred Street, Milsons Point, Sydney, NSW 2061, Australia,
in New Zealand by Random House New Zealand Ltd,
18 Poland Road, Glenfield, Auckland 10, New Zealand
and in South Africa by Random House (Pty) Ltd,
Endulini, 5a Jubilee Road, Parktown 2193, South Africa.

Printed and bound in Great Britain by
Cox & Wyman Ltd, Reading, Berkshire.

Papers used by Transworld Publishers are natural, recyclable
products made from wood grown in sustainable forests. The
manufacturing processes conform to the environmental
regulations of the country of origin.

For Claudia, Jack, Louisa and Sam.
And Mum and Dad.

ACKNOWLEDGEMENTS

Thanks to Constantine Beloroutchev, for conducting key research in St Petersburg, Moscow and Yalta, for showing me around and advising me on all matters pertaining to the history of the period, Russian culture and language (all mistakes are mine not his); to my mother, Sally Bradby, for assistance with historical research in the UK; to my editorial team, Bill Scott-Kerr and Jason Kaufman, for their support, endless encouragement and clever insights; to Mark Lucas, for being the greatest agent known to man; and to my inspirational wife, Claudia, for more reasons than there would be space to list.

ST PETERSBURG (PETROGRAD), 1 JANUARY 1917

Vengeance is mine,
And I will repay.

From *Anna Karenina*

CHAPTER ONE

The arctic wind sliced through Ruzsky's thin woollen overcoat. His boots were damp and his toes numb with cold, but he was oblivious to everything except the frozen expanse that lay before him. All he could see was ice.

He tried to place a foot upon it, then shifted his weight back to the steps that led down from the road. He looked down at his boots, but his vision was blurred. He fought to control his breathing. 'Christ,' he whispered to himself. His first day back and it would have to begin like this.

The constables were ahead of him, in the centre of the frozen river Neva, illuminated by a ring of torches. The snowfall had tapered off through the night and the sky was now clear. The narrow spire of the St Peter and St Paul cathedral on the far side of the river was bathed in moonlight.

There was a flurry of movement, and a burly figure broke away from the group, the flame of his torch dancing as he walked. Ruzsky watched his partner stride towards him.

'Are you waiting for an escort?' Pavel Miliutin

halted in front of him, one hand thrust deep into his pocket. Snow crystals were lodged in his beard and along his drooping moustache.

'No.'

'Is it the ice?' They'd had to deal with a body on the ice once before, years ago, on a small lake outside the city.

Ruzsky cleared his throat. 'No,' he lied.

'It's January. The river's been frozen for months. If anyone was going to fall through, it would have been me.' Pavel had a round face that exuded warmth even when he was frowning. He was right, of course.

'Oh, shit,' Ruzsky muttered. He closed his eyes and stepped forward, trying to ignore the jolt of fear as his foot crunched on the frozen surface.

'The city's bravest investigator afraid of the ice,' Pavel said. 'Who would believe it?'

Ruzsky opened his eyes. They were walking forward briskly and he was breathing more easily.

'I didn't mean that,' Pavel said.

'I know.'

'I don't blame you, my old friend. You've barely been back twelve hours and look what the damned ice has delivered up to us.' Pavel nodded in the direction of the Winter Palace. 'And here, of all places.'

They walked with their heads bowed against the damp, bitter wind that whistled in from the Gulf of Finland. It was several degrees colder out here on the river. Ruzsky thrust his hands deep into his pockets. Only his head, beneath one of his father's old sheepskin hats, was warm.

The constables stood smoking next to the bodies. They were dressed in long greatcoats and black sheepskin hats, the uniform of St Petersburg's city police.

16

The woman was closest to Palace Embankment and lay on her back, her long dark hair spread out around her head like a fan. 'Torch.' Ruzsky held up his hand.

One of the men marched forward. He couldn't have been older than seventeen or eighteen, with a pronounced nose, narrow eyes and a nervous expression. He was lucky not to be fighting at the front, Ruzsky thought, as he took the torch and bent over the woman's body. He sank to his knees.

The victim was – or had been – pretty, though with poor skin. He removed one of his gloves and put his hand against her cheek. Her skin was frozen solid. Her face was almost peaceful as she stared up at the night sky. The fatal wound was to her chest, probably to her heart; he could see that she had lost a good deal of blood. He tried to ascertain where she'd been stabbed, but her clothes were rigid and he decided to leave any further investigation to Sarlov.

Ruzsky's hand was already numb, so he put it back into his glove and thrust it into his pocket. He got up, looking at the gap between the two bodies. The area around them had been well trodden by the constables, so he couldn't determine a pattern of events from the footprints. 'Don't they teach them anything these days?' he grumbled, gesturing with the torch at the trampled snow.

'It's good to have you back.' Pavel offered him a flask.

Ruzsky shook his head. He walked round to the other body, the spitting of the torch's flame and the crackle of his boots in the snow the only sounds above the whistle of the wind.

The man lay face down, surrounded by a sea of crimson. He had bled like a fountain.

17

'Turn him over,' Ruzsky said. Two of the constables moved forward and heaved the body on to its back.

Ruzsky breathed out.

'Holy Mother of God,' Pavel said.

There were stab wounds to the man's chest, neck and face, one through his nose, and another peeling back his cheek.

'Who were they?' Ruzsky asked.

'I don't know.'

'Have you checked their pockets?'

'Of course. Nothing, except this.' Pavel handed over a roll of banknotes – small-denomination Russian roubles.

'That's it? No identity papers?'

'Nothing.'

'Cards? Letters?'

'There's nothing.'

'Have you looked properly?'

'Of course I have.'

Ruzsky bent down and pulled back the man's over-coat. He thrust a gloved hand into the inside pocket. It was empty. He straightened again and shoved the roll of roubles into his own coat. 'The girl?'

'Same.'

'Any sign of a knife?'

'No.'

'How far have you looked?'

'We were waiting,' Pavel said slowly, 'for you.'

The constables were moving about again. 'Stay where you are,' Ruzsky instructed them. He went back to the girl. She was young, probably no more than twenty; well dressed, too. They both were. It was difficult to be sure, but he didn't think she had been stabbed more than once. He looked across

18

at the other body. They were about seven yards apart.

'You've checked *all* of their pockets?'

'Twice.'

'We'll have another look when we get them inside,' Ruzsky said, mostly to himself. He didn't want to take off his gloves again.

He looked up towards the Admiralty spire above Palace Embankment, and the golden dome of St Isaac's cathedral in the distance. They were in full view of the austere blue and white façade of the Tsar's Winter Palace, but at a distance of fifty yards or more. Pavel followed his gaze.

'Perhaps a servant saw something,' Ruzsky said.

'Not if they were killed in the middle of the night.'

'We should make it our first port of call.'

'Of course. We'll get the Emperor out of bed.'

Ruzsky didn't smile. They both knew the Tsar hadn't spent a night in the Winter Palace for years – not since the start of the war, at any rate.

Ruzsky raised the torch higher. 'Tell them not to move, Pavel.' He walked slowly and carefully until he found the footsteps he was looking for, implanted in the thin layer of snow that covered the ice. He examined them, then returned to the bodies to check the size and shape of the victims' shoes.

Once he was away from the mêlée around the murder scene, he found the trail easily enough. The couple had been walking close together, perhaps arm in arm. He followed their footprints for about twenty yards, then stopped, turned and looked back at the scene of the crime. Pavel and the constables were watching him.

He swung around ninety degrees, held the wooden oil-flame torch in front of him and walked in a wide circle around the bodies, watching his boots make imprints in the fresh snow. He expected to encounter another set of footprints – or several – left by the killer, but there was only virgin snow.

Ruzsky returned to the original path and got down on his knees again. He looked at the tracks, moving the torch closer to the ground so that it hissed next to his ear. He raised his hand.

Pavel was marching out to meet him. 'You search like a hunter,' Pavel said.

'I used to track wolves with my grandfather.' He was struggling to throw off the vestiges of a hangover.

'It's New Year,' Pavel went on, 'the couple are lovers out for a romantic stroll.'

'Perhaps.'

'Just the two of them, alone. They leave Palace Embankment, walking close together, arm in arm. They turn towards the Strelka, then gaze up at the stars above. The city has never looked more beautiful. Some bootlegged vodka, perhaps, all troubles forgotten.'

Ruzsky was now absorbed in his task, the fragility of the ice only a dim anxiety at the back of his mind, the biting cold a dull ache in his hands, feet and cheeks.

He began to trace the victims' path backwards once more, ignoring Pavel, who followed him in silence. It was not until they had almost reached the embankment that Ruzsky found what he was looking for.

The killer had followed the tracks of the dead man, both before and after he'd struck. Only at the very last moment, barely three yards from the embankment, had he lost patience and stepped outside them.

Ruzsky reached into his pocket, took out a cigarette

case and offered it to his colleague. He felt more confident within reach of the steps.

They lit up – no easy task with gloved hands numbed by cold – and turned their backs against the wind. The smoke was pleasantly warm, but Ruzsky could feel his temperature still dropping.

'They must have been lovers,' Pavel said. 'Their footsteps are close.'

'Why didn't the girl run?' Ruzsky asked.

'What do you mean?'

'How many times has the man been stabbed? Ten? Twenty? In his chest, his heart, his nose, his cheek. Does the girl just stand there watching?'

'Perhaps she knows her attacker.'

Ruzsky stared out across the river.

'It was planned. She knew of it.'

'Possibly.' Ruzsky turned to his colleague. 'But why did she have no idea that she was also to be a victim?'

Pavel shook his head. He flicked his cigarette high into the air and they heard it fizzle as it hit the ice.

Ruzsky gazed at a cloud passing across the face of the moon. A photographer walked over from the St Peter and St Paul fortress. They watched as he prepared his camera and lined up the first shot. He bent down, his head beneath a cloth and they saw a light flash. The noise – a dull thump – reached them a split second later.

'Were there any witnesses?' Ruzsky asked.

'Do you see any?'

'We should begin at the palace.'

Pavel's expression told him that he did not wish to go anywhere near it. 'So I'm taking orders again?'

Ruzsky looked up sharply, embarrassed. 'Of course not. I'm sorry.'

Pavel smiled. 'Better things return to the way they were. Welcome back, Chief Investigator.'

Ruzsky met his affectionate gaze and tried to smile back, but his frozen face wouldn't obey. He reached into the pocket of his greatcoat for a notepad and pencil, then handed Pavel the torch and bent down. Shakily he traced the outline of one of the footprints the killer had left in front of the steps, then put his own boot alongside it. 'About my size. A little bigger.'

'Why didn't he go over to the Strelka?'

'Who?'

'The killer.' Pavel gestured at the Winter Palace. 'There are guards here, the road is busy. Much less chance of being seen if he'd gone on to Vasilevsky Island.'

Ruzsky did not answer. He was staring at the group out on the ice, deep in thought.

'Oh, by the way,' Pavel added, 'New year, new happiness.'

It was the traditional New Year's Day greeting. 'Yes,' Ruzsky answered. 'Quite.'

CHAPTER TWO

They climbed on to the embankment and approached the riverside entrance of the Tsar's Winter Palace.

Ruzsky stepped forward to knock on the giant green door. There was no answer, so he tried to look through the misted window to his right. He climbed up on a stone ledge for a better view.

'Be careful or they'll shoot you,' Pavel said.

A light was dimly visible in the hallway. There was little obvious security, but it was well known that the Tsar and his family preferred their country palace outside the city at Tsarskoe Selo.

Ruzsky stepped forward and knocked again. He glanced up at the light suspended on a long iron chain above him. As it swayed in the icy wind, its metal links creaked.

'This cannot be right,' Pavel said.

'If anyone saw anything, it will have been the guard.'

Pavel hesitated. 'Let's go round to the office of the palace police at the front.'

'Then we'll never find out who was on duty back here.'

They waited, listening to the wind. Pavel forced his hat down on his head. 'Maybe it's colder than Tobolsk.'

Ruzsky saw the guilt behind his uncertain smile. 'It's the damp here,' he said. 'You know how it is. In Siberia, it's a dry cold.' He wanted to assuage his friend's guilt, but did not know what else he could say. Pavel had been responsible for his exile, but Ruzsky did not hold it against him – in fact, far from it.

Just over three years ago, in the darkened, piss-stained stairwell of a tenement building in Sennaya Ploschad, they had arrested a small-time landlord who'd assaulted and strangled the ten-year-old daughter of one of his poorer tenants. The man had not imagined the terrified mother would dare complain, but his insouciance, as they led him down to the cells in the city police headquarters, should have set their alarm bells ringing. Throughout that night, both Ruzsky and Pavel had struggled to keep their temper as the fat, sweaty toad had drummed his pudgy fingers on the table and answered all questions with a contemptuous insolence.

Pavel had always taken these crimes hard, and while Ruzsky was upstairs dealing with another matter, he'd decided to put the man into a cell with a group of armed robbers. He'd informed the men of the nature of their new companion's crime.

Ruzsky had no moral objection to this solution, but it had resulted in the world falling on their heads. The man turned out to have been the foreman of an arms factory over in Vyborg and an agent of the Okhrana, the Tsar's vicious secret police. Within a few hours of his lifeless body being dragged from the cell, the city police headquarters had been swarming with hard-faced Okhrana men in long black overcoats.

Pavel tried to take responsibility, but Ruzsky had overruled him. It had been his own idea, he told the secret police chief, Igor Vasilyev, and his thugs. His punishment had been banishment to Siberia as the chief investigator of the Tobolsk police department.

Ruzsky tried to return his friend's smile. They both knew that Pavel would have fared much worse. Ruzsky might be the black sheep of his distinguished, aristocratic family, but the Ruzsky name and the fact that his father was a government minister still carried weight. It had limited the scale of punishment – back then, at least.

Ruzsky heard a bolt pulled back and the door swung open. Three men in the distinctive uniforms of the Yellow Cuirassiers emerged from the darkness. The eldest – a sergeant – had white hair and a moustache like Pavel's. His two young companions held their rifles firmly in both hands. In the grand hallway behind them, Ruzsky could just make out the tip of a chandelier.

'City police,' Ruzsky said. He wasn't in the mood to offer felicitations for the dawning of a new year.

'You should have come to the other side.'

'There have been two murders on the ice.'

The sergeant walked forward, followed by his companions. They stood in a small group looking out towards the torches in the middle of the river. 'Yesterday it was a drunk,' he said, pointing at the deserted road in front of him. 'Froze to death just here.'

'I fear this is a little different. The victims were stabbed—'

'A week ago, someone was stabbed in front of the Admiralty.'

'A domestic dispute,' Pavel corrected him. 'Two brothers. Both still alive.'

'Have you been on duty all night?' Ruzsky asked.

'Of course.'

'You're on detachment?'

The Yellow Cuirassiers – officially His Majesty's Life Guard Cuirassier Regiment – were based out at Tsarskoe Selo, in the small town that surrounded the royal palaces there. It was about an hour's train ride from the capital.

The sergeant did not answer.

'There are other guards?' Ruzsky went on.

The man shrugged. 'On Palace Square. They don't move unless we call for them.'

Ruzsky looked down the embankment towards the Hermitage. 'There is no one out here?'

'A sentry at either end until midnight. After that, it is not necessary. The shutters on the ground and first floors are closed. We would hear any commotion.' He was defensive.

'There are no patrols?'

The sergeant flushed. Ruzsky didn't wish to press the point: it had been New Year's Eve, after all. 'What time did you and your men come on duty?'

'If you wish to ask questions, you will have to apply to the head of the guard detachment or the office of the palace police.'

'Come on,' Pavel said softly, before Ruzsky could get annoyed. 'A couple of lovers have been sliced up out there. We just want to make sure no one saw anything, then be on our way.'

The man's face softened. He breathed out.

'Cigarette?' Pavel asked, taking out a tiny tin case and offering it round the group.

The men hesitated – smoking on duty was strictly forbidden – then each took one in turn. They lit up and smoked in silence, suddenly conspiratorial.

The sergeant looked out at the constables guarding the bodies on the ice. It was marginally less cold here, in the shelter of the giant porch. 'We came on duty at midnight. I did my last rounds about an hour later. I walked along the embankment to check for drunks, then locked the door.'

'You stand here, inside the hallway?'

'We check the rooms periodically but, as I said, all the shutters are locked, except those by the door.'

'You didn't see or hear anything?'

The sergeant shook his head and so did his young companions. Ruzsky could see they were telling the truth. He suspected they'd been playing cards as the new year dawned. That, and the fact they had accepted a cigarette while on duty, was a sign of the times, he thought. He wondered if they had seen action at the front. The sergeant, certainly. The others looked too young.

'When you came out at one o'clock, you didn't see anyone at all?'

'There was a group further down, by the Admiralty. I think they'd just crossed the river, but they were going home. It was quiet after that. If we'd heard any-one else, we'd have moved them on. We don't allow people to linger.'

'Could anyone have seen something from one of the upstairs windows? A servant?'

'These are all state rooms at the front. There are family bedrooms on the top floor, but none are

27

occupied.' The sergeant gestured towards the group on the ice. 'It's quite far out.'

'But extremely visible on a clear night.'

'Yes.' He looked apologetic. 'You can talk to the head of the household later. He could tell you whether there might have been anyone in the front rooms, but I'm afraid I cannot help you.'

The sergeant turned and retreated, taking the younger men with him. The door shut with a loud bang and silence descended once more, save for the iron chain above them that still creaked in the icy wind. An ambulance had parked on the Strelka and two men were carrying out a stretcher to retrieve the bodies.

'It's a strange place for a murder,' Pavel said, 'at this time.'

Ruzsky glanced over his shoulder. Here, they were only a few minutes from his parents' home, and he thought of his son Michael sleeping, curled up with his teddy bear pressed to his nose. 'We'd better start looking for the knife,' he said.

He returned to the edge of the ice. As he reached the bottom of the steps, he heard the sound of a car door being shut and turned to see two men in fedoras getting out of a large black automobile further down the embankment. The men leant over the wall and surveyed the scene on the ice.

'The Okhrana?' Ruzsky asked quietly.

It was only half a question. They both knew perfectly well that these were Vasilyev's men. The change in Pavel's demeanour was almost palpable.

'What are they doing here?' Ruzsky asked.

Pavel did not answer. He was staring at them, trying to conceal his unease.

The two men sauntered back to their automobile and got in. The car returned the way it had come. Ruzsky and Pavel watched as it disappeared down the embankment before turning left over the bridge in the direction of the St Peter and St Paul fortress.

CHAPTER THREE

Ruzsky didn't want to go back on to the ice so he told Pavel to instruct the constables, then stood on the embankment and watched as they searched across the river. It was a huge area and they moved quickly, reminding him of a pack of hunting dogs eager to pick up a trail. Maybe they just wanted to get home. The wind had dropped a little, but it was still bitterly cold. The dim light gave the appearance of fog and Ruzsky could now only just make out the spire of the cathedral on the other side of the river. It wasn't going to make their search any easier.

It was still early, but they were not alone on the ice: two constables from the marine police had begun working the section of the river around the Strelka. As Ruzsky watched, one probed gently with his foot, then took a pole with a red flag from his colleague and stuck it into the ice.

The pair appeared oblivious of the murder investigation going on around them. They were looking for hazards, patches of black water, where a thin covering of ice concealed a pocket of five or six feet of water and a thicker layer of ice underneath.

Pavel was marching back towards him. Ruzsky wondered why none of the constables had bothered to tell the marine policemen to be on the lookout for a murder weapon.

'Not helping with the search, Deputy Chief Investigator?' Ruzsky asked Pavel, as he climbed the steps towards him.

'They'll never find anything.' Pavel glanced at him. 'You look terrible, by the way.'

Ruzsky did not respond. Pavel had picked him up from the station on his return last night and they had demolished a bottle of bootlegged vodka in the dingy room Pavel had rented for him. They stood together, their breath billowing out into the morning air. Pavel coughed.

The bodies had been removed by the ambulance, but as he watched the constables scanning the ice, Ruzsky had a clear vision of the dead girl's face. He could picture her laughing, her head resting on her companion's shoulder as they stared up at the stars and the cold beauty of the city around them. The dawn of another year. Had they been wondering what it would bring? How could they not?

Ruzsky heard movement and turned to see a servant brushing snow from the porch of the Winter Palace behind them. He was a tall Tartar in the distinctive cinnamon-coloured coat of rough cloth and cap trimmed in silver braid worn by the most menial palace staff. He, too, stopped what he was doing to watch the dark figures on the ice.

'You must be excited about seeing your boy,' Pavel said.

Ruzsky frowned. His wife Irina had left him in Tobolsk six months ago and returned to the capital with their son. Pavel knew the bare facts but, so far, Ruzsky had avoided all but the most cursory discussion of the subject. 'She won't allow me to see him,' he said.

'She won't allow it?'

Ruzsky could see that Pavel also blamed himself for the state of his marriage, but the surprise was not that Irina had left him but that she had agreed to go to Siberia in the first place and had stuck it out for two and a half years. It had been a last attempt to make the marriage work and for a few months it had looked as if it might succeed.

'Irina has gone to stay with my father,' Ruzsky explained. 'She's sheltering behind them.' With a talent for deliberate provocation, which he now recognized as one of her most striking attributes, Irina had upon her return to Petersburg – or Petrograd as it had been renamed at the start of the war – gone to live with his father rather than her own parents. The old man doted on his grandson and would deny him nothing.

'He's your son, Sandro. Just demand it,' Pavel told him.

He seemed about to go on, so Ruzsky forestalled him, wishing to change the subject. 'When you think about it—'

'I'm not paid to think any more,' Pavel interrupted.

'No, but seriously—'

'I am serious. It doesn't do any good.'

'I can't understand those last three paces. He doesn't come back and make any attempt to conceal them, and they're clearly visible even to the most ignorant detective.'

'It shows you what people expect.'

Ruzsky stared at the steps in front of him. He wondered what the man had done to encourage such brutality in his assailant. 'Who found the bodies?' he asked.

'An old woman walking home.'

'Did you speak to her?'

'Of course. She didn't see anything.'

'What time did the constables call you out?' Ruzsky asked.

'I don't know how you stand it, Sandro,' Pavel went on. 'I wouldn't manage a month without seeing my boy. Why did she leave?'

Ruzsky watched one of the constables talking to a marine policeman. His wife had detested their stifling provincial life in Tobolsk, from the exaggerated respect afforded the governor, a petty tyrant from Petersburg, to the crumbling homes and small-town attitudes of the local gentry. He didn't blame her. Not for that. 'A disintegrating marriage is not attractive,' he said quietly, reflecting upon the arguments that had raged in the tiny house at the end of the dusty street. He took a pace forward and surveyed the river once more. 'Is there anywhere else from where someone might have witnessed the murder?' he asked. The wide expanse of ice answered his question.

The constables were working their way back towards the embankment.

'Well, we survived another night without a revolution,' he said, turning towards his deputy. It was a teasing reference to Pavel's vodka-induced doom and gloom the night before.

'I told you what is said in the *khvost*.'

The *khvost* was a phenomenon talked about even in faraway Tobolsk, but you had to see the lines of people snaking round windy street corners to believe it. The poor had to queue for anything and everything, these days: food, oil for their lamps, clothes. They joined lines even when no one knew what lay at the front; it was bound to be something in short supply.

'What you don't understand,' Pavel went on, 'because you have not been here, is that people don't read newspapers any more. No one believes what little slips past the censors. They treat what is said in the *khvost* as news, not rumour. They believe it.'

'Maybe the war will be over soon.'

'Maybe I'll become the Tsar.' Pavel leant forward earnestly. 'The word in the *khvost* – and it has been so for months – is *treason*.'

'That's not new.'

'One of our neighbours was in a line last night for bread. She told Tonya it was a four-hour wait. One woman said she'd heard from a cousin in the Life Guards that the Imperial Family had already left for England. Another said China had invaded. The day before, the *khvost* talk was that the Empress had agreed to be paid by the Germans to starve the peasants to death. Last week it was said she had promised to sell the western half of Russia to Berlin. And the things that have been said about the Empress and Rasputin . . .'

'Perhaps things will improve now that the priest's no longer with us,' Ruzsky said. They'd talked about Rasputin's murder last night. The case had been taken over by the Okhrana.

'No. And it was too late, anyway. Do you know where the biggest *khvost* is? There's a new railway-ticket bureau since you left, in Michael Street. Now that so few trains run, the line there is five deep. Thousands are leaving – to the Crimea or the Caucasus, or Haparanda.' Haparanda was just over the border, in Sweden. 'And here's another thing,' Pavel was getting into his stride, 'who would defend them? Tell me that. Who would fight to save the Romanovs?'

They'd had this discussion last night too. 'The same people who always have.'

Pavel shook his head violently. 'The blue bloods are not here. They're at the front. Dead. You have seen it yourself – the capital is full of reservists, the wounded, deserters.'

'There's one lot who would defend him,' Ruzsky said, pointing at a group of dark figures who had left the Strelka and were walking towards the Winter Palace. They were dressed in black and the man at the centre carried a picture of the Tsar mounted on a wooden pole. They were singing the national anthem '*Bozhe, Tzaria Khrani*' – 'God Save the Tsar' – in loud, tuneless voices. 'Another night of Jew-baiting,' Ruzsky muttered, as he and Pavel watched their approach. The Black Bands were gangs of street thugs funded by the secret police to attack opponents of the Tsar. Mostly they spent their time organizing pogroms against the Jews.

The men mounted the steps, still singing. The figure carrying the portrait was a young man with a fleshy face flushed red from alcohol and exertion, and a thin, pencil moustache. In his left hand, Ruzsky could see a knuckle-duster. The man stopped. 'New year, new happiness,' he said.

Neither Ruzsky nor Pavel answered.

'God save the Tsar!'

This was what all of these gangs did: demanded a show of loyalty as an excuse to beat anyone who wouldn't offer it. 'Go away,' Ruzsky said.

The man took a pace forward, his face livid.

'We're police officers,' Pavel added. 'There's been a murder. Move on, please.'

Pavel's tone had been more conciliatory, but the leader of the group brushed him aside. 'If you're police officers, you should want to show your loyalty to the Tsar.'

'Go away, before I arrest you,' Ruzsky snapped.

'You? Arrest us?' The man did not move and, for a moment, he looked as if he would strike them. Ruzsky felt the weight of the Sauvage revolver in his pocket. As it had been often before his exile, the temptation to cut such scum down to size was overwhelming.

There was a shout from the river. Close to the embankment – about fifty feet away – a constable was holding something above his head.

Ruzsky and Pavel pushed past the thugs and strode out on to the ice. Behind them, the men of the Black Bands began to sing 'God Save the Tsar' again.

'I've found it, sir!' the constable shouted, as they approached him. He offered Ruzsky the knife.

'Christ,' Pavel whispered.

It was an old, crude black dagger. Ruzsky held it up so that he could see the twisted iron handle more clearly. There was an inscription at the base of the blade, partly obscured by dried blood. It looked like Sanskrit, or Arabic. He turned it over in his hand, then passed it to Pavel. He faced the embankment. The thugs had disappeared, the sound of their singing now just a faint echo across the river. 'Why would he do that?' Ruzsky asked.

'Do what?'

'He follows them so carefully out here, then throws away the murder weapon.'

'He must have been wearing gloves. There won't be any fingerprints.'

'It's still careless. Why throw it away?'

'Panic.'

'He wasn't panicking when he retraced his steps, going backwards.'

Pavel returned the knife to the constable. 'Take it straight to the office and give it to Veresov. If he's not in his room, telephone him at home and say the chief investigator would like his help and he is to come in immediately.'

The constable ran off in the direction of the palace. They watched him go. 'In its way, it's all a bit theatrical, isn't it?' Pavel said, gesturing towards the patch of blood in the centre of the ice. 'Following in the footsteps and so on.'

'If you can call being stabbed a dozen times theatrical.' Ruzsky turned to his partner. 'It's certainly not straightforward, I'll grant you that.'

CHAPTER FOUR

Pavel was hungry, so Ruzsky agreed to go to a café for breakfast. The route to their favourite haunt took them round the front of the Winter Palace, past the Hermitage and into Millionaya Street, where the wind, funnelled down from Palace Square, had swept deep drifts against the walls of the houses. Outside the barracks of the first battalion of the Preobrazhensky Guards – Ruzsky's father's regiment – a sentry stamped his feet.

As they walked down Millionaya Street, they heard a muffled shout and turned to see a detachment of the Imperial Guard cavalry entering the street behind them, the horses' hoofs clattering on the treacherous cobblestones, their breath hanging on the cold air.

Ruzsky and Pavel waited as they passed. The men were from the élite Chevalier-Guard Regiment, mounted on their distinctive chestnut mares. They were in full parade uniform, the soldiers' white and red jackets visible beneath long blue overcoats, their swords clanking beside them, the scabbards bright in the moonlight. The officer wore a cape over his blue and red jacket, fastened at the throat with a gold buckle. All of the men had upon their heads the curved brass helmet of the guard, with the large Imperial eagle at its peak.

There were no shouts or barked commands: they were trying to avoid waking the aristocratic residents of one of the city's wealthiest districts. As they reached a stretch of the street that was covered in snow, their progress was suddenly silent.

Half-way down, Ruzsky stopped outside a house with a delicately sculpted, soft yellow façade. The shutters were closed. This had always been his family's home in the city. He'd been born here. So had both his brothers. Pavel stood behind him and Ruzsky found it hard to move on. In the cold dawn light, a sense of overpowering loneliness settled on him.

He thought of Michael in his room in the attic and wondered which of his own toys were still on the shelves above the small bed.

Pavel waited patiently. 'They'll still be asleep,' he said quietly.

Ruzsky forced himself to walk on. As they emerged from the far end of the street on to the Field of Mars, past the Pavlovsky Guards barracks, he felt like a champagne cork escaping from the neck of a bottle. Just to be in the street was to feel the pressure of his own history.

The Field of Mars was a sandy expanse designed for military training, now shrouded in a thick layer of snow. The detachment of cavalry cantered around it, turning and wheeling, exercising as a unit, still quiet but for the snorts of the horses, the clank of metal and the occasional barked command.

Pavel and Ruzsky walked round the square, past the giant yellow-stone palaces that faced on to it. All the windows were dark. Outside one a private sled-driver stood next to his horse, banging his hands together. Just in front, beneath a gas lamp, another servant waited for a small, dirty-white Pekinese to do its business. Neither man acknowledged them as they passed.

As they went on towards the Summer Garden, Ruzsky's heart lurched when he saw a tall man striding in their direction, trailing behind a big brown hunting dog. The man's purposeful gait and the type of hound – big dogs were unusual in Petersburg houses – made him think for a few seconds that it must be his father and the realization, as they came closer, that it wasn't brought both relief and disappointment.

The café was on the ground floor of a large tenement block on the other side of the Moyka canal. Pavel ate bread. Ruzsky sobered himself up fully with Turkish coffee and cigarettes. Their drinking had gone on into the early hours and the alcohol was still circulating in his bloodstream. His feet were sore and damp, and he regained feeling in his toes only gradually.

The café was run by a short, swarthy Ukrainian from the Crimea and was full even at this time in the morning, the air thick with steam, body heat and cigarette smoke. A small group of the abjectly poor milled around outside, glancing in at the warmth and the food, their faces gradually obscured by the mist gathering on the windows.

The black Romanov eagle was etched in the centre of the panes at either side of the door, and there was a line drawing of the royal palace in Yalta on the wall above Pavel's head. The owner's father had been a member of the Imperial Household at the Tsar's summer home in the Crimea, and the son remained fanatically loyal not only to the Tsar and his family but to the principles of autocracy. But his food was good and, more importantly, cheap.

Sitting there that morning, Ruzsky felt as though he had never been away. Had he been inclined by nature to self-pity, the scene would almost have been poignant: the last time he had been here, before his fall from grace three years ago, he had felt happier than at any point since the early days of his childhood.

It had been mostly because of her. Instinctively Ruzsky touched the letter in his jacket pocket. Like Michael, Maria would still be sleeping.

'It hasn't changed,' Pavel said, as Ruzsky looked around him.

'Clientele still as shabby as ever.'

'It's no place for a prince,' Pavel went on, stretching. 'Dear me, no.'

Ruzsky smiled too. It had been a long-standing joke between them. The Ruzskys drew a continuous line of service and loyalty to Tsar and empire stretching back more than a hundred and fifty years to the reign of Peter the Great. The eldest son always served in the empire's most prestigious infantry regiment, the Preobrazhensky Guards. Ruzsky's decision to shun the Guards and, as a result of a childhood passion for Sherlock Holmes, enter the service of the St Petersburg police department – as lowly an occupation for a man of high birth as it was possible to imagine – had provoked a final severance of any connection with his father.

Ruzsky looked at Pavel. With his drooping

41

moustache and lugubrious expression, he seemed to have aged dramatically these past three years. He made a sudden decision and stood up. 'I'll see you back in the office.'

'Where are you going?'

'I won't be long. Make sure Sarlov is in.'

In the street, Ruzsky walked at first but then gathered speed, so that by the time he reached Millionaya Ulitsa he was running. His father's home was one of the most beautiful on the street. It was four storeys high, not including the attic or the basement. To the left of the steps leading up to the doorway was the yard in which the family's transportation was kept. Ruzsky watched a servant oiling the runners of one of his father's up-ended sleds, with its distinctive green and gold livery.

He climbed the steps and knocked. The door was opened, but not by Ivan.

Ruzsky stared at the young man before him. He was tall and thin, handsome but for his pimples, with wavy dark hair curling over his collar.

'Can I help you, sir?'

It took Ruzsky a few moments to get over the shock of not being recognized in his own home. 'Where's Ivan?'

'He is not here. And you are?'

'The son of the house,' Ruzsky said, as he walked forward into the hallway. He stopped, realized his manner had been churlish, and offered his hand. 'I apologize, I'm Sandro.'

'Master Sandro, sir, yes.' The young man's hand-shake was firm. 'I'm Peter. I believe your father is out.'

'I'm here to see my son.'

'Yes, sir. Would you like me to find him?'

Ruzsky forced himself to smile. 'I will be all right, thank you.'

'Of course. New year, new happiness.'

'And the same to you.'

The young man shut the door and withdrew discreetly down the wooden stairs towards the kitchen in the basement.

Ruzsky stood for a moment in the semi-darkness of the hallway. He had been holding his breath.

He shoved his hands into the pockets of his coat and exhaled slowly. Ahead of him was a fir tree, decorated for Christmas. He took a pace closer and touched one of the round pink and white ginger-breads his mother had always instructed the servants to bake. The decorations were the ones she had bought at Peto's all those years ago: tiny sedan chairs, violins, bears, monkeys and thin candles in tin candle-sticks. Ruzsky imagined Michael helping his grandfather and the servants to decorate the tree. He thought of the excitement that would have lit his son's face. He'd heard that Christmas trees had been banned as too Germanic, but the rule clearly did not apply to such high servants of the Tsar.

The hall was wide, leading on to the formal rooms to his right and left. His father's study and the winter room were at the back, before the stairs leading down to the kitchen. The hall was dominated on one side by a giant gilt-edged mirror above an ornate chestnut dresser, and on the other by a dark tapestry hanging from a long metal pole. There was an iron coat-stand in the corner. Beside it, on top of a wooden pillar, was a bust of Ruzsky's grandfather. In the style of Roman emperors, his brother Dmitri had always said, and with similar pretensions to grandeur.

Next to it was a portrait of their mother, a cold smile playing at the corners of her mouth. Ruzsky stared at it for a moment. The memory it triggered was of the scene in this hallway on the day Ruzsky had begun as a cadet at the Corps des Pages – the last time he had seen her. Standing by the door in the uniform of the school, next to his father, he had raised his hand to her to say goodbye and she had failed to lift her own in response.

He had hesitated, waiting for something more, his face reddening as he realized that nothing would be forthcoming.

The drawing-room door was open and Ruzsky walked in, conscious of the noise of his footsteps on the wooden floor. The place was in semi-darkness. His father forbade the servants to light a fire until after four in the afternoon, even in the depths of winter. It had been redecorated since Ruzsky's last visit, with a rich red wallpaper that matched the Persian rugs. On the wall closest to him a curved sabre hung below a painting of a mountain in the northern part of the Hindu Kush. Next to the sabre was a tall wooden table upon which stood an elaborate, bejewelled box and, on the wall above that, portraits of his two brothers.

His mother had wanted a society artist, but his father had chosen someone cheaper and less fashionable. Ruzsky could no longer remember the man's name, although he had forced them all to sit for long enough. He pulled back the curtain, to allow in a little natural light. The man had caught none of Dmitri's charm, but the portrait of Ilya – Ilusha as he had been known to them all – had greater warmth, and captured perfectly his impish grin.

Ruzsky wondered what his father had done with

his own portrait. Even though it had been many years since it had hung alongside the others, its absence still caused him pain. It was as if he did not exist.

He let the curtain fall, haunted by the resemblance between Ilya and Michael. Or was it just that his own son had almost reached the age at which Ilusha had been taken from them?

Ruzsky walked swiftly from the room and along the hallway. He glanced out of the rear window and caught sight of his son in the garden. Michael was on his own. He had built a wall of snow and behind it assembled a small mound of snowballs. Ruzsky watched as the little boy came back behind the wall, picked up the first missile and hurled it towards its target. He missed, so repeated the exercise with the second, then with all the others, ducking down between each throw, as if dodging gunfire. When he had finished, he mounted an imaginary horse and rode out beyond his rampart. Then he dismounted and ran around the small garden, with his arms outstretched. He was a plane, or perhaps a bird. He was alone in his world.

His son's isolation reminded Ruzsky of his own in the years after Ilusha's death. He rested his forehead against the window. How the months had dragged since he'd last set eyes on him.

'Perhaps you should leave him.'

Ruzsky spun round. His father stood quite still in the hallway, apparently unchanged by the past three years. He was an older, more distinguished version of his eldest son. He was no taller than Ruzsky and not much broader, but he carried about him the gravitas of his wealth and position. His moustache was white now and drooped neatly at the edges of his mouth.

His hair was longer than usual, a distinctive silver-white. Neatly brushed across his forehead, it was wavy and thick. 'If only you were as handsome as your father,' Irina had once said to him, with a sigh.

Today, Russia's assistant minister of finance wore a morning suit, his gold pocket-watch chain looped across the front of a dark waistcoat, highly polished boots catching what little light filtered through the window.

'I'm sorry?' Ruzsky said.

'He's your son. It's your choice.'

'What is?'

'Whether to see him.'

Ruzsky faced the window again. Michael had discarded his hat and was standing in the middle of the garden staring at the grey sky. 'Why is that a choice?' he asked.

Irina emerged from the kitchen below and hurried towards the child. She tried to shoo him back inside, but he was reluctant to go. She picked up his hat and pushed it on to his head. She was not an unattractive woman. Her dark hair had been recently cut and styled to frame her narrow face. She glanced up briefly, but did not appear to see him.

'Perhaps you should give him more time.'

'Time for what?'

'To settle in.'

Ruzsky had forgotten how much authority his father carried in his voice. 'To settle in where?' he asked.

'You know perfectly well what I mean.'

Ruzsky watched as Michael allowed himself to be led into the house. He heard the door shut below and could dimly make out the sound of their voices in the kitchen.

'Fatherhood carries responsibilities.'

Ruzsky turned and, as he did so, caught sight of a wooden train in the corner of the doorway to his father's study, by the base of a large palm tree. 'What do you mean by that?'

'Sometimes you have to act in the best interests of the child rather than your own.'

'And what are the best interests of my child?'

The elder Ruzsky gazed solemnly at his son. His face was deeply lined, his forehead creased by a severe frown. 'If she finds you here, there will be a confrontation.'

Ruzsky stared at the train. It was part of a set his father had commissioned for him on his seventh birthday from St Petersburg's leading toymaker. Once, they had enjoyed playing with it together in the attic room at the top of the house. He forced himself to meet his father's eyes. 'He would be better off without me. Is that what you think?'

There was no reply and Ruzsky felt the weight of the past upon him. He was no longer the chief investigator of the Petrograd police department, but a frightened eleven-year-old boy in the study at Petrovo.

Ruzsky lowered his eyes and kept them on the train as he fought to contain his emotions. He breathed in deeply. 'Can a man never escape his past mistakes?' he asked.

The elder Ruzsky did not flinch. 'It is the boy's welfare that concerns me now.' He walked slowly towards the study door. At the entrance, he bent down to pick up the wooden engine and then, without a further glance, shut the door behind him, leaving Ruzsky alone in the corridor.

The house was silent.

Ruzsky heard banging below, like a wooden bowl being hammered on a table. One of his father's Great Danes gave a single bark, then was quiet. He waited. Ever since Ilusha's death, his life had been about that closed door. He wanted to move beyond it, but felt paralysed. He could hear the Tompion clock on the mantelpiece in the drawing room, and recalled the dark winter afternoons of his childhood, marked out by its steady, rhythmic ticking. It was the sound of the inflexible regimentation of his father's world.

Ruzsky closed his eyes and let himself return to that day at Petrovo. He could almost feel the icy water's embrace as his mind drifted towards a place where he knew, deep in his heart, the pain and guilt would end for ever.

He had not been present when his brother had taken those fatal steps, but there was no one who blamed Ruzsky for the tragedy more than he blamed himself. His father had instructed him to make sure that Ilusha did not play on the ice now that spring was upon them. Ruzsky had left his side for only a few moments, but it had been long enough. All his attempts to save his little brother had been to no avail.

He should have gone with Ilusha.

It was snowing heavily when Ruzsky emerged, but he didn't take this in, or his surroundings, until he had reached the corner of the Nevsky Prospekt. He stood on the street corner opposite the Alexander Garden, now, in winter, just dark, skeletal trees reaching for the sky, and tilted his face upwards.

He tasted the flakes as they fell.

A detachment of soldiers in long greatcoats marched past him, then wheeled right on to the Nevsky. Ruzsky recognized them as members of the Semenovsky regiment, but they hardly did justice to its reputation. They looked scruffy and marched without the precision that had been expected before the war: then, no regiment had moved anywhere in Petersburg unless immaculately turned out and in perfect order.

Ruzsky thought of the painted soldiers he had kept neatly in boxes in his attic room in the house in Millionaya Street. He wondered if they were still there, and if Michael played with them. The contrast with the St Petersburg of his childhood was pervasive. It was the first day of the new year, but he was certain there would be no reception in the great halls of the Winter Palace. Aside from the soldiers, the capital's main thoroughfare was almost deserted. Two private sleds waited outside the Wolf and Beranger café and beyond them, a motor-car was clanking noisily in his direction.

Ruzsky pulled out his pocket watch. It was not yet ten o'clock; the city was only slowly coming to life.

But if the soldiers on its streets were cut from a different cloth, and the atmosphere strained, this section of the city had borne few physical changes. The huge windows of Alexandre's were packed with scarves of woven Persian silk, jade, ivory, leather goods of all descriptions and jewels beyond the imagination of most passers-by. Druce's, the famed *magasin anglais*, still had Harris tweed and English soaps in its smaller windows, and Cabassue's displayed fine French silk ties and linen along with the fashionable *botiky*, or low-cut velvet boots with rubber soles, so favoured by the rich. All the stores had signs that declared, 'English spoken,' or '*Ici on parle français*,' though, of course, they had all lost the once common '*Man spricht Deutsch.*'

Ruzsky stopped dead. He had reached Wolff's, the capital's largest bookstore and his childhood favourite. The latest casualty lists from the front were posted in the window. The names stretched for column after column. He read through them all, then turned away, deep in thought.

Beyond the shop, tucked into the corner of the wall he saw a bearded Circassian in traditional sheepskin coat, his wares – mostly silver bangles and brooches – spread out on a coloured rug. The man was clutching the coat around him, head bent. These traders were a commonplace sight in summer on the Nevsky, but Ruzsky had never before seen one here in winter.

A red, orange and green electric tram rattled past, heading south, its windows dirty and fringed with ice. Ruzsky felt someone tugging at his coat and swung round again. A beggar in filthy rags stood before him, arm outstretched. His face and teeth were blackened. '*Khrista radi,*' he whispered. A copper, for Christ's sake. Ruzsky reached into his pocket, found a ten copeck coin, shoved it into the man's hand and stalked off.

The windows of the Elisseev Brothers' grocery store, he noticed, as he turned off the Nevsky, appeared to be full of provisions. Some people, at least, were not going short.

A *droshky* driver – one of the ubiquitous *vankas*,

drivers of the city's cheapest form of hired transport, mostly peasants who had come to the city to make their fortune – pulled his sled over and started touting for a fare, but Ruzsky waved him away. This morning, he wanted to walk.

CHAPTER FIVE

The City Police Department was housed in a grand, classical building situated on Ofitserskaya Ulitsa – Officers' Street – not far from the Mariinskiy Theatre. Pavel was waiting for him by the gate and the pair strolled in through the side arch of the courtyard, past a group of horses being exercised in a tight circle. Behind them, men from the transport department had already hauled out sleds and carriages from the stables, ready to be hitched up.

Ruzsky led the way into the lobby. It was warmer in here, but gloomy and run-down, the blue and gold paint peeling from the walls.

Directly ahead of them was the duty desk, then the incident room and the narrow stone steps leading down to the cells. To the right, behind a closed door, was the senior officers' mess. Ruzsky stepped into the constables' mess opposite, where small groups of men gossiped, sipping tea or perhaps vodka from steel cups. Few lamps were lit in the vault-like room, and the warm air was thick with the smell of tobacco smoke, wet leather and wool. The three constables who'd been out on the ice earlier sat on a bench in the corner, smoking. One had his boots off and was rubbing the circulation back into his toes.

The men got to their feet immediately. 'I should have introduced myself out on the ice,' Ruzsky said. 'Chief Investigator Ruzsky.'

They thrust out their hands and announced their names in turn, with an eagerness born of the fact that service here earned exemption from the front.

'You searched well,' Ruzsky said.

They did not reply. They were just boys, and looking into their faces made him feel old. He hesitated, wishing he had more to say, then went back into the hallway. He didn't recognize the constable at the duty desk either, and Pavel didn't bother to introduce him as he pulled across the report book. 'Anyone missing last night or this morning?' he asked. A glass-fronted cabinet behind the desk was filled with rifles and revolvers.

'No, sir.' The man had a wide, flat face. He wasn't from Petersburg. Probably one of his parents was from the far eastern provinces.

'They must have some form of identification on them,' Ruzsky said.

'They haven't,' Pavel responded. 'I've just been down to check again. We have two nameless victims.'

Ruzsky watched his partner flick back through the pages of the report book. 'Would you get us the missing-persons book?' Pavel asked.

The desk clerk went into the room behind, ran his hand along the rows of files.

Pavel slammed the incident book shut. Ruzsky leant back against the desk, examining the posters on the wall. He moved closer. Alongside the grainy police photographs of wanted men, there was a caricature of Rasputin dancing with the Tsar and the half-naked Empress. Next to the Tsar sat his English cousin George. The caption read, 'Little Father plays with Georgie, little Mother lies with Grigory.'

Next to the poster were photographs of Rasputin's body. The first was a close-up of his face, which looked as if it had been rubbed in soot. There appeared to be a bullet hole in the centre of his forehead. The other two showed the priest's frozen corpse, with its legs and hands bound, arms raised above his head.

'I thought you told me we were not called to the scene,' Ruzsky said.

'The photographer arrived first. By the time I got there, Anton had handed jurisdiction to the Okhrana.'

Ruzsky frowned at his friend, who seemed nervous or embarrassed, his eyes evasive. Last night he'd told Ruzsky that the constables had called the Okhrana direct – indeed, they'd had a mild altercation over it. The Tsar's secret police normally dealt only with sedition and terrorism and the ruthless suppression of opposition to the Tsar. This was the first time they had taken direct control of a murder case.

'You think Anton should have fought for the investigation?'

'No.'

'But you still had a look?'

Pavel didn't answer and Ruzsky turned back to the photographs. 'This was taken by Great Petrovsky Bridge.'

'Yes.'

'So it's true that he was still alive when they threw him into the river. His arms are like that because he was trying to escape when his body froze.' Rumours had even reached Tobolsk about the manner of

Rasputin's death – that he had been almost impossible to kill, and had still been breathing after being shot, bound and thrown into the ice.

'I don't know,' Pavel said.

'And you weren't curious?'

Pavel stared at the photographs.

'We should have insisted on making it our investigation,' Ruzsky said easily.

'There was no investigation. The dogs on the streets knew who had done it. If the relatives of the Tsar want to murder his wife's lover, then who are we to get involved?'

'You don't really believe that they were lovers?'

Pavel shrugged. 'People do. I was called out to an incident – about a year after you left. It was at one of the new gypsy restaurants. He was drunk.'

'Rasputin?'

'Yes. Someone telephoned to complain and I happened to be working late. When I arrived he was dancing in the middle of the restaurant, boasting of how he could make the Empress dance like this . . .' Pavel shoved his hips forward. 'Then he dropped his trousers and started waving his penis at the spectators.'

'I don't believe it.'

'On my son's life.'

Ruzsky had met the peasant priest only once, just before the war: the Imperial favourite had appeared at the police department late at night, drunk, claiming incomprehensible threats on his life.

The constable shuffled back with the book and pushed it across the desk. There had been no entries for more than a week. 'I suppose it's too early for anyone to have missed them,' Ruzsky said.

He led Pavel past the entrance to the armoury and up to the first floor. The door to Anton's office at the top of the stairs was shut, the corridor dark. To their right were the administrative offices – finance, the records library, constables' and senior officers' administration – but Ruzsky flicked on the light and turned left to the criminal-investigation division.

Their office was small – far too cramped for the number of people who worked there – a series of wooden cubicles arranged round a group of desks in the centre reserved for the secretaries and the junior constables on attachment. Vladimir's cubicle had the words 'Investigator, Street Crime' inscribed on the door. Next came Sarlov, under the heading 'Pathology', then Maretsky under 'Modus Operandi', and finally the corner office that Ruzsky and Pavel had shared for many years with the words 'Chief Investigator/Deputy Chief Investigator, Murder' inscribed heavily in black. Ruzsky pushed open the door of his cubicle, flicked on the wall light, took off his coat and threw it on to the stand in the corner. He removed his gloves and stamped the last of the snow from his boots before sitting down at his desk.

'See? I tidied up,' Pavel said.

Ruzsky was gratified that no one had occupied his desk, but it was obvious that Pavel had simply spread the mess during his absence, then swept it up and dumped it back on his own desk prior to his return. 'You're a pig,' Ruzsky told him.

Pavel took a piece of chalk and wrote the date at the top of the blackboard on the wall beside him. Underneath, in capitals, he scrawled 'Neva bodies'. He turned. 'A great start.' He moved to the city map, took a black pin from its edge and placed it in the centre of the river. 'Black for murder, red for muggings, green for random street violence, orange for anti-Jewish violence. Vladimir puts his pins up. It's a kind of competition. We get five points per pin to Vladimir's one. We ran out of pins so many times last year I got bored with it, but today we can begin again . . .'

'Did you call Sarlov?'

'Yes.'

'He said he was on his way?'

Pavel raised an eyebrow. 'This is Sarlov we're talking about. He didn't say anything.' He straightened and left the office. A few moments later, Ruzsky heard the door to the toilets bang at the end of the corridor. He reached into his pocket, pulled out the roll of banknotes taken from the dead man's jacket and put it into one of his drawers.

He sat down. In the centre of his desk was a piece of wood with a carved inscription carrying the words of the oath all soldiers and officers of the Imperial Army swore to the Tsar. 'I promise and do hereby swear,' it read, 'before Almighty God, before his Holy Gospels, to serve His Imperial Majesty, the supreme Autocrat, truly and faithfully, to obey him in all things, and to defend his dynasty, without sparing my body, until the last drop of my blood.' It had been given to Ruzsky by his brother as a joke. In the light of the carnage at the front, it no longer appeared funny.

Ruzsky pulled over his in-tray and took out the only item that had been placed in it. It was a clipping from the newspaper *Novoe Vremia*.

He glanced at it. The article had been written by the liberal Maklakov and it compared Russia to an automobile being driven at breakneck speed towards a precipice by a mad chauffeur whose passengers were too scared to attempt to seize control of the steering-wheel.

Ruzsky opened the central drawer of his desk and was surprised to find that his old notebook was still there. He flicked through the notes of his last case, that of the ill-fated girl from Sennaya Ploschad. He turned over a fresh page and wrote, 'Neva Murders'.

Pavel's telephone rang and Ruzsky got up to answer it.

'Pavel, it's Veresov.'

'Veresov? It's Ruzsky.'

'Sandro?'

Ruzsky was heartened by the pleasure he detected in Veresov's voice. He was a small, studious man who occupied the tiny fingerprint bureau, located, much to his chagrin, in the basement between the canteen and the cells.

'You're back,' Veresov said.

'Don't sound so surprised.'

Veresov was silent. 'Bad timing, anyway,' he said.

'Why?'

'Oh, you know.' There was a moment's silence. 'I have the dagger. Is it criminal suspects only?'

'What do you mean?'

'We don't have automatic access to the Okhrana's files any more. If I have to apply to work through their records as well, it's going to take twice as long.'

'I thought we shared files?'

'New regulations.'

'Well,' Ruzsky said, 'it doesn't look like a political case. Start with your own files.'

'Petrograd or Empire-wide?'

'Start with St Petersburg, Moscow, then work through the other cities.'

Ruzsky put the mouthpiece back on its hook. It rang again immediately.

'It's Sarlov. You can come down now.'

Sarlov's laboratory was next to Veresov's fingerprint bureau in the basement. It was equally damp and even tinier. Sarlov always complained about this, but Ruzsky thought the pathologist enjoyed having to force the detectives to stand close to the bodies. There was a bright lamp in the ceiling and the two victims lay side by side beneath it. The steel table had been designed for one and the man's body looked as if it was about to tumble on to the floor.

Sarlov wore a mask over his face and a white apron spattered with blood. He had a small saw in his right hand. 'Ruzsky,' he said, surprise in his voice. 'I didn't know you were back.'

'Well, I am.'

'To what do we owe the pleasure?'

'Did you see Rasputin's body?' Ruzsky asked, ignoring his question.

'No.'

'Is it true he was still alive when they put him in the river?'

'I don't know.'

'Don't you doctors talk?'

'Sometimes.' He leant over the man's body and raised the saw.

'Please, Sarlov,' Pavel said. 'Not now.'

'You can see for yourself. There's not much to tell you. I'll give you a full report upstairs when I'm finished.' Sarlov leant back and pulled down his mask. 'The man was in his early forties, died around three a.m. Between three and four. Severe loss of blood from the stab wounds. Seventeen in all. Look at him.'

Ruzsky realized his eyes had been avoiding the victims. The man was bulkier than he'd imagined, a thick pelt of hair running from chest to waist. His body had been punctured repeatedly, but his face looked less distorted now that the wounds had been cleaned. He'd not been a handsome man, Ruzsky thought, his cheeks too fleshy and nose too broad. The girl, by contrast, was prettier than she'd appeared. She had a neat face, with a small nose and long eyelashes. She'd been stabbed only once, precisely, in the centre of her chest. She was naked and Ruzsky wanted instinctively to cover her.

'So?' Pavel asked.

'They were followed from behind,' Ruzsky said, 'yet stabbed from the front.'

'I can confirm that they were stabbed from the front,' Sarlov said.

'The man has no marks on his arms, so the first blow must have been unexpected. He was caught unawares.'

'Very good, Ruzsky. I'm pleased to see that provincial life has not dulled your powers of observation.' Sarlov's eyes twinkled with laughter. He liked to hide his affection beneath a manner that was alternately curmudgeonly and playful.

'Who was killed first?' Ruzsky asked, failing to return the smile. He knew the game. He was supposed to be the butt of their humour – now more than ever.

'I don't know. Common sense dictates it must have been the man.'

'One of them knew this would happen,' Ruzsky went on, 'because neither ran. Perhaps the girl was killed first, but the man was expecting it, so he stood and watched. Then the murderer turned on him.'

'And stabbed him seventeen times?' Pavel asked.

'Have you found anything on them, Sarlov?'

'No. Their pockets had been cleared out.'

'But nobody took the money we found.'

Sarlov shrugged.

'Have you any clues at all?'

'The man has had some dental work,' the doctor said. 'It's gold foil treatment, very elaborately performed. That is not to say it couldn't have been done by a dentist here, just that it is more likely to have been done in Europe or, maybe, America.'

'A foreigner, then?'

'His shirts have no markings, and the labels from his jacket and overcoat have been removed. His underpants were Russian, his boots made to measure, probably somewhere in the empire, I couldn't tell you where.'

'The man was the real target,' Ruzsky said.

'Perhaps.'

'Why else would he have been stabbed seventeen times?'

'He was certainly no Rasputin. I should think he was dead after the first blow.'

'Anything else?'

'No – oh, yes. I almost missed this. Look here, on his shoulder.'

Ruzsky and Pavel examined the man's skin. There was a small, branded black star.

'What does that mean?' Pavel asked.

'I have no idea,' Sarlov said.

'Have you seen anything like it before?'

'No.'

Ruzsky noticed the pile of clothes on the far end of the shelf. The man's were stiff with dried blood. His overcoat was thick and, Ruzsky thought, expensive. There was nothing in the inside pocket and the outline where the label had been was clearly visible. He pulled out the pocket, but there was nothing, except a little dirt.

The jacket was made of thick, dark wool, probably of cheap Russian manufacture since the stitching appeared primitive. He turned all the pockets inside out, but again found nothing. Then he studied the boots. They were old and worn down; if the maker's name had ever been visible in the sole it had long since faded.

Ruzsky pushed the pile to one side and turned to the girl's clothes. He was struck immediately by their quality. The seams were immaculately stitched. He started with her corset, then picked up the dress and saw the tiny label sewn into the hem. 'Pavel,' he said, 'tell one of the constables to go down to the Nevsky and bring Madame Renaud here, whatever her objections.'

'Why?'

'Because my wife's expensive taste in frocks may finally have served a purpose.'

Pavel went to talk to the desk officer.

Upstairs, as he reached the first floor, Ruzsky saw that Anton's office door was ajar. He had always come to work on a Saturday morning. It was a ritual. He was bent over a drawer, searching for something. The desk was covered, as always, with loose papers. On the wall, below a white clock, hung a picture of Napoleon's retreat from Moscow. The bookcase was full of leatherbound volumes, some Anton's own work.

Anton straightened. He had his glasses in his hand and spun them slowly.

'You're in early,' Ruzsky said.

Anton looked at him for a moment more, then bounded towards him. 'My boy,' he said, gripping his shoulders, 'how wonderful to have you back. Come, we celebrate.' He reached down to the bottom drawer of his desk and pulled out a bottle of vodka. As he filled two glasses, a mop of dark hair flopped over his forehead, the grey now visible at his temples. His face exuded the warmth of a loving father, his manner the absentmindedness and eccentricity of the college professor he had once been.

He pushed one glass across the desk and raised the other. He looked carefully at his subordinate. 'It's good to have you back.'

They drank. Ruzsky almost choked. 'Christ.'

'I know – it's dreadful.'

'It's worse than dreadful.'

'The city is an island, cut off from decent vodka.'

'I should have brought you some from Tobolsk.'

Anton raised his eyebrows. 'Better keep your voice down. It's still illegal, you know.'

Ruzsky smiled. 'I'm sure prohibition has been observed to the letter, especially inside this building.'

Anton took another slug. 'It's been an excellent idea which, as the chief of the city police, I have, of course, fully supported. It has made a huge contribution to improving the general level of sobriety.'

Ruzsky moved to look at the photograph on

63

Anton's desk. It was of the five of them. 'Good God,' Anton said. 'A proper reunion is in order. Where's Pavel?' He picked up the telephone earpiece. 'Professor Maretsky,' he told the operator, then, 'Maretsky. Anton. Come round, will you? I've got a surprise. And bring Vladimir.' Anton listened. 'What about Sarlov? . . . All right, just get over here.' He put down the receiver and refilled their glasses.

'Pavel will be back in a minute.' Ruzsky threw the vodka to the back of his throat and put the glass on the desk. He picked up the photograph and looked at the faces that stared back at him, one a much younger version of his own.

'You were a baby then,' Anton said.

'So were you.'

Ruzsky examined the picture. The words 'Criminal Investigation Division, St Petersburg City Police Department' and the year, 1900, had been written across the bottom. He took out his cigarette case and pushed it towards Anton, who removed one and shunted it back.

'Have you seen her?' Anton asked. Ruzsky saw the warmth that shone in his friend's eyes.

'Irina? No.'

'I wasn't talking of Irina.' Anton was smiling. 'I saw you together, don't forget. That night at the Mariinskiy.'

Ruzsky did not answer. He wondered how his feelings could have been so transparent.

'One of the dancers told me she kept a photograph of you on her dressing-table after you went.'

Ruzsky flushed with embarrassment and pleasure.

Anton stretched his legs. 'So?'

'It's complicated.'

'I know that you will say I should not, but I cannot

help feeling responsible in some way for this mess.'

Ruzsky sucked heavily on his cigarette. Irina had been one of Anton's students. 'Pavel has been filling me with the usual gloom,' he said, anxious to change the subject.

Anton leant forward again. 'This time he's right. I never imagined that the Tsar's absence would be a handicap, but since he ran off to the front to try to win the war singlehandedly, it has got worse. It is like being on a ship headed for an iceberg with a madman at the controls.'

'I got the article.'

'Yes, but the worst of it is that the woman is at the steering wheel. That's what's frightening.'

'Do you still attend the weekly meetings at the interior ministry?'

'Yes.'

'What do the Okhrana say?'

'We don't need them to tell us what is going on. Stand in a line for bread. You'll get the idea.'

Anton came round the desk and leant against it. 'I took a look at the bodies,' he said.

'And?'

'People are desperate, but that kind of savagery . . . Have you identified the victims?'

'No. Their bodies had been systematically stripped.'

Anton looked up. His eyes were washed-out and bloodshot. Deep concern showed in them. 'It troubles me. At this time, right out there on the ice, in front of the palace, in the heart of the city.'

Ruzsky wondered what lay beneath the other man's anxiety. 'I don't think the location was chosen for its symbolic value, if that is what you mean.'

Anton toyed with his spectacles.

'I don't understand what you're driving at,' Ruzsky said.

'These are complicated times, Sandro.'

'What has that to do with us?'

He sighed. 'It's a time for caution. The progressives and even some members of the Government have been writing to senior generals at headquarters to demand the Empress be arrested on her next visit to the front line and sent to the Crimea. I've heard that some of your contemporaries at the yacht club discuss in hushed tones whether it would be justifiable to assassinate the Tsar.'

'And what has that to do with us?'

'Nothing, I just want you to be aware.'

'Of what?'

'No one operates in a vacuum, that's all.'

Ruzsky did not see what he was driving at. 'And our friend Vasilyev?'

'The chief of the Okhrana sits in his office playing the loyal police chief. The plotters' letters are opened, their contents divulged to the Empress. She in turn writes to her husband and demands another round of ministers be sacked and sent into exile. We call it ministerial leapfrog. At a meeting yesterday, the latest bulletin to be sent up to Tsarskoe Selo was pushed around the table. It contained extracts from a letter written by the Grand Duchess Maria Pavlovna to a leading member of the Duma, demanding that the Empress be . . . annihilated.'

Ruzsky did not answer. Maria Pavlovna was one of the most senior members of the Romanov family and what Anton was telling him was not *khvost* gossip. 'Pavel tells me Vasilyev tolerates no opposition,' he said, the memories still fresh of his confrontation three years ago with the city's secret-police chief.

'You have to question the currency of a regime that relies for its survival on such a man,' Anton expanded.

'You exaggerate.'

'No.'

'And he is rewarded for his loyalty?'

'Yes, but you're missing the point. Vasilyev is not stupid. Think about it for a minute. Some of these strikes . . . what lies behind them? Are the Okhrana up to their old tricks? We know they have *provocateurs* in these factories and strike committees. Is Vasilyev deliberately stirring up trouble so that whichever group of revolutionaries he favours can seize power under the guise of saving the Empire?'

'The incorruptible Vasilyev? Devoted servant of the Tsar?'

Pavel appeared in the doorway. 'What's this? A wedding reception?'

Maretsky was half a step behind him. 'Professor,' Ruzsky said, unable to conceal his pleasure. Maretsky stepped forward, offered himself for a bear-hug, and Ruzsky ducked into it as he would with his son. Maretsky held him tightly, then took a pace back, unsteady for a moment. He sat down next to Anton. His legs didn't quite reach the floor and he looked like a child in an adult's chair. His face was round, a few wispy strands of grey hair protruding from the top of his shirt belying an otherwise almost feminine appearance. He wore a grey jacket and shorter boots than was the fashion.

'You look thinner,' Maretsky told him. 'Don't they have food out there?'

'It's more than can be said for you, Maretsky,' Pavel said.

'How was Tobolsk?'

'Cold and dull.'

'Is it true they eat each other when they get hungry?'

'More or less.'

Anton clinked his glass against the metal vodka bottle, then poured out a measure for each of them. He pushed the glasses across the table and they raised them together. 'Older, wiser,' he said, looking at them meaningfully, 'but still here.'

They drained their glasses.

An awkward silence followed. Their attempt to pretend that nothing had changed only served to reinforce the fact that something had. Maretsky – even Anton, or was he imagining that? – seemed almost wary of him, Ruzsky thought.

'How is Irina?' Maretsky asked.

'She's fine, thank you. Or so I believe.'

Maretsky frowned. 'She survived Tobolsk?'

'Just about.'

'I'm surprised she went. My wife wouldn't have.'

'It's surprising,' Ruzsky said, 'what guilt can make you do.'

They were silent once more.

Ruzsky heard Madame Renaud's haughty voice at the other end of the corridor.

CHAPTER SIX

Madame Renaud burst into the room, an anxious constable alongside her.

'*Bonjour*, Madame.'

'You are Irina Ruzskya's husband.' It was an accusation. She surveyed the room, glanced coldly at his colleagues.

'I am.'

'You should be ashamed of yourself.'

Ruzsky stood up, then leant back on his heels. They stared at each other like predators. 'We have the body of a woman downstairs, wearing one of your dresses.'

'I have a business to run, don't you know that? You drag me in here like some common criminal, and in these times! Don't you have anything better to do?' She glared at them.

'As the constable will have told you, Madame, we are the criminal-investigation division and we are investigating a murder. I'm sure the Okhrana has better things to do with its time, if that is what you mean.'

'How can you be sure it is one of my dresses?'

'A man whose wife is bankrupting him recognizes the cause.'

'Only cheap husbands complain.'

Madame Renaud exuded a haughty arrogance. She had a long, bony nose, narrow eyes and white skin heavily powdered in a vain attempt to conceal her age. Her fingers were thin and, like her neck, bedecked in jewels that sparkled even in this dull light.

Her expression reflected disgust and astonishment that the scion of a great family could work in such surroundings.

'These are my colleagues, Anton Antipovich—'

'I did not come to attend a social occasion.'

'You make no concession to the times,' Ruzsky said, pointing at her diamond necklace. 'For that I admire you.'

'I am not normally dragged through the streets.'

'Your sled was not ready. I apologize. But this is a murder case, the victim one of your clients. I thought you would wish to help us.'

She relaxed a little, breathing out. It dawned on Ruzsky that his irritation and hostility had more to do with Irina. He imagined the two of them together, clucking and cooing over a dress that would cost ten times more than most people earned in a year. Since their marriage, Irina had received an allowance direct from his father, as well as a smaller stipend from her own parents. Behind the desk, Anton was staring at his empty glass.

'I'd be grateful if you would accompany us to the basement,' Ruzsky said.

A hint of a smile played at the corner of her lips. 'You make the invitation sound so attractive, Prince Ruzsky.'

He could tell that both Pavel and Maretsky were watching him. 'We're not in the habit of such formality here, Madame Renaud.'

'Are you ashamed of your fine ancestry?'

Ruzsky saw Pavel roll his eyes theatrically. Without replying, he led them along the corridor and down the stairs. Madame Renaud kept both hands in a fur muffler and her back rigidly straight.

As they went down the last flight of stairs, Ruzsky could hear Sarlov working with the saw and he hurried along the dark corridor. 'For God's sake,' he said, and Sarlov looked up, startled. 'I thought I asked you not to do that.'

'I have a medical practice to run, Ruzsky. I can't wait on your pleasure all day. As even you must be able to see, the bodies are rock hard and will take a considerable time to thaw properly.'

Sarlov's coat, mask and face were splattered with tiny flecks of frozen blood and flesh. There was an incision across the woman's chest, a small pool of thawing blood on the metal table beneath him, a thin stream dripping on to the floor.

Ruzsky heard a sharp intake of breath from Madame Renaud behind him and rushed forward to pull a sheet over the body. 'My apologies, Madame Renaud. I was not aware that this process had begun.'

He expected her to turn away, but found instead that she was struggling to compose herself. Pavel stood alongside her. Maretsky and Anton had remained upstairs.

'Come forward, if you would.'

She put a black gloved hand to her mouth, then took out a white lace handkerchief from her bag and placed it over her nose. She stepped forward and looked calmly at the girl's face. Then she shook her head confidently. 'I don't recognize her.'

'Are you sure?'

'Of course I'm sure.'

Ruzsky walked over to the pile of clothes in the corner and picked up the dead girl's dress. He carried it to Madame Renaud, pulling the hem through his hands until he found the label. She took the dress from him and half turned, holding it up towards the light. She returned it to him and removed a pair of spectacles from her bag. She examined it once again. 'Yes,' she said, simply. She let the hem drop, holding the dress by its shoulders. 'I see you are as capable as your wife claims.'

Ruzsky felt momentarily confused.

'Sherlock Holmes, she calls you. Isn't that so?' She was taunting him.

'This is one of your dresses,' he said.

'It is much too big for the dead girl. A terrible fit.' She gave him a caustic smile. 'Surely you can see that.'

'Who did you make it for?' Ruzsky didn't expect an answer.

'Vyrubova,' she said.

'*Anna* Vyrubova?'

'Yes.' She was enjoying her power now. Ruzsky saw the colour drain from Pavel's face again.

'The intimate friend of the Empress, that Anna Vyrubova?'

'The same. It's an old dress – two or three years. She must have given it to the girl.'

Ruzsky hesitated. 'You haven't seen this woman before?'

'No.'

'Definitely not?'

She tilted her head to one side, but it was a gesture of amusement, not irritation. 'No.' She was watching him. 'Your wife came in this morning.'

He didn't answer.

'She wishes to have a dress for the Vorontsov ball.'

'Of course.'

'She said you would not accompany her.'

Ruzsky stared at the floor.

'She says you were once handsome, but she does you a disservice.'

Ruzsky looked up. He could hardly believe that this harsh-faced woman was attempting to flirt with him in front of two half-dismembered corpses. 'Thank you for coming in, Madame Renaud.'

Pavel was silent as they walked upstairs to the office.

The dagger had been placed on the corner of Ruzsky's desk, with a tag attached stamped 'Petrograd City Police, Criminal Investigation Division'.

Ruzsky opened the drawer, took out the notebook and slipped it into the inside pocket of his jacket. He replaced it with the piece of paper on which he had drawn the outline of the footprint traced from the snow.

'What do you want me to do?' Pavel asked.

'Go down to the embankment and start checking all residential buildings in the neighbourhood. Go to the Winter Palace and try to get hold of the head of the household. See if there is a chance that anyone saw anything. And, if you have time, try the embassies, British, French, American. Ask if they've received any reports of a missing national. We'll see if Sarlov was right about the man being a foreigner. I'm going out to Tsarskoe Selo.'

'You don't want me to come with you?' Pavel didn't sound enthusiastic.

'We'll make more progress if we split up.'

'Who are you going to see?'

'Count Fredericks. One of the other senior household staff. Vyrubova herself.'

'Why don't you telephone?'

Ruzsky frowned at Pavel's caution. 'If I call, they will decline.'

'They will decline to see you anyway.'

Ruzsky looked up and saw Maretsky going into his cubicle. He picked up the dagger and went to join him. Pavel followed.

Maretsky was scanning a document, his glasses pushed to the top of his head. He looked up at them, chewing his lip, as if concentrating on something else, his round, piggy eyes staring into thin air.

Ruzsky held up the knife.

'It's a dagger,' Maretsky said.

'Correct.' Ruzsky handed it to him.

'It has blood on it.'

'That's not uncommon in murder cases.'

Maretsky pulled his glasses down and glanced at Ruzsky. He held the dagger up to the light.

'There's some writing on the blade,' Ruzsky said.

'I can see.'

Ruzsky waited as Maretsky turned it over in his hand. The professor handed it back without comment. 'And?' Ruzsky asked.

'And what?' Maretsky glanced at Pavel. For some reason, Ruzsky thought, the professor never felt as comfortable when Pavel was around.

'Have you ever seen this kind of knife before?'

'You're the chief investigator, Chief Investigator.'

74

When the professor had joined the department, a protective bond had formed between him and Ruzsky. Maretsky had once been a highly regarded academic at St Petersburg University – a professor of philosophy – but an incident with a young male student had destroyed his career. Anton had offered him a home here, but for some reason Maretsky thought Ruzsky was the only other member of the department who did not judge him. Over the years this had paid dividends more often than Ruzsky could remember.

'The Black Bands?' Ruzsky asked. 'Political organizations? Revolutionaries? Does this kind of knife, or the inscription, have a connection with any of them?'

'I've not seen anything like it.'

'What is the script?'

Maretsky shrugged.

'Can you find out?'

The professor sighed, which Ruzsky took as a sign of acceptance. He examined the knife once more. 'It's an unusual weapon,' he said.

'Do you still do liaison work?' Ruzsky asked.

Maretsky had been made responsible a long time ago for liaison with the Okhrana, but since Vasilyev's appointment, relations between the two organizations had grown so hostile that there was virtually no communication between them at any level.

'I never wanted to.' There was a note of bitterness in Maretsky's voice.

Ruzsky looked at the professor. Perhaps it was his imagination, but all of his colleagues seemed more evasive these days. Had his fate frightened them? Or something else? 'Have you heard any whispers about this case?' Ruzsky asked. 'Has anyone called you?'

'No.'

Ruzsky nodded at Pavel, who returned a minute later with the photographs. Ruzsky spread them out on the desk and waited as Maretsky examined them. 'No,' the professor said.

'You don't recognize either of them?'

'No.'

Maretsky was saved from further questioning by the appearance of one of the constables, his face puce with exertion and alarm. 'Sir. You had better come.'

CHAPTER SEVEN

Sarlov's voice was audible from the top of the stairs.

Three men in long dark overcoats waited outside the laboratory. Sarlov and Anton stood between them. 'This is outrageous,' Sarlov said, his face red with anger.

Ruzsky pushed past them. Ivan Prokopiev was standing in the centre of the room, smoking a cigarette. He was a tall man, bigger even than Pavel, with a bulbous, ruddy nose and close-cropped hair. He wore only a jacket and shirt – which, despite the cold, was open to the middle of his chest – with dark trousers and high leather boots. The head of the Okhrana's internal division still held himself with the swagger of the Cossack officer he had once been. He was watching two of his officers wrap the bodies in a single canvas sheet.

'What are you doing?' Ruzsky asked.

'Prince Ruzsky, what a pleasant surprise. Welcome home.'

There was a moment's silence as they stared at each other. Prokopiev made no attempt to offer an explanation.

Ruzsky came closer to him. 'You've no authority to do this.'

'Sandro,' Anton said, taking his arm.

Prokopiev's expression was dismissive.

'Let's see your authorization.'

'Sandro,' Anton said again. His and Pavel's faces were white with shock. Only Sarlov echoed Ruzsky's anger.

Prokopiev finished his cigarette and ground it out under his boot. From the inside pocket of his jacket, he took a piece of paper and handed it to Anton, who looked at it, then gave it to Ruzsky. It contained a single sentence instructing the Okhrana to remove the bodies for 'urgent political investigation'. It was signed by Major General Prince Alexander Nicholaevich Obolensky, the city mayor and titular head of all Petrograd's police departments.

'Did Obolensky see this?' Ruzsky asked. 'Or did you just sign it yourselves?' In theory, Obolensky was the most senior police official in the city, but they all knew he would never dare stand in the Okhrana's way. Prokopiev might easily have forged his signature to save time.

Prokopiev lit another cigarette, then pointed at the pile of clothes on the side. 'Where are the contents of their pockets?'

'Are you assuming control of the investigation?' Ruzsky pressed.

'I don't believe any mention has been made of it.'

'Then why do you wish to remove the bodies?'

'You have emptied their pockets?' Prokopiev countered.

'They had been stripped of all personal items by the time we arrived.' Ruzsky omitted to mention the roll of banknotes.

Prokopiev nodded, his face expressionless. Ruzsky

thought it was the answer he had expected, or wanted.

Anton stepped aside and forced Ruzsky to do the same as Prokopiev's men took hold of the canvas sheets and began to carry the corpses out of the room and down the corridor. Prokopiev clicked his heels. 'We shall return them when we are done. Good day, gentlemen.'

Ruzsky followed them, shaking off Anton's restraining hand. Pavel stared at the floor as he passed.

Upstairs, Ruzsky's constables stood and watched as the corpses were carried out into the courtyard and thrown into the back of a large truck. The Okhrana men climbed up beside them. Prokopiev made his way round to the cab.

'"Urgent political investigation",' Ruzsky said. 'What does that mean?'

Prokopiev turned back.

'Who were they?' Ruzsky asked.

'I have no idea.'

'Then why do you want them?'

'They were murdered in front of the Winter Palace. That will do as a reason for now.'

'So, in your estimation it was a political murder?'

'I didn't say that, did I?' He raised his finger. 'You mustn't misquote me, old man.' He stepped back. 'I'm glad you're home. See how our city has changed?'

Ruzsky said nothing.

'You haven't, perhaps, but you will. You'll telephone me if you ever need anything, won't you?'

Ruzsky still held his tongue.

'So much crime, such difficult times. We need to

79

help each other, isn't that so? How is your son, by the way?'

Ruzsky went cold. 'He's fine, thank you.'

'Michael, isn't it?'

'Michael, yes.'

'A good name. Perhaps if I ever have a son I'll call him Michael.' Prokopiev looked at him, with his piercing blue eyes. 'Good day, Prince Ruzsky.' He climbed up into the truck. 'And, once again, welcome home.'

The engine started up and diesel fumes billowed across the courtyard.

Ruzsky watched until it had disappeared from view. He turned to find Anton standing on the step behind him. 'So, we let them get away with it?' he asked quietly.

Anton stared up at the sky. 'Sometimes you're not very bright, do you know that?'

'So I've been told.'

'If they had the power to send you into exile before, imagine what they could do to you now.'

'Was the dead man one of theirs?'

'How should I know?' Anton turned towards him. 'If you want to be a martyr, be my guest, but be careful of Pavel.'

'Why?'

'He bears a huge burden of guilt. He carries it like a yoke.'

'He shouldn't.'

Anton sighed. 'Don't take me for a fool, Sandro. I know what happened. He'll follow you into the jaws of hell if it comes to it. Remember that, please.'

Ruzsky shook his head.

'You know what I mean, and don't pretend that you don't. Your desire to take the blame places others in your debt, but you're stubborn and, in these times, that is dangerous.'

'So, what do you want us to do?'

Anton didn't answer.

'It was only authorization to move the bodies. We still have responsibility for the overall investigation.'

'Well, then, it's up to you,' Anton said, eventually, and walked back into the building. Pavel passed him on the threshold, coming out into the courtyard.

'They frighten you?' Ruzsky asked Pavel.

'It's you they should frighten.'

'I won't be their lap-dog,' Ruzsky said.

'No, well . . .' Pavel trailed off.

'What do you want to do?'

'I don't know. You're the boss.'

'It's still our investigation.'

'Fine.'

'Did they know who they were?'

Pavel studied his boots. 'I don't know.'

Ruzsky turned around. Pavel did not move.

At his desk, Ruzsky sat back in his chair and thought of the fear he'd seen in Pavel's face, and even Anton's. He glanced at the clock, then took out his wallet and removed the photograph of Irina and Michael that he kept there. He put it on his desk, switched on the lamp and bent over it. He told himself Prokopiev was only dangerous if he made another mistake. He would just have to be careful. Tackling the thugs of the Black Bands this morning would have been unwise.

Ruzsky stared at the face of his son. Michael was a handsome boy, with straight dark hair and a solemn face. He was shy, just as his father had been, stubborn and loving. When he was difficult – which he had become more frequently as his parents' arguments increased – he would cling to his rebellion tenaciously, only to cry his heart out once it was over.

Irina smiled, with the easy lopsided grin that now failed to touch anything within him. Ruzsky thought of their departure from Tobolsk six months ago. He recalled Michael's desperate affection and Irina's impatience. He thought of her standing in the tiny kitchen of that house, screaming, 'I wasn't made for this!' Michael would think his father had abandoned him. At only six, it was a terrible conclusion to reach.

Ruzsky stood and, as he had done at home, rested his head against the damp cold glass of the window. It was not possible, surely, that a boy could be better off denied a father's love. Wasn't he himself testimony to that? He put his hand into his jacket pocket and pulled out an old printed programme from the Mariinskiy Theatre. He opened it to the relevant page and placed it over the picture of Irina on the desk, so that Maria and Michael both looked up at him. He gazed at their faces, allowing his fantasy free rein. Was a happy family too much to ask?

Ruzsky noticed the pile of newspapers next to Pavel's desk and went over and pulled off the top copy, which turned out to be Friday's *Petrogradskie Vedomosti*. He ignored the war news and flicked through to the theatre section. *Romeo and Juliet* in the Mariinskiy, it announced, but there was no reference to her.

Pavel came back into the room and sat down at his desk. Ruzsky pushed aside the newspaper, scooped up the photograph and the programme and slipped them into his pocket.

Pavel had recovered and his manner was

businesslike, but he still had an uncanny knack for perceiving his partner's mood. 'You've been dreaming?'

Ruzsky leant back against the window. 'No. But if I had it's not a crime.'

'Depends who you are. In my case, no. I dream only of the possible. More vodka, more money, more sex. But with you, I'm not so sure.'

'Sex with you? I'm not so sure either—'

'You're a dreamer by nature. You dream of the impossible, I think, and that is a kind of prison.'

'Tobolsk was a prison. Without dreams, I'd have been dead from the neck up.'

Pavel stared at the floor. 'So, where do we go?'

'The thing is, political murders don't involve someone being stabbed seventeen times. Do they?'

'It depends on the motive.'

Five minutes later, as Ruzsky left the building, he collided with a man who barely reached his chest. 'Sandro!' the man exclaimed. 'They let you back!'

It was Stanislav. The wind had dropped and snow was falling in big, fat flakes, some of which perched on top of his head.

'They let you stay!' Ruzsky retorted. 'I can hardly believe it.'

'Well, you know . . . Even a sinking ship needs its rats . . .' He was a small, lean man with greasy hair, a long nose, round glasses and oily, pockmarked skin. Pavel called him 'the Rat' and the name had stuck. He had been a journalist originally, and still called himself one, although he had been employed by the department for more than a decade. His official job was to provide information on city police activities to the newspapers – which mostly meant murder cases, since that was all they were interested in – but Ruzsky had other uses for him. Stanislav, more than any of them, was at home in the city's sewers.

'I hear you've got a case for me,' Stanislav said, revealing an atrocious set of yellowing teeth. He wore woollen gloves with the fingers cut off.

'Possibly.'

'What do you want me to tell them?'

'Nothing, but if you have to, two unidentified bodies found on the Neva. We're searching the missing-persons file, and we urge anyone who cannot locate a loved one or colleague to come forward.'

Stanislav's eyes narrowed. 'I also hear they've taken your bodies.'

Ruzsky looked over the man's shoulder. Clearly he had only just arrived in the office. 'How do you know that?'

The Rat leant forward. 'As always, my friend, better not to know how I know.'

'All right.' Ruzsky stared at him. 'I need to know who the victims were. Can you find out?'

Stanislav raised his hands to the skies, palms up. He took a step past Ruzsky, then stopped. 'I never thought to see you back here.'

'Why?'

'Oh, I don't know.' He pointed a long, bony finger at him. 'But you be careful.'

'I've had enough warnings.'

'Maybe, but the rules have changed.'

Ruzsky frowned.

'Your street investigator, Vladimir, had an assistant a year back, a young army officer, invalided out of the war. Honourable man, like you. He started trying to bring to account some of those thugs in the Black Bands. He wasn't standing for any nonsense.' Stanislav's stare was grave with meaning. 'He was found in the Moyka with a knife in his back. No one here will tell you that. They don't like to think of it.'

'Who put it there?'

'You don't have to ask.'

'Was there an investigation?'

'There had to be.'

'Who ran it?'

'The deputy chief investigator, murder.'

Ruzsky stared at the man. He wasn't sure what he sought to imply. 'I'm sure Pavel did his best.'

'Maybe. Vladimir helped. He was upset.'

Ruzsky stared at the snow falling in the courtyard. Vladimir would have been upset. He was a strong man, like Pavel, but equally decent at heart. 'Did the Okhrana know who these corpses were today?' Ruzsky asked. 'And if so, how?'

Stanislav turned back. 'How did they know you'd sealed the fate of the man who killed that girl three years ago? You or Pavel, whoever it was.'

'There are hundreds of people in this building. Constables gossip.'

'There may be hundreds of people, but few who know exactly what is going on inside the criminal-investigation division.'

CHAPTER EIGHT

The front door of the Mariinskiy Theatre was ajar, and as Ruzsky slipped through into the foyer, he heard the noonday gun being fired from the St Peter and St Paul fortress on the far side of the river.

Ahead of him, two young women stood by the main entrance to the auditorium in animated conversation. He interrupted them with less grace than he had intended. He felt, suddenly, as he had on the ice.

The women looked taken aback. 'Who wants to know?' one asked.

'Chief Investigator Ruzsky, city police.' Ruzsky fumbled in a pocket for his dog-eared identification card, but the girls were not interested. They nodded towards the wooden doors that led into the auditorium.

The door snapped back as he entered and one of the dancers on the stage turned in his direction. It wasn't her. Ruzsky's mouth was dry. He pulled his shirt collar away from his throat.

He stood beneath the royal box, the blue and gold décor of the auditorium sumptuous even in the semi-darkness. At the centre of the small group of dancers on the stage the ballet master was bathed in light. He had dark hair and a long moustache. He stepped back to allow his dancers room. 'And again,' he shouted. 'And one and two and *jump* . . . No, no, *no*.'

He became aware of the dancers' distraction and spun round to face Ruzsky. '*Yes?*'

It was a moment or two before Ruzsky acknowledged that the remark had been directed at him. 'Maria,' he said, 'Maria Popova.'

'What about her?'

'I was just looking—'

'And who are you?'

'Ruzsky, Alexander Nicholaevich, chief investigator, city police.'

'Has a *crime* been committed?'

'No. I mean, yes. But it's not . . .' Ruzsky recovered his wits, spurred on by the theatrical exasperation on the man's face. 'Where is she?'

'So it's a private matter?'

'It's certainly none of your concern.'

The ballet master's smile told those around him he understood exactly the nature of Ruzsky's confusion.

'Where will I find her?' he asked again.

'Dressing room number one. Through the side door.' The man dismissed him with a peremptory flick of the hand.

Ruzsky walked slowly towards the side exit. He glanced up at the huge gold crown above the royal box and then at the seats his family customarily occupied. He knew where to find the dressing rooms. It was quiet backstage and he stood alone in the dark corridor outside number one.

He ran a hand through his hair, then rubbed distractedly at his lower lip with his index finger.

Now that he was here, he did not know what to do.

A dancer appeared from one of the rooms further down the corridor. She was in a hurry. 'Can I help you?' she asked, as she ran past him towards the stage, but Ruzsky had failed to reply by the time she turned the corner.

He took another pace forward.

He felt the blood pound in his head. He didn't need the ballet master's help to feel that he didn't quite belong there.

For a moment, he was transported back to their first meeting at Krasnoe Selo just outside the capital – the site of the summer camps of many of the Guards regiments – shortly before the outbreak of war. On that bright day, the French president had joined the Tsar for an inspection of the serried ranks of guardsmen on a dusty field leading down to a shimmering sea. Ruzsky had not forgotten a single detail. Standing here, he could almost feel the intense heat and smell the acrid odour of burning turf from a distant forest fire. He recalled the sight of the Emperor on his grey horse, the stillness in the crowd, then the cheers rising with the strength of an approaching storm.

Irina had persuaded him that they should accompany his father. After the inspection was over and a sinking sun cast shadows across the grey battleships anchored in the bay, he had been introduced to Maria. They had exchanged only a few words, but as she walked away, in a cloud of dust kicked up by a thousand horses' hoofs, she had turned to look back at him, the wide brim of her white hat pushed up and a hand shielding her eyes from the fading sunlight.

Ruzsky took another pace forward. In that moment, his life had been transformed, yet he had nothing better to go on than an instinct for her feelings.

He thought of Anton's assertion that she had kept a picture of him on her dressing-table. Was he too late? He knocked.

'Come in.'

Adrenalin pumped through him. He put his hand on the door and pushed it gently.

Maria stood on the far side of the room, in front of a mirror, half turned towards him. She was tall, with long dark hair that stretched all the way down the centre of her back. She had a slim nose, long eyelashes, rich green eyes and full, slightly upturned lips. She was a woman of heart-stopping beauty, talented, womanly and clever, yet the sight of him made her flush. Her smile was girlish, filled with unsophisticated pleasure. 'Hello, Sandro,' she said softly.

Ruzsky's stomach lurched.

She wore a simple, elegant cream and gold dress. 'You're back,' she said.

'Yes.'

'You've come home.' Her voice was warm.

Ruzsky did not know how to reply, so he said, 'You haven't changed.'

She gave a tiny smile. 'Is that a compliment?'

'Of course.'

'You look older.'

'And that isn't.'

'I don't know. It suits you.' She paused, her face serious again. 'It's been so long, Sandro.'

'A lifetime.'

'How was Tobolsk?' she asked.

'It was cold.'

'You missed Petersburg. City of our dreams.'

'And yet it got along without me.'

'That's a matter of opinion. I was told that your wife came home.'

Ruzsky wanted to ask by whom. 'She did, yes.'

'I'm sorry for that.' Then, evidently, she caught sight of the hole in his boot. 'Don't you have anyone to look after you?'

'No,' he said, with a rueful smile.

It had been intended, he knew, as a joke, but her face was instantly concerned, and warmth flooded through him.

Maria took a step towards him, then leant against the dresser upon which she stored her makeup. Her dress was tight and low-cut, the swell of her breasts almost sculpted. He caught sight of a single rose in a cut-glass vase behind her, and imagined another man kissing the smooth skin of her neck. Ruzsky fought to keep his emotions in check, but it was an unequal battle. He was forty – *forty* – an investigator hardened by more experience than was good for a man; he was married, betrayed, alone. And yet when he was with her – a girl not much more than half his age – the cares of the world fell away.

Opposite her dresser, a photograph of the male dancer Vaslaw Nijinsky as the golden slave – the role that made him famous – took pride of place alongside one of Maria and Kshesinskaya, the prima ballerina *assoluta*. Russia's two best-known ballerinas had draped their arms around each other for the camera. 'How is she?' Ruzsky asked, inclining his head.

'Much the same as before,' Maria replied. 'Still collecting Romanovs.'

'Perhaps not the best currency in these times.'

'The world is at war, Sandro. How many million

dead? How many yet to die? Our fantasies count for little.'

Ruzsky felt as if she could look right through him.

'Was it so bad, what you did? To send you away for so long.'

Her gaze was intense. Was it hurt he saw there? Ruzsky sighed. 'I helped cause a man's death.'

'But he was a terrible man.'

Ruzsky stared at the floor.

'And you took the blame, Sandro.'

Ruzsky did not answer.

'So you're the kind of man who will not cheat on his wife, even though she betrays him openly, and who will happily go into exile to protect a friend.'

'I wouldn't say happily—'

'An example to us all.'

'I'm afraid my father would not agree.'

'Is what he thinks still so important?'

'Yes.' Ruzsky realized he had said too much. 'No.' He forced a smile. 'Are you rehearsing today?'

There was a shout from the corridor. 'Maria Andreevna!' Then another, when she did not answer. She was still looking at Ruzsky. 'Something for next month. Two more nights of the Stravinsky and then I go home to Yalta.'

'It's a long way, at a time like this.'

'My sister is not well. Sandro, I . . .' As she tried to find the words, her face was more achingly beautiful than ever. This was how he had remembered her. 'I would like us to be friends,' she said.

Ruzsky's heart banged like a drum. Friends . . . He was not sure if she meant only friends and no more. 'We are friends.'

Now he saw sorrow in her eyes. Longing, or just a

deep loneliness that was the mirror of his own? Ruzsky looked at her, but something prevented him speaking.

'Maria!' the man shouted again.

She touched his cheek, her fingers cool on his skin as her eyes searched his. Then she was gone.

Ruzsky stayed rooted to the spot. By the time he had followed her out of the door, she had disappeared.

At the end of the corridor, he stopped. He could hear the ballet master already barking instructions. 'And one and two and *no . . . Again!'*

He waited. He listened to his own breathing in the silence of the corridor. After a minute, he continued on his way.

CHAPTER NINE

It was still snowing heavily as Ruzsky walked across the square towards the Tsarskoe Selo station, head down and deep in thought. He could see no sign of any police presence, so he assumed the trains must be running today. The elegant yellow station took its name from its principal destination: trains from here ran out to the town an hour away that was home to the current Tsar. Whenever Nicholas wanted to come to the capital on *his* train, the station was sealed off, sometimes all day.

Ruzsky barely registered the long *khvost* on the far side of the square until he heard shouts and looked over to see a group of soldiers fighting in the middle of the queue. He hesitated, then walked on until he heard the crack of a shot, then another.

A tram rattled past, almost encased in ice, and Ruzsky ran round the back of it, slipping as he narrowed his eyes against the driving snow. A large group of men was fighting, perhaps ten or more, and there was another shot. The mêlée was too confused for him to tell who was firing or at what. He reached into his pocket for his Sauvage, pointed it in the air and fired once. 'Police! Get back in line.'

The men continued to fight. He fired twice more. 'GET BACK IN LINE!' he bellowed.

They stopped and, as Ruzsky moved closer, turned to stare at him. Two were on the ground, covered in snow, and got up slowly. All were in long greatcoats, but one at least had large holes in the top of his boots. He was an older peasant conscript with a long, unkempt beard. He had knocked over a woman and her son in the scuffle and Ruzsky helped them to their feet. The woman almost slipped over again, but he caught her. She was dressed in a thick jacket and a scuffed, dark pair of *valenki* – knee-high rough woollen boots.

He retreated once more, and it was only then that he could see the line was more than a hundred yards long and stretched all the way round the corner of the block. 'You're waiting for bread?' he shouted.

The men stared at him, snow gathering on their faces. Most of those ahead and behind them were women, wrapped up in headscarves so that only their eyes were visible.

He saw himself from their point of view. A detested servant of the Tsar. He thought of the article on his desk. No wonder the educated classes feared the mob.

'You're waiting for bread?' he shouted again, wanting to break the mood. Still no one answered him.

Ruzsky walked swiftly along the queue and turned the corner to see that the bakery they were waiting outside was not even open. He pushed through the middle of the crowd and went to the door, then put his face to the cold glass and peered in. There was no light on inside, but he could see that the shelves were empty. He turned back to them. 'There's nothing in there.'

Nobody spoke.

At the front of the queue, a woman waited with her son and an old man on a makeshift wooden barrow. Snow and ice had gathered in the old man's beard and his eyes were beyond caring.

'They said there would be bread later,' the woman said. 'No one wishes to lose their place in the line.'

Ruzsky walked back towards the group of soldiers. 'It will be a long wait,' he said, as he approached. 'If you must stay, be patient. Fighting serves no one.' Even as he spoke, he felt the patronizing futility of his words. He stared at them for a moment more, then went towards the station steps. As he did so, he felt a thousand eyes upon his back.

'Officer!' someone shouted. Ruzsky swung round. The boy who had been at the front of the queue stood before him. He thrust a piece of paper into his hands. Ruzsky looked down at it.

A PROPHECY

A year shall come of Russia's blackest dread;
Then will the crown fall from the royal head,
The throne of tsars will perish in the mud,
The food of many will be death and blood.
                    Mikhail Lermontov, 1830

Ruzsky looked up. Even through the veil of falling snow he could see the hatred in their eyes. He folded the piece of paper, put it into his pocket and walked away.

He climbed the stone steps to the platform level of

the station and emerged on the concourse. A guard blew his whistle loudly and the engine closest to him released a burst of steam that flooded across the platform. Light spilled through the glass panels of the curved iron roof.

Ruzsky walked past the shops selling sweets and cigarettes and noticed how bare their shelves were. Before the war, they'd also have sold pastries and bread, but now there was no sign of either. Only a man standing next to a brazier selling baked *lavasky*, the wafer-thin round cakes, appeared to be doing any trade.

Ruzsky grasped the brass rail at the entrance to one of the carriages and pulled himself up, then shut the door behind him. He took his seat and pushed up the window next to it; a few crystals of snow and ice floated down on to his lap. On the platform, three women in fur coats and hats stood next to an officer in the dark blue and green parade uniform of Her Majesty's Cuirassier Regiment – the Blue Cuirassiers. Next to them, a newspaper boy in a flat cloth cap was shouting: *'Petrogradskie Vedomosti! Novoe Vremia!'* beside a crudely inscribed headline board: 'Western Front: No Changes. Romanian Front: No Changes. Caucasian Front: No Changes. Bravery of Russian Soldiers! Shaliapin Charity Concert to be Announced in Moscow.'

As Ruzsky watched, the officer ordered the boy to be quiet, then said something to the women and roared with laughter as the whistle sounded. For all his rebellion, Ruzsky could not help sharing his family's prejudice against cavalry officers. The Preobrazhensky – his father's regiment – was in the infantry division of the Life Guards. He stood up and returned to the platform to buy a copy of *Petrogradskie Vedomosti*. He gave the boy a large tip.

The carriage was empty, save for a couple in the far corner staring out of their window. Ruzsky stretched his legs and sank back in the leather seat. There was another whistle and the train began to move. The view across the rooftops, through dull light and dirty windows, appeared endless.

The girl at the end of the carriage leant her head affectionately on the man's shoulder. They were young, possibly palace household staff.

Ruzsky pulled his thin overcoat tight, trying to ignore the cold. He took out his silver case and almost smoked a cigarette, before thinking better of it. He flipped the case over and looked at the family crest. Like the Romanovs', it depicted a giant eagle, but single-headed.

He closed his eyes. Train journeys always transported him back to his youth and the times when his family left Petersburg for what had been his father's favourite country estate at Petrovo. Sometimes Ruzsky revisited that journey in his mind: the packing of the household, the excitement that invaded everyone, even the servants, for days beforehand, the hampers, the first-class compartment, the soporific rattle of the train as it moved slowly south, the horse-drawn *troikas* at the station, and the thrill of that last stretch when he, Dmitri and Ilya would run through the woods to the house. He could see, even now, the village sparkling through the pine trees as they crested the last hill, the house ablaze with light.

He wondered if he would ever go back.

The train rattled past a frozen lake upon which a boy of six or seven was skating with halting, uncoordinated movements. Ruzsky saw him fall and sat upright, craning his neck to see if he had gone through the ice. But the boy got up, dusted the snow from his clothes and skated away. Ruzsky kept his eyes on him until the train had rattled round the corner of the wood and out of sight.

He picked up his newspaper. There was a long article on the front page that contained the usual fantastic assertions about the progress of the war, and a claim that the radical political changes demanded by some would 'shatter the foundations of Russian society'. This was the newspaper his father had always treated as a conservative bible. He flicked through it. A group of criminals had robbed the Mutual Credit Bank in Kharkov of a million roubles, drilling through a wall from a neighbouring house.

He put down the paper. Perhaps it was a sign of the times. When a ship hit bad weather, it was every rat for himself.

When he reached the station in the town of Tsarskoe Selo, Ruzsky climbed into the back of a *droshky*, and a few moments later the wind was cutting into his cheeks as he was hurried along Sadovaya Ulitsa, past the formal gardens of the Catherine Palace. The weather was much clearer out here, and the magnificent blue, white and gold baroque façade of the palace sparkled in the sunlight. Above it, the Imperial standard of the Romanovs crackled in the breeze.

Ruzsky watched a green ambulance with a red cross on its side slide through the gates of the palace. It was the grandest of all the Romanovs' homes, and since the start of the war a section had been used as a hospital for officers. Not that that had done the ruling dynasty any favours. Ruzsky smoked a cigarette to calm his nerves. He had been here as a child, when his father had been summoned to a meeting with the present Tsar's father, Alexander III – a rare event since Alexander had preferred his home at Gatchina. Even as a son of privilege, Ruzsky had found the opulence awe-inspiring. So many servants, he had told his mother. He could not forget the look of rapture in her eyes.

The *droshky* slowed as they approached the Alexander Palace and the driver stopped short of the gate. Ruzsky paid and sent him on his way. He waited for a moment as he pushed his bundle of roubles back into his pocket. Two guards stood by the gate. The emperors did not like to see servants arriving and leaving, he had once been told, so an entrance to the palace complex had been built underground. He was surprised by how ordinary it all seemed. Somehow, given the climate in the capital, he had expected to find hundreds of guards and thick barbed-wire fencing.

'Ruzsky, Alexander Nicholaevich, chief investigator of the Petrograd police,' he told the guards, producing his identification papers.

The men were soldiers from the Cossack Escort regiment, but as he handed over his papers, Ruzsky noticed another man – an officer of the police of the Imperial Court – watching him from inside the gate. A minute later, the man, in a long, elegant grey overcoat, slipped out and walked towards him.

'An investigator from the city police,' one of the guards explained, as the man took Ruzsky's identification papers and examined them.

He looked carefully at the photograph, then up at Ruzsky. 'It says here you're the chief investigator.'

'Yes.'

'I don't know you.'

'I've been away.'

'To the front?'

'No.'

The man frowned. 'You are still the chief investigator?'

'I suppose so.'

'You suppose so?'

'Yes, I am.'

'Your papers are out of date.'

Ruzsky looked at him, not sure if he was joking. 'I apologize,' he said, then realizing that the officers charged with the Tsar's personal protection had nothing to smile about. 'You're quite correct, they are out of date, but I'm conducting a murder investigation.'

'Not Rasputin?'

'No.'

'Who have you come to see?'

'Madame Vyrubova.'

'Vyrubova?'

'Yes.'

'You have made an appointment?'

'No, I'm afraid not.'

The officer looked suspicious. 'I'll have to ask you to wait while I telephone.'

'Of course.'

The policeman retreated to the small wooden box beside the gate, the guards alongside him. Ruzsky walked forward to the railings and looked through to the yellow and white colonnades. The Alexander Palace was infinitely more modest than the Catherine Palace, its neighbour.

He took out his case and lit another cigarette. It was almost warm now that the sun was out, though his feet were still numb with cold. He stamped in an effort to get the blood flowing.

He noticed two faces in an upstairs window of the house closest to the gate. He assumed they were also officers of the palace police, watching the entrance. The aura of calm was deceptive. He faced the gate again and watched a gardener chipping ice from the steps to the nearest wing of the palace.

Ruzsky thought about the faces of those waiting in the bread queue. Were they really talking about revolution? Now that people discussed it openly, he found himself recoiling from his earlier insistence that change was inevitable and desirable in whatever form. It frightened him: he no longer believed that it always made things better. He thought of the arguments with his father. If only they had spent less time being so certain they were right . . . but, then, the same could be said for the whole country.

'All right, Chief Investigator. I'll get someone to accompany you.'

Ruzsky was so surprised that he did not answer. The man returned to his box and Ruzsky waited, his hands thrust into his overcoat pockets.

There was a burst of activity as three soldiers ran down from the near wing to open the gate. A long, low black saloon car followed them, the yellow and black Imperial flag fluttering over the bonnet.

It skidded on the ice as it pulled out on to the road, affording Ruzsky a brief glimpse of the man inside. The Tsar of All the Russias glanced at him, then settled back into his seat.

One of the soldiers walked over. 'I will take you.'

'I thought the Emperor was at the front,' Ruzsky heard himself say.

The guard gave him a sour look, but did not deign to reply.

They began to walk, stepping on to the side of the road into the snow where the footing was surer. 'How is Petrograd?' the man asked.

'Cold.'

'We hear only bad things.'

'It will be better when there is more bread.'

They rounded the corner of the palace and saw a group of children playing beneath the terrace. They were making something from the snow – from here it looked like a house – helped by two men and a woman. As they moved closer, Ruzsky recognized two of the grand duchesses, the Tsar's daughters, and the Tsarevich, his only son. He could not take his eyes from them. As with the car, it was almost like seeing an apparition. If he told Pavel he'd witnessed the Tsar's children playing in the snow – just like any others in Russia – the big detective would never believe him. It reminded Ruzsky of his childhood conviction that the Tsar was not a mere man but a being from another world. It was an impression that he could still not entirely dispel, even though he had once exchanged a few words with the young Nicholas Romanov at a New Year's Day reception at the Winter Palace.

The Tsarevich laughed. He was a pale child, with a thin white face, but there was no sign of the haemophilia with which rumour said he was afflicted. As the guard led him towards the group, Ruzsky tried to tear his eyes away from the boy, but could not.

'Madame Vyrubova,' the guard said. A round-faced

woman looked over towards them. She was dressed in a long white coat with a fur collar. 'This gentleman has come to see you. He is the chief investigator for the Petrograd police.'

The woman frowned. The two grand duchesses looked at Ruzsky with frank curiosity. They were strikingly beautiful. The men – tutors, he assumed – stopped what they were doing and appraised him also. Both were dressed in long overcoats and suits.

Ruzsky realized that he was staring at them as he would at a caged animal. He had to force himself to look away.

'I've not seen him before,' Vyrubova said.

The Tsarevich looked like his own son, Ruzsky thought. They shared the same gentle solemnity. As he watched, the woman drew the boy to her, but the gesture was proprietorial rather than affectionate.

'I'm new,' Ruzsky said. He was required to offer an explanation.

'You're too late.'

The Tsarevich slipped his other arm through that of the older of his two sisters. She must be Olga, Ruzsky thought, or perhaps Tatiana. It was many years since he'd seen either of them. They projected a luminous innocence, in sharp contrast, he thought, to the caricature he had seen on the office wall earlier of their half-naked mother dancing with Rasputin.

'Take him to my house. I will see him there,' Vyrubova said. Her manner was imperious and dismissive. He turned reluctantly and the guard led him away down the central path.

Ruzsky glanced back. The group still watched him. He was chivvied on by the guard. The icy path had been scattered with small stones to give a measure of grip, but he walked uncertainly.

The path ran through a long line of trees, which stood out starkly against the snowy landscape. Ruzsky could see the Catherine Palace to his left and stopped as he reached the point where the paths leading to both palaces met. He could still see the children playing beneath the curved terrace behind him. The guard moved him on again. They passed a chapel. 'Is that where they buried him?' Ruzsky asked. 'Rasputin, I mean.'

The guard stopped, his face severe. 'You have no power or jurisdiction here. Is that understood?' Ruzsky noticed how red the man's cheeks were from the cold, the capillaries so pronounced that they reminded him of the painted wooden maps they'd studied at school. 'This is the home of the Tsar of All the Russias. You will confine yourself to addressing Madame Vyrubova, and no one else.'

Ruzsky concealed his irritation as the man marched him swiftly down to a small house in the far corner of the park. It was a pavilion that had been transformed into a comfortable, solid residence, with a white wooden fence around the garden.

The guard left him at the door in the hands of a young housekeeper with pretty dark eyes. She smiled and led him through to a drawing room, which was neatly but not lavishly furnished. He accepted her offer of tea.

The room was bright, sunlight spilling in through large windows. Ruzsky stood with his back to the fire blazing in the hearth. On the far wall there was a framed photograph of Rasputin with a collection of icons beneath it. Next to it was a picture of Anna

Vyrubova sitting beside the Tsar on a thin strip of sand in what looked like the Crimea. The last picture, next to a bookcase, was of her surrounded by the Tsar's five children.

Her desk was arranged neatly, a pen and inkwell placed beside a pile of writing paper. On the right-hand side, alongside a small carriage clock, the Tsarina stared out at him severely from an ornate silver frame.

He heard someone come through the front door and returned to his position in the centre of the room.

'What do you want?' Vyrubova asked as she entered.

'I—'

'You didn't come to see us about Father Grigory. If you are indeed the chief investigator, we should have seen you then.'

'I have just returned to Petrograd, and I believe such an important case was always likely to be treated as a political and not simply a criminal matter, for reasons that will be obvious to you.'

She stared at him. 'It has brought shame on our country, and our class.'

Ruzsky didn't answer. He wondered exactly what relationship this woman enjoyed with the Empress. Technically, he recalled, she was a lady-in-waiting, but she was clearly much more. This was the woman whom much of Russia believed to be her lesbian lover, and a participant in orgies that were said variously to involve both the Tsar and Rasputin.

'If your business is not important,' she went on, 'why do you trouble me with it?' Her small eyes were fixed on his. He sensed her suspicion, and cunning.

'The body of a woman was found on the Neva this

morning. She was wearing a dress made by Madame Renaud.' He paused. 'A dress made for you.'

Her expression did not alter, but he saw her eyes flicker. 'Who was she?'

'That's why I'm here.' Ruzsky reached into his pocket for the photographs. He handed her one of the girl's head and shoulders. 'I was hoping you would be able to tell me.'

Vyrubova took it. 'How do you know the dress was mine?'

'Madame Renaud confirmed it.'

'How did you know it was one of her dresses?'

Ruzsky was about to explain, but thought better of it. 'Do you recognize her?'

'Yes.' Vyrubova handed back the photograph, her face expressionless.

'And?'

'Her name was Ella.'

They heard the front door open and shut, and a voice in the hall. A moment later, the Tsarina appeared, in a black overcoat, gloves and hat, a diamond brooch at her throat.

Ruzsky did not move. After a few moments, he realized that his mouth was open and he shut it. She was taller than he remembered, but there were deep lines around her eyes and her face was harsher, thinner, more angular than he'd imagined. The last time he had set eyes on her had been on the day of his arrest. He had been with his brother in the general-staff building, overlooking a packed Palace Square, as the Tsar and his wife came out on to the balcony of the Winter Palace to read a proclamation declaring the Russian empire to be at war with Germany and Austro-Hungary. Even now, Ruzsky could recall every detail of that crisp day: the giant crimson drape that hung almost to the ground, the Tsar dressed in the uniform of a colonel in the Preobrazhensky regiment, his wife in white, the gigantic crowd falling to its knees and chanting the national anthem '*Bozhe, Tzaria Khrani*', over and over again, the Emperor raising his hand against the din as he read the proclamation, his wife bowing.

That day the swell of emotion had touched even the most cynical hearts. In the eyes of the uniformed young men around him Ruzsky saw nothing short of ecstasy. Now most of them were dead, and the woman who ruled an empire stood before him dressed in black. His education failed him. He had no idea what he should say if she chose to address him.

'Who is this?' she demanded.

'He says he's a chief investigator from Petrograd.'

The Empress snorted in derision, as if he wasn't there. 'It's not good for Alexei to be out in the cold so long.' She spoke Russian with a heavy German accent.

Vyrubova's expression was soothing. 'He seems better today.'

'He's no judge of his own well-being.'

'He wants to be out with the girls.'

'I know he does, but that doesn't mean it is good for him.'

The Empress of All the Russias turned to Ruzsky. 'What is he doing here?'

Vyrubova handed the Tsarina the photograph. She studied it, then looked up again, her mouth taut. 'I suppose you think it is our fault.'

Ruzsky did not know what to say.

'She was murdered,' Vyrubova explained. 'It wasn't—'

The Empress looked confused. 'Murdered?'

It appeared to be a question for him. 'Yes,' Ruzsky said. He cleared his throat and bowed slightly. 'It would appear so, Your . . .' Ruzsky wondered if he should address her as 'Your Imperial Highness', but a hint of resentment at his mother's fawning approach to the Imperial Family acted as its own check. Their manner was damned rude.

'It would appear so? Surely you must know.'

'Yes, Your . . . That is correct.'

'How was she murdered?'

Ruzsky glanced at Vyrubova to see whether he should continue to answer, but received no signal. 'She was stabbed. Once. The man with her, seventeen times.' Ruzsky handed a photograph of the man's head and shoulders to the Empress. She looked at it, then passed it to her companion.

'How did you know she worked here?' the Empress asked.

Ruzsky looked at Vyrubova, whose face was impassive. 'I didn't,' he said. He thought he saw a slight flush developing in the Tsarina's cheeks.

'Ella worked in the nursery,' Vyrubova explained, 'and was very fond of the children.'

'She was a pretty girl,' the Empress said, 'but unreliable.'

'She was fond of the family,' Vyrubova went on, 'and was sad to go.'

They were silent. Their sudden garrulousness confused him. 'If I may ask,' Ruzsky said, 'to go where?'

'She was dismissed,' the Empress said.

There was another long silence.

'Would it be impertinent . . .' Ruzsky kept his eyes

on Vyrubova so as not to offend the Empress. 'May I ask why?'

The Empress frowned, tilting her head to one side. 'You may not.'

'I apologize, Your Highness.'

'She stole from us,' the Tsarina said suddenly. She sighed. 'There was no choice but to dismiss her. It upset the children. She upset the children.'

'She was too close to them,' Vyrubova added. 'To the Little One, to Sunbeam, especially.'

The Empress's irritation with Vyrubova began to show again.

'She was sad to leave here?' Ruzsky asked.

'Devastated. Of course.' The Empress seemed to remember herself. 'I did not expect anyone to be here,' she told Vyrubova. 'Telephone me when you have dealt with this man.'

She walked out. They watched her pass the window and the white fence around the garden.

Vyrubova did not look at him. There was an intimacy between them now, as if he had witnessed a domestic scene normally kept from prying eyes. She stared at her shoes, a rueful smile on her lips.

'What did this girl . . . Ella . . . steal?'

'Oh, I don't know.' Vyrubova was evasive again.

'You don't know what she took?'

'No.' She looked out of the window. The Empress was now some distance away. 'No.'

'Some money?'

'No. I mean, yes. Money.'

'How much?'

She turned back, still not meeting his eye. 'I don't know.'

Ruzsky smiled encouragingly. 'You seem to keep few secrets from each other.'

'Who?'

'You and the Empress.'

'That is not your business.'

'No. Of course. I just imagined that she would have told you the cause of this girl's dismissal.'

'She rules the Empire during the Tsar's absence at the front, commanding our great forces. She doesn't have time to deal with the minutiae of the household. The girl was unimportant.'

'But the children were upset.'

'They will quickly recover. It is best to be removed from unsuitable influences.'

'How was she unsuitable exactly?'

'Oh . . . I don't know.' Ruzsky saw her impatience, but did not understand why she should make such heavy weather of the lies she was telling. 'You must ask the household staff.'

'As you wish. May I go over now?'

'No.' She was shocked. 'You must apply in writing.'

'To whom?'

'To the household. To Colonel Shulgin. He deals with such matters.'

Ruzsky tried to control his annoyance. 'Was Ella from Petersburg?'

'No, she wasn't. Yalta or Sevastopol. Somewhere on the peninsula.'

'How did she come to be employed here?'

'I have no idea. You'll have to ask the household staff.'

'Did you know the girl well?'

'Ella? No. Not at all.'

'But you gave her one of your dresses?'

'Yes, but . . . she had not worked here long.'

'How long?'

'A few months. Perhaps a little more.'

'Did she ever talk about her life outside of her work?'

'Not to me. I don't believe so. No, she didn't.'

'Did she have any family or friends that you know of?'

'I've no idea.'

'What was her family name?'

'Kovyil.'

Ruzsky noted it. 'So you saw her when you were with the children. She was a nanny. To Alexei?'

'She helped in the nursery.' Vyrubova's expression clouded. 'It was disgraceful to steal like that. Disgraceful. The Empress has always been most generous.'

Ruzsky doubted, from her tone, that this was true. 'But you knew the girl well enough to give her one of your dresses.'

'I hardly spoke to her.'

'It was an act of great generosity.'

'She mentioned how much she liked it one day. It no longer fitted me. After she was dismissed, I sent it round to her.'

'But Madame Renaud's dresses are not inexpensive . . .'

Vyrubova looked at him, assessing him properly for the first time. She took a pace away. 'I must go to the palace.'

'I would ask you to stay a few moments more,' he said quietly.

'I have work to do.'

'And I too.' Ruzsky's tone checked her. 'This girl

was walking arm in arm with her lover under the moonlight in the first hours of the new year. The man's face was so severely lacerated it will be hard to identify him. Even in these troubled days, murder must not go unheeded, surely.'

She stared at him. He wondered if she had privately expressed such sentiments at the way in which Rasputin's killers had escaped justice.

'Who are you? What is your name?' she demanded.

'Ruzsky. Alexander Nicholaevich.'

She frowned. 'You are related to the assistant minister of finance?'

'My father.'

She assessed him with inscrutable eyes. 'I cannot help you further.'

'*Did* you recognize the man?'

Vyrubova still had the photograph. She returned it to him. 'No.'

'He wasn't a member of the household staff also?'

'No.'

'You haven't seen him before?'

She shook her head.

'Did Ella ever speak about a male friend, a lover, perhaps?'

'I told you, I hardly knew the girl.'

Ruzsky breathed in deeply to hide his impatience. 'When you say Ella was upset, what do you mean? Did you—'

'It was the Empress who said she was upset. I did not see her.'

This was so obviously a lie that Ruzsky became angry. 'From everything you've said, Madame, I find that—'

112

'I have to go now. The Empress is expecting me.'
She began to walk away.

'Madame?'

She glowered at him.

'Could you give me the number of the house to which you sent the dress?'

She looked puzzled.

'You said that you had sent the dress round to her after she left.'

He thought Vyrubova might explode as she sought a way out of the trap into which she had led herself. 'The household staff dealt with it. You must speak to them.'

'To Count Fredericks?'

'No, no. He has many more important things to deal with.'

'Colonel Shulgin, then?'

'Yes, but you may not do so now. You must make an appointment.' There was something close to panic in her voice.

'Tomorrow, perhaps.'

'Tomorrow, yes. Tomorrow.'

Ruzsky was led back the way he had come. The children were still playing with the snow house. Alexei was standing on a block of ice and sweeping snow on to the heads of the two men helping them. He was laughing.

One of the girls threw a snowball at her brother, and he threw one back. Ruzsky noticed that the boy dragged his right leg as he tried to run away.

'Keep up,' the guard said. 'Or I shall be forced to call for assistance.'

'The boy tries hard to overcome—'

'It is not your business.'

'I don't recall suggesting that it was.' Ruzsky thrust his hands into his pockets. 'It's a good life here. Quiet. I can see why they hate coming to Petrograd.'

The guard looked at him, then turned on his heel. Ruzsky studied the boy for a few moments more, then followed. When he turned back, he saw that the heir to All the Russias was watching him.

CHAPTER TEN

By the time he got back to the office, the only light in his department was from Pavel's desk lamp, but his partner's coat was not on the stand in the corner. Ruzsky walked over to his own desk. Propped up against the telephone was a letter. He recognized Maria's hand. He tapped it once against his fingers, then tore it open. 'My dear Sandro,' she had written, 'it was so good to see you today.' Folded in it was a ticket for *The Firebird* at the Mariinskiy the following night.

Ruzsky sat down. He put the letter on the desk and pushed it gently to and fro. He stood up again and looked out of the window into the darkness. Was this just an act of friendship? But hope made him want to dance.

'Want to tell me what you're doing?' Pavel stood in the shadows just inside the doorway.

'I thought you'd gone,' Ruzsky said.

'Russia's most beautiful woman,' Pavel said. 'She delivered it herself. I hope you know what you're doing.'

'It's not what you think.'

'I'll take your word for it. I should imagine she has many admirers.'

'What do you mean?'

'Exactly what I said.'

Ruzsky folded the letter and slipped it back into the envelope.

'So,' Pavel continued, 'how did you get on?'

'You'll never believe what I have to say, so you first.'

Pavel raised his eyebrows. 'Nothing from the embankment. I spoke to some junior official in the Winter Palace household who assured me it was not possible that anyone could have witnessed anything from an upstairs window.'

'We'll go and see him together tomorrow.'

'I don't think there's much point. He was adamant that the rooms on the top floor are the preserve of the family and none of them was present last night. I don't think he was lying.' Pavel yanked up his trousers. 'But I've just come from the American embassy, and that sounded promising.'

Ruzsky waited.

'The official we need to speak to has gone out of town and won't be back until the morning, but one of his colleagues said they'd had a report from home six weeks ago asking them to ask us to be on the lookout for a Robert White, an armed robber from Chicago. They said they'd passed it on to the Okhrana. I told them a lot of good it would do them.'

'What has that to do with the couple on the ice?'

'Someone from the Astoria telephoned the embassy this morning. Apparently, a man calling himself Whitewater checked into the hotel just over a week ago, saying he was a diplomat and writing "care of the embassy" on the registration form. They suspected him of having left without paying his bill because his room was empty and they hadn't seen him for two days.'

'Did you go down to the Astoria?'

'Give me a chance. I'll go first thing. Come on, I need a drink.' Pavel spoke with feeling.

'I can't afford it.'

'Neither can I, but there is a place nearby. I've threatened it with closure. They're very co-operative.' He led the way down the darkened stairwell.

Outside, the snow was thick on the ground. The wind had dropped, but the air was still crisp and the night cloudy. Ruzsky's feet were instantly cold again.

'Tell me what happened at Tsarskoe Selo,' Pavel said.

'You won't believe it.'

'Try me.'

Ruzsky smiled to himself. It was hard to believe that the episode had not been a figment of his imagination – and yet it had been so ordinary. 'I went to see Vyrubova, but the Tsarina arrived.'

'You're not serious.'

'On my honour.'

'She had horns growing from her head?' Pavel asked.

'Mmm. And she carried a flaming pitchfork.'

'No, really, what happened?'

'As I said, I went to see Vyrubova.'

'She received you?'

'Not exactly. I saw the Tsar depart in his car and then I was taken to her house. We walked past the Imperial children, or some of them, playing in the snow. Then the Tsarina arrived.'

'Just like that?'

'More or less.'

'On her own?'

'Yes.'

'No staff, no officials, no fanfare?'

'It was very ordinary.'

'No strange priests?'

Ruzsky did not answer.

'And?' Pavel went on.

'Have you ever seen her close up?'

'Of course not.'

'She looks very tired.'

'Don't tell me she answered questions?'

'The girl's name was Ella and she worked in the Imperial nursery. She was originally from the Crimea. Yalta or Sevastopol.' Ruzsky watched his feet in the snow. 'Vyrubova insisted she'd taken pity on the girl and given her an old dress, but if she had cared for her enough to do that, she seemed strangely indifferent to news of her death. The Tsarina forgot herself and answered some questions, but they were both evasive and . . . cold. I didn't know what to do. Should I ask the Empress of All the Russias questions?' Ruzsky shrugged. 'And they didn't seem to know whether or not to dismiss me out of hand.' He thought for a while. 'Vyrubova was obviously lying, or at least not telling much of the truth, but I found it difficult to guess why.'

'What did they say?'

'The girl was close, or so they said, to the Imperial children. She was dismissed for stealing. That's as far as I got.'

'For *stealing*?'

'Yes.'

118

'Stealing what?'

'They said money, but I'm fairly certain it was something else.'

Ruzsky and Pavel waited as a Finnish sled drove past, bells jangling, then crossed the street. This side was darker, with no light from the houses and the gas-lamps unevenly spaced. Ruzsky's hand closed instinctively on the butt of the Sauvage revolver in his pocket.

'So we know her name, but nothing more,' Pavel said.

'I'll telephone the Imperial household staff tomorrow and find out who she was and exactly why she was dismissed.'

'What about the man?'

'They said they'd never seen him before.'

'Were they lying about that as well?'

'I don't know.'

'So what do you think did happen with the girl?'

'I don't know.'

Ruzsky and Pavel passed a tall brick building that looked like a warehouse, and came to a small door with a white sign above it. Pavel knocked once. It was opened by an enormous man with a round face and a long beard. He nodded at them and stepped back to allow them inside. Light, warmth and music spilled down the stairs.

In the centre of the floor of the room above, an old man played a violin with manic energy, two men and two women sweating as they danced before him. A young gypsy girl led them to a table and returned a moment later with an unmarked bottle and two glasses. She was pretty, Ruzsky noticed, with serious eyes and curly dark hair that spilled over her shoulders. She laughed as she leaned forward to touch his arm.

The restaurant was packed. All the tables were full, and a crowd lurked in the shadows behind them. Everyone was drinking from the same unmarked bottles. Prohibition had been introduced at the start of the war, to reduce drunkenness and boost national effectiveness, but had instead robbed the treasury of substantial revenue, reduced the quality of the vodka and contributed to rampant alcoholism. That expensive wines and champagnes were exempt from the ban did little for social equanimity.

Ruzsky had heard about these illegal cafés, where people danced and drank to forget the world around them, but this was the first time he had been into one. They'd not existed before his departure. 'They keep this table for you?' Ruzsky said.

'A man must have somewhere to relax.'

Pavel filled the glasses and they looked at each other over the rims. '*Santé*, as you would say,' Pavel said, before they both drank.

Ruzsky spluttered – the vodka was rough. Pavel refilled the glasses and they drank again. Ruzsky watched the dancers. The women were voluptuous, aware of the hungry eyes on them, and their dancing was sensual and provocative. He dragged his eyes away from the floor, took out a cigarette and leant forward to light it in the candle flame. He pushed the case across to Pavel, who declined. 'You're going to go back to Irina?' Pavel asked.

'No.'

'Why not?'

'She won't entertain the notion.'

'Is she aware that you know of her latest affair?'

120

'No.' Ruzsky had confided in Pavel during a moment of weakness before his departure to Tobolsk.

Pavel sighed. 'Isn't that a little perverse?'

Ruzsky's eyes were on the prettier of the two gypsy girls, who was dancing with her back arched, her chest thrust high and forward, her forehead glistening with sweat. He thought of Maria on stage in the last performance he had seen before his exile, her long, sinewy body and graceful movement.

'Why haven't you told her?' Pavel asked.

'Who?'

'Irina.'

'About what?'

'That you know about her affairs. That you have known for years.'

'I don't know.'

'You want to occupy the moral high ground,' Pavel sounded annoyed, 'even if it costs you your boy.'

'I want to leave Michael out of it.'

'That's not possible, and you know it. It's killing you, not seeing him, so tell her, tell your father.'

'I don't want her, I've no desire to see her, and it's not going to cost me Michael. I'm determined it won't.'

'If you say so.'

'How are Tonya,' Ruzsky asked, 'and your boy?'

'You won't want to know that they couldn't be better.'

'I don't begrudge anyone happiness, especially you.' Ruzsky looked at his friend. 'I mean that.'

'I just want to be at home all the time with them.' Pavel looked as if he might burst with longing.

Ruzsky patted his bunched fist. 'The little fellow must be – what? Four?' Ruzsky always avoided referring to the boy by his name, Sandro, because Pavel's decision to call his son after him had always made him feel uncomfortable.

'He had his birthday two months ago,' Pavel said. 'He laughs all the time. He's got a great Russian sense of humour and he's big like a bear.'

'Like his father, in other words.'

'I don't laugh enough any more.'

'You worry too much.'

'And you don't worry enough.'

'Go home, Pavel. That's where you should be.'

'I want to be with you.'

Ruzsky laughed. 'No, you don't.'

Pavel filled both glasses again. 'Once more.' They drank. 'I shouldn't leave you here,' Pavel said.

'This is exactly where you should leave me, and you know it. Go home to your wife and child.'

Pavel gazed into his empty glass. 'Do you think we should . . . pass on this case? Leave it?'

'Leave it?'

Pavel looked up, deep unease in his eyes.

'How can we leave it?'

Pavel shrugged. 'The Empress, the palace. The Okhrana. I know you saved me last time, lied for me, but I couldn't . . . Tonya wouldn't come to Tobolsk, and these are bad times.'

'We broke the law. I was the chief investigator. If anyone was going to be punished, it should have been me.'

'Do you think that was what it was about?'

'What do you mean?'

'You think that you were punished because we broke the law?'

'I think Vasilyev wanted to bring the whole

department down a peg, show us who was boss in this city.'

Pavel shook his head. 'Sometimes, you're not such a brilliant investigator, after all.'

'I don't understand.'

'You think he gives a shit about breaking the law?'

'No, but—'

'He's the devil. You, more than Anton, posed a threat. You like digging around in things, you're high-born and disdainful of anyone who doesn't operate on the same moral plane.' Pavel raised his hand. 'I mean it as a compliment. Above all, you're difficult to control and impossible to intimidate. You're dangerous. And I don't like this case.' Pavel leant back. 'I don't like it.'

'Why not?'

'It smells dirty. We should push it on to the Okhrana. They're equipped to deal with that kind of stuff. Why fight for it?'

They stared at each other in silence. Pavel lowered his eyes. 'You're thinking of what love has reduced me to,' he said, reading Ruzsky's mind.

'Of course I'm not.'

'I don't mind if you are. They're all I care about, Sandro.'

'Of course.'

'You think that I think you're emotionally reckless,' Pavel went on, 'but I don't. We're just different. Or perhaps you've never been in love.'

Ruzsky stared at the dancers. 'Perhaps.'

Pavel stood up reluctantly, but Ruzsky could tell he wanted to be at home, and he was determined not to accept charity. 'Go on, go.'

'Be careful, Sandro.'

'I'm not a child.'

'I suppose this means we're working tomorrow.'

'It's up to you.'

'I know you will be.'

Ruzsky shrugged. 'It's a Sunday, you have a wife and family. Stay at home. Go to church.'

Pavel put one giant hand on his friend's shoulder then ambled towards the door. Ruzsky watched him go, then turned back to the dance floor and the bottle of vodka. He poured himself another glass. He was watching the prettier of the girls on the dance floor again when the waitress put down a wooden tray and slipped in beside him. The tray contained fresh and pressed caviar, salted cucumbers and herring fillets. There was a cup of tea with lemon. She looked like the girl on the dance floor. They might have been – and probably were – sisters. She was smiling at him, her hand on his knee, her body tilted towards him so that the smell of her cheap French scent caught in his nostrils.

The audience cheered and clapped as the dancers reached a climax. The waitress poured two glasses of vodka with her left hand. The right was massaging his thigh. They drank and, as he put his glass down, her hand reached his groin. The girl's face was in front of his now, her dark eyes searching his own. Her mouth was warm and her hand worked beneath the table as the music seemed to get louder. 'Come,' she said, shifting away from him and taking his hand.

'No,' he said.

'You want to come.'

'No.'

'Upstairs.'

'No.'

She looked disappointed. 'Your friend has gone.'

'And so must I.'

She stared at him, then got up angrily. Ruzsky was too drunk and tired to care. As she flounced away from him, he pushed himself to his feet, dimly aware of the eyes on him as he tried to walk steadily to the door. On the other side of the room, he saw – or thought he saw – Stanislav the Rat, watching him.

Immediately Stanislav disappeared beyond a red curtain. Ruzsky pushed through the crowd and followed him up a dingy staircase. It smelt of varnish, dirt and cleaning fluid. He reached a long corridor with rooms off each side. Ruzsky heard the unmistakable sounds of copulation. He stopped. 'Stanislav?' He wondered why Pavel had brought him here. Was this what his friend had thought he needed? Or was there something else?

'Stanislav?' he called again.

He moved forward slowly to the source of the sounds and glanced in through the gap in the door. He saw a girl astride a large man, long blonde hair hanging down her back. Whoever it was – and Ruzsky could not see the man's face – he did not see how it could be the Rat. He retraced his steps.

He had not taken off his overcoat, and had felt warm in the restaurant for the first time that day, but the impact of the cold air was exacerbated when he stepped out into the street. It was snowing heavily again, the wind whipping the flakes into tiny cyclones. He began to walk, head bent, mind spinning. He knew that this was how people died in the winter. They emerged drunk from the warmth, fell over in a dark corner and froze to death.

On the far side of the street, two *likhachy* drivers

eyed him. It was a matter of honour that drivers of the better-sprung carriages, with soft rugs and velvet cushions, never touted for or haggled over a fare. There were no *droshky* drivers in sight – another indication of the kind of place to which Pavel had taken him.

Ruzsky kept walking. He tried to shake the vodka from his mind. It was a few moments before he realized that he was not heading back to his apartment, but towards his family home on Millionaya. He passed a doorway, then stopped, his head spinning. He struggled to focus. Two girls were huddled together. 'Anything you like,' one said. 'Good price.' They could not have been more than thirteen or fourteen. One was blonde, the other dark, and both were deathly thin, clinging to each other for warmth. Their clothes were ragged, their shoes threadbare and holed. 'Both of us together?'

On the wall above them, crudely drawn, was another depiction of the Empress of All the Russias. She lay on her back, her skirt above her waist, stockings visible, her legs wrapped round a half-naked Rasputin whose trousers were by his ankles. The caricature was graphic and above it was the word *Niemka* – the German woman.

For a moment, Ruzsky was paralysed as the girls appealed to him. Then he reached into his pocket, found a few roubles and thrust them into their outstretched hands. He stumbled away.

The girls cried out, and Ruzsky turned back to see them running towards a car that had pulled over by the side of the road, almost tripping over themselves in their eagerness to reach the open back door. Like Ruzsky, they instantly recognized its occupant. He stepped back into the shadow of the wall. The girls climbed into the car and the door banged shut. The driver revved the engine and the wheels slipped on the icy road as the car belonging to the chief of the Petrograd Okhrana moved off. Ruzsky caught a glimpse of Vasilyev's square face. He watched until the car disappeared over the canal, then marched on through Palace Square and into Millionaya.

He stopped before the yellow stone façade, the snow settling on his face. He hammered on the door and stepped back. A light came on in one of the upstairs windows. At the same time, he heard a growl from within and the door was flung open.

CHAPTER ELEVEN

His father stood before him in a red silk dressing-gown.

'I want to see my son.'

'You're drunk.'

'I want to see him.'

'He's asleep.'

'Then I want to see him asleep.'

The senior Ruzsky's stare revealed the depth of his contempt. 'How low can you sink?'

Irina emerged from the shadows, a tiny figure in a white gown, her black hair dishevelled, eyes full of sleep.

'I want to see our son,' Ruzsky said.

'He's asleep.'

'Then I want to see him asleep.'

'Don't make a fool of yourself, Sandro, any more than you already have.' She looked up at her father-in-law, who placed his arm round her shoulders and drew her to him. 'Give me a minute, Papa,' she murmured.

Reluctantly, the older man withdrew, turning his back on his son as he climbed the stairs.

Irina took Ruzsky's hand and led him through to the drawing room on the left. It was an oddly intimate gesture. She closed the door behind them. The fire was dying in the hearth. She took a step closer to him. Her mouth was tight, her eyes narrow and without warmth in the fading light. Her hair, which had once been sleek and dark, was shot through with grey. 'You're drunk,' she said.

'No.'

'By doing this, you make it worse.'

'How could it be any worse?'

'You lower yourself still further in the eyes of your father.'

'That's hardly possible.'

Ruzsky was facing two giant silver candlesticks and a carriage clock in front of a bookcase that stretched to the ceiling. This was his home, yet his wife had succeeded in making it more alien to him now than it had ever been. He glanced wearily at the portraits of Dmitri and Ilya. 'You said I could see Michael but when I telephone you don't speak to me. You never return my calls or reply to my letters.'

For the first time, she looked shamefaced. Ruzsky grasped that it was not merely anger that had fuelled her evasiveness. 'We thought it—'

'We?'

'Your father thinks Michael would be better away from your influence. I don't—'

'You've talked about it.'

'I don't agree with him, but it has been hard for Michael. The arguments, the upheaval. I thought . . . think it would be better if he were allowed to settle for a time, without the upset of seeing you.'

Ruzsky thought of his boy upstairs, sleeping

peacefully, unaware of his presence. 'I want to see him.'

He moved towards the door, but she grabbed his arm. 'Please don't,' she said.

Ruzsky stared into the fire. How much better it would have been never to have married than to have come to this. 'You believe you understand this family,' he said, 'our history, and yet . . .' he shook his head '. . . you know nothing.'

'If that's what you want to believe.'

'No outsider can truly understand, Irina.'

'That's your conceit.'

Ruzsky opened the door. His father was in the hall-way, but his brother was coming down the stairs. 'Give me a minute, Papa,' Dmitri said, as he took Ruzsky's arm and led him on to the stone steps outside. He pulled the door shut behind them. His face was solemn, but his eyes sparkled. A smile tugged at his lips, and then they clasped each other so tightly and for so long that when they parted they were both breathless.

Ruzsky grasped his brother's shoulders. 'I thought I'd lose you,' he said. 'You don't look a day older.' His delight at seeing Dmitri alive and well was sobering him up.

'I wish I could say the same for you.' Dmitri patted his hair affectionately, and lowered his voice to a whisper. 'If you're not careful, you'll end up looking like the old man.'

'How's your arm?'

Dmitri raised it. 'Strong enough to resist a bear-hug from you.'

'I'm sorry.'

The snow was falling silently around them.

'A real soldier now,' Ruzsky said. 'A veteran. The ancestors would be proud.'

'Spare me their judgement.'

'You survived,' Ruzsky said. 'That's all I care about.'

Dmitri dropped his gaze and Ruzsky touched his brother's cheek, his protective instinct not dulled by the years. Relief and warmth flooded through him, but he'd calmed down enough to understand what a fool he had been making of himself. 'I'll go.'

'We'll work something out, Sandro.'

'Have you seen him?'

Dmitri hesitated. 'He's fine. He's a strong boy. Ingrid helps to look after him.'

'How is Ingrid?'

'Still German. She hides away here.'

'Good night, Dmitri.'

'Telephone me. We'll get together.'

'Of course.'

'I mean it. Tomorrow. We'll have Sunday lunch at the club. Agreed?'

Ruzsky was silent.

'Tomorrow. Promise me.'

'I'd like that. We have a lot of work. I—'

'Sandro, there is a war on, and I'm an officer in His Imperial Majesty's army. If I can find the time, so can you.' Dmitri was still smiling.

'Of course,' Ruzsky said. 'I'll be there.'

'One o'clock. Don't be late.'

Ruzsky began to walk away. After a dozen paces, he stopped and turned. The front door was shut, Dmitri back in the warmth of their childhood home, but when he looked further up he saw Michael in the attic window of the bedroom that had once been his. The

131

boy's small dark head was illuminated by a flickering candle. Ruzsky moved closer, urgently, his heart thumping, tears in the corners of his eyes. The little boy was watching him. Ruzsky raised his hand. He mouthed his name, and Michael raised his in response, his eyes never leaving his father's. Then Irina was behind him, her hostile face replacing his. She tugged the curtains shut.

Ruzsky tried to convince himself that he had been right not to insist on seeing his child. He was drunk. He was a disgrace. Michael would have been embarrassed.

During the night, Michael's face appeared beneath the ice, his cheek pressed against it, eyes wide with fear, fingers scrabbling for freedom. Ruzsky knelt above him, hammering with his fist against ice as solid as brick until blood seeped from beneath his nails. Panic gripped him. He was shouting for help, but no sound came. And all the time he could see the desperation in Michael's face as he lay trapped beneath him, fighting the current, struggling to breathe . . .

Ruzsky awoke to the sound of rifle shots and leapt out of bed. He was sweating and shaking but not even the intense cold of the darkened room could shake the images from his mind. He heard a dog bark, and scratched a patch of ice from the window so that he could see out into the night. It was clear now, the moon bright. His breath froze against the glass.

His head hurt. He went to the door, his boots – he had fallen fully clothed into bed – noisy on the floorboards.

The room Pavel had rented for him was in a large tenement building on Line Fourteen, a street that ran through the centre of Vasilevsky Island. It was not far from, but much less respectable than, the apartment he and Irina had occupied before his departure. The rents had gone up and, of course, he no longer had the allowance given to his wife by his father, so all Pavel had been able to get for the budget Ruzsky had wired him was a small, bare room in a building that stank of cabbage and cat urine. A photograph of Michael stood above the fireplace, and a dark wooden dresser along the opposite wall between two scruffy armchairs.

Ruzsky took out his cigarette case and reached for the box of matches. He lit up, exhaled heavily and steeled himself for a long night. He thought of his son's face in the attic window. At what point, he asked himself, should a man accept that his life had been a failure? His mind went back to the summer of 1908 when he and Irina had fallen in love. Anton had still been a part-time lecturer in law at the university and Irina one of his students. She had been admitted to one of the special courses for women, since ladies were not officially enrolled in the university. Ruzsky recalled the long, heady nights in the back garden of Anton's small country home north of the city, the midnight sun bringing a soft glow to faces flushed with vodka and good food. His friend had lectured Irina on how admired her clever paramour was in the department, how bright his future, even if it was not the one his father had wished for him.

Ruzsky got to his knees and put a light to the fire Pavel had laid the previous evening. He sat cross-legged and watched the flames climb from the kindling towards the blackened walls of the chimney. After a few minutes they died down again, the wood too damp to sustain them. Instead he took a full bottle of vodka from his bruised leather suitcase, and placed it on the table beside his bed.

CHAPTER TWELVE

Ruzsky awoke to the peal of church bells across the city. He rolled on to his back and listened, his head pounding and his throat dry. It was still dark and he reached for his pocket watch. It was just after nine. He fell back and studied the ceiling. He was cold, but reluctant to move. The smell of damp cabbage from the stairwell was pervasive.

He could not help recalling spring Sundays in Millionaya Street when he had lain in bed with the windows open, listening to the sound of those time-less bells. He thought, too, about Petrovo, where there were no bells, no noonday guns, no shouts, no carriages rattling over cobbles, no horses or soldiers, neither opulence nor squalor – just the silence of the immense Russian forests.

He got up, spurred by the recollection that he had once seen Maria in a quiet corner of the Kazan cathedral on a Sunday morning. It was a painful process, even for a man used to Siberia. He lit a fire in the tiny stove and melted a bowl of ice. After half an hour the water was still only tepid, but he could wait no longer. He washed, shaved, trimmed his moustache with an old, blunt pair of scissors, then dressed and stepped on to the landing.

The stairwell was festooned with clothes hung up to dry, most of which had frozen overnight, and there was no light, so he picked his way down with care. Most of the apartments had been subdivided so that each room was occupied by a different family, but at least this morning no one was sleeping on the stairs. Perhaps it was just too cold.

The stench of the hallway latrines and refuse caught in his throat as he made his way towards the big oak door and stepped out into the chill pre-dawn air of the courtyard. Ahead, two *droshky* drivers had up-ended their narrow sleds. The nearest was oiling the runners, while the other was packing the inside of his with hay for passengers to rest their feet on. The horses stood in the corner, beneath one of the slimy, covered wooden staircases that led up to the rooms on the first floor on the other side of the yard.

Ruzsky pulled down his sheepskin hat and crossed the courtyard. A gas-lamp glowed dimly through the archway from the street and he nodded to the lanky *dvornik* – yard-porter – who sat in his cubicle by the gate.

He almost fell over the figure crouching in the shadows. The man was wrapped in a blanket and had a long, unkempt beard, encrusted with filth. He stared up at Ruzsky with hollow eyes. Ruzsky ignored him, but twenty paces down the street, he changed his mind and went back. He pulled the man to his feet, ignoring the indignant shouts of the fat *schweizar* – the porter – who emerged from nowhere as Ruzsky half carried, half dragged the man up the stairs.

He had intended to leave him inside the entrance to

the building, but carried him instead up to his room and placed him in front of the stove. He straightened and looked at the man as if he were a wounded animal. He stoked the fire, went to his bed and brought back a second blanket to put round his shoulders. 'What's your name?'

The man stared into the flames.

'When you are warm, I'd be grateful if you would leave. I have things to do.' Ruzsky waited for a response, but none was forthcoming. He crouched beside him. 'I have work to do. There is nothing here of value, so I will leave you. Please let yourself out when you are warm.' The man continued to stare straight ahead. Ruzsky moved to the door, wondering if he would return to find a corpse.

Outside, he stopped to clear the foul smell of the hallway latrines from his nostrils, then set off. Line Fourteen was close to Maly Prospekt, the seediest of the main three streets that cut across the island. Down at the far end, close to the great massif of the stock exchange and the honey-coloured buildings of the university, around Bolshoy Prospekt and down to about Line Five, the island had a faintly well-bred air. But the area around Maly was more or less a slum, run-down ochre-coloured houses interspersed between shops with small grimy windows. Most had signs above their doors announcing, 'Credit not allowed. Do not come in unless you can pay.'

This had never been a good part of the city, but now it was downright depressing. It was close to the narrow streets of the Gavan, St Petersburg's first port, which lay at the western tip of the island and, as he walked, Ruzsky brushed past several merchant sailors emerging from the area's seedy bars. Maly had no restaurants, but plenty of tea-houses. However, even these *chaynaya*, which had once served basic fare at a reasonable price – before the war you could get a decent stew with sausages here for five copecks or so – no longer had anything appetizing to hang in the window. The only activity appeared to be in the secondhand-clothes shops, which had multiplied along the street.

Ruzsky was hungry, so he walked down to the St Andrew's market, which ran in narrow alleys off the back of the cathedral on Line Six, but he was shocked to find that the war had stripped even this colourful quarter of its character. If Irina had never got over having to move away from the south side, she had at least enjoyed helping the servants with the shopping here – it had always been bustling with loud pedlars touting their wares in competition with each other. This morning a grim silence hung over the alleys. The only stall-holders were families trying to offload junk in return for a few copecks. Between the piles of old furniture and books, all Ruzsky could find was root vegetables, so he continued in the opposite direction.

He passed a group of four students emerging from a café: a pretty girl in an astrakhan cap and three young men in tattered clothing. As Ruzsky examined them, their anxious faces brought to mind Judge Porphyre's words in *Crime and Punishment*: 'Raskolnikov's crime is the work of a mind over-excited by theories.'

As he reached the waterfront, he saw a few *droshky* drivers waiting for hire, but he ignored their shouts and passed Konradi's sweet shop on the corner, where the servants had brought him and Dmitri to spend their weekend pocket money. He waited for a tram to cross in front of him as he was buffeted by a gust on the Nicholas Bridge. The dawn sun washed the sky a subtle shade of red. The lamps hissed. Those on the waterfront were the last to be lit and put out.

It was cold, the Arctic wind whistling down the Neva with startling ferocity. Ruzsky's cheeks stung and his feet grew numb. He recalled running across the bridge to Konradi's – he still shuddered almost every time he thought of his schooldays. As he turned on to Horseguards, he considered, as he often did, how different his life would have been if he'd followed the course prescribed for him.

Would it have been easier?

The giant semi-circular colonnade of the Kazan cathedral had been inspired by St Peter's in Rome and this morning, as always, beggars were standing on the steps at its entrance – mostly women with young children. Ruzsky reached into his pocket and pulled out a few copecks to thrust into each hand. There were four or five times more than usual and by the time he reached the main doors he was handing out larger-denomination notes.

Ruzsky stepped into the relative warmth of the cathedral, which was packed already. Small groups stood in front of icons and candles, their heads bent in prayer. Ruzsky bought a candle from the nearest booth and joined a group close to the altar. He lit the candle and placed it in the metal holder, crossing himself as he did so. The priest's murmured prayers were answered by a choir on the mezzanine floor at the far end of the cavernous hall. Ruzsky did not believe in God but, for as long as he could recall, he had found the Church's ritual soothing. He crossed himself once more and began to wander among the worshippers.

All around, pale blue spirals of incense drifted up towards the vaulted ceiling. He walked behind one of the great columns and stood directly before the altar, beneath the great chandelier that hung from the dome.

He searched the faces around him without success, and was moving towards the darker corners down one wing of the cathedral when he saw her. Her expression in repose, it seemed to him, had a wistful quality, but a slow smile spread across her face as he approached. 'Hello, Sandro,' she whispered. 'I thought you might come here.'

They stood close together, looking at the golden sun above the altar and listening to the priest's mournful liturgy. 'I got your note,' Ruzsky said.

'You will come?'

'Of course.'

Maria was still looking towards the altar. 'Perhaps I should not have asked you.'

Ruzsky's heart beat a little faster.

'You are chief investigator once more?'

'Yes.'

'So we can sleep easily in our beds again.' She smiled at him, then gazed back towards the altar.

'We found two bodies on the Neva yesterday. In front of the Winter Palace.'

'Who were they?'

'We don't know,' Ruzsky said. He recalled Irina's accusation that he never communicated about anything. 'They were badly mutilated.'

'Sandro, I . . .' She was biting her lip and he could see the confusion in her face.

'My wife has left me,' he said quickly, before she could go on. 'She made her choice.'

'It may be that we now live in a world without choices.'

'Things change.'

'Yes.' Maria looked into his eyes. 'Things change. But we must stay friends. We can achieve that, can't we?'

'Of course.'

'I have to go.' She was flustered now.

He nodded, not trusting himself to speak.

He watched her leave. When she reached the door, she hesitated, then slipped out into the cold light.

Ruzsky went first to the duty desk, where the officer with whom he'd dealt yesterday was slumped forward, his face on the report book, fast asleep. His mouth was squashed open and he snored quietly. 'Good morning.'

The man sat bolt upright, with startled eyes. 'I'm sorry, sir.'

Ruzsky grinned. 'It is Sunday, after all. How long have you been on the night shift?'

'Two weeks. This is my last one.'

'Good. Evidently you need some sleep.' Ruzsky reached for the report book and glanced at the previous day's record of assaults, burglaries and random acts of street violence. Many more than he remembered from the old days. 'Get me missing-persons again, would you?'

The officer hurried to oblige.

There were no new entries.

'Nothing there, sir?'

'No.'

'Who were they?'

Ruzsky looked at the man for a second. 'We don't know,' he said.

'Revolutionaries?'

Ruzsky frowned. 'Why do you say that?'

'It's what the others think. Out there in front of the palace.'

Ruzsky assumed the men had been talking about yesterday's visit from the Okhrana. 'I think they're wrong. When's your relief?'

'In an hour, sir, if he's on time.'

'Tell him that if there's any report of someone missing I want to be told immediately.'

There was a pile of papers on his desk, placed there after he'd left the previous evening. On top was a note from the fingerprint bureau asking for written authorization to begin a search. He filled in the form, ticked the box marked 'criminal suspects only' and placed it in his out-tray. The one thing common to all departments of the Tsar's government was the insane level of bureaucracy.

Ruzsky looked at his pocket watch. He took down the telephone earpiece and waited for a connection, then asked the operator for the line to Tsarskoe Selo. It was answered immediately. 'May I speak with Colonel Shulgin, please?'

'Who is calling?'

'Investigator Ruzsky of the Petrograd police department.'

'What is it concerning?'

'I'd rather explain to the colonel in person.'

'One minute, please.'

Ruzsky waited and waited, drumming his fingers impatiently on his desk.

'Are you still there?' the voice asked eventually.

'Yes.'

'I'm afraid Colonel Shulgin is engaged. He will

telephone you later this morning.'

'I'd like to speak to him now.' Ruzsky heard the sharpness in his voice.

'He is otherwise engaged.'

'I'll wait.'

'He will be engaged for some time.'

'This is a murder investigation.'

Ruzsky heard the man sigh. 'Colonel Shulgin will telephone you later this morning.'

'Do you have any idea how long he will be? I have to go out.'

'I'm afraid not.'

Ruzsky terminated the call. The arrogance of the palace staff in the face of the current popular mood defied belief. He consulted his pocket watch again.

Downstairs Sarlov was drinking from a tin cup of strong Turkish coffee. There was another corpse on the slab, covered by a single white sheet, folded back at the top, an old man. 'A drunk,' he explained. 'Froze to death.'

There was a light on in the corner, but the room was mostly in shadow. The smell made Ruzsky gag, but he didn't recoil. It irritated Sarlov when detectives were in a hurry to get away. He appeared to prefer the company of corpses to that of the living. There were times when Ruzsky couldn't blame him.

'So?' Ruzsky said.

'So . . . what?'

'Any further thoughts?'

'I'm thinking about whether you have a cigarette.'

Ruzsky took out his silver case and walked round the corpse's head. Sarlov took a cigarette, and Ruzsky lit one for himself. They smoked in a silence that was

143

almost companionable. Ruzsky stared at the old man in front of him, whose face was as white as marble.

'It's Sunday morning,' Sarlov said. 'I'm not officially working.'

'I can see.'

'You don't know who they are, do you? Or why they were taken?'

Ruzsky pointed with his cigarette. 'The girl was called Ella. She worked in the nursery at Tsarskoe Selo—'

Sarlov whistled quietly.

'She was dismissed, apparently for stealing.'

'That's what they told you?'

'Yes.'

'But you didn't believe them?'

'I'd hesitate to say that. It was the Empress who told me.'

'You spoke to her? She consented to see you?' Sarlov couldn't keep the incredulity out of his voice.

'I wouldn't put it quite like that.'

'I was forgetting . . . your fine lineage and noble connections,' Sarlov said, with what might or might not have been irony.

'I went out to see Vyrubova,' Ruzsky said, 'and the Empress walked in during the course of our interview.'

'This is the same Vyrubova who is, or was, an intimate of both Rasputin and the Empress?'

'Yes.'

'What is the girl supposed to have stolen?' Sarlov asked.

'Money, they said. But I'm not sure I believed that either.'

'How did she look?'

'Who?'

'The Empress.'

Ruzsky ignored his colleague's puerile humour. 'Tired.'

'She stays up late to telegraph our war secrets to the Germans.'

Rumours had circulated since the outbreak of war that the Empress fed information to the country of her birth. Ruzsky looked at the dead couple's effects, which were still piled in the corner. He dropped his cigarette on the floor, trod on it, and picked up the man's overcoat. 'Why didn't Prokopiev take their clothes?'

'He looked at them.'

Ruzsky spread out the coat. 'A cursory glance or a proper examination?'

'Pretty thorough.'

'A few seconds?'

'A minute or more. I don't see what you're driving at.'

'What was he looking for? That's what I'm driving at.'

'He looked like he was checking there was no incriminating evidence,' Sarlov said.

Ruzsky glanced at his colleague. This was exactly what he had been thinking, but he'd not expected the doctor to articulate it. 'You said the man was American,' Ruzsky went on.

'Possibly foreign,' Sarlov said, correcting him.

'We might know by later on this morning, or perhaps tomorrow. Pavel has a lead down at the United States embassy.' Ruzsky looked at the patch where the label in the overcoat had been removed, then turned out the inside pockets. 'Did the girl die instantly?' he asked Sarlov.

'Most unlikely. Why?'

'I can't get a clear view of this. Once we establish both their identities, in what direction should we be looking? Is it a crime of passion, a professional assassination, a family feud? What do you think? I mean, forgetting the Okhrana's behaviour for a moment and just considering the crime scene.' Ruzsky put down the overcoat and turned to the man's jacket. The labels had been removed from the collar and the inside pocket.

Sarlov stubbed out his cigarette on the corner of the table, then flicked it into the iron wastepaper bin. 'I've been thinking about it, too. Let's start at the beginning. I would say the murderer was tall. Take the woman. From what I could see, a healthy incision, but high. Forceful. Overhand.' He simulated the action. 'Then the man.' Sarlov looked at the position the victim had once occupied on the slab. He pushed his glasses up his nose. His hair was wilder than it had been yesterday. 'Stabbed once initially, also overhand and quite high, coming down – remember the cuts on his face.' He raised his arm once more. 'Then again. And again. And again, and again, and again, and again—'

'All right.'

'You see what I'm saying?'

'No.'

'The murderer is angry. More than angry. This is a deep, atavistic rage, certainly not the work of a professional assassin. You do not stab so many times to be certain of a man's death. Nor do you plan to do it in the snow in full sight of the Winter Palace. This isn't some petty squabble over money or . . . something trivial.'

'I agree.'

'Do you?'

'Yes.'

'The murderer's anger is directed principally at the man – that is my other point. It is an elementary but important observation. The murder of the woman is purely functional. There is no anger against her – he just needs to get that done before he turns to the man. That is why he is here and . . . *Bang!* An explosion of rage. I'm not sure I've ever seen anything quite like it.'

'You make it sound like a lovers' quarrel,' Ruzsky said.

'It might have been.' Sarlov was interested in drawing conclusions from the medical facts at his disposal, not in finding explanations.

'And the branded star on the man's shoulder doesn't mean anything to you? You've never seen anything like it before, don't recall hearing of anything similar?'

Sarlov shook his head.

'Can you think of any potential explanation?'

'That's your job.'

'What created it, then? What was it made with?'

'As you have observed, it is a branded star.'

'An imprint of loyalty to an organization, group, society?'

'I don't know.'

'A religious sect?'

Sarlov didn't answer.

Ruzsky made a mental note to pursue that possibility. He went back to the clothes. The branded star rang a bell somewhere in his mind. In a case he had investigated, or something he had read about? He picked up the man's boots. There were tiny holes in both soles, like his own. He glimpsed something on the heels and held them up to the light. 'Have you got a magnifying glass?' he asked.

The physician fumbled around in a drawer, then came over, cleaning his spectacles. Ruzsky held both the boots and the magnifying glass to the light. 'Do you see that?'

'No.'

'The maker's name has been worn down, but I can see something. I think it is "amburg". The "H" has gone. Hamburg. That's where they were made.'

Sarlov nodded. 'He might have been German.' He took the magnifying glass and returned it to his drawer. Ruzsky examined the man's trousers, turning them inside out. 'If the murderer was so angry,' he said, 'so insane—'

'I said angry, not mad. Sane men do diabolical things,' Sarlov insisted, with some feeling.

'His blood is up and yet, once he is done, the girl, according to you, is probably still alive, bleeding to death on the ice. The murderer bends over her and rips the labels he can see from her clothes. Then he or she goes to the man and does the same. The man's body is covered in blood, which is everywhere, freezing quickly. This all takes time. Five minutes. Longer. It is the middle of the night, but the moon is bright and the danger of being seen must be high. There is no easy escape. You must walk far in each direction to get away from the scene and the murderer has decided that he must leave no prints. It's brutal, methodical, but also amateurish. He goes to the trouble of placing his footprints in those of his victims, then abandons that plan as he gets close to the embankment.'

Looking at the overcoat, Ruzsky could not quite

believe that the murderer had been able to remove all clues to the man's identity so thoroughly in a few rushed minutes on the ice. 'Do you think he bought his coat in Hamburg as well?' Ruzsky asked, holding it up to the light.

'Do I look like an expert in international fashion?'

'No,' Ruzsky conceded. 'To be honest, you don't.'

Pavel was sitting at his desk. 'Progress,' he said, holding up a photograph of the male victim's body. 'It's Whitewater, the man from the Astoria hotel. I checked on the way in. And I got hold of the American official. He's waiting for us at the embassy.' He stood up. 'There's a note on your desk. Another messenger. You're a popular boy.'

Ruzsky picked up the envelope and turned it over. It had the seal of his brother's regiment, the Preobrazhensky Guards.

The letter was on thick, yellowish paper: 'My dear Sandro,' Dmitri had written, 'I shall be at the yacht club at luncheon and hope you will join me there. I shall make the assumption that your answer is affirmative, unless you get a message to me by noon.'

Ruzsky sat down and took out of his drawer the roll of roubles they'd found on the dead man. He realized that there was more money than he'd first thought – the outer notes were of low denomination, but there were higher ones within. He leant forward to count them, and narrowed his eyes. He extracted one note and held it up to the desk lamp. He did the same with another, then with the rest. 'Come and have a look at this,' he said.

The big detective heaved himself from his chair.

'See?' Ruzsky held up two to the light.

'See what?'

'Here.' Ruzsky pointed. There was a series of tiny marks, in black ink, underneath the serial numbers. He looked closer, then at the other notes once more. 'Look. They're all in some kind of order. Each note is marked with a minuscule figure in black ink inside the double-headed eagle. By the left-hand beak. You see, one, two, three and so on. Then on each note some of the serial numbers are underlined with tiny dots.'

'That could mean anything. A bank teller fiddling around on a slow afternoon.'

Ruzsky spread out all the notes in front of him. He rearranged them in order of the numbers inscribed by the left-hand beak of the eagle. He could see that he was right. 'We've got numbers one to fourteen here. So it's a code, and the message has fourteen letters, which are to be assembled in this order. The digits underlined in the serial numbers must be page references from the code-book. If we had that, we could see the message.'

'But we don't,' Pavel responded.

'It gives the whole case a new perspective.'

'Maybe.'

CHAPTER THIRTEEN

They found themselves faced with a long wait at the United States embassy over on Furshtatskaya. A fat, middle-aged Russian woman sat behind the reception desk and became more irritated every time Ruzsky went to enquire how much longer the official they sought might be.

He strolled around the entrance hall, glancing at the pictures crowding the walls. The subject of each was inscribed on a brass plaque at the bottom of the frame. There was a watercolour of beach life in California, and another of a town-house in Boston. Some government buildings in Washington were depicted in oil, along with a grand plantation house in Georgia and a panoramic view of New York.

He sat down again. The remnants of Pavel's breakfast were still visible in his moustache and on his chin. 'You smell of herring,' Ruzsky said.

'I forgot to tell you. I received a call from Anton when I got home last night. We have to chair a briefing later today.'

'For whom?'

'Vasilyev and an official from the Ministry of the Interior.'

'Where?'

'Alexandrovsky Prospekt.'

Ruzsky's heart sank at the mention of the Okhrana's gloomy headquarters. 'You can do it. I don't need to go.'

'Oh, no.' Pavel shook his head. 'If you want to be back in charge, you do it.'

'Do you think,' Ruzsky said, 'that our corpse was an American intelligence agent?'

'Why do you say that?'

'Think of the banknotes. If they contain a cipher, an encoded message . . .'

'I still think that's quite a leap.'

Ruzsky could see Pavel knew he was right.

'You're seeing conspiracies where none exists,' Pavel said. He had become defensive again.

'True, but it makes me wonder. Perhaps it explains why the Okhrana was so quick off the mark. Did you check his room at the Astoria?'

'Inch by inch. Nothing.'

They sat in silence.

'Nothing at all,' Pavel emphasized.

'Come on,' Ruzsky said, glancing up at the clock on the wall again.

'I'd have thought Tobolsk might have cured you of your chronic impatience.'

'I saw Vasilyev last night outside that club.'

'And?'

'He was in a car and opened the door to pick up two young street girls.'

A tall man with small glasses, short hair and a long, bony nose came through the door opposite them. He had an ungainly walk. 'Good morning,' he said, speaking Russian with a perfect Petersburg accent. 'Abraham Morris. I'm sorry to have kept you waiting.'

They introduced themselves.

'Come through,' the man said, smiling. His voice was soft and cultured.

Morris led them up several flights of stone steps. His office was on the top floor and it enjoyed a spectacular view of the Neva. His desk was uncluttered. The filing cabinet next to it was covered with what looked like sporting trophies. On the wall, the only painting depicted a white clapboard house overlooking a long, sandy beach.

Morris invited them to sit, then went to the other side of his desk and pulled over a chair, tugging up his trousers a fraction as he lowered himself into it. Ruzsky was entranced by the picture: the artist had captured perfectly the extraordinary quality of the light. He'd forgotten how much he missed being surrounded by fine paintings.

'Have you been to America, Chief Investigator?'

'No,' Ruzsky said, 'but I'd like to go. That's a fine painting.'

'I'll take that as a compliment.'

'Is it one of your own?'

The man smiled modestly. 'I telephoned the Astoria a short time ago. You have already been to see them.'

'Yes,' Pavel said.

Morris took a sheet of paper from a desk drawer. He glanced at it to refresh his memory, then replaced it. He raised his right hand, palm up. 'How can I help you gentlemen?'

Ruzsky reached into his pocket for a picture of the dead man. 'Do you recognize him?'

The American took the photograph and pushed his spectacles on to the bridge of his nose. 'No.'

'You have been made aware,' Ruzsky asked, 'that we are conducting a murder investigation?'

'Yes.'

'You don't recognize the man?'

'No.'

Ruzsky looked at him. His gaze remained steady. 'This isn't the man you warned the Okhrana about?'

'I don't know.'

'My colleague here was informed that you warned the Okhrana to be on the lookout for a man called Robert White, an armed robber from Chicago.'

'Correct.'

'Is that the same man as the Robert Whitewater who has not paid his bill at the Astoria?'

'It's likely, but I cannot say for certain.' Morris handed back the photograph.

'But you don't know if this is him?'

'No, as I've said.'

'The man at the Astoria gave his address as care of the American embassy.'

Morris shrugged.

'He's nothing to do with you?'

'No.'

'His real name, then, is Robert White?'

'He travels under many names. He prefers to amend genuine passports, of which he appears to have an unlimited number.' Morris tugged at his trousers and adjusted his spectacles once more. 'His real name *is* White.'

Ruzsky waited for him to go on, but the American continued to regard him with the same level gaze. 'Well, who is he, and what is he doing in St Petersburg?'

Morris studied his feet. 'The warning concerned his presence.'

'White was an agent of yours?'

Morris looked up, but didn't blink. 'Quite the reverse. He's a criminal and labour agitator of the worst kind.'

'A labour agitator?'

'In the steel mills.'

'Does your State Department have time to treat all American criminals in this way?'

'Robert White has incurred the wrath of some important and wealthy people.'

'What has he done?'

Morris shook his head slowly.

'So you were looking for him?'

'Yes.'

'And you found him?'

'We had reason to believe that he was returning to St Petersburg.'

'Why?'

Morris was progressively abandoning any attempt to appear co-operative, but Ruzsky found it hard to fathom why. 'You warned the Okhrana?'

'We asked for more information on White's previous activities here, and those of one of his Russian associates.'

'But none was forthcoming?'

Morris didn't answer.

'Who was the Russian associate?'

'You will have to ask your colleagues in the Okhrana.'

Ruzsky thought he detected a hint of a challenge in Morris's eyes. He held up the photograph. 'Is this White?'

'If not, he has slipped the net again.'

'The man had no identification on him, but our pathologist thought his dental work might identify him as an American.'

'I couldn't say.'

'Could you ask your State Department for a description?'

Morris looked from Ruzsky to Pavel and back again. He seemed to be assessing them. 'Your photograph fits the description.'

'So this is White?'

'I didn't say that.'

'But, then, you're not saying anything much.'

Morris stood up. 'I'm grateful to you gentlemen for stopping by.'

Ruzsky did not move. 'Why here?' he asked. 'Why now? A criminal and labour agitator?'

Morris was staring out of the window towards the Admiralty spire.

'An American with a history of labour agitation in his native country comes to Russia at a time when all the talk is of revolution against the rule of the Tsars.'

'Mr White is considerably more interested in crime than revolution,' Morris smiled warily, 'and your colleagues in the Okhrana are adept at keeping watch on political activists.'

'So they knew this man was in Petersburg?'

'I informed them six weeks ago, just as I have told you.'

'That you believed White was on his way to Russia?'

'Precisely.'

'And the Okhrana did not reply?'

'No.'

'You have heard nothing from them?'

Morris gave them a tight but knowing smile. Ruzsky got the impression he didn't like the Okhrana very much.

'Who did you speak to?'

He did not answer.

'Something tells me, sir,' Ruzsky said gently, 'that there are other things you could choose to share with us.'

Morris's eyebrows arched. 'An investigator's instinct?'

'The look on your face.'

'It is not my city,' Morris said, 'and not my country.'

'Not the American way.'

Morris smiled again. 'Not the American way, no.' He looked at Pavel and then back at Ruzsky. 'Good day, gentlemen. And good luck.'

For a moment, in the cold street outside, Ruzsky and Pavel stood in silence, each with his own thoughts, Morris's evident suspicion of the Okhrana hanging between them. 'So it was White,' Pavel said.

'Yes.'

'Robert White. What do you think he was doing here?'

'I have no idea, but I think Morris probably does.'

'He's suspicious of us,' Pavel said.

'Or of the Okhrana, or of the city, or of Russia. He looked to me like a man with too much knowledge, who no longer feels confident of drawing distinctions.'

Pavel stared disconsolately at the ground.

'Will you telephone the Okhrana records office? See if you can get some hint of what they have on White?' Ruzsky asked.

157

'You're not serious?'

'You might slip through the net. Why would the records library know what the senior officers are doing?'

'You've been away, don't forget. No one does anything over there without authorization now, even the most basic query. Vasilyev's orders.'

'Well, try. See what their reaction is, at least.'

'What are you going to do?'

'I have to see my brother.'

'Lunch at the club?'

'I've been in Tobolsk, he's been at the front.'

'Well, I hope there isn't another murder this afternoon. I'd hate anything to get in the way of your social arrangements. Don't forget you've a briefing to do.'

'When?'

Pavel stopped. 'In your own good time.'

'I think we should go back out to Tsarskoe Selo this afternoon.'

'If you can fit it into your schedule.'

'We'll go out straight after lunch and we'll brief them when we get back.'

'Whatever you say, boss. Enjoy your lunch.'

'Could you do me one more favour?'

'I doubt it.'

'Put out an all-stations bulletin. Ask if any of them have anything on White.'

Pavel spun on his heel and walked away.

CHAPTER FOURTEEN

At the Imperial Yacht Club, time had stood still for more than a hundred years. From the carriages parked outside, alongside those for the Astoria, the drivers stamping their feet against the cold, smoking and gossiping, to the ornate, dimly lit stairwell and the gilt-edged mirrors of the dining room, it had remained resolutely the preserve of the élite within the élite.

Ruzsky walked past the boarded-up German embassy and across St Isaac's Square, stopping to allow a car to pass. He heard the noonday gun as he reached the grand grey building's front entrance. Parked outside stood two sleds with the distinctive gold crowns and crimson velvet upholstery of grand dukes of the Romanov dynasty.

The doorman, dressed in the club's bright livery, nodded. 'Good day, sir. Your brother is waiting in the dining room.' For the first time since he'd been sent to Tobolsk, and perhaps for much longer than that, Ruzsky felt like a member of one of Russia's leading families. He took off his hat and overcoat and gave them to the doorman, who brushed a few shards of ice on to the entrance mat, then handed them to a porter standing behind him.

Ruzsky wondered who he would see.

He walked up the curved staircase towards the dining room on the first floor.

Grand Duke Boris Vladimirovich stood on the landing, propped against the wall beneath a huge painting of the Neva at sunset, his portly frame straining the buttons of his uniform. He was talking conspiratorially through a cloud of cigar smoke with a man Ruzsky did not recognize. The shock of seeing him again made Ruzsky stop dead. He could feel the hairs standing on end on the back of his neck. The grand duke noticed him, but made no acknowledgement. Ruzsky felt the weight of the man's contempt and the colour rose in his cheeks before he had recovered enough to walk on.

The dining room was full. The clink of champagne glasses carried across the tables, and the dust in the air, illuminated by the dull winter sun filtering through the windows, looked like gauze. Everywhere, uniforms groaned with gold braid and medals earned by acts of bureaucratic audacity.

To his right, a huge oil of the royal yacht *Standart* dominated the nearest wall; the others were covered in gilt-edged mirrors. Ruzsky steadied himself. Anyone who recognized him here would see the disgraced scion of one of the country's leading families. If they appreciated the circumstances to which he had been reduced – a dingy one-room apartment near Line Fourteen of Vasilevsky Island – he'd have been thrown out on to the street.

Dmitri was already seated at the family's favoured table at the far end of the room, reading a newspaper, a tall, solitary figure.

Ruzsky approached slowly, studying his brother in a way he hadn't been able to the previous night. Dmitri's hair was longer, the first flecks of grey creeping into his temples. His face was fleshier, though his build was still slight. His eyes were bloodshot; he looked dissolute. He was in the dark green and red uniform of the Preobrazhenskys, but it looked less distinguished on him than on either their father or their uncle.

Dmitri turned and, for a moment, neither man moved. Ruzsky searched his face and saw the same things deep in his brother's eyes that had always been there: love tinged with loneliness, joy at their reunion tempered by the shadows of the past that nothing could dispel. Then he went to him. They hugged each other, Dmitri's fingers digging into Ruzsky's back. Neither man wanted to break the embrace. Eventually, they stepped apart.

'You look terrible,' Dmitri said. He had already been drinking.

Ruzsky grinned. 'So do you.'

They both sat down. Dmitri's eyes were drawn towards the door and Ruzsky half turned to see the grand duke enter, still chomping on his cigar.

'Do you know what the tragedy is?' Dmitri's face was earnest, but he had lost none of his impetuous, exuberant charm. 'Father knows everything. In his heart, he understands what is going on, but nothing will shake his faith in the system. He doesn't – or won't – understand that, to the people, Boris Vladimirovich and his kind *are* the system. Vulgar, lecherous, crass, whoring, drinking, debt-ridden and corrupt beyond redemption.' Dmitri took his brother's arm. 'Please tell me it doesn't upset you.'

'What doesn't?'

'You know what I mean.'

Ruzsky sighed. 'That my wife is having an affair, or that my father turns a blind eye to it because he does not like me, and the recipient of her affections is a grand duke?'

Dmitri sighed despairingly.

'If it is what Irina wants, so be it,' Ruzsky said. 'It's only Michael's situation that upsets me.'

'The whole thing disgusts me,' Dmitri said. 'Michael is a *Ruzsky*, though, isn't he?'

Ruzsky looked up into his brother's eyes and saw exactly what Dmitri was thinking – that Michael could have passed for Ilya, even if his words had not been intended to convey it. Dmitri immediately looked away. Ruzsky's pulse quickened. They were silent. The noise in the dining room – the hubbub of conversation and the sound of silver scraping bone china – seemed unnaturally loud.

Ruzsky picked up the menu. The front was embossed with the yacht-club insignia and, inside, a handwritten sheet had been glued to the board.

A waiter approached, took a white linen napkin from the table and placed it on Ruzsky's lap. 'Something to drink, sir? Champagne, perhaps?' He was French, as were all the waiters in the club.

'Damn right, Armand,' Dmitri said loudly, overcompensating for the awkwardness of the moment. 'It's a reunion. Brothers back from the dead.'

'Dom Perignon?'

'Let me look at the wine list.'

Armand hurried away and returned with it a few seconds later. Dmitri perused it, then looked up. 'Dom Perignon, yes. Make sure it is properly chilled.'

'Of course, sir.' An assistant scurried away.

Ruzsky stared at the menu. He was crucifyingly hungry.

'*Vous avez choisi*?' The waiter smiled.

Ruzsky examined the menu with exaggerated care. 'The fish and the venison.'

'The same,' Dmitri said.

Another waiter approached with a silver bucket and their champagne. He opened the bottle and poured it into tall crystal glasses. Ruzsky wondered if his brother was still in debt. Before the war, Dmitri had always eaten here because he could use their father's account.

'Begin at the beginning,' Ruzsky said. 'Tell me what happened.'

Dmitri waved a hand dismissively, then lit a cigarette. 'What is there to say? Everything you hear is true. Thankfully I nearly lost an arm or I'd be buried in six feet of mud by now.'

'At least you went. I meant it when I said the ancestors would have been proud.'

Dmitri snorted. 'Yes, but I've never consciously chosen to do anything in my life, and you know it. All I've done is take the easy way out, and that included going to war. It would have been impossible not to go. You know how Father is. And as for our ancestors being proud, believe me, no one could do anyone proud out there, it's not possible. The war is a disgrace – not just to Russia but to mankind – and someone will be made to pay for it.'

Dmitri's voice had risen an octave and they had attracted a few curious and disapproving glances from a group of older men at the neighbouring table. 'It's as bad as they say?'

'Bad? Unless you've experienced it yourself I don't think you could possibly imagine the corruption and incompetence. The Germans are fighting a war, but we're being massacred. I've seen battalions of our finest troops going into battle against machine-guns armed with revolvers.'

'Where did you fight?'

Dmitri sighed. 'Father secured me an appointment as ADC to Bezobrazov.'

'What's he now, commander-in-chief of the Guards?'

'The old man thought it would be good for my career. We started out in Warsaw, then transferred to the southern Lublin front to join the Fourth Army and roll up the Austrian left.' Dmitri stared out of the window. 'That was where we lost most of the Pavlovsky, all laid out in the morning sun, like brothers. I found Bibikov without his head. I only recognized him by his family ring. You remember Bibikov from the Corps des Pages?'

'Yes.'

'Too conscious of himself for you, perhaps. He wasn't a bad sort.'

'I know he was a friend.'

Dmitri looked down at his hands, then returned his gaze to the window. 'From Lublin to Ivangorad, then Warsaw, then Lomja. Back to Warsaw, south to Kholm just as the Great Retreat was getting under way. And so on. We were always short of everything so I toured the railheads searching for ammunition, like a beggar scavenging for food. I pulled a revolver on the commandant of the station at Keltsi and almost shot him. Our men were going to their deaths with solemn faces and a few rifles to share between them and meanwhile all the fat bastards in the rear, friends of Rasputin or some grand duke, were lining their pockets. You should look into the eyes of the men, Sandro. It would break your heart. They march to a certain death fully understanding the futility of their sacrifice. When the Germans started using gas, the respirators we were promised in Lomja ended up in Warsaw by mistake and a telegram from Head-quarters suggested we tell the men to urinate into a handkerchief and tie it round their faces.' Dmitri's eyes were on Ruzsky now. 'And, among all this, the poor sods are commanded by officers who, with a few honourable exceptions – and they perish soon enough – billet themselves to the rear of the front and visit it only to shout at their men for not polishing their boots, when they're lucky enough to have boots. I've seen soldiers fighting barefoot.'

'How did you get hurt?'

It took Dmitri a few moments to gather his strength. 'The Great Eastern Offensive in July. We were ordered to advance to the section of the front between the Third and the Eighth Army. The idea was to break through at one spot and cavalry charge the Germans.' Dmitri took a sip of his champagne. 'A ridiculous plan. I went out as an observer with the Rifle Division, and the section chosen for our attack turned out to be a bog. Brusilov told us not to advance, but our commander knew better so in we went. Some of the men sank and drowned. Since the Germans were on high ground, the rest were mown down. We lost more than fifty thousand officers and men, and it was my good fortune to be cut down in the first arc of fire before we hit the swamp.'

Dmitri took a gulp of champagne, then drained the

glass. He took the bottle from the silver bucket and refilled it. 'And, forgive me, but Father tolerates the wife of his eldest son having an affair while living under his roof because she is fucking a *grand duke*. All is well and good, then. Boris Vladimirovich. Look at him.'

The group at the next table were now staring at them. Ruzsky felt a powerful urge to turn towards the grand duke on the far side of the room, but he resisted it.

'It's *disgusting*.' Dmitri drained his glass again. 'It is *all* disgusting. But it is all *over*. We are on the edge of the abyss now, there is no question about it, and you should be careful, Sandro.'

'About what?'

'You see yourself differently from the way others perceive you. You know you're Sherlock Holmes, but the mob doesn't have the faintest idea who he is.'

'The mob? Isn't that going a bit far?'

'No.'

Ruzsky thought the champagne was forming his brother's words. 'I'll be all right.'

'You think so? Do you know that . . .' Dmitri glanced ostentatiously around the room. 'I'm prepared to make you a very large wager – your annual police-department salary, or more – that at every single table in this room, conversation has already turned to how much longer Nicholas II is going to be the Tsar of All the Russias. Boris Vladimirovich wouldn't give him more than a month. And that's just as a result of the five plots *he's* involved in.'

'They always talk.'

'It's gone beyond that.' Dmitri leant forward and almost knocked over his glass. 'They killed Rasputin, for Christ's sake.' Dmitri had spoken loudly and now they were attracting scandalized glances. 'The woman's lover. And got away with it!'

'Keep your voice down.'

'Why? Surely you don't think that's heresy any more? Look into the faces of soldiers you pass in the street. All those who have been to the front know the truth. The regime is morally bankrupt. Finished. The occupants of this room chat about what will replace it while the rest of the world waits for the whole thing to go up with an enormous bang.'

A waiter arrived with their fish. Ruzsky inspected it, twisting the plate. '*C'est bien, Monsieur?*'

'*Bien sûr.*' Ruzsky smiled. '*Bien sûr.*'

'When was the last time you had anything decent to eat?'

Ruzsky peeled back the fish skin. 'I don't know.'

'You should come to the house during the day when Father's at work. One of the servants will feed you.'

'Irina's there.'

'Of course.' Dmitri showed no interest in his food. He refilled his glass once more. 'Why is she there, anyway?'

'She enjoys the effect it has on me.'

'Surely even she is not *that* . . .' Dmitri smiled again. 'All right, she is that evil.'

'How is Ingrid?'

'She is fine. Fine, fine, fine. Always fine. We tolerate each other.'

'She tolerates your wandering still?'

'In a manner of speaking. From time to time I even wander into the marital bed, although I can't say it's a stimulating experience . . . It's good to see you smile, brother Sandro.' Dmitri paused. 'However, my occasional forays into doing my duty do not seem to have achieved the requisite result. We are heirless, unlike you.'

'Another reason why Irina stays at home.'

'I still don't understand that. Her own parents are alive.'

'But not as rich.'

'She's a witch!' Dmitri laughed. Ruzsky had forgotten how much he enjoyed his brother's company. 'Burn her!'

The old men on the next-door table frowned at them again, but now Ruzsky was enjoying their discomfort. He refilled his glass before the waiter could reach the bucket.

'Actually,' Dmitri said, with a sly smile, 'I have acquired another little asset.'

'Who is she?'

'That's for me to know and you to speculate about.'

'Are you going to tell me, or do I have to beat it out of you?'

'You have my permission to try to drink it out of me.' Dmitri raised the champagne bottle. 'Another, Armand!' He looked at Ruzsky. 'After all, it is not every day I have a reunion with my long-lost deeply loved elder brother.' He held up his glass. 'I drink to you, Sandro – the only true Ruzsky among us all – and to the end of empire.'

This was too much for the men at the next table. Rather than risk a scene, they gesticulated to the head waiter and demanded to move. The only vacant table was at the back of the room, under the picture of the *Standart*. They glowered as they went.

'Pompous farts,' Dmitri said. 'They think they're

saving us, you know, with all this talk, but we're doomed and they don't know it.'

Ruzsky didn't reply. He finished his fish. 'Have mine,' Dmitri said, pushing his plate clumsily across the table.

'I'm not that hungry.'

'You look thin.'

'I never look thin,' but Ruzsky began to eat. 'So, tell me about her,' Ruzsky said. 'This "little asset".'

'I know what you're thinking, but it's different.' Dmitri waved his finger. 'Three years, and no one else.'

'Apart from your wife.'

'Don't mock.'

'No more carousing until dawn? No more shocking Society? Just *one* mistress?'

'You can laugh at me all you like.'

Ruzsky looked into his brother's bloodshot eyes. 'You're telling me you're in love?'

'It is not, you know, solely the preserve of Sandro the poet.'

'Is she married?'

'No. She lost the love of her life shortly before we first met – or so she says.'

'Why?'

Dmitri shrugged. 'Off to the war, I suppose.'

'She wishes to be your wife or is happy to be your mistress?'

'She revels in the term.'

'Does she know Ingrid?'

'Now you *are* joking.'

'So who is she?'

'It's a secret, damn it.'

'I'm not going to beg you to tell me.'

169

'It would make no odds if you did.'

'Nothing is a secret in Petersburg. It never has been.'

'Well, you're the chief investigator. You find out.' Dmitri smiled. A wave of hair flopped down on to his forehead. His nose and cheeks were red. 'I shall tell you one day.'

'I won't hold my breath.'

'You know,' Dmitri said seriously, 'I would do anything for her. Anything.' He paused. 'Have you ever been in love, Sandro? Truly in love.'

'I don't know.'

'We've talked about it so many times.'

'You scorned the idea, as I recall.'

Dmitri drained his glass.

'How are your soldiers?' Ruzsky asked.

'My *soldiers*?' Dmitri laughed, perhaps pleased that his brother had changed the subject. 'They're a rabble – worse. Do you know, there is not a single regular battalion in Petrograd? All the units you see are reserves, full of peasants. Every time we go out on a training exercise I feel this itch in the middle of my back and wonder which of them will shoot me. It's pathetic, not like the old days at all, but that's what happens if you send Russia's best to be mown down. Father came to dinner at the mess last week and complained bitterly on the way out about the slovenly way some of the men had dressed and how he'd seen several slouching on duty.' Dmitri guffawed. 'As I've said, the older generation thinks everything is somehow going to stay the same.'

'If things are as bad as you say, what will you do?'

'What do you mean, what will I do?'

'You will leave Petersburg?'

'Of course not. Don't be a fool, man. I've survived the front. What could be worse than that? If it is as bad as we all fear, I will go down in flames, all hands on deck, firing until the good ship disappears below the waves. Armand! Where's our main course?' The waiter hurried away again. 'The service here is a disgrace.' Dmitri took hold of his brother's wrist. 'I'll assist you, Sandro, in any way I can. I'll bring Michael and we can arrange to meet. Every day, if you like. Ingrid will help. She loves Michael and, anyway, Irina is always out in the afternoons.'

Ruzsky flushed again. Despite himself, the idea of Irina hurrying from the house to spend her afternoons with the bloated figure behind him – no doubt in a suite at the Astoria or the Hôtel de l'Europe – gnawed away at him. He thought of Michael playing alone in the garden.

Dmitri was staring at him, with a familiar expression: an earnest seeking of approval. Ruzsky locked hands with him and tried to return his affection, recalling Dmitri's distress on the night of their brother's death, the urgency with which he had clutched him on the way down to their father's study, the gabbled assertion that he had been too far away to reach Ilya, and had shouted and shouted in an attempt to stop him.

Ruzsky withdrew his hand. The intervening years fell away.

'I'll do anything to help, Sandro. Anything at all.'

CHAPTER FIFTEEN

Ruzsky was glad of the time alone with Pavel on the train to Tsarskoe Selo. For most of the way they sat in companionable silence, looking out at the pine forests and fields covered in a thick blanket of snow. He watched a woodsman clambering up towards the track. He carried an axe and had a stack of firewood on his back, snow and ice in his beard and thick leather skins wrapped round his feet and shins.

Pavel was a comforting presence. Ruzsky envied the way he kept his life simple, envied his unwavering loyalty to the people and causes he believed in. It occurred to him again, however, that his friend wasn't quite his old self. He appeared more nervous and defensive, but perhaps it was just a sign of the times. Perhaps Pavel was right: the case was best ignored. But Ruzsky knew it had moved well past the stage where he could ignore it. He'd once told Irina in an argument that the foremost talent an investigator could possess was persistence, to be like a dog with a bone. 'Persistence is not a talent,' she had replied, 'and I don't want to be a bone.'

'When you're on the run,' Ruzsky said, 'you surely

don't head for the most aggressive police state in the world? If you're an American, I mean, like this man White.'

Pavel didn't answer.

'What do you think?' Ruzsky asked.

'You know what I think. It smells rotten. You know it, I know it. That's why Morris behaved as he did.' Pavel lapsed into silence.

At the Alexander Palace, a servant took their coats and led them into an ornate antechamber. Pavel looked ill at ease. 'Don't stare,' Ruzsky whispered.

'It's all right for you. You were born to this.'

'Hardly.' Ruzsky walked to the windows. The children were skating on the ornamental lake. He could see the grand duchesses, but not the Tsarevich. They were wearing tight-fitting dark overcoats and fur hats, hitting a ball to each other across the ice with sticks under the careful watch of two men seated on the bank. Ruzsky wondered how much they knew of the politics of the empire their brother would inherit. The scene felt more normal to him than it had on his first visit, but Pavel seemed dumbstruck.

Although he had once told his father during an argument that it was inevitable, Ruzsky found it hard to imagine life without a Tsar.

He turned to see a tall man striding across the room towards them. The head of the palace household was in uniform and wore a monocle: an officer of the old school. To his chest was pinned the dark blue ribbon and silver star of the Order of the White Eagle, marking him out as being of the highest rank in the Civil Service, not that there would have been any doubt.

'You are Ruzsky?'

'Yes.'

'How can I help you?'

'Colonel Shulgin?'

'Yes.'

'I am the chief investigator for the Petrograd city police, and this is my deputy. One of your employees was murdered two nights ago. Her body was found in the centre of the Neva.'

'A former employee.'

'So I gathered from the Empress.'

Colonel Shulgin pursed his lips. 'It was most inappropriate that you came to interrogate Madame Vyrubova. You should have approached me.'

Ruzsky gave a half-bow. 'My apologies, Your High Excellency,' he said. 'Our enquiries led me to discover that the dress the girl was wearing had been made for Madame Vyrubova. I followed my nose.'

Shulgin glanced from Ruzsky to Pavel, then back again. 'Yes,' he said. 'Unfortunately, I do not believe we can help you in this case. All matters pertaining to members of staff are confidential.'

Ruzsky took out his pocket watch and glanced at it, to give himself a moment's pause for thought. Clearly Shulgin was going to concede nothing easily. 'The girl and her companion were murdered, Colonel. Brutally.' Ruzsky lowered his voice. 'In the climate of the times, out there, in front of the Winter Palace . . .' he inclined his head '. . . and the victim a palace employee. Naturally it troubles us.'

Shulgin eyed them cautiously. 'If there was a suggestion of . . .' he chose his words carefully '. . . *political* motivation I would have expected to deal with the Okhrana.'

But Ruzsky could tell from the old man's face that

Shulgin had no desire whatsoever to deal with Vasilyev's men.

Shulgin hesitated for a few moments, then pointed at two stiff-backed chairs pushed up against the wall. He pulled another over from the table in the centre of the room. 'I have only a few minutes,' he said.

'Ella was dismissed,' Ruzsky offered. 'If you do not mind me asking, Your High Excellency, why was that?'

The colonel admired his highly polished boots. 'That, I think, must remain a matter for the palace alone.'

'For stealing?'

Shulgin looked surprised.

'Madame Vyrubova told us as much.'

'Madame Vyrubova?'

'And Her Imperial Highness.'

Shulgin was evidently appalled that Ruzsky had been able to converse with the ruler of Russia, but was once again unwilling to dismiss him and Pavel. 'Stealing. Yes. A disgraceful episode.'

'How much money did the girl steal?'

Now the colonel looked confused. 'Money?'

'Isn't that what she stole?' Vyrubova had told Ruzsky it was money, even if he had not wholly believed her. Now it looked as if his hunch had been right. Shulgin had frozen and appeared ready to ask them to leave, so Ruzsky changed tack. 'The girl worked in the nursery.'

Shulgin seemed to be trying to work out how much they had already been told. 'That is correct, yes.'

A maid in a blue uniform with a starched white front came in with a single porcelain cup and saucer on a silver tray. Shulgin took it, stirred it with a silver spoon, then put it to his lips.

Ruzsky took the two photographs from his pocket. 'These are only head and shoulders . . . The man was stabbed seventeen times, the girl once. The murderer followed them out on to the ice . . .'

Shulgin stared intently at the image of the man. 'Who was he?'

'We were hoping you might be able to tell us.'

Ruzsky watched his face for any reaction, but he shook his head. 'No, I've never set eyes on him.'

Shulgin reminded Ruzsky of his father: obstinate and opinionated, but honest.

'Could you give us a few more details about the girl? When she was employed, where her family lives and so on.'

Shulgin stood up. 'Give me a minute, please.' He marched abruptly out of the room, then returned holding a file, which he was reading. He sat down and flicked through a series of loose sheets of paper until he found what he was looking for. 'Ella was from Yalta,' he said. 'She was twenty-two.' He ran his finger down the page. 'She started work at Livadia. She was employed to work in the nursery there in the summer of 1910. She would have been sixteen.'

'1910?'

'Yes. Her father died the following year and her mother moved to stay with her sister in Petersburg. Ella asked to be transferred.'

He turned further pages. 'Exemplary record until . . .'

'Until the theft?' Ruzsky prompted.

Shulgin cleared his throat. 'Until then, yes.'

'So she worked in the nursery here?'

'Yes.'

'What did her duties involve?'

'She assisted in the nursery.'

'Looking after the Tsarevich?'

Shulgin didn't respond.

'When he was sick?'

Shulgin flushed. 'The Tsarevich's health is not a matter for public discussion.'

'Of course not, but as a member of the household staff, and one with such an important role, she would have had access to other sections of the palace.'

Shulgin frowned.

'Presumably the money she stole wasn't kept in the nursery.'

'As I've said, the events surrounding her dismissal are a matter for the palace alone.'

'What if I said that the man in the photograph I just showed to you was a notorious American criminal and labour agitator?'

Shulgin looked at him uncomprehendingly. 'I do not understand . . .'

'Was she ever seen with the man? Would any of the other palace staff have met him? Who were her friends?'

'She was a very quiet girl. A labour agitator?'

'Yes.'

'An American?'

'Yes.'

'What was he doing in Petersburg?'

'That is what we would like to know.' Ruzsky leant forward. 'If Ella stole something – a sum of money or perhaps something else – then isn't it possible, indeed probable, that this man was involved? Assuming that she had never behaved in this way before.'

Shulgin stared out of the window, deep in thought.

'What Ella stole is of significance to us, Colonel Shulgin, do you see that?'

He still did not answer.

Ruzsky glanced at Pavel. They waited.

'Ella . . . she was not a bad girl. I did not know her well, but she was quiet, shy, quite solemn. What you have said . . . a man leading her astray, it would make some sense of her actions. The Empress . . . we were all surprised. Shocked.' Shulgin gazed into the middle distance. 'The Empress was cast down by this. It was a sign of the times, in her eyes. With so many difficulties outside the palace, to be betrayed by one of your own staff, from within . . . You understand.'

'She confessed to her crime?' Ruzsky asked.

'Yes.'

'And regretted her actions?'

'I believe so.'

'Did she mention the American?'

'No.'

'Or any man?'

'No.'

'You never heard her refer to him in any way?'

'No.'

'So why did she do it?'

'I have no idea.'

'Was she short of money?'

Shulgin's jaw tightened. 'As I have said on several occasions I am not prepared to discuss the circumstances of her dismissal.'

'May we speak with other members of the staff?' Ruzsky asked. 'Those who knew her best – in the nursery, perhaps.'

Shulgin placed the teacup on the table in front of them. 'I will consider your request.'

Ruzsky stretched out his hand. 'Colonel Shulgin, may I look at the file?'

Shulgin opened it again and leafed through it, removing several pages before he handed it over. 'It is of no further use to us.'

Ruzsky and Pavel decided to walk back to Tsarskoe Selo station, but stopped by the railings as soon as they had got far enough away from the gate to be beyond the eyes of the palace police. 'What did you make of that?' Pavel asked.

'It wasn't money.'

'Why not?'

'I'm just certain it wasn't. Vyrubova *was* lying. If Ella really had stolen money, why not tell us and have done with it? No, she stole something much more embarrassing that Shulgin couldn't talk about.'

'Perhaps he had her killed.'

'Shulgin? Never. I'd say he's as confused as we are. And he's no fool. He knows everything hangs by a thread, and he's worried. Three years ago we'd not have got through that gate under any circumstances.'

'I think you're being too soft on them,' Pavel said. 'If she stole something embarrassing, who's to say they didn't arrange to have her killed? Maybe they got the Okhrana to do it. Maybe the Empress herself arranged it.'

Ruzsky opened the file. 'Ella Kovyil,' it read. 'Born Yalta 12 April 1895. Father Ivan, postal worker, mother Anna, 14 Ilivichi Street. Employed 29 June 1910. References: Schoolteacher Madame Ivinskaya, father Ivan Alexandrovich (former NCO, Preobrazhensky Guards 1890–1906).'

'That's why she got the job,' Ruzsky said. 'Her father was in the Preobrazhenskys. He must have retired to the Crimea.' He read on: 'Unmarried.

Employment record: summer 1910, assistant in nursery at Livadia, and summer 1911. Autumn 1911, requested full employment and transfer to Tsarskoe Selo. Assistant nanny with special responsibility for Tsarevich. Remains in post.'

Somebody had written at the end of the first sheet: 'Reliable. Category One.'

Ruzsky showed this to Pavel. 'Categorizing staff by loyalty,' he said.

'Yes, I suppose so.'

Most of the rest of the file was given over to evaluations of Ella, which had been completed in December of every year she had worked at Tsarskoe Selo. They were written by hand, never stretched to more than a paragraph, and signed at the bottom by Shulgin himself, alongside the palace seal. The first sheet read:

Performs her duties adequately and is in possession of a cheerful manner. Claims to have formed a strong bond with the Tsarevich and has expressed a desire to concentrate on looking after his needs . . .

Ella can be somewhat careless over detail (and other nursery and household staff have had occasion to complain of poor moods and sloppy manners), but is considered reliable and honest . . .

Shy character, well suited to work in the nursery . . .

Time off is spent with mother in Petersburg . . .

Continued employment and security clearance granted.

In the evaluation for 1915, Ruzsky noticed the line, 'acquaintance of Father Grigory'. The next year, Shulgin had written, 'Spends time with Rasputin and Vyrubova, at cottage here, but also in Petrograd.'

The last sheets contained details of her salary. She had earned ten roubles a month in Livadia, the Tsar's palace in the Crimea, but her pay had not risen by much over the years and remained low until her dismissal.

Pavel had been reading the notes over Ruzsky's shoulder. 'It's good to know someone is paid less than us,' he said.

'Why give us this?' Ruzsky asked.

'What do you mean?'

'The details about Vyrubova and Rasputin. He removed several pages from the file, but he left this one in. Why?'

'I don't see what you're driving at.'

'I think Shulgin was trying to help us, as far as he feels he can.' Ruzsky held up the file. 'He didn't have to give us this, and he made a point of removing several pages. Therefore we have it for a reason.' Ruzsky looked down again. 'He has given us her background, and he's linked her to Rasputin and Vyrubova.'

Ruzsky turned the page. The last sheet contained an address for Ella's mother in Petrograd. 'Something tells me,' he said, 'that Ella was the real victim.'

CHAPTER SIXTEEN

Ella's mother lived in a squalid tenement building in the Alexander Nevsky quarter, but the door was locked and her neighbour told them she worked nights and had only just gone on shift.

Ruzsky and Pavel hurried back on foot to the department through the darkened, snow-covered streets, but when they got to the office, there was a note on Ruzsky's desk saying that a briefing had been fixed for Vasilyev at Alexandrovsky Prospekt at six. They were already late.

They took a *droshky* over the ice-packed Troitzky Bridge. The spire of the St Peter and St Paul fortress, bright in the moonlight, was a visible reminder at the heart of the city – as the place where the regime's enemies were confined – of the power of the man they were heading to meet.

As they disembarked outside the dimly lit entrance to Alexandrovsky Prospekt, they heard a dull mechanical roar and turned to see a green liveried car sliding to a halt behind them. The nearside door opened and Vasilyev stood on the running-board, his outstretched arms and wide black cloak making him look like a bird of prey. He stepped down and stalked towards them with the slow, deliberate gait that Ruzsky recalled so well. He drew level and stopped. His hair was short, and deep crow's feet at his temples led down to hooded, pale blue eyes, washed out with too much knowledge. A man who could look the devil in the eye without blinking, Anton had once said. He had a pronounced scar on the right side of his forehead.

'Chief Investigator,' he said. His voice was low and measured. 'Welcome back.'

Vasilyev led the way up into the gloomy hallway. Just as in their own headquarters, a reception desk faced them. The corridor was full of newspaper-sellers, cabbies and tramps – men from the External Agency, or the Okhrana's street-surveillance division. As Vasilyev walked in their conversation became instantly subdued.

They marched behind him down the long corridor. Ruzsky glimpsed the giant black presses in noisy operation as they passed the print room. He saw several leaflets scattered on the floor, but read only one headline: 'Vermin of Russia'. The Okhrana's notorious anti-Jewish propaganda machine was in full swing.

Ruzsky glanced at Pavel, who was staring straight ahead, determined to avoid confrontation.

They walked into the lift and the attendant closed the cage, pushed the button and stood ramrod straight as they ascended to Vasilyev's office; they did not stop at any other floor.

Anton was already at the round wooden conference table, alongside Maretsky. There was a bespectacled official next to him – perhaps the man from the

Ministry of the Interior – whom nobody bothered to introduce and who avoided Ruzsky's eye. Next to him sat Prokopiev, in a shirt and thick leather braces. Vasilyev's *protégé* might have been wrought in his image. They were physically different – Prokopiev was tall and lean, where his master was stocky and short – but they had the same coloured hair, cropped close, and a similar intensity in their eyes that gave no hint of warmth or humanity. Prokopiev was head of the Internal Agency, the division of the Okhrana responsible for running agents within organizations hostile to the state.

As they sat down, Pavel leant towards Ruzsky. 'Be careful,' he whispered.

'Would you care to share your thoughts with us, Deputy Chief Investigator?' Vasilyev asked. He was standing behind his desk, his back to a tall window that afforded an astonishing view of the fortress and the frozen river beyond.

Pavel flushed.

'He told me to remember to be respectful,' Ruzsky said.

'Ah,' Vasilyev responded. 'No need to stand on ceremony.'

The chief of the Okhrana moved a round metal weight from some papers and shuffled them to the centre of his desk, then walked over to the bookcase. Above him hung a line of religious icons and pictures of the Tsar and Tsarina. He took a silver case from the inside of his pocket. 'Cigarette, anyone?'

No one answered. He was immaculately turned out, from his neatly groomed moustache to his highly polished shoes. His manner was precise and meticulous, and he still had the habit of obsessively

184

removing small specks of dust from his waistcoat as he spoke, Ruzsky noticed.

'Would you like some English tea?' Vasilyev asked. It was a question to all of them, but directed at Ruzsky.

'No.'

'Your father is well?'

Ruzsky wondered if the question was designed to humiliate him. 'I believe so.'

Vasilyev lit his cigarette. He held it away from himself so that the ash did not fall on his suit. 'Anton Antipovich has told me a little, but perhaps you would care to expand. You found two bodies on the Neva. Who were they?'

Ruzsky scrutinized the table in front of him. It was inconceivable that Vasilyev had called the meeting in ignorance: he wondered how much he already knew, and how little he could get away with telling him. 'You have the bodies,' he said caustically.

Vasilyev betrayed no visible reaction. 'But you have still been working on the case, is that not so?'

'The girl was called Ella.'

'Her family name?'

'Kovyil.'

'Kovyil?' Vasilyev glanced at Prokopiev. 'Does that sound familiar?'

Prokopiev shrugged, but Ruzsky could see it was a charade. They both knew precisely who she was. 'She worked in the nursery out at Tsarskoe Selo,' he said, since he was certain they must know that, too.

'You should have informed me immediately that the girl was a palace employee.'

'We only found out this afternoon,' Ruzsky lied.

'And the man?'

'As I said, you have the bodies.'

'We wished to ascertain that the murder was not the work of a political assassin.'

'And have you done so?'

'Indeed we have. But I repeat, it is your belief, is it not, that the course of the overall investigation remains under the jurisdiction of the Petrograd city police department?'

To buy himself time, Ruzsky pulled out his own cigarette case and lit up. 'We believe the dead man was probably an American called Robert White.' He watched Vasilyev's face for a reaction.

Apparently unperturbed, the man drew deeply on his cigarette. 'An American?'

'So it would appear.'

'How did you discover this?'

'Sarlov thought he might be, from his dental work. We went to the embassy and asked.'

'And they confirmed it?'

'Yes.'

'How could they be sure?'

'They were looking for him.'

'Looking for him? Here?'

Ruzsky watched his opponent. 'He was a criminal and labour agitator.'

'A labour agitator?' Vasilyev turned back to Prokopiev. 'Ivan?'

Prokopiev shrugged again.

'You've never heard of him?' Ruzsky asked.

Prokopiev blinked, but evidently did not feel the need to reply.

'You've spoken to Shulgin?' Vasilyev asked. Clearly he knew that they had.

'Yes.'

'What did he have to say?'

'Ella worked in the nursery at the Alexander Palace. She was from Yalta. Perhaps you remember her?' Ruzsky noticed a muscle twitch in Prokopiev's cheek. 'I believe you were chief of police in the city at the time, and Ivan your deputy?'

'Why should either of us remember her?' Prokopiev asked.

'No reason.'

They were silent. The man from the Ministry of the Interior stared at his notepad. Ruzsky needed no further evidence that the city's overall chief of police, Prince Obolensky, was no longer in control. In the deteriorating political climate, all power had passed to Vasilyev.

'Go on,' Vasilyev said.

'Ella was dismissed for stealing.'

'Stealing what?'

'I don't know.'

'Money?'

'Probably.'

Vasilyev was now standing with his back to them, gazing out of the window.

'The man had a small branded star on his right shoulder,' Ruzsky said.

The official from the ministry looked up and scribbled something on the notepad in front of him. But Vasilyev remained unmoved.

'In addition to which, the killer went to considerable effort to strip both victims of anything that might identify them.'

'So you *are* saying it was a political crime,' Vasilyev remarked.

'The man was stabbed seventeen times—'

'But the girl was a palace employee.' Vasilyev's tone was emphatic.

Ruzsky glanced around the room. Anton shifted nervously in his seat. Pavel stared dead ahead.

Vasilyev took a pace forward. 'Thank you, gentlemen. That will be all.'

For a moment, nobody moved, then Pavel stood up, looking relieved.

'A word in private, Sandro,' Vasilyev said, as he turned to leave.

The others filed out, but the man from the Ministry of the Interior stayed where he was. He seemed to relax a little in his chair.

Vasilyev still had the remains of the cigarette in his hand. 'It is difficult,' he said, 'isn't it, when we cannot be certain of the victims' identity, especially in these times, when our manpower is stretched so thin?'

'Criminal investigations are rarely as straightforward as we would like them to be.'

'But times have changed, Sandro. Our concerns are so . . .' Vasilyev spread his hands '. . . broad. I think we could view this as a lovers' argument. A man, a woman . . .'

'So, they killed each other?'

'Don't play the fool with me, Ruzsky.' Vasilyev chose his words carefully. 'I had a telephone call this morning from the Alexander Palace. From the Empress herself. You can, perhaps, imagine my dilemma.' Vasilyev stubbed out his cigarette, in a manner that hinted at the anger bubbling under the cloak of his self-control. 'Or could if you weren't so damned *arrogant*.'

Ruzsky fought hard to keep his voice level. 'This is a murder, a criminal case, and therefore under the jurisdiction of the chief of the city police, according to the dictates of the Ministry of the Interior.' He paused.

'There is no sign of political motivation. As soon as there is, we will pass over the evidence we have accumulated to this department.'

Vasilyev glared at him.

'Will that be all?' Ruzsky asked.

'There are other matters that require your attention, I'm sure.'

'But none as important.'

'So the Tsar is no longer to be obeyed?' Vasilyev's voice was like velvet. 'Is that what you think?'

'I think that now, more than ever, there is a need for justice.'

Vasilyev's face darkened. 'It is the Tsar or the mob, Ruzsky. You would do well to remember that.'

Ruzsky could almost feel the fury at his back, propelling him down the corridor.

CHAPTER SEVENTEEN

At the headquarters of the Petrograd city police department, they were waiting for him in Anton's office. Ruzsky sat down heavily, opposite the picture of Napoleon's retreat. He could see that the others were apprehensive. 'He invited me to close the case on the grounds that it had proved impossible to establish the identities of the victims.'

No one replied.

'He said he had received a call from Tsarskoe Selo, and that I must understand his *dilemma*.'

'Do you think that's true?' Pavel asked.

'Why wouldn't it be?'

'Shulgin seemed concerned to me, and uncertain, rather than hostile.'

They considered this. Ruzsky looked into the eyes of his colleagues. They wanted to appear defiant, but none could hide their fear.

Anton sighed. 'Vasilyev is a powerful and dangerous enemy, now more than ever.'

'But still not omnipotent.'

'I'm not so sure.' Suddenly Anton looked old. 'It has a pleasing hint of irony about it, don't you think? In the dying hours of the regime, we loyally carry out the tasks assigned to us in the name of a tsar none of us believes in, while those who once professed fanatical loyalty to the absolute monarch now prepare themselves for when he is no longer with us.'

'I don't understand,' Ruzsky said.

'What do you think our friend Vasilyev has been doing these past weeks?'

'I can't imagine.'

'He's been a very, very busy man. Meetings and telephone calls. Reading telegrams and letters. Those addressed to him and those that have been intercepted. He speaks to generals, politicians and grand dukes, even to revolutionaries.' Anton raised his hand. 'You won't believe it but, trust me, he does. How can I manage this for maximum advantage? He could stay loyal to the Tsar, as he claims, but he knows it's moving beyond that. Change is coming. Which way is it going to blow and how can he be seen to assist it? Strikes, demonstrations, protests, the appearance of disorder, he can orchestrate them all. The generals, politicians and grand dukes could claim they were forced to take resolute action. But, of course, if Vasilyev and his agents get it wrong . . . who knows what might happen?'

'He just told me that the choice was between the Tsar and the mob.'

'And he is right.'

'If he is so preoccupied, then why bother to interfere with us?'

They sat in silence again. No one could answer this.

'It doesn't smell good,' Pavel said. 'They were warned that this American was coming back, and when he does he gets seventeen stab wounds for his trouble.'

'And yet,' Ruzsky went on, 'we cannot get away from the fact that, to all of us, their deaths still feel personal.'

They looked to Maretsky, who examined his chubby hands. As a professor of philosophy at the university, he had developed a passionate interest in the criminal mind and had been brought in by Anton – after his disgrace – on a part-time basis to assist in investigations. Shortly afterwards, Vasilyev had seen the value of his work and had requested – or, rather, they believed, coerced him into offering – his assistance too. 'I see only files,' Maretsky said, 'and sometimes individuals. I would be the last person they would tell.'

'What do you think lies beneath this case?'

'I don't know. I've never heard of White or the girl. Never seen any paperwork on either of them. But, then, if it was something they wanted to keep from you, I wouldn't see it.'

'Why have they warned us off?'

'I don't know.'

'Did they—'

'Sandro, I can see the questions. I just don't know the answers.'

They all glanced at each other. Pavel seemed less than pleased at the idea of being one of a band of brothers, but there was warmth in Anton's eyes.

'We cannot easily trace the American,' Ruzsky said, 'so we must begin by following the path of the girl. If any of you want to stay officially neutral, now's the time to make that clear.'

There was an awkward silence.

Pavel got to his feet. His face was strained. He came level with Ruzsky, then slapped him so hard on the back that he almost choked. 'God, Sandro,' he guffawed, 'you're a pain in the backside.'

Pavel went home and Ruzsky retired gratefully to his office. He shut the door, switched on his lamp and sat behind his desk in the half-darkness. He pulled out of his pocket the ticket Maria had sent him for the ballet, and glanced up at the clock. It was almost eight: the performance had already begun. He put down the ticket, moved it from one side of his desk to the other. He reached for his in-tray. On top was an internal envelope containing a note from the finger-print laboratory: they needed a signature of authorization before they examined the prints from the dagger.

Ruzsky put down the form, dipped his pen in the inkwell, scrawled, 'Is this bureaucracy really necessary?' put it back into the envelope and re-addressed it.

Next was a thick sheaf of telegraphs responding to Pavel's all-stations bulletin. Only three showed any promise. The Moscow city police had made two sight-ings of an American wanted on suspicion of espionage, theft and affray, who travelled under the name of Douglas Robertson.

Kazan reported that a Canadian travelling as Robert Jones had failed to pay his hotel bill in August 1914.

The most encouraging was from Yalta. 'American wanted in connection with armed robbery, October 1910. Fits description. More details upon request. Detective Godorkin, Yalta 229.'

Ruzsky rested his feet on the edge of the desk, and stared at the religious icon hanging on the wall. He imagined Ella as she might have been when she was alive. He pictured her as shy and timid; the American, aggressive and manipulative. A pretty Imperial nanny and a thieving brigand; it was an unlikely romance.

The minute hand on the clock moved with a loud clunk.

Ruzsky headed downstairs. The machines in the communications room were idle. The solitary operator was drinking coffee and reading his newspaper. Ruzsky handed him the three telegraphs and asked him to get on to Moscow, Kazan and Yalta for further details.

Back in his office, he glanced at the clock again, although he had been acutely aware of the time all evening. He sat down, pulled open the drawer and took out the roll of roubles removed from the dead man's pocket. He spread them out in order of the numbers outlined on the left-hand side of each.

He stared at them, looking for a flaw in the theory he'd shared with Pavel. If you assembled the notes like this, you got the order of the letters. The numbers on the right could refer to a page and line number. But he could get no closer to breaking the code without knowing what had been used as the key.

Ruzsky shifted a paperweight to and fro, deep in thought. After a time he noticed that a figure had crept into the doorway and was watching him. 'Only a rat moves that quietly,' he said.

'Only a fool allows himself to be burnt twice.' Stanislav sauntered over to Pavel's desk. He perched on the end of it, short legs not quite reaching the floor. His leather boots were in as advanced a state of disrepair as Ruzsky's own.

'Did you talk to the newspapers?' Ruzsky asked.

'I tipped off one or two.' Stanislav was sober, but he

looked tired, his thin face yellow with ingrained dirt.

'Was that you last night?' Ruzsky asked.

Stanislav didn't answer. He was stroking his stubble and looking at the floor.

'Up to something you'd rather I didn't know about?'

He still didn't reply.

'What are you trying to tell me?'

Stanislav took out a packet of cigarettes, lit one and threw the carton to Ruzsky, who sent it straight back.

'How did Prokopiev know about the bodies?' Stanislav asked.

'I've no idea. Probably from one of the constables.'

'That's a coincidence.'

Ruzsky frowned. 'That's what you said last time. You – or, rather, Pavel, with your agreement – put that pervert in the cell at the end of the corridor and told his fellow inmates what he'd been up to. When I asked you who told the Okhrana, you said, "Probably one of the constables." But Prokopiev was here within an hour of the man's death.'

'I still don't see your point.'

'Almost without exception we now have a different set of constables. So, one hour after the bodies are brought in from the ice this time, Prokopiev is here to remove them.'

'So?'

'They knew. Someone high up is singing down the wire.'

Ruzsky did not respond.

'In another time, maybe that wouldn't matter, but you took three years in exile and Vladimir's man wound up in the Moyka with a knife in his back. If that can happen to the assistant to the head of street crime, then it's not a game any more.'

195

They were silent. The clock ticked loudly on the wall.

'Spell it out,' Ruzsky said.

'If I had the answers, I'd tell you.'

'I've got to go.' Ruzsky stood up and put on his coat, slipped the ballet ticket back into his pocket, and walked briskly along the corridor.

He arrived in time for the interval. The first-floor lobby was thronged with theatre-goers discussing the performance, the hubbub rising towards the curved ceilings as liveried waiters, balancing silver trays, wove through the throng. The men were dressed in white tie and tails, the women long dresses and gloves, diamonds glittering in the light spilling from the chandeliers.

Here, outside the dress circle, tradition dictated that theatre-goers walked slowly around the edge of the room, arm in arm.

At the top of the stairs, Ruzsky was momentarily dazzled by the finery on display. Petersburg and Russia were two different countries. This city was as sophisticated, European and rich as most of Russia was backward, remote and poor. The salons of the capital and the endless pine forests of the interior bore no relation to each other, and he belonged wholly to neither world.

He glanced at his ticket, then at the signs directing him to the top floor.

As Ruzsky stepped on to the stairs, his father's booming laugh stopped him in his tracks. His family had spilled out of their box and into the corridor. The landing was crowded, but not enough for him to pretend credibly that he had not seen or heard them.

He found himself propelled across the rich red carpet behind the dress-circle boxes. They were drinking champagne, clustered round a low wooden table laden with bottles in silver buckets. His father stood at the centre of the group.

Dmitri's German wife, Ingrid, was at his shoulder. She was coldly beautiful, her long blonde hair framing a neatly formed, perfectly made-up face. She had a long, straight nose and a small mouth, her personality so shy and reserved that Ruzsky had rarely been able to penetrate much beneath the surface. But her kiss tonight was warm and her eyes sparkled as he stepped away from her. The natural empathy between betrayed spouses? he wondered.

Dmitri stepped down from the box, his face flushed. 'Sandro,' he said, glowing with pleasure. Vasilyev was behind him, followed by Irina.

'I believe you know each other,' Ruzsky's father said stiffly, gesturing towards the Okhrana chief.

'Yes.' Ruzsky was stunned by the man's presence in the bosom of his family. 'Yes,' he said again. 'I believe we do.'

Dmitri stepped forward and hugged him so tightly that his ribs almost cracked. 'The prodigal returns,' he said, to the silent company. 'Come on, this ridiculous feud cannot go on for ever.' His tone was laced with jollity, but it carried an unmistakably serious plea. He stood next to his brother, his arm round his shoulder.

Ruzsky found it impossible to avoid Vasilyev's hooded gaze.

Irina's face was flushed, her eyes barely concealing her anger at his presence. Perhaps the grand duke was close by.

'Sandro must join us,' Dmitri exclaimed. 'A

benchmark performance.' Ruzsky saw the hurt in Ingrid's eyes, and realized how drunk his brother was.

They remained silent. Vasilyev continued to stare at him intently. Ruzsky tried to summon enough energy to retreat with grace, but caught his father's eye. Just for an instant, beneath the severe frown, he thought he saw his expression soften. 'Sandro must join us,' he said. 'Of course.'

Dmitri stepped away from him and lit a cigarette, looking suddenly sober.

Ruzsky cleared his throat. 'No.' He saw relief in Irina's eyes, regret in Ingrid's. 'No, it's a kind offer. Another time, perhaps.'

'You're here anyway,' his father said.

'Yes, but I'm . . . on duty, in a manner of speaking.'

His father glanced at Vasilyev.

'One must take time to relax, Sandro,' Vasilyev said, but his unyielding glare belied the soothing tone of his words.

'Of course.' Ruzsky looked at his father, whose face had not quite returned to the hostile set of previous encounters. 'Have a good evening.' He did not look back as he climbed the stairs. He slumped into his seat at the far end of the front row with some relief, and gazed down at the empty stage. He was very high up here and it was pleasantly warm.

He only became aware that the performance was about to resume when he noticed that the seats around him were full once again. The orchestra was warming up discordantly.

Ruzsky glanced down at the royal box. He could see the Tsar's brother, Grand Duke Michael, in earnest conversation with Teliakovsky, director of the Imperial theatres, and Count Fredericks, minister of the Court.

The lights faded, the lavishly embroidered stage curtain was raised, and the overture began.

Maria appeared, in pure white against a startling blue backdrop. Her presence was as intoxicating as it had been when he had first watched her here, all those years ago. A young girl next to him craned her neck for a better view, her face alive with excitement.

Ruzsky forced himself to relax, in the semi-darkness far above the stage.

She was tall for a ballerina. Her long, willowy body moved with such supple grace that nothing she did, no step she took, no pirouette or twist, ever seemed less than perfect. He watched her in a daze, oblivious to the music, the onlookers, even the careful choreography of the dance, and he allowed himself to wallow in the sensation of being close to her.

But, as he watched, he was gripped by doubt. Only a fool would wait three years for a man who had let an unfaithful wife stand in the way of their fragile chance of happiness. He tried to stem the growing tide of dismay and self-reproach, but without success. He stood up and pushed his way along the row, to a chorus of disapproval from those around him.

Outside, as he rounded the corner of the stairs, he almost knocked Ingrid over. He grabbed her to steady them both, and as he looked into her eyes, Ruzsky saw the depth of her pain.

'I'm sorry,' she said.

He stepped back. 'No . . .' He wondered what his brother had done or said on this occasion. 'You are . . .' He could not think what to say. It was obvious that she was too upset to join Dmitri.

'You're leaving?' she asked.

'Yes.' He could see she assumed that he had been upset by the exchange with his father. 'I have work to do.' He moved past her. He thought of offering words of comfort, but a sense of decorum restrained him. Whatever the cause of her unhappiness, she was his brother's wife. 'Good night,' he said.

Ruzsky went on down the stairs. At the foot, he looked back and saw that she was still watching him. He raised his hand briefly – in a gesture of support – then was gone.

CHAPTER EIGHTEEN

Ruzsky waited beside the canal that ran along the rear of the theatre. It had started snowing again. The visibility was poor in the glow of the widely spaced gas-lamps, but it was warmer tonight. The last of the audience was making its way out of the Mariinskiy, some heading for sleds or carriages, some on foot. There was the occasional burst of laughter, but then the street grew quiet.

The stage door opened and a familiar figure appeared. The chief of the Petrograd Okhrana adjusted his fur hat, then moved into the darkness. Ruzsky ducked into the shadows until he could no longer hear the rhythmic crunch of Vasilyev's departing footsteps. He walked over the bridge, hands in his pockets, leant against the railing and looked down at the icy canal.

It was a few moments before he realized that she had left the theatre and was heading away from him. Snowflakes gathered in her hair. He almost called out, but thought better of it and took off in pursuit. When he caught up with her he touched her arm, and she spun round. 'Sandro!' Relief flooded her face.

'Are you all right?'

'Yes. You gave me a fright.'

'Who did you think I was?'

The stage door banged and two men hurried towards them. Ruzsky recognized one as the ballet master with whom he'd crossed swords. 'You'll catch your death of cold,' he told her, in French.

'*Ça ne fait rien*,' she responded.

'*C'est qui?*'

'*Un ami.*'

The other man took a pace closer and eyed Ruzsky. 'We have something to eat and some vodka at home.' He pointed down the canal, in the opposite direction. 'Just there, number 109.'

'*Je suis fatiguée*,' Maria said.

Ruzsky recognized the man as the legendary Fokin.

'You're going home?' he asked Maria.

'Yes.'

Fokin smiled. 'Well, be good.'

He walked briskly away with his companion.

Ruzsky and Maria set out in the direction of the St Nicholas cathedral. 'What did you think?' she asked.

'Of Fokin?'

'Of tonight.'

'Oh, it was good.'

'Good?' She laughed, kicking up fresh powder snow around her. Her mood was suddenly much lighter. '*Good*, Sandro?'

'All right, very good.'

'*Very* good?' She had walked a few paces ahead and faced him now, laughing. She scooped up some snow into his face. 'Very good?'

'Astounding.'

'Astounding?'

'You're Russia's finest prima ballerina. What more can I say?'

'*One* of Russia's finest.'

'Such modesty . . .'

'You were bowled over by the scale and ambition of the choreography, or the physical perfection of the dancers. You—'

'All of them.'

'I wager you don't even like the ballet.'

'On the contrary.'

'Don't you mean "*au contraire*"?'

'What's so funny?'

'I bet you were asleep.'

He grinned. 'If only I had been.'

'It was that boring?'

'Tedious beyond words.'

They were beside the cathedral now, its golden domes towering above them.

'My father used to take me to the ballet,' Ruzsky said quietly.

'Now there is a story.'

'Mmm . . .'

Maria looked into his eyes. The snow fluttered down, big flakes melting as they touched her cheeks. His feet were cold, but he had no wish to hurry. She began to walk again, half turning to examine her footprints in the snow. 'You went with your father alone? Just you and him?'

'Yes.'

'What about your brothers?'

'I don't know. Perhaps he thought they were too young.'

They crossed another bend in the Griboedov canal and walked past the covered market. Ruzsky glimpsed figures huddled inside its entrance, seeking shelter. 'Poor devils,' Maria murmured.

Ruzsky took a few more steps. 'Do you know Vasilyev?'

'Of course. Of him, anyway.'

'You don't know him personally?'

She frowned. 'No. Should I?'

'I saw him leaving the theatre by the stage door. I wondered if you had known him from Yalta?'

'He's an admirer of a colleague,' she said. 'Poor girl.'

Maria's apartment was on the top floor of a faded yellow building just beyond the Nicholas market. It was not far from where she had lived three years ago. She did not ask him to come up, but neither did she turn to say goodbye at the entrance.

They climbed the stairs slowly. Ruzsky watched as she found her key and placed it in the lock. He had to resist the temptation to reach forward and brush the snow from her hair.

They stepped inside. Maria turned on a lamp by the door.

Ruzsky's throat was dry.

She led him down a narrow corridor to the drawing room, their leather boots noisy on the wooden floorboards. He could hear the water squelching from the holes in his own.

Maria lit a candle above her writing desk, slipped off her coat and threw it across the end of a *chaise-longue*. She wore a white dress, and he caught a glimpse of stocking above her boots. On the wall beside her was a painting of the bay at Yalta, at sunset.

'Are you still planning to go home?' Ruzsky asked.

'Tomorrow night.'

'It will be warmer.'

Maria shrugged.

'It was a wonderful place for a holiday,' Ruzsky said.

'Then come again. I'll show you around.'

'One day I'd like that.'

'One day I would too.'

'It's a long way. Perhaps more than two days, with the railways in the state they are.'

She did not answer.

'How did you get a ticket? They say the *khvost* at the railway bureau is five deep.'

'I have a friend at the Ministry of War.'

Ruzsky wondered what kind of friend.

'Would you like some vodka?' she asked.

'No. Thank you, no.'

'Whisky? I have bourbon in the dresser.'

Ruzsky refused it, then changed his mind. 'I'd love some.'

Maria shook out her long dark hair. It was a simple gesture that still had a devastating effect on him. She gathered it at the nape of her neck as she went to the dresser, picked up the single glass and what was left of the bottle of American whisky. Ruzsky knew few people who drank bourbon. It was Dmitri's favourite, but hard to come by these days, he imagined, even in Petersburg. Maria handed him the glass. 'I'll make us some tea too.'

'I should go,' he said.

'If you wish . . .'

He didn't move, and she went to the kitchen.

Ruzsky sat on the *chaise-longue* between the book-case and the fireplace, his heart racing. He looked about him. On the wall opposite was a framed poster, in dark red, advertising her first performance as a prima ballerina at the Mariinskiy Theatre in *Swan Lake*. The year was 1911.

Ruzsky stood up again, went over to the window and looked down at the street. It was deserted, but for a sled standing by the iron railings, the driver hopping from one foot to the other to keep warm.

He turned back to the room. A fire had been laid and he reached into his pocket for some matches to light it. It caught quickly and he sat back on the rug, watching the flames. He didn't hear her return.

'I've been hoarding fuel,' she said. 'They say the bakeries don't have enough to keep their ovens working.' She put down a silver tray and unloaded its contents: a silver teapot, milk jug and sugar bowl, with two china cups and saucers. Ruzsky watched her pour the tea through a strainer.

She returned to the kitchen and brought back a plate of English biscuits. He took one, then sipped his bourbon.

'How do you survive, Sandro?'

'What do you mean?'

'You said your father had cut you off without a rouble, and I don't have the impression that much has changed.'

'I have my salary.'

Maria raised her eyebrows. 'You're a Ruzsky.'

'So I survive. Like others do.'

'By not eating. You look thinner. It doesn't suit you.'

He ignored her. 'You should leave Petersburg,' Maria told him.

'I've done that. Tobolsk was not an improvement.'

206

'I'm serious. You may see yourself as the guardian of justice, but for all that you are a policeman.'

'I'm a detective.'

'You expect the mob to care?'

Ruzsky remembered what Dmitri had said, and the hostile faces outside the bakery. He propped himself against the *chaise-longue*. She was looking at him, as if in a trance, her mind somewhere else. 'You know what really saddens me?' he said. 'The way everyone assumes change is going to make things better.'

'You *have* changed your tune.'

'You were the radical,' he said.

'Well, everyone is a radical now.'

Ruzsky turned to gaze into the fire.

'What of the bodies you found on the ice? The girls were asking.'

Ruzsky liked the idea that they had been talking about him. He wondered again if it was true that Maria had kept a photograph of him with her during his exile. 'Still a mystery,' he said.

'I like mysteries.'

'We could swap.'

'Sandro the ballet dancer? I'm not sure.'

'I'd be perfect. Apart from the boots.' He raised one foot. 'No. Perhaps you're right.' He took another sip of bourbon. His natural instinct was not to talk about the case, but he did not want to repeat the mistake he had made with Irina. If need be, he would force himself to communicate. 'The girl was from Yalta. Ella Kovyil. Ever heard of her?'

She smiled. 'Yalta is small, but not that small.'

'No, well—'

'What was she doing here?'

'Ella was an Imperial nanny.'

207

Maria tilted her head in surprise. 'Why was she killed?'

'We don't know.'

'A lovers' quarrel?'

Ruzsky shrugged.

'Who was the other?'

'An American.'

'What was he doing in Petersburg?'

'We don't know.'

'So you don't know much, really.'

Maria glanced at the clock and her smile vanished. It dawned on him that he was expected to leave. He felt suddenly disoriented.

He stood opposite her, gazing into her big, dark eyes. 'I'm sorry, Sandro,' she said softly. 'It's just ... I'm sorry.'

'For what?'

But her eyes told him everything he needed to know. Her loneliness was the mirror of his own, and her apology was for the opportunity they had lost.

Ruzsky went out slowly into the corridor.

'Sandro?' She was at the door. 'Thank you for coming tonight.'

They looked at each other for a moment more, then Maria closed the door.

Ruzsky was rooted to the spot. Then he forced himself to walk down the stairs.

He took a few paces along the street, then stopped. He looked up and saw her face in the window. He lowered his head and moved on. It was a minute before he recognized the figure hurrying down the snowy street towards him.

Ruzsky could hear his brother's voice in his head: *Actually, I've acquired another little asset.* He slipped into the shadow of a doorwell, watched every jaunty step his brother took.

Ruzsky waited, listening to him pound up Maria's stairs. It had stopped snowing and the night was uncannily still, the footsteps echoing like rifle shots.

He crossed to the far side of the street and looked up at her window. He caught a glimpse of them together before Maria unfolded the shutters and blocked out the night.

Ruzsky did not move: his eyes were fixed upon the darkened window above.

In his barren room a short time later he tried to sleep, but could not. He tossed and turned until he could stand it no more. He got up to dispel the images and paced around the silent room until he turned to the window and the deserted, snow-covered street for solace, or at least distraction. He heard a dog bark.

He placed the tips of the fingers of his right hand against the window and waited until they grew numb. Then he pulled out his last bottle of vodka. There was no trace in the apartment of the tramp he had rescued that morning, except for a lingering smell of decay.

Ruzsky upended the bottle, gulped down the harsh liquid. Oblivion came quickly. His head swam, but even the fire of the vodka in his belly could not extinguish his fury. He raised the almost empty bottle above his head and smashed it against the edge of the dresser next to the door, slashing the palm of his hand. Blood oozed from the cut, but he felt nothing. He staggered towards his bunk and fell, face first, out cold.

But if Ruzsky slept, peace eluded him. He found

himself returning to the lake at Petrovo, the images that assaulted him stark against a clear blue sky. He could see the ice cracking and feel the freezing water and then he was plunging back into the darkness, arms flailing as he sought Ilya's outstretched hand. He could hear the dull swish of his movements in the water and the sound of the bubbles ascending as the air escaped from his lungs. He could see, through the shimmering surface, his father's long hand stretched towards him.

And then he was flailing in the darkness once more.

Ruzsky kicked and swam, down and down. But all that touched his grasping fingers was weed and all he could hear was the beating of his own heart.

Ruzsky closed his eyes and began to shout, the pain searing his soul.

Then he could see light slicing through the surface and his father's hand pawing at the water. He felt the lake wrapping him in its icy embrace.

He could no longer summon the will to resist. He slipped further and further away, the hand at the surface receding. At last, he was enveloped in water the colour of night and, with it, a kind of peace.

The banging had risen to a crescendo in his dream long before it woke him. Ruzsky had been curled up beneath his blankets like a foetus, and only reluctantly stuck out his head into the night. His hand was painful, his throat dry, and his head pounded like a locomotive. The shattered bottle shimmered in the moonlight.

Someone was thumping insistently on his door.

'Who is it?' he yelled.

Ruzsky heard a muffled cry, so he pulled back the

covers and dived for his overcoat. As he walked across the room, he pulled out the Sauvage revolver. He winced as he gripped it with his injured palm. By the door, he considered turning on the light, then thought better of it. 'Who is it?'

'It's me.'

'Who's me?'

'Don't be an ass.'

Ruzsky pulled back the bolt and left Pavel to push open the door. Pain exploded in his head.

'Get dressed,' Pavel said.

'It's the middle of the night.'

'We have another body.'

CHAPTER NINETEEN

The victim lay crumpled in the shadow of the arch. they were not far from the Mariinskiy Theatre, next to the Lviny Most, the Lion Bridge, a well-known haunt for lovers. It was about six in the morning, the city around them still shrouded in darkness. Ruzsky was standing next to one of the white stone lions, wondering how he could avoid going down on to the ice. His injured hand throbbed. 'Do you want us to bring him up?' Pavel asked. 'He was pushed over from the parapet.'

Ruzsky looked around him. The path was too well trodden to trace any footprints. 'All right.'

There were three constables, the same men who'd been on duty when the bodies had been found on the Neva. They listened to Pavel without enthusiasm, then walked down on to the ice behind him.

Pavel bent over the body. One of the constables glanced up towards Ruzsky. The chief investigator muttered a curse, then walked down to the ice. The Griboedov canal curved to the left here, its frozen surface ghostly in the light of the gas-lamps. As he stepped on to it, Ruzsky twisted involuntarily, slipped, and struggled to control his breathing. He became aware that he was under the scrutiny of the constable closest to him, lowered his head and marched towards the body.

The man lay curled up, frozen. Ruzsky waved to indicate that the constables should move back, then took hold of the corpse with his good hand and dragged it out into the moonlight.

He bent down again.

For all his experience of crime, his stomach churned. The man had been stabbed so many times in the neck that his head was almost severed. The blood had frozen and crystals of ice had collected in his moustache and along his eyebrows.

'Christ,' Pavel whispered.

The man had a young, lean face and yellow teeth. He would have been only marginally more attractive in life than he was in death. Ruzsky pulled back his overcoat. There were no markings on it and, at first, he thought the body had been systematically stripped again. In the right-hand pocket he found a disordered fistful of banknotes. He riffled through them, then held them up to see if any had been marked in the same way as the American's but they had not. In the middle of the bundle was a return rail ticket from Sevastopol to Petrograd, issued from an office in Yalta. The card for the first leg of the journey had been stamped three days ago at Sevastopol, so he must just have arrived in the capital.

Ruzsky tried the other pocket. He pulled out some identity papers, which appeared to be genuine. 'Boris,' Ruzsky said. 'What does that say?' He pointed to the name.

'Molkov,' Pavel said, scrutinizing it closely. 'Or

Markov. Markov.'

'Yalta. Thirty-four years of age.'

Pavel pulled the coat further back to be sure that there were no other wounds. 'Almost certainly the same killer, wouldn't you say?'

Ruzsky took two paces back and scanned the buildings overlooking the canal. They were residential apartments or houses, backing on to the Conservatory. 'More chance of someone having seen here,' Ruzsky said.

'Not at that time in the morning. He's been dead for several hours, at least.'

Ruzsky looked at his pocket watch. It was almost seven. He wondered if the man had already been dead when he had left the theatre with Maria.

'This time,' Pavel said, 'the killer wasn't stalking his victim.'

'An arranged meeting?'

'Don't you think so?'

'Yes, but it's a strange time to choose.'

They heard a group of horses whinnying and turned to see a green police-department sled pulling up. Prokopiev jumped down before it had stopped and strode towards them. He vaulted off the bridge and landed squarely on the ice – a silly, theatrical gesture. 'Thank you for your assistance, gentlemen. We shall take over from here.'

Prokopiev's shirt was still open at the neck, as though he, too, had just got out of bed. He looked at them with his head tilted down a fraction; in the dark, it made his stare still more intense. Two other Okhrana men hung over the bridge above them.

Ruzsky slipped the dead man's identity papers and the wad of money into his overcoat pocket.

Prokopiev was too busy preening himself to notice.

'By order of the interior minister,' Prokopiev said.

'What is?'

'We'll deal with the case.'

The two groups glared at each other. 'Is there something I'm missing?' Ruzsky asked.

As he spoke another sled rounded the corner and drew up. The chief of the Okhrana climbed down and strode towards them. He stepped awkwardly on to the ice. The moonlight made his face seem older, the lines exaggerated and his skin bloodless. He nodded once. 'Good morning, gentlemen.'

No one replied.

'We need more constables, I see.'

It was a moment before Ruzsky realized that this had been an attempt at humour. 'Yes,' he said.

'What is the situation?'

Ruzsky frowned. 'What is what situation?'

'You have discovered another body and the constables have reported that the killing was aggressive?'

'Something like it.'

'*Something* like it?'

Ruzsky looked at the dead man. 'It's similarly savage.' He glanced at the constables, each of whom avoided his eye.

'So the same killer?' Vasilyev asked.

'Possibly.'

'Possibly?'

'Or someone who wants us to think that.'

'You can go home now,' Vasilyev said. He'd spoken so quietly that it was a moment before Ruzsky grasped what had been said.

'What did you say?'

'Ivan will deal with this.'

Pavel tugged at Ruzsky's sleeve. 'Isn't that Anton's decision?' Ruzsky asked. 'Or does the Okhrana have an interest in the case that we should know about?'

'The same frenzied attack,' Vasilyev continued smoothly. 'We should have let Ivan deal with the couple on the ice.'

'Why?' Ruzsky asked. Pavel tugged again at his sleeve.

'Ivan has many agents at his disposal, Sandro. A member of the Imperial staff . . . It must have been the work of terrorists.'

Ruzsky was about to go on – he wanted a confrontation – but he sensed Pavel's nervousness. He made them wait. 'Good luck,' he said finally, then clambered back on to the bridge.

'Will they get Sarlov to do the autopsy?' he asked when they had turned the corner.

'I don't know.'

'We should get him out of bed and explain what's happened.'

'What's that going to achieve?'

'Forewarn him, Pavel.'

'We should leave it.'

'And how did they find out so quickly?' Ruzsky went on, ignoring his partner. 'Which one of the constables is in their pay?'

'Calm down, Sandro.'

Ruzsky stopped and stared at him.

'All right,' Pavel said, 'but let's slow down, can we? By the way, you look terrible.'

Ruzsky wasn't surprised. He pressed his eyes into their sockets. His head was pounding. 'I don't understand,' he said.

'Understand what?'

'When they took away the bodies from the Neva, why didn't they assume control of the case? It doesn't make sense to me. Their actions aren't consistent.'

Pavel didn't answer. 'What happened to your hand?' he asked.

'Oh.' Ruzsky looked at the rag he had bound round his palm. 'An accident with a vodka bottle.'

'You should be more careful, my friend.'

CHAPTER TWENTY

Back at his desk, Ruzsky unhooked the telephone earpiece and asked the operator to put him through to Dr Sarlov at home.

'Yes?' The pathologist sounded sleepy.

'We've had an incident with the Okhrana.'

'I don't want to know.'

'Another victim. Same kind of attack. The head was almost severed. They have removed the body. Will you do the autopsy?'

'I have no idea.'

'If you do—'

'Consider who is listening,' the doctor said, then abruptly terminated the call.

Ruzsky sorted through the telegraphs he'd received the previous night. He reread the one from Yalta. 'American wanted in connection with armed robbery in Yalta, October 1910. Fits description. More details upon request.' He took up the telephone again and asked to be put through to Detective Godorkin. The line went dead, but he held on. He heard a loud crackle, as though someone was screwing up newspaper next to the mouthpiece. 'Detective Godorkin, please,' he shouted again.

'Godorkin here,' a voice said calmly. The line was suddenly clear.

'Detective Godorkin?'

'I am he.'

'This is Chief Investigator Ruzsky, Petrograd city police.'

'Chief Investigator, I was trying to contact you.'

'I don't know how long the line will last,' Ruzsky said, 'so let's dispense with the niceties. We've got three dead bodies, including two from Yalta – a girl from the palace called Ella Kovyil, who was murdered with her American lover on the Neva, and a Boris Markov.'

'I see.'

'What can you tell me? Could the American have been the one you're searching for? His name was White . . .'

The line faded again and Ruzsky cursed. It came back, but he caught only the end of a sentence. 'I missed that,' he shouted.

'Robert Whitewater,' Godorkin said.

'Whitewater?'

'Yes. That was his name. An American . . .'

The line failed again. Ruzsky tried repeatedly to get another connection, but without success. He sat back in his chair as Pavel walked in with a newspaper under his arm. He threw it across the desk at Ruzsky. 'Page three.'

It was a copy of *Novoe Vremia*. Ruzsky flicked past the advertisements on the front page. The article was a factual account of the discovery of the original bodies on the river and only the headline, 'Blood on the Neva', exhibited the sensationalism for which the paper was known. It did not give either Ella's or the American's name. The last line posed the question, 'In these difficult times, is a killer on the loose in Petrograd?' The piece alongside it followed one woman's daily struggle for survival while her husband was fighting at the front. 'While the rich drown in excess,' it said, 'the struggle of the poor gets daily more impossible.'

The news item at the top of the page appeared under the headline 'Further explosion of crime: Petrograd's streets more dangerous than ever.'

Ruzsky glanced up at the clock. It was almost time for the morning conference. 'Are we going?' he asked.

Pavel shrugged.

Ruzsky stood up and took his coat from the stand. Through the open door, he watched Vladimir roll into the room opposite. The investigator, street crime, was a barrel of a man, no taller than Ruzsky's shoulder, but with the strength of an ox. He trailed a young assistant – a new one. He caught sight of Ruzsky, altered course and charged across the room towards him. 'Here's trouble,' he said, loud enough to be heard downstairs. 'Welcome back.'

They clasped each other. 'This is my new assistant,' Vladimir indicated the young man standing awkwardly in the doorway, 'Constable Shavelsky.' Shavelsky's handshake was firm. It made Ruzsky wince, though the other man appeared not to notice. Ruzsky wondered whether he knew of the fate of his predecessor.

'So,' Vladimir said, 'they finally let you come home.' The fat detective took out a cigarette and offered one to both Ruzsky and Pavel, but not his assistant. When they declined, he lit his own and smoked it with the other hand in his pocket, looking out towards the secretaries who were taking their places at the desks outside, steam rising from mugs of tea alongside their giant black typewriters. They were sitting forward in their chairs, gossiping. 'How was Tobolsk?' Vladimir asked.

'Cold.'

'He should never have let you go.'

Ruzsky remembered the last morning conference before his exile, when Vladimir had launched a vicious attack on Anton for not fighting harder to protect him.

'They're keeping you busy, I see,' Ruzsky said, holding up his copy of *Novoe Vremia*.

In response, Vladimir held up the sheet of paper in his own hand. It listed a series of crimes and incidents. 'Last night alone.'

'Who?'

'Deserters, the desperate. Sometimes serving soldiers. Our friends in the Okhrana. Another three Jewish properties burned last night.'

Ruzsky put on his coat. 'How do you handle that?'

'We take a look. If it is the Okhrana, which it usually is, we leave it. What choice is there? Are you coming to the conference?'

'Not today,' Ruzsky said.

'What happened to your hand?'

'An accident.' Ruzsky raised his hand, took off the rag and threw it into the bin in the corner. A little blood was still oozing from his palm.

Ella's mother lived on the top floor of the tenement block, and it was a slow climb. Pavel wheezed heavily. They stopped to catch their breath, surrounded by

221

clothes that had been hung up to dry on lines criss-crossing the landing. A thin trickle of water ran down the stairs, forming a pool by their feet. There was an overpowering smell of urine.

The door closest to them opened and a young girl appeared. She had wild black hair, hollow cheeks and staring eyes. She wore high boots and stood with her feet close together, watching them. There were six or seven people at least in the gloomy room behind her, lying in bundles on the floor.

At the top, they saw that the trickle of water on the stairs had come from thick ice around the windows, some of which was melting. Pavel ducked under another line of frozen washing and knocked on the door at the far end of the corridor. They waited.

'Who is it?' a voice asked.

'Madame Kovyil? City police.'

There was another pause, and then the door was opened by a tiny woman who barely reached Pavel's waist. She stepped back to allow them to enter. 'This is Chief Investigator Ruzsky,' Pavel said, as if he himself was unimportant.

The woman forced herself to smile. 'My husband once served under—'

'My father. Or perhaps my uncle.' Ruzsky clasped her wrist with his left hand. 'Sandro.'

She placed a small cold hand in his and tried to hold her smile in place. She looked up at him with hollow eyes.

'Madame Kovyil, I'm afraid I have to tell you that . . .' But he could see she already knew. From the palace, he assumed, Shulgin, probably. She was crying and Pavel was at once next to her, ushering her into a chair close to the fireplace and holding her arm until she had recovered her composure. Ruzsky wondered how long ago she had been told.

'I'm sorry,' she said. 'I'm so sorry.'

'There is no need to apologize, Madame Kovyil,' Ruzsky said.

'Anna. Please call me Anna.' She pushed herself forward in her chair. She seemed even frailer than when they had arrived. 'Would you like something to drink? I'm afraid I have no vodka, but tea perhaps?'

Ruzsky and Pavel both declined. The room was small and neat, but the fireplace was too clean to have been used at any time in the recent past, and if she ever heated any kind of pot, they could see it was a rare event.

The only light in the room emanated from one small window, covered in frost. Ruzsky peered at the photographs on the mantelpiece. The first was of Anna and her husband on their wedding day, the second of him in the regimental uniform of the Preobrazhensky Guards and the third of Ella, aged fourteen or fifteen. As Ruzsky had imagined, she had a shy, sweet smile, like her mother.

'She was your only child?' Ruzsky asked.

Anna nodded once and then, slowly and with dignity, placed her head in her hands. Pavel patted her shoulder.

She composed herself. 'I'm sorry,' she said again.

Ruzsky took a seat. Even in this light, he could see that its cover had been carefully stitched together. Like everything else, it spoke of threadbare respectability.

'This is a terrible time, Madame . . . Anna, but if you feel strong enough to answer questions, we'd greatly appreciate your assistance.'

She nodded. 'Of course.'

'We don't believe that Ella's murder was an isolated incident.'

Anna stared at him unseeingly. Her face was narrower than Ella's and if, as the photograph suggested, she had once been beautiful, her features were ravaged now by age, cold and poverty. 'I told your colleagues,' she said quietly, 'but if there is something else—'

'Our colleagues?'

'Yes.'

'Which colleagues?'

'They came this morning, just a few minutes ago.'

'Did they give their names?'

'No, they just said they were from the police department.'

'Was it they who told you of your daughter . . . of Ella's death?' Ruzsky asked

She shook her head.

'You were informed by palace officials?'

'Yes.'

'Yesterday, or the day before?'

'The day before. On New Year's Day, in the evening.'

'Colonel Shulgin came to see you?'

Anna did not respond, but he could see that this had not been the case. Ruzsky had seen no telephone in the flat. Had they sent a messenger? Informed her by letter? He looked at Pavel and then back at Anna, unable to conceal his disgust at the way she had been treated. 'What did they look like, the men who came this morning?'

'The man in charge was tall. Like you, but bigger. He had short hair and poor skin and a large . . .' She indicated, with long bony fingers, a pronounced nose. 'He didn't tell me his name.'

'And what did he want?'

'There were four of them. They asked questions about Ella and . . . some others.'

'Which others?'

Anna sighed. 'Some I didn't know.'

'Did they give names?'

'I can't remember all of them.'

'It would help if you could recall one or two, Anna.'

She was overtaken by confusion. 'Were they not policemen?'

'Not really, no.'

'Who were they?'

'Government officials.' Ruzsky glanced at Pavel again. 'Okhrana. I don't think they would be interested in finding your daughter's killer.'

Anna kneaded her hands. Ruzsky hoped he'd not frightened her into silence. 'They asked about Ella's friend.'

'The American?'

'Yes.' Anna looked up, pleadingly.

Ruzsky showed her the photograph. 'This man?' He was on the point of apologizing when he saw a hint of satisfaction in her eyes.

'He was charming, of course, but I didn't like it. He was so much older than her. He . . .' She trailed off.

'He manipulated her?' Ruzsky suggested.

'I wanted her to marry a man like her father, like my . . . He was such a good man, so loyal, to the Tsar and to us.'

'Where did Ella meet her friend, Anna? Here in Petersburg?'

'At home.'

'In Yalta?' Ruzsky's pulse quickened.

'Such a long time ago now. I thought she had forgotten him.'

'She met the American on a holiday, or before you moved here?'

'Yes. That's why I left. I wanted to get her away. But I didn't know.'

'You didn't know that they remained in contact?'

'How could I? She never told me. I thought perhaps she would have met some nice man at the palace, which would have been so much more . . . appropriate. I always asked her about it and she said no, there was no one, that she was devoted to the Tsarevich and to her work . . .' Anna stopped again, apparently frightened that she had revealed something she should not.

'We know your daughter worked with the Tsarevich,' Pavel said. 'We have been to the palace. They spoke highly of her.'

Anna seemed relieved. 'She was a good girl, such a good girl.'

'You met the American in Yalta?' Ruzsky asked.

'Only once.' Anna sat forward and pushed the scarf back from her head. She appeared stronger now, bolstered by hostility to her daughter's lover. 'That summer, he came to the house just after Ella's father had died. He was charming.' She shook her head. 'I don't know what it was. He was so much older than her. She was just a young girl.'

'Did you sense that your daughter—'

'I'm not a fool, Chief Investigator. I knew that they were lovers, but I thought it was an infatuation that would run its course. She said he'd encouraged her to apply for a job at the royal palace and I thought she would soon forget him.'

'He encouraged her to get a job at Livadia?'

'Yes.'

'This would have been . . . what year?'

'1910.'

'How old was she then, Anna?'

'Sixteen.'

'Did Ella tell you why he'd encouraged her to apply for a job at the palace?'

Anna didn't understand the significance of the question. 'Her father had died,' she said defensively. 'It was a difficult time for both of us, of course. Ella was at that age . . . she wanted to find her own feet. It was understandable.'

'But the American specifically encouraged her to get a job in the Imperial Household?'

'My husband had worked at Livadia. He had always hoped she would find employment there but—'

'She had been reluctant to work in the Imperial Household?'

Anna stared at her hands. 'She was just a young girl.'

'She didn't like following in her father's footsteps. It felt too—'

'A lot of people filling her head with silly ideas.' Anna smiled. 'We dealt with it. After the move to Petersburg, it was so much better.'

'Silly ideas?' Ruzsky asked.

Anna did not answer.

'Revolutionary ideas?'

Anna looked worried again but then her face cleared, as if she had realized that her daughter's death had absolved her of any need to fear this at least. 'It was different in Petersburg,' she repeated.

'The American was a revolutionary and Ella was influenced by him?'

'My husband would not allow discussion of politics in the house. They . . . he and Ella argued in the last year of his life. It upset him greatly.'

'She met the American in revolutionary circles in Yalta?'

Anna looked at Pavel, then back at Ruzsky. 'I don't know about that, but I didn't like him. After my husband died, I wanted to move away. It would be good to begin again. It was my gift to him.'

'To your husband?'

'Yes.'

'He had been worried about Ella?'

'She would never have brought the American to the house when her father was alive.'

'Did the American ever explain what he was doing in Yalta, Anna?'

'Travelling, he said.' Anna shrugged contemptuously. 'Just travelling. That was all he said. Ella told me his father was a millionaire from America and he liked to visit other parts of the world. He boasted that he had no need to work.'

Ruzsky could see how the poor, respectable Kovyils must have hated the charming interloper who had bewitched their daughter with strange ideas and the prospect of another life. 'Did you meet any of Ella's other friends from the same circle?'

'From the same circle?'

Ruzsky tried to remember the name of the man they had found at the Lion Bridge this morning. 'Boris Markov? Perhaps just Borya?'

'I don't know.'

Ruzsky dug the man's identification papers from

his pocket and showed her the dark, smudged photograph. She shook her head. 'Who did the men this morning ask you about?'

Anna handed back the papers. 'I'm not very good with names.'

'What did they want to know?'

'If Ella had brought him home, and whether I had met him.'

'The American?'

'Yes.'

'And had you, this time?'

Anna's face quivered briefly, then she recovered her composure. 'How could I know she had taken up with him again? I thought he was on the other side of the world, where he belonged.'

'Did she bring him here?'

'No, but I knew he had come here.'

Ruzsky could tell he was upsetting the woman. He crouched in front of her. 'Anna, can you think of anything over the last few months that would give us an indication of why someone would want to kill Ella?'

Tears welled in her eyes. 'She was a loving girl, Officer, so loving.'

'When did you last see her?'

Anna gestured to the photograph of her daughter on the mantelpiece and the religious icon hanging above it. 'Last Sunday. She always came to see me on Sunday. It was her day off and she would catch the train into town and we would go to church together.'

'And what happened last Sunday?'

Anna stared at the wall. The silence dragged on, but Ruzsky did not push her.

'It was just a Sunday,' she said, 'like all Sundays.'

'You went to church?'

'She was so happy, Officer. That smile, I wish you could have seen it. She was such a pretty girl.'

'Why was she so happy, Anna?'

'I thought she was just . . . happy. To be with me. To be close to the Lord. Such a fine, clear, bright day, the city so beautiful. I felt happy too – happier, I think, than on any day since I came here. It was wonderful to see her so bursting with joy.'

'What did you do?'

'We came home. She had brought some food. She was a kind girl.'

'Did she tell you of any reason why she was so happy?'

She couldn't hold her emotions in check any longer and collapsed, burying her face in her hands, her thin shoulders heaving. Pavel held her. 'It's all right, Anna,' he said quietly. 'It's all right.'

Ruzsky took her arm and squeezed gently. She was all skin and bone.

They waited until the convulsions had stopped, then averted their eyes while she took out a handkerchief and blew her nose. 'I cannot bear the thought of it, do you understand?' she said simply. 'Those Sundays were my life.' She wept once more.

'We're intruding,' Ruzsky said. 'Perhaps we could come back another time.'

'No, please.' She wiped her eyes again. 'I would like to help.' She put away the handkerchief. 'Please ask me whatever you wish.'

'Was there anything unusual about that Sunday, Anna? Did she say or do anything out of the ordinary?' Ruzsky said.

'There was an argument, that's all I can think of. Not even an argument.'

'What about?'

'She asked me a question and I was offended.'

'What did she ask you?'

'It was unlike her. And I said her father would have been disgusted.'

'What did she ask you?'

Anna stared at Ruzsky. She was uncertain again. She glanced at Pavel for reassurance, then steeled herself. 'She asked me whether I thought it was possible that the Empress and Rasputin had enjoyed intimate relations. Whether they had been lovers.'

'Why do you think she asked that?'

'I don't know.'

'Surely, Anna, your daughter, more than anyone, would have been in a position to know the answer to that question. Do you think she was seeking reassurance for something she already suspected?'

'Someone had been poisoning her mind.'

'There have been many rumours. You must have heard them.'

'The work of revolutionaries. What do they want, these people?'

Ruzsky rose again and moved to the mantelpiece. 'Anna, your daughter knew Rasputin. On the records kept by the household staff, it is said that she met him both at the palace and in Petersburg.'

'She would never have consorted with such a man.'

'By all accounts, he was able to cure the Tsarevich of his bouts of haemophilia, or so the Empress believed. That would have encouraged Ella's approbation.'

Anna did not answer.

'Did she give any intimation as to why she was asking you the question?'

'No.'

Ruzsky glanced at Pavel. 'We must go. Thank you for your assistance.' He touched her shoulder.

As they stepped out into the corridor and pulled the door shut behind them, they heard her begin to sob violently.

They listened, debating whether to go back and try to comfort her once more.

'God in heaven,' Pavel said, as they walked away.

CHAPTER TWENTY-ONE

Outside, the sun was so shrouded by cloud that it was difficult to tell if it was day or night. The wind whistled along the narrow alley between the tenements, and the few people out on the street moved quickly, their heads bent.

A funeral procession rounded the corner. Four men dressed in black carried a coffin draped in a simple scarlet cloth. Behind them a group of women huddled together against the cold, holding their veils to their faces as the wind worried at their billowing robes. Three soldiers in dirty grey overcoats and woollen hats walked beside them.

Ruzsky and Pavel waited as the procession passed, the only sound that of boots crunching in the snow. None of the mourners met their eyes. Ruzsky thought of the soldiers he had seen going off to the front on the day of his departure for Tobolsk three years ago. Then, the capital had been full of khaki-clad men marching with grim but determined faces. Now only the politicians claimed that the war could be won; defeat was in the face of every man in uniform.

For a moment, after the cortège had disappeared,

the detectives gazed after it, both deep in thought. As they turned back, they saw a man huddled in the front of his cab at the far end of the alley, clutching the reins to his chest as his horse shifted restlessly. Once he saw that they were looking at him, he moved off.

They were being watched. It came as a shock to Ruzsky, although he knew it shouldn't.

'A rouble for whoever's first to spot the next one,' Ruzsky said, but Pavel wasn't smiling. 'Just ignore them,' he said. 'If they've got nothing better to do—'

'But they have,' Pavel said.

They had breakfast in the canteen. It was the first working day of the new year, and it showed. Pavel got a full tray of cold meat and pickled cucumbers; Ruzsky made do with Turkish coffee – the vodka had killed off his hunger. They went to sit in the far corner so that they would not be overheard.

'I knew Rasputin would come back to haunt us,' Pavel said.

Ruzsky offered him a cigarette and they smoked in silence.

'Why would Ella ask her mother that question?' Pavel asked.

'A guilty conscience.'

'I don't understand.'

'Ella was a shy, somewhat naïve girl,' Ruzsky said. 'She knew little of life outside the palace and the respectable but dull world of her parents. For all her talk of revolution, she never quite came to terms with what her American had asked her to do.'

'To steal something?'

'Something personal.'

'To do with Rasputin.'

Ruzsky nodded. 'It starts to make sense of things, don't you think?'

'And he justified it to her on the grounds that the Empress and Rasputin were lovers. So what did Ella steal?'

'A diary?'

'If it had been a diary, she'd have been thrown into the darkest dungeon of the fortress over the river.'

'Perhaps they don't know for sure what she stole.'

'Then how did they know she'd stolen anything?'

'I don't know,' Ruzsky said, 'but I think we should try Shulgin again today. See if we can talk to some of the people Ella worked with.' He squashed his cigarette butt into the ashtray. 'What were Prokopiev's men doing there? I don't understand why he would be asking Ella's mother questions to which we assume he already knows the answers.'

Pavel gestured towards the street outside. 'I can understand why they might want to take over the case, but why would they want to watch us? The country stands on the brink and they have time to watch two Petrograd city policemen going about their business?'

'We should go to Yalta,' Ruzsky said.

'Good idea. I need a holiday.' Pavel hadn't taken him seriously.

'Everything leads to Yalta. We'll go tonight.'

The colour drained from Pavel's face.

'You don't wish to come?'

'It's up to you.'

Anton and Maretsky came in. Anton was smoking a cigarette and raised it in greeting as they went to get a cup of coffee. Ruzsky and Pavel watched their progress in silence until they came to join them.

'So, they're officially taking over the case,' Anton said, as he sat down. 'I just got a call from the interior ministry.' He took off his glasses and placed them on the table, rubbing his forehead and eyes. He ground out his cigarette on the hardwood table top, threw the butt on to the floor at their feet and lit another. His eyes were bloodshot: he looked the way Ruzsky felt.

They sat in silence. None of them wished to take the matter further.

Maretsky was drinking hot water, which steamed up his glasses as he bent over it. He slid the mug to and fro, restlessly.

'We're going to Yalta,' Ruzsky said. 'Tonight.'

'Why?' Anton asked.

'The man we found this morning was from Yalta,' Ruzsky went on. 'Ella was from Yalta. We think the dead American is wanted for armed robbery in Yalta.'

No one spoke.

'I don't particularly want to live in a world where the chief of the Okhrana can do whatever he likes. Do you?'

Maretsky and Pavel kept their eyes on the table. 'We already live in that kind of world, Sandro,' Anton told him.

'Well, we shouldn't just accept it.' Ruzsky knew what his colleagues were thinking – that he, of all of them, had nothing to lose. All that had awaited him upon his return from Tobolsk was a cold wife and a son he couldn't see. He tried to block Maria from his mind.

By contrast, Maretsky had a family, despite the incident with the student. Anton had a daughter on one of the university courses for women: she would not want her fellow students to know that her father

236

was a policeman – even one in the city police. And Pavel had Tonya and his boy, who were, as he so readily admitted, all he cared about. But Ruzsky was reluctant to let go.

Anton's lips thinned. 'This isn't the time for a crusade. They've made it official. We can't ignore that.'

'Since when has doing our job been a crusade? We've got three bodies and at least one killer. That makes it a murder case. That's what we're here to do.'

'It *was* a murder case. Now it's a series of atrocities carried out by a suspected revolutionary cell. And if you don't believe me, call the interior ministry.'

'Revolutionaries don't stab their victims seventeen times.'

No one responded.

'Let's ask ourselves some questions, then. Why do the Okhrana want this case? Maretsky?'

The professor continued to stare at the table.

'Maretsky? You work with them. You don't think this was the work of revolutionaries, do you? And what are the Okhrana doing?'

The professor's face was strained. 'I go over there when I have to. I do not work with them.'

'Well, what do you—'

'Do you know why you were sent into exile?' The professor's eyes flashed at Ruzsky. 'Because he didn't know what to make of you. He was still feeling his way then. You're high-born. You had connections. You were an unknown quantity. Better to play safe and get you out of the way. But it's all changed, Sandro. You've seen him up close. You know that.'

Ruzsky thought of Vasilyev at the ballet, in the midst of his family, which had largely disowned him. 'I see nothing behind his eyes.'

'Precisely. We're not talking about exile to Tobolsk any more.'

They contemplated this in silence.

'He's the chief of the secret police, not God,' Ruzsky said.

'We're not here to give you a sense of purpose,' Anton responded.

Ruzsky reddened.

'The Okhrana has taken over this case. There is nothing we can do about it.'

'We could take it up with the interior ministry.' It was a weak argument and he knew it.

'Vasilyev can pick up the telephone and call the palace any time he chooses,' Anton reminded him.

'But the palace doesn't like the Okhrana,' Pavel said quietly. He smiled at Ruzsky, his earlier anxiety apparently forgotten.

Anton sighed.

'They can't punish us for continuing to amass information on a murder case,' Ruzsky went on.

'Of course they can.'

'We can say we were still seeking to assist them.'

'They can suspend us, dismiss us, send us to where you've just come from. Or worse.'

To Ruzsky, Anton seemed suddenly terribly tired. It was as if he had given up, not just on his work but on life. It was hard to recall the witty, outspoken man who had kept them laughing during those evenings at his country home overlooking the Gulf of Finland.

'They have removed us from the case. Categorically. Explicitly,' Anton said. 'They left no room for me to claim a misunderstanding. I'm going to have to ask you to desist from further enquiries.'

'But why?' Ruzsky asked. 'That's the question. Why are they so determined to block us?'

'That may be the question, but it is not one to which we have to find an answer. My instructions are clear. It would have been difficult to get to Yalta, anyway. You've heard what it's like.'

Anton stood up and walked out. Maretsky followed him.

'So now we are two,' Pavel said, once they'd gone. 'Well done.'

CHAPTER TWENTY-TWO

The train to Tsarskoe Selo moved slower than ever, the rhythmic hiss of the steam engine and the gentle roll of the carriages sending Pavel to sleep. His head was between the seat and the window, his mouth open.

As Ruzsky looked out at the snow-covered landscape, he could not imagine leaving the country of his birth.

'What are you thinking?' Pavel asked. His head hadn't moved, but his mouth was shut now and he'd been watching him.

'Nothing much.'

'A girl?'

They pulled out of the trees. The window was dirty and the landscape here so monotonous that it was hard to distinguish between snow and sky.

'Is it love?'

Ruzsky didn't answer.

'Who is it? The ballerina?'

'No,' Ruzsky lied.

Pavel whistled quietly. 'She's beautiful. I wouldn't blame you. What will you do?'

'Nothing.'

'I don't believe you.'

'Believe what you want.'

'Love has a habit of overcoming most obstacles,' Pavel said.

Ruzsky looked out of the window. Two young boys in thick winter coats were standing on the bank, waving at the passengers. Ruzsky waved back. 'Sometimes the obstacles are impossible to overcome,' he said.

'But you don't believe it. That's your secret.'

Ruzsky had a sudden vivid image of Maria and his brother naked in front of her fire, the soft light dancing over their bodies.

'Now what are you thinking?' Pavel asked.

'That I wish you'd keep quiet.'

'I'm here to torment you until you talk.'

Ruzsky attempted a smile. 'Nothing profound. About Russia. About home.'

Pavel searched his face. 'Did you ever think of escape?'

Ruzsky thought of the ice cracking, of the water's embrace. 'And leave Michael in the hands of the grand duke?'

Pavel nodded ruefully. 'I could never live anywhere else.'

'Neither could I.'

Pavel straightened. 'Perhaps you could take him with you. I'm not saying you wouldn't miss home – you do miss it – but whatever it was that happened in your . . . well, you know. You could go.'

'You sound like my nanny.'

Pavel's demeanour showed that he had taken the remark as a compliment, although it hadn't necessarily been meant as one. 'We've known each other a long time. It's been a privilege to be your friend.'

Ruzsky frowned. 'Am I missing something?'

'I like things to be said. I don't like them to be hidden, you know that.'

Ruzsky turned to the window again.

'Do you enjoy your job, Sandro?'

'What do you mean?'

'Exactly what I said.'

'This is a strange series of questions.'

'You're an idealist. You didn't have to work—'

'Neither true, alas.'

'You could have reconciled with your family, if you'd wanted to.'

Ruzsky didn't answer.

'I started out as a constable – I had little choice – but I enjoy what I do. I was just thinking about it—'

'I don't know where this is leading us, Pavel,' Ruzsky interrupted.

'I've always assumed that I understood what made you do this job, but I've never asked.'

'Yes. I suppose the answer is yes. I enjoy what I do, but you're wrong about a lot of things. I don't think of myself as an idealist.'

'Why not?'

'Because what you see as idealism, my old friend, I know to be obstinacy. It's not the same thing.'

Pavel pressed his forehead against the window. 'What will become of us?'

'We'll be all right.'

'Do you think so?'

'Yes.'

'I don't. Not any more.'

'What are you worried about?' Ruzsky asked.

'About Tonya. About my boy.'

'They'll be all right. If anyone, it is you who should worry.'

'Exactly. And where would they be if something happened to me?'

'I'd look after them.'

'Would you?' Pavel's eyes glistened.

'Of course. I'd steal one of my father's paintings.'

Pavel looked uncertain, then grinned sheepishly. 'Very funny, Sandro,' he said.

At the Alexander Palace, they were shown through to the same anteroom and told to wait. Ruzsky walked to the window and looked out at the frozen lake, but there was no sign of the Imperial children. A skein of mist curled round the trees in the distance and stretched across the ice.

'This was a bad idea,' Pavel said. 'Just because we didn't see them watching us on the way here doesn't mean that they weren't.'

'Shulgin doesn't like the Okhrana, or at least the Petrograd Okhrana,' Ruzsky said, 'and I think the feeling's mutual. We'll see what happens.'

'It's crazy to come here.'

Ruzsky didn't reply. They'd had this argument three times already.

They heard footsteps. The guard who had brought them appeared again. 'Come with me,' he said, without grace or ceremony.

Their coats were returned to them in the hallway. 'Are we not to receive an audience?' Ruzsky asked, with equal curtness.

'Please come with me.' The guard led them out, past the columns at the front of the palace and the two curved archways, to the far wing. The door swung open and they were admitted by a tall houseboy in a bright red and gold uniform. Two others stood behind him; a fourth took their coats.

He took them up two steps and marched them down a long corridor.

'What's going on?' Pavel whispered.

'These are the family quarters,' Ruzsky said.

Their footsteps echoed. Martial paintings lined the walls. Ruzsky's eye was caught by a giant portrait of Nicholas I on a white charger. A shrill peal of laughter rang out from somewhere on their left.

They were led past two large golden urns and into a formal room decorated, too, in red and gold. They stood at the entrance, flanked on either side by a phalanx of white marble busts, beneath a vast tapestry of Marie Antoinette and her children.

The houseboy invited them to sit on an upholstered gilt-edged sofa, between two inlaid grand pianos, then withdrew. They listened to his footsteps receding.

'What's going on?' Pavel whispered again.

Ruzsky was staring up at Marie Antoinette. He turned to Pavel and put his finger to his lips. He mouthed, 'Empress,' and pointed to the open door on the far side of the room.

They heard more footsteps in the corridor. Shulgin entered, scowling. 'You did not telephone.'

'Please accept my apologies, Your High Excellency,' Ruzsky said quietly, knowing that the colonel's performance was not entirely for their benefit.

'That does not—'

Shulgin stopped as both Ruzsky and Pavel became aware of a figure standing in the shadows beyond the doorway.

'What do they want, Shulgin?' the Tsarina asked.

'They are investigating the death of Ella Kovyil, Your Majesty.'

'I asked, what do they want?'

'They wish to speak to some of the household staff who worked alongside her. I have told them already, on a previous occasion, that this is a matter that requires discussion with other senior members of staff . . .'

The Tsarina stepped forward. She wore a black dress, with an oval mother-of-pearl brooch pinned to the collar. 'I saw you before,' she said to Ruzsky. 'Two days ago.'

'Yes, Your Majesty.'

Ruzsky stood and made a small bow, then gave a sidelong glance at Pavel, who was sitting with his mouth open. He snapped upright and did the same.

'What do you want now?' she asked.

'They fear a conspiracy,' Shulgin said, his tone dismissive. 'Some political skulduggery.'

'Is this true?' the Tsarina demanded. She looked at them for the first time, concentrating her attention on Pavel, but her gaze was neutral: neither censorious nor inquisitive.

'It is one possibility,' Ruzsky said.

'Then it should be a matter for the Okhrana.'

'If it pleases Your Majesty.'

'*Is* it a matter for the Okhrana?' She made no attempt to conceal her impatience.

'Yes.'

'Then why are they not here instead of you?'

'I don't know, Your Majesty. Perhaps they will be.'

'You give swift answers, Detective, yet I do not

believe them. Why have you not found Ella's murderer?'

Ruzsky looked at Shulgin, whose expression now carried more than a hint of apology for his mistress's haughty manner. 'We are working tirelessly, Your Majesty,' Ruzsky said evenly, 'but our resources are few. As I'm sure you are aware, the city has known better times.'

'What do you mean by that?'

Ruzsky recognized his mistake. 'The war, Your Majesty, a strain upon us all, but especially on yourself.'

'The Tsar is returning to the front,' she said. Perhaps realizing this had little relevance, she added, 'We will prevail.' It was said with finality, but she did not move.

Shulgin coughed. They all peered at the highly polished floor.

'Why do you think Ella was murdered by a revolutionary?' the Tsarina asked.

'It is only a theory,' Ruzsky said, not wishing to contradict her.

'Tell me about it.'

Ruzsky glanced at Shulgin again, but was given no lead.

'Your Majesty, Ella's lover, the American, was a notorious agitator.'

'An American?'

'Yes.'

'What was he doing in Petrograd?'

'We don't know.'

'You have spoken to the Okhrana – to Vasilyev, to that other tiresome, arrogant man . . .' She snorted.

'Ivan Alexandrovich, ma'am,' Shulgin said.

'Prokopiev. Yes. Have you spoken to them?'

'We have.' Ruzsky answered.

'What do they have to say on the matter?'

'I believe they were informed some weeks ago that the American would be returning to the capital.'

The Tsarina looked at him sharply – Ruzsky had known that he was playing with fire, but had been unable to resist. 'Who told you that?' she asked.

'The American embassy.'

'The American embassy? That ridiculous man!'

'A Mr Morris, ma'am,' Shulgin offered.

The Tsarina stared at Ruzsky. 'You don't seem to have achieved very much, Chief Investigator . . .'

'Ruzsky.'

'Ah, yes. Your father is the assistant minister of finance.' The Empress seemed on the verge of making some dismissive remark, but evidently thought better of it. 'So, am I to understand that a member of the Imperial Household was stabbed in the centre of our city yet you know nothing of who killed her, or why?'

'We believe that the American might have had something to do with whatever she stole from you.'

'Who told you that she stole from me?' The Tsarina glared at Shulgin.

'With respect, Your Majesty, you did,' Ruzsky said. He could no longer recall if this was true, or whether he had first learnt of Ella's alleged crime from Anya Vyrubova, but he wanted to see if he could catch the Empress off-balance.

'You must try harder,' she said, before turning on Shulgin. 'This is an absolute disgrace. Speak to Vasilyev and—'

'I was under the impression that it had already been done,' Ruzsky said.

In the uneasy silence that followed, he could see that the Tsarina was caught between fury at the interruption and curiosity as to what he had meant.

'We were led to believe,' Ruzsky went on, 'that the palace considered it in the nation's best interests that the matter be given . . .' Ruzsky caught Pavel's eye. He looked as if he was about to faint. 'We were under the impression,' he said carefully, 'that the palace had dwelt upon this matter and did not consider it an item of high priority.'

Again Shulgin became the focus of the Tsarina's fury. 'What's this?'

'I have no idea.'

'What do you mean?' She turned back to Ruzsky.

'Exactly as I said, Your Majesty. But I must have been mistaken. I apologize. You wish the matter to be given the highest priority?'

'Of course. An attack on one of our members of staff? What could be more important than that?'

Shulgin breathed in deeply as the Empress retired. For a moment, they were all co-conspirators, but his reserve reasserted itself. He took a step back, as if to distance himself from the exchange that had just taken place.

'Please wait here,' he said.

CHAPTER TWENTY-THREE

It was almost an hour before he came back – during which they had more or less sat in silence – and when he did his manner was off-hand. It took Ruzsky only a moment to decide that this was from anxiety rather than irritation. Shulgin, he thought, as they followed him down the corridor, was not a bad sort. He reminded Ruzsky even more forcefully of his father.

Their coats were returned and they were led back to the library, where a silver tray with a samovar awaited them, between two low chairs and a long settee, covered with crimson velvet and gold piping. 'Please have a seat,' Shulgin said, then disappeared.

They did as they'd been instructed and looked around. It was a beautiful room, less ornate and there-fore somehow more intimate than the antechamber they'd just left. A fire burned on the hearth between two enormous bookcases filled from floor to ceiling with leatherbound volumes. In the centre of the room there was a giant globe with a three-dimensional, topographical map of Russia similar to the ones Ruzsky had studied at the Corps des Pages. It stood beside a grand piano. Ruzsky had an almost irresistible desire to play it.

'Could you please explain what is going on?' Pavel asked.

'I have no idea.'

Shulgin entered the room, accompanied by a man in a sailor's uniform and a girl of about Ella's age. The man looked resentful, the girl nervous. They sat awkwardly on the chairs, while Shulgin took his position on the long settee. He poured tea, though only Ruzsky accepted it.

'These are two of Ella's colleagues from the household staff,' Shulgin explained. 'They knew her as well as anyone.'

Ruzsky waited in vain for them to be introduced, then got up and offered his hand to the man, who took it reluctantly. He seemed about to open his mouth when Shulgin intervened: 'I don't think there is any need for you to know their names.'

Ruzsky sat down.

'For their own safety,' the colonel added.

'Of course.'

Ruzsky dug a notepad and pencil from his jacket pocket. He turned to the girl. 'You knew Ella well?'

'Quite well, sir, yes.'

'You worked alongside her in the nursery?'

The girl glanced at Shulgin. Her vulnerability made her seem even prettier than she'd first appeared.

Shulgin nodded, and she turned anxious eyes back to Ruzsky. 'Yes,' she said.

'Did you know her from Yalta, or from Petersburg?'

'Just here, sir. I'm from Moscow.'

'You've never been to Yalta?'

'No, sir.'

'How long have you worked at the palace?'

'About two years.'

'I served with her father,' Shulgin said. 'Her background is second to none.'

Ruzsky ignored the interruption. 'You both looked after the Tsarevich?' he asked. 'You and Ella?'

'I worked with Ella,' the sailor said.

Ruzsky swung towards him. 'You looked after the Tsarevich together?'

'Yes,' the man said.

'Did you know Ella before she came here?'

'No. I'm from Petrograd.'

'How long have you been working at the palace?'

'Three years. Before that, Kronstadt. Before that the Barents Sea.' It was said without pride, almost like a prisoner rattling off the length of his sentence.

'You liked Ella?'

'Of course. Everyone liked her.'

'You were lovers?'

Shulgin almost choked on his tea. 'Investigator, I must warn you—'

'No,' the man said. His gaze was steady.

'Ella already had a lover?'

'So she said.'

'Did she say who?'

'I knew he was an American, someone she'd met at home.'

'What did she say about him?'

'Nothing. Not to me, anyway.'

'Nothing?'

The man had a wide, strong face and held himself well. His naval uniform was immaculately pressed.

'She was secretive?' Pavel asked, finding his voice.

'About him, yes.'

'What about other friends?' Pavel asked.

'She went to see her mother on Sundays. She wrote letters. That was all. She led a quiet life and didn't deserve to have it ended like that.'

'Few do,' Ruzsky said. He turned towards Shulgin. 'Do you have any of her letters, or other belongings?'

The colonel shook his head.

'Did she ever talk about politics?' Ruzsky asked the sailor.

'Not to me.'

'Not to you, or not at all?'

'Not to me.' A muscle was flexing in the man's cheek. Why was he angry?

'To others?'

'I can't say.'

Ruzsky turned back to the girl. 'And you, Mademoiselle?'

'Not to me. No, of course not.'

'Why of course not?'

'This is the Imperial Household, Chief Investigator,' Shulgin said.

'Did you ever hear her discussing politics with others?' Ruzsky asked the girl.

'No, sir.'

'Did you know that her American lover was a well-known revolutionary criminal?'

'No, sir.' Her shock was genuine.

Ruzsky addressed the sailor: 'You?'

'No.'

'But you knew that she went to see Rasputin in Petersburg on her days off?'

It took Shulgin a few moments to react. 'That is a confidential matter,' he said, 'and no business of other members of staff.'

'But you knew?' Ruzsky asked the sailor.

'She had the good sense not to discuss any relationship . . . friendship,' he corrected himself.

'Why do you call it "good sense"?' Ruzsky asked.

'This has no bearing on the investigation,' Shulgin said, before the other man could speak. 'I really must ask you—'

'Tell us about her last few days,' Pavel said.

The sailor placed his elbows on his knees and rubbed the palms of his hands together. 'What do you want to know?'

'Was there anything different or unusual about her behaviour?'

The sailor looked at the girl.

'No,' she said.

'She was happy,' the sailor added.

Shulgin stood. 'Chief Investigator, a word, please.'

As they stepped outside, Ruzsky said, 'There is no point in allowing us to meet these people if you're going to prevent us asking them any pertinent questions.'

'*Remember where you are*,' Shulgin whispered.

'I can see exactly.' Ruzsky looked down the corridor. 'Now, do you want to find out who killed your girl or not?'

'We shall call the Okhrana,' Shulgin said.

'Be my guest, but they're unsuited to anything that might require a modicum of patience to unravel.'

'You have your father's arrogance.'

Ruzsky hesitated. 'How well do you know my father?'

'He was in my year at the Corps des Pages.'

Ruzsky realized that, despite his own lowly position, Shulgin had deliberately accorded him the respect due to someone of his background.

'I can't have you rampaging about in there—'

'They're as stiff as boards.'

'They're nervous.'

'That's not the reason, and you know it. You want us to get to the bottom of this or we'd not even have got through the door this morning. And so, by the sound of it, does the Empress. What is it? You don't trust the Okhrana?'

'You have not served your cause well.'

'Did you telephone the police department after our first visit?'

Shulgin looked at him with incredulity.

'After we first came out here, did you telephone the department to request that the investigation be dropped?'

'Why would I do such a thing?'

'We humble members of the city police,' Ruzsky said, 'were led to believe that the Empress did not wish the investigation into Ella Kovyil's death to proceed.'

'That's preposterous. Who told you that?'

'Your friend Vasilyev.'

Shulgin glanced down the corridor in the same direction Ruzsky had. Weary resignation replaced his confusion. He removed his monocle and tucked it into the pocket of his uniform.

'It would be better if you were not there while we talk to them,' Ruzsky said.

'That's out of the question.' Shulgin raised his arm to indicate that they should return.

Ruzsky resumed his seat. 'A few final matters, if you would be so kind. Did she . . . did Ella talk about the American's return?' He had been looking at the sailor, but now turned to the girl. 'Mademoiselle?'

'She was very happy that Robert . . . Mr White had

come back. Several months ago she received the news that he would in a letter.'

'Did you ever meet Mr White?'

'No, sir,' the girl said.

'How did you find her over these past few months?' he asked the sailor, making a conscious effort to soften his tone. 'You must have seen her every day. Was there anything you noticed that would help us, anything unusual?'

'She was moodier. One minute happy, the next withdrawn.'

'Did she give any hint as to why?'

'I thought it was . . . women's matters.'

The girl nodded. 'One minute she would . . . talk about it, I mean. She would say something like, "Natasha, he is coming, he really is." And then she would say, "Natasha, I don't know what to do, but he is wonderful." When I asked her what she meant, she would say, "It is nothing." She received many letters, addressed by the same hand, one or two a week in the last months. They are placed on a table outside the kitchen. She would fall upon them and, no matter how late she was or what duties awaited her, she would race up to her room and stay there for half an hour, sometimes more.'

'There were . . . *incidents*,' Shulgin said.

'She loved the boy more than anyone,' the sailor snapped back. Ruzsky saw now that the man's anger was directed against his superior.

'She harmed him?' Ruzsky asked.

'She raised her voice, that was all,' the sailor said. 'The boy was unwell, it was not his fault, but we're all under pressure.'

There was an awkward silence.

'How did she behave in the last day or two, immediately before the incident that caused her dismissal?' Ruzsky asked.

They both shook their heads.

'She gave no sign of being under any additional strain?'

They were silent.

'What exactly happened?'

'Chief Investigator—'

'I'm not asking what she stole but how she was caught,' Ruzsky told Shulgin. 'Surely we can be informed of that.'

'One of the footmen found her in the Empress's study,' Shulgin said. 'Naturally he had no choice but to inform me, and I the Empress. It was not a place she was entitled to be.'

'What was she doing there?'

'The footman in question said that she started in a guilty manner when discovered.'

'She was at the Empress's desk?'

Shulgin had taken out his monocle again. 'I don't see how this can have any direct bearing on the case.'

'So she didn't steal anything?' Ruzsky asked.

Shulgin looked at him. 'The Empress believes she did.'

'What?'

'I'm afraid—'

'What on earth could this girl have been searching for in the study of the Empress of All the Russias?'

'I don't know.' Shulgin could no longer conceal his own exasperation. 'I simply do not know.'

'The Empress told you she had stolen something, but not what? I thought you said Ella readily confessed to her crime.'

'She didn't steal anything,' the sailor said.

'Then what was she doing in there?' Ruzsky asked.

'We have taken this as far as it can sensibly go.' Shulgin stood up. Neither of the others now met Ruzsky's eye.

As soon as they had been let out of the wrought-iron gates, Pavel breathed an enormous sigh of relief. 'Christ,' he said, 'has Tobolsk done something to your mind?'

Ruzsky took out and lit a cigarette.

'Going on with the investigation is not exactly sane, but that was pure madness.'

'It gives us a degree of protection. Don't you see that?' Ruzsky expostulated.

'No.'

'That was the most bizarre interview we have ever conducted. Correct?'

'Indisputably.'

'They're completely in the dark. They're suspicious of the Okhrana and Vasilyev.'

'That may be, but it's not going to help us. We're just caught in the middle.' Pavel pointed at him aggressively. 'You have taken us into the middle of a minefield, and you know it.'

'If the Okhrana has been following us this morning, they'll know now that they have to tread carefully.'

'Rubbish. We've just increased the stakes in a game whose rules we don't even begin to know. And we're still no nearer to working out what's going on.' Pavel had flushed. 'Tell me what that was all about.'

'I don't know.'

'You're damned right you don't know. We're invited into the family apartments. The woman who

257

rules us is lurking in the doorway like a ghost. It's all completely unreal. She asks us whether the Okhrana is involved. She doesn't know what's happening beyond her own doorstep.'

Ruzsky raised his hand. 'But Ella did steal something.'

'The sailor denied it.'

'But they're worried. Worried enough to entertain the notion of interrogating a couple of lowly city policemen, then allowing us to interview members of the household. Is that normal? Hardly. And a few months ago it would have been unthinkable.'

'So we go crashing in like a couple of ignorant peasants—'

'That girl stole something important.'

Pavel stared miserably into the distance.

'It is the only rational explanation for the episode. They can't admit she stole something, let alone what it was, but they don't trust the Okhrana. Or, at least, they were talking to us as a way of finding out how the investigation is proceeding.'

Further down the street a cab driver stood beside his horse, waiting for a fare. Ruzsky had never seen a *droshky* waiting there before.

There was a young, dark-haired boy in the far corner of their office, looking out of the window.

For a moment, Ruzsky felt a surge of excitement. Then Pavel bellowed 'My boy,' bounded over and took his son into his arms.

A woman appeared next to Ruzsky. 'Sandro,' she said, and embraced him.

'Tonya.' Ruzsky stepped back. Pavel's wife was thinner, her blonde hair framing a face that seemed more careworn than before he had gone away. Her lips were pinched and her cheeks hollow. The effect in another woman would have been to make her look mean, but Tonya had always possessed an air of fragility. She gave him a shy smile.

'What do you say to your Uncle Sandro?' Pavel said. He still had his son in his arms.

'Hello, Uncle Sandro.' The boy was younger than Michael. He had long eyelashes and big blue eyes and, apart from his hair, was the image of his mother.

The sight of him, the innocence in his voice, made Ruzsky's heart miss a beat. He had been back more than forty-eight hours. Why had he not seen his child?

Tonya picked up a suitcase and put it on Pavel's desk. 'A holiday in Yalta!' It was a poor joke and, when she turned to face Ruzsky, he saw the fear in her face. 'You will look after him, won't you, Sandro?'

'I was hoping it would be the other way round.'

'I don't trust him to look after himself.' Whatever confidence Tonya had projected a few minutes before had vanished.

'He'll be fine,' Ruzsky said. 'I'll see to it he's kept out of trouble.'

'I can tell, even on the telephone, when he's uncertain about something.'

'Tonya—'

'Please, Sandro.' Her eyes burned. 'You will look after him, won't you?'

'Of course.'

'Tonya . . .' Pavel's face softened as he took his wife into his arms and drew their son into the narrow gap between their bodies. Ruzsky was transfixed for a moment, then quietly withdrew.

CHAPTER TWENTY-FOUR

There was a low archway to one side of the front door to the house in Millionaya Street, and beyond it a gate into the garden. Ruzsky slipped through and climbed the stone steps that led up to the lawn. He saw Michael immediately, but a woman was with him so he ducked instinctively into the shadows. It took him a few moments to determine that the woman was Ingrid. They were building a snowman, and Michael was perched on a wooden chair, working on the eyes and mouth. They were both in dark overcoats, but neither was wearing a hat. Ingrid's long blonde hair had shaken loose down her back, and shone in the dim light. Suddenly Ruzsky wanted to reach out and touch it.

Michael concentrated on scooping holes carefully in the centre of the snowman's head, until he got bored and threw a handful of snow at his aunt. Ingrid roared and chased him round the garden as he shrieked with laughter. She allowed him to escape several times, then caught him and rolled him in the snow until he was in hysterics.

She straightened and caught sight of Ruzsky. 'Stop, *Liebchen*, stop,' she said, blushing. 'It's Papa.'

For a moment, Michael was frozen to the spot. Then he ran headlong into his father's outstretched arms. Ruzsky hugged his son so tightly that the boy groaned. 'Papa,' he said, eyes shining as Ruzsky released him. Then he looked down, unsure of himself.

'It's all right, my boy.'

'Where have you been?'

'I've been . . . working.'

'Mama said you didn't want to see us,' Michael told him solemnly.

Ruzsky gathered his son into his arms again. 'You know that's not true, don't you?'

Michael nodded, but Ruzsky mourned the fact that the look of playful innocence he had radiated during the game with his aunt had disappeared.

He walked over to Ingrid, who was adjusting her hair. 'I'm sorry, Sandro. I didn't see you.'

'Why should you apologize?'

'It was just a game.'

'Of course. We can play on.' Ruzsky put Michael down, inclining his head towards the house. 'Is . . . ?'

'No.'

'Out all afternoon?' Ruzsky said.

'I don't know,' Ingrid answered. 'She never says.'

'Let battle commence,' Ruzsky went on. He built himself a small wall, scrabbling around in the snow and glancing across to where Ingrid and Michael were preparing their ammunition. Once or twice, he caught the bewilderment in his son's eyes, but sought to divert it by chasing him round the garden. They collapsed in a corner and Michael stuffed snow into his father's shirt as Ruzsky laughed and yelled for help. Ingrid stood above them, face flushed, chest

261

heaving. Ruzsky thought again that she was even more beautiful than he remembered.

He wrestled with Michael until he was cold and knew his son must be, too. 'Enough,' he cried, stood up and tossed Michael over his shoulder, then strode towards the house. Michael wriggled with delight, then lay still, his head against his father's, a small hand clutching Ruzsky's collar.

Outside the kitchen, Ruzsky peeled off the boy's overcoat, scarf and boots. As he hung the coat on the low hook by the kitchen door, his nostrils were filled with the aroma of baking bread and he was overcome by a wave of nostalgia. He took Michael's hand and pushed open the kitchen door with his foot. Katya was bent over the oven. A young assistant he didn't recognize eyed him while Katya pulled out a baking tray. When she straightened and saw him, there was a hint of anxiety in her eyes, but she smothered it. 'Master Sandro.' She beamed, bustled towards him and put her round, red face against his. Then she was fussing over Michael. 'You're freezing cold, young master,' she said. 'Look at the state of you!'

Michael rolled his eyes.

'You need a cup of hot milk,' Katya said, as she returned to the stove and pulled across a pan. 'Would you like some English tea, Master Sandro?' She glanced at Ingrid, who was standing behind them. 'Madam?'

'Why not?' Ruzsky said.

'Your father is here,' Ingrid blurted.

Katya hurried across the room, and Ruzsky sighed quietly. How they all jumped to the old tyrant's tune.

'Why is Grandpapa always angry with you?' Michael asked.

262

Ruzsky lifted his son on to a side table. 'It's a long story.'

'Mama says that Grandpapa won't let you into the house, so I told him it was unfair because it's your house, too.'

Ruzsky forced himself to smile. 'And what did he say?'

'He said he'd think about it.'

'I'm sure he will.'

'I love Grandpapa. Some people, like the servants, say he's frightening, but he doesn't frighten me.'

'I'm pleased to hear it.'

'He gave me a wooden train set and we play with it together.'

Ruzsky put his hands into his pockets and tried to hold on to his smile. 'You must like playing with Auntie Ingrid,' he said.

'Yes, I do. Auntie Ingrid is kind. She always plays with me. Mama never does.'

Ingrid stroked Michael's hair. 'That's not true, *Liebchen*.'

'It is.' Michael's face was sorrowful now. 'She's always busy. Why don't you live with us any more, Papa?'

Ingrid looked embarrassed. 'I'll go.'

'You don't have to.' Ruzsky took his son's hand. 'I'll explain in a minute. We'll go upstairs and play together. Would that be all right?'

'Yes!' Michael jumped off the side. 'We can build a big train track!'

'In a minute. Have your milk first.'

Michael walked over to Katya and the housekeeper hugged him to her, as she had his father when he was a boy, the child's head resting against her ample thigh while she finished warming the milk. She reached up and took down a large mug from the shelf. It had a familiar picture of Peter the Great on one side, holding a hammer, and the dates of the city's bicentenary: 1703–1903.

'Is it true, what he says?' Ruzsky asked Ingrid.

'I don't know, Sandro.'

'She ignores him?' he whispered.

'He misses you.'

Ruzsky closed his eyes. Should he try to patch up some kind of relationship with Irina for Michael's sake? Would she allow it? Could he bear it? He thought of their violent, bitter rows, of her screaming at him, teeth bared. 'I don't know what one can do,' Ruzsky said. 'Perhaps you should be grateful you don't have children.'

'I could never be grateful for that,' Ingrid responded.

Ruzsky saw the deep sadness in her eyes. 'I'm sorry.'

She smiled. 'There is no need.'

'What will you do?'

Now she laughed, which brought light and warmth to her face. 'What *can* I do? A German in wartime Petrograd. I'm a prisoner.'

'It can't be that bad, surely.'

'These last few months . . . My accent is still strong.'

They both watched Michael sitting at the table with Katya, drinking his milk.

'I'm pleased that you're back,' she said quietly. 'Will you live together again, you and Irina?'

'We couldn't afford to,' Ruzsky said. 'Not in the style she would insist on, anyway. Irina's parents are embarrassed by me, and as for my own father, you know the situation well enough.'

'I'm sure Dmitri could—'

'No.' Ruzsky turned towards her and smiled. 'It's not possible any more.'

'Have you talked to him?' she asked.

'Yes.'

'Did . . .' She was unable to go on.

It was painful to watch her struggle with herself. 'I'm sorry,' Ruzsky said.

She raised her head. 'Did he tell you?'

'No.'

'It is common gossip?'

Ruzsky wished he could ease the desolation he saw in her eyes. Had she not known of his brother's reputation before? Was it only Maria she was aware of? Her pain fuelled his own. 'I do not believe so,' he said kindly.

'Then how—'

'I guessed.'

She did not believe him. 'He has been arguing with your father.'

'What about?'

'I don't know, but it puts him in a foul temper.'

For a moment they stared at each other. Then Ruzsky walked over to his son and bent down. 'Come, my boy. Shall we build that train track now?'

They left Ingrid with her head down and her hands over her eyes.

The house in Millionaya Street was almost dark. Ruzsky led his son quietly past the door of his father's study. Like their home at Petrovo, the walls were filled with portraits and banners from the family's martial past. The floors were covered with rich red rugs from Central Asian campaigns, and the mantelpieces laden with strange and exotic artefacts – masks, daggers, even jewels. They turned the last corner and, still hand in hand, climbed the narrow stairs to the attic. On their right was the door to what had been Dmitri's room when they were children. Ilya had shared it with him, because he hadn't liked sleeping alone. Ruzsky stepped towards it.

'Come on, Papa,' Michael said.

Ruzsky felt the nerves tighten in his stomach as he depressed the metal latch.

'Grandpapa says that room will be for Uncle Dmitri's son.'

Ruzsky pushed open the door, ducked through and tugged back the curtains. Grey light filtered through the dust that hung heavily in the air. The two wooden box beds were still in place under the lee of the sloping roof. Ilya's tattered elephant lay on his pillow. A painted wooden soldier in the uniform of the Preobrazhenskys stood guard at the end of his bed. On a shelf, a photograph of Ilya, flanked by two short brass candlesticks, made the alcove seem like a shrine.

On the other side of the room, above Dmitri's pillow, was the box in which all his toy soldiers were stored, arranged neatly by regiment. His old polar bear was sprawled across the lid, its head drooping.

'Grandpapa doesn't like me to come in here,' Michael said quietly.

Ruzsky stared at Ilya's elephant. One ear had fallen off and his trunk had been loved almost out of existence. Its remaining eye was fixed on him.

'Grandpapa doesn't like me to come in here,' Michael repeated.

Ruzsky put a hand on his son's head and drew him closer, then picked him up. 'I love you, my boy.'

'I love you, Papa.'

Ruzsky carried him out on to the landing and pulled the door shut behind him. He lowered Michael to the ground and let the boy lead him into his bedroom. The floor was littered with bits of train track and other wooden toys. Ruzsky saw his own bear sitting above Michael's bed, also now a shadow of its former self. He picked it up. 'I always sleep with him,' Michael said. 'And my own bear, of course.'

Ruzsky felt tears creep into the corners of his eyes.

'What happened to Uncle Ilusha, Papa?'

Ruzsky wiped his eyes. 'Did anyone ever tell you that you look like him?'

'Does that mean I'm going to die too?'

'Of course not.' Ruzsky was gathering together the pieces of track. 'Of course not,' he said again.

'How did Uncle Ilusha die?'

'It was an accident.'

Ruzsky concentrated on assembling the track, and soon Michael was doing the same. The sections were beautifully made, and easy to fit together. There was a station, three bridges, a group of wooden houses and a sprinkling of pine trees. The houses had been modelled on the village at Petrovo. There was even a replica of the big house itself, which Ruzsky set on top of a *papier-mâché* hill. While he assembled the track, Michael put the train together, then pushed the engine around, imitating the sound of escaping steam as the wheels turned.

Ruzsky was working on the signal box when he looked up to see his father standing in the shadows by the doorway. He tried to think of something to say but couldn't, so he returned to what he was doing.

The silence grew.

Did the old man expect him to stand up and be polite? Did he expect him to apologize for coming to his own home to see his own son?

Michael was steering the train round the other side of the track, oblivious to the tension, as if having his father and grandfather with him was an everyday occurrence.

The old man sighed, squatted down and took the signal box from Ruzsky's hands. He looked at it, then slotted it together and placed it next to the track. He picked up the roof of the station building and slotted that into place too, then gathered up all the people from the box beside him and placed them in position on the platform. There was a station-master, a newspaper-seller, several passengers.

'No wounded soldiers,' Ruzsky said.

The old man grunted. His lined and distinguished face was solemn, tension visible around his eyes.

'Why were you arguing with Dmitri?' Ruzsky asked.

'That woman will be the death of him.'

'Which woman?'

'You know damned well which one.'

Ruzsky flushed with embarrassment. He wondered if, after all, Dmitri's affair with Maria was common knowledge in the city.

His father rearranged the toy figures so that the passengers were more obviously waiting for a train. 'The world's gone mad,' he said.

'Mad enough for you to be entertaining a man like Vasilyev at the ballet?'

Ruzsky hadn't intended to be provocative, but his father didn't flinch. 'Vasilyev is a swine, but I don't know if he is a necessary or treacherous one. However, this is a time of moral relativism.'

'What are you talking about, Grandpapa?' Michael asked. He had sat back on his haunches, his hand still protectively over the train, his face creased with confusion.

'What indeed?' Ruzsky's father asked.

'Mama says that you two hate each other.'

There was a long silence. Ruzsky rearranged some of the pine trees into a small coppice in front of the house. 'Then Mama, on this occasion, is wrong,' his father said quietly.

Ruzsky didn't dare meet the old man's eye. He watched him check his gold pocket watch, then twist in his direction. 'She'll be back in a minute,' he said softly.

Ruzsky nodded and straightened, but his father was on his feet first and took a step towards the door. 'Have a few moments more in peace.' He opened it. 'Come again . . . won't you? Sandro?'

'Of course, Father.'

The old man paused, and Ruzsky turned away. A few seconds later he heard his father's retreating footsteps.

CHAPTER TWENTY-FIVE

As the night train to Moscow prepared to pull out, Ruzsky and Pavel watched the last burst of activity on the platform from the red velvet window-seats of their second-class compartment. A pair of swarthy Tartars selling shashlik competed volubly with two Chinese touting illegal hooch in tin bottles. The last of the third-class passengers bustled past, clutching straw baskets and clumsy bundles. A newspaper-boy running the length of the train, his wares held aloft to display the headline, was lost in a cloud of steam that poured from the engine.

As the steam drifted slowly along the platform towards the rear of the train, all Ruzsky could see was soldiers in greatcoats. Some were sitting on benches, others standing talking in small groups; a handful lay, crudely bandaged, on stretchers. They didn't appear to be in a hurry to go anywhere.

But, then, the train was already full of soldiers. Ruzsky and Pavel shared this compartment with four – rough peasant conscripts, uncommunicative and sullen, from south of Moscow, on their way back to the ancient capital. There were others in the corridor who had not found a berth, but showed no sign of disembarking.

'The country's like a military camp,' Ruzsky said.

'You're policemen?' the man next to Pavel demanded.

They didn't answer him.

'I thought so. I can smell it.'

The man nodded curtly at his colleagues. He had big, full lips and a greasy, unshaven face. He put his boots up on the seat opposite, forcing Ruzsky to move his own legs out of the way. It would be better after Moscow, he told himself. Most of the soldiers would disembark there. The train on to Yalta would be more or less empty.

The train lurched. The steam engine behind them hissed violently as the iron wheels turned.

Despite the circumstances, Ruzsky found it hard to contain his excitement. As the train departed, he recalled how Dmitri and Ilya would stand with their noses pressed against the glass, waving to the servants who were staying behind to look after the house on Millionaya Street. Just as quickly as it had come, the thrill of those memories melted into something more melancholic. In every sense, the journeys to Petrovo were history now. They were gone for ever.

The train gathered speed, pulling out of the Nicholas station and gliding past the moonlit spires of the city. The moon was bright until they reached the suburbs, and then it was engulfed in a bank of cloud and the world around them was swallowed by the night.

There was a single dim light in the compartment, but Ruzsky was happy to evade the scrutiny of his companions. 'When will we see it again?' Pavel asked.

'See what?'

'Home.'

'We're going to Yalta, not the moon.'

'Thanks for your understanding.'

'You're going to Yalta?' the man opposite asked, pausing in the process of lighting a cigarette.

Ruzsky didn't answer.

'Running away?'

Ruzsky offered his hand. 'Sandro.'

The soldier stared at him, smoking nonchalantly, until Ruzsky withdrew his hand. 'Officer class,' he said, 'but not your friend.' He grinned. He had almost no teeth.

Ruzsky glanced at his pocket watch, then closed his eyes. He had not checked the passenger lists before they'd embarked – partly because he couldn't think of an excuse to give Pavel – but he had climbed on to the train brimming with confidence that she would be aboard. Her presence was like a magnet: it took a conscious act of will to remain seated.

Ruzsky tried to put her out of his mind. He listened as the soldiers opened a bottle of vodka and drank. They didn't offer it to their travelling companions, but didn't talk much among themselves either. When Ruzsky opened his eyes briefly, the man opposite was staring at him. Pavel was snoring gently.

He could contain his impatience no longer. There were still soldiers in the corridor outside, as surly as those in his compartment, but they allowed him to pass. His passage was slow: most of the blinds in the compartments had already been drawn, so Ruzsky had to knock on a succession of doors and open them, nodding to passengers within when he saw that she wasn't there. He worked his way down the train to the first-class carriages.

Here, a guard stood on the inside of the door, barring entry, and was reluctant to open it even to speak to him. Ruzsky tried putting his weight against it, but it was locked. He gesticulated, but the glass was thick and the rattle of the train loud; the man looked away from him.

Ruzsky pulled out his identification papers, placed them against the glass, then hammered hard. 'Police,' he shouted.

Reluctantly the guard unlocked the door and let him through, looking warily behind him to make sure that he was on his own. As soon as he was past, the guard slammed the door and locked it again.

It was quieter here, and warmer. The curtains had been pulled shut all the way along the corridor. The guard's face was visible in the dim glow of an over-head lamp. 'Maria Popova,' Ruzsky said.

The man pointed down the corridor, without needing to consult the passenger list in his hand. 'Next carriage. At the end,' he said. 'Cabin number eight.'

Ruzsky strode down the richly carpeted corridor and through the door into the next carriage, his nerves sharp again. He breathed in. It was a relief to have left the soldiers behind. He knocked.

'Who is it?'

'It's me, Sandro.'

He waited. A thin sheen of sweat gathered on his forehead.

The door was pulled open.

There was no light in her eyes: she was not pleased to see him. 'I thought I would find you here,' he said.

Her gaze remained steely.

'I have business in Yalta,' he went on. He was trying too hard to fill the silence that hung between them. 'I am on the train with my partner and I recalled you saying you would be travelling south tonight.'

'I suppose you had better come in,' she said. She stepped back and sat down.

Ruzsky shut the door and seated himself opposite her. She wore a long, navy blue dress, buttoned with pearl studs high around her throat. Her dark hair spilled over her shoulders and down to the swell of her breasts.

There was a single reading lamp, with a red lantern, casting shadows across the walls and ceiling, and the drawn blinds behind it.

Maria reached up to the leather suitcase on the rack above him, stretching on tiptoe to remove a bottle. She poured a large measure of whisky into one of the glasses on the table by the window and handed it to him. She filled another for herself, then replaced the cork stopper and slipped the bottle under her pillow.

'Thank you,' Ruzsky said. His voice felt as if it was coming from someone else.

They drank.

Maria raised the blind closest to her and stared out of the darkened window, but because of the light inside he knew it was impossible for her to see anything.

'So many soldiers on board,' Ruzsky said. 'All ill-mannered.'

'Wouldn't you be, if you'd been fighting with the Tsar's army?'

'Probably.'

They sat in silence, each avoiding the other's eye. Ruzsky sipped his whisky, then took out his cigarette case and offered her one. She declined, so he slipped it back into his pocket. He thought she had never looked more beautiful.

Maria shut her eyes. Ruzsky watched a pained expression take hold of her face, then relax its grip. He listened to the steady rattle of the wheels on the iron rails beneath them. 'Have I done something wrong?' he asked.

Maria opened her eyes, but continued to stare out of the window. 'No.'

'You seem . . . angry.'

'It was foolish,' she said, almost inaudibly, 'to think that we could be friends.'

'Why?'

'You know why.' She turned on him, anger burning in her eyes. 'What are you doing here?'

'I thought that—'

'What kind of fool do you take me for?'

'I made a mistake.'

'I'll say you did.' Maria faced the window again. 'I'd have waited for you until the end of the world, Sandro, if you had given me just the faintest breath of hope.'

'I could not—'

'Compromise? No. Of course not. I know. It's not in your genes.'

'I had a wife and an eighteen-month-old son.'

'A wife who is a liar and a cheat.'

'And a son who looks up to her as his mother.'

'Well, where is she now, Sandro?'

'I know I made a mistake.'

'You wouldn't lower yourself.'

'Don't be absurd.'

'You didn't touch me.' She was almost shouting now. 'Your sense of honour would not allow you even

275

to *touch* me. Your wife fucked like a whore that . . . *disgusting* man – and others – yet you would not, *could* not, bring yourself to touch the woman you professed to love.'

'I was . . . I wanted you so much—'

'You were right!' Her face was strained to breaking point, her eyes wet with tears. 'You were right not to touch me.'

'If I'd known—'

'What? That I would become your brother's mistress? His whore . . .'

Ruzsky swallowed. 'Don't talk like that.'

'Does it disgust you, Sandro?'

Ruzsky found that he was holding his breath. He exhaled. 'I made a terrible mistake.'

'You made your choice, and now we can both pay for it. Does it disgust you to think of him touching me? To think that he can do as he wishes with me?'

'Stop it.'

'Does it disgust you to think of him naked beside me, inside me? Your brother—'

'Control yourself.'

'And now it is too late.'

He saw the emotion swelling in her eyes and in her breast, then breaking like floodwater. She curled herself into the corner of her bunk, her body convulsed. He moved instinctively to her. 'Maria,' he said, but she pushed him away.

'Get away from me!' she screamed.

There was a knock at the door. She did not reply. 'Are you all right, Mademoiselle?' the guard called. Ruzsky moved back to his seat.

'Yes,' she said weakly.

276

'Please open the door so that I may ascertain that you are not being threatened.'

Maria did not move. The guard turned the lock and pulled back the door. He glared at Ruzsky. Maria was wiping tears from her cheeks.

'Is this gentleman upsetting you, madam?'

'No, it is all right.'

'He's not from the first-class compartments.'

'It's all right. Truly. He's a friend.'

The guard eyed Ruzsky suspiciously. 'There are all kinds of bad sorts on the train,' he said. 'I only let him in because he showed me police papers. I'll check them again if you wish.'

'It's all right. I know the gentleman.'

The guard shot her an admiring glance, then reluctantly withdrew. 'If you need anything, Miss Popova, please don't hesitate to call.'

'I won't. Thank you.'

He pulled the door shut and relocked it from the outside. For a moment Maria looked composed, then began to shake once more.

'Maria, please—' Ruzsky was leaning forward, but she had raised her hand to prevent him coming closer.

She switched off the lamp, and the landscape beyond the window sprang instantly to life, illuminated by a bright moon in a cloudless sky. 'You really don't understand, do you?' she asked.

'Understand what?'

Her anger had gone, and in its place Ruzsky saw only regret, which was worse. 'You would not compromise,' she said, 'but I did.'

Ruzsky's eyes pleaded with her.

'And you don't understand why, do you?'

'I—'

'I'm your brother's mistress because I loved you.' Maria rested her head against the window. 'I'm your brother's mistress because you would not bend. And now that you will, *my* compromise has put love beyond our reach. Don't you see?'

Ruzsky could not answer. He shook his head, as if to deny what they both knew to be true. 'Christ,' he whispered.

'I'm sorry, Sandro,' she said.

'No,' he muttered.

'I've hurt you . . . I'm sorry.'

Ruzsky attempted to lose himself in the rhythmic beat of the pistons. 'Do you love him?' He had not wanted to ask the question and did not wish to have an answer.

Maria wiped her eyes.

'I'm sorry. I shouldn't have asked.'

'I'm very fond of him, Sandro.'

'Fond?'

'I'm moved by him, by the sadness in his heart, and by his devotion to you . . . I am nothing more than an adornment for him. I know that he will never be in love with me.' She sighed. 'I do not believe he can love – *really* love – another.'

'Why not?'

'Because he does not love himself.'

'I don't understand,' Ruzsky said.

'Oh, Sandro . . .' She seemed to look right into the depths of his soul. 'I think you understand better than anyone.'

Ruzsky waited for her to continue, but she did not.

They sat quietly in the dark. From time to time, the moon disappeared behind a stand of pine trees, then burst out again, making brilliant the snow-covered fields and washing her troubled face with light.

'Why him?' Ruzsky asked at length. 'Of all people, why him?'

Maria's head rocked from side to side. Her hands rested on her lap. 'I have told you already,' she said. 'Because, at his best, he is like you.' She gave him a look of almost infinite sadness. 'And because I can't have you.'

They listened to the sound of the train and watched the changing patterns of light and shadow as it carved its way across the landscape. They were silent for a long time.

'What do you want of me?' he said.

'I don't know any more.'

He watched her face.

'It is too late for us,' she said. 'But it doesn't change the way I feel.'

Ruzsky's throat was dry. 'Should I go?'

'No.' Her voice was just a whisper.

'Do you want me to stay?'

Maria did not answer immediately. 'Can we escape from the world just for a heartbeat?'

She lay down on her bunk, her head on the pillow. A long, elegant arm stretched out towards him in the moonlight. He marvelled at the cool perfection of her fingertips, desperate for her touch. Then he moved across the compartment and lay down beside her, his arm over her waist, his lips brushing the nape of her neck. She lay quite still, her breast barely rising and falling as she breathed. At length, she turned towards him, her lips close to his, her eyes searching his. 'Are you nervous, Sandro?' she whispered.

'Yes.'

With her thumb and forefinger, she smoothed the

lines on his temples, then caressed his cheek. Her lips were parted, her breath warm. 'So many wasted years,' she said.

'Maria, I cannot—'

'Don't punish me,' she said, placing a finger upon his lips. She brushed his eyes closed, then smoothed his brow. 'Just rest, Sandro. You need to rest.'

They lay side by side. The compartment was warm. He wished he could stay there for ever.

CHAPTER TWENTY-SIX

Maria's cheek was resting on his shoulder and he thought she might be sleeping. He listened to her breathing. On the train journeys he had made with his family, he and Dmitri had always occupied the top bunks in the same compartment and lain awake deep into the night as the train rattled south.

'I love to listen to the train at night,' she said, 'the snow outside, the warmth within. It makes me feel safe.'

Ruzsky didn't move. He didn't want to break the spell. 'Do your parents still live in Yalta?' he asked.

'No.'

'Where did they move to?'

Maria did not answer.

'You said you were going to see your sister.'

'Yes.'

Ruzsky sensed he was skating on thin ice, but had to continue. 'Why don't you talk about your past?' he asked.

'For the same reason you don't.'

'Are your parents in Petersburg?'

'No.'

'So you moved up alone?'

'They died a long time ago.'

'I'm sorry.'

Maria slipped away from him and rolled on to her back.

'How old were you when they died?'

'Young, but old enough to remember how wonderful they were, which should make it better but only makes it worse.'

'What—'

'It was an accident.'

Ruzsky watched the shadows crossing and recrossing her face. 'Who looked after you?'

'My uncle.'

'Is he still in Yalta?'

'He's dead now, too.'

'Were you fond of him?'

'Of course. He was a good man.'

Ruzsky detected a reservation in her voice. 'But it was still—'

'His wife never wanted us.'

'Is she alive?'

'Yes.'

'Will you go to see her?'

'No.'

'Where is your sister now?'

'In a sanatorium.'

'What happened to her?'

There was a long pause. 'I don't know,' Maria said. 'I don't know.' She closed her eyes.

He recognized the cold, brittle place within her all too well. In the darkness, he could feel his love growing and deepening. He reached over and held her to him. For a moment, her fingers dug into his shoulders as she hugged him and then she let go.

'Did your—'

'Sandro, I don't want to talk about it any more,' she said. 'Tell me about Petrovo. Tell me about the house there.'

'Why do you want to know about it?'

'Dmitri won't talk about it, yet it's such an important part of you both.'

Ruzsky contemplated her request. It was many years since he had talked at any length about Petrovo, but it was so intimately enmeshed in the fabric of his existence that he didn't need to. The house, its atmosphere, its history – he carried it with him all the days of his life. 'What do you want to know?'

'Paint me a picture.'

What harm could it do, just to describe the house? 'It's tall,' he said, 'with a series of ornate pillars along its façade, but not too grand. Inside, it's a family home, with fireplaces as big as my father and rugs, military portraits and souvenirs gathered by the Ruzskys over the years, from campaigns in the Caucasus, the Far East and Europe. There were sabres and lances, and primitive, rusting muskets, banners and giant silver plates. There was a shaded veranda along the front where we used to spend the summer evenings . . .'

'Go on.'

'I—'

'Please go on, Sandro.'

Ruzsky twisted away from her. Long-suppressed memories made him feel as vulnerable as he had as a child. 'In the summer, my mother would sing. She had a lovely voice and we joined in, even my father. The sound carried across the valley. Sometimes Father

283

would go into the drawing room and play the piano. I would sit with my feet over the edge of the balcony, my toes brushing the top of the thick lilac bushes that surrounded the house.' He was silent for a minute, perhaps more.

'One year, when our time there usually came to an end, Father and Mother said we wouldn't be returning to the house on Millionaya Street until the end of the following summer. A whole year at Petrovo. I was about eleven, and for us boys it brought unexpected joy. No school. Father hired a tutor, but it was still a magical time. Every day, after lunch, we would go out and play in the woods, in the snow. We made camps, staged battles, played on the ice, all the things that boys do.'

Ruzsky ground to a halt. He had a vivid memory of them all skating on the lake, their breath billowing in the chill air as they chased each other round the island in the middle. He heard again their laughter and the swish of the blades cutting across the ice.

'It's as far as Dmitri gets.'

'What is?' Ruzsky asked.

'His story always stops in the same place. When Ilusha was still alive.' She caressed his brow, then placed a soft hand against his cheek. 'It's all right, Sandro,' she whispered. Then, 'We should go back . . .'

'Go back where?'

'The house is one day's ride from Mtsensk, isn't that so? On the way to Yalta.'

Ruzsky swung his legs over the edge of the bunk, and sat with his back to her.

'You cannot run away from it for ever, Sandro.'

'I'm not running away from anything.'

'You both are.'

'And you're the expert on us.' Ruzsky regretted the sharpness in his voice.

'I'll come with you,' she said.

'Why?'

'I told you.' Maria raised herself on to one elbow. 'Because you need to go. And because I want to escape from the world. Just for a moment. It's all changing, Sandro . . .' She lay down again. 'You asked me why I'm going to Yalta. I want to see my sister. I want to make sure that she will be cared for, no matter what happens to me or to Russia. But, first, I want to escape.'

As he returned to the second-class section of the train, Ruzsky pulled the door shut and heard it locked behind him. A soldier slouched in the corridor, his back to him, smoking a cigarette. As Ruzsky squeezed past, he saw that it was one of the men who had been in their compartment earlier. The man quickly averted his eyes.

It took him a further twenty minutes to pick his way through the sleeping bodies that now lined the corridor. When he reached his own compartment, the blinds had been drawn against the moonlight. He waited for his eyes to adjust to the darkness. He saw that one of the top bunks was empty, put a foot on the ladder and swung himself on to it.

He lay still. One of the men was snoring. He didn't think it was Pavel. He turned on his side and tried to make out the shape of his friend.

'Where in hell have you been?' Pavel asked.

'I'm sorry.'

'These men haven't seen a woman for months. I've been lucky to escape with my virtue intact.'

'Don't flatter yourself.'

Pavel grunted. 'Some friend you are. After the revolution I'm not sharing a cell with you.'

'Even revolutionaries need policemen, Pavel. You should remember that.'

Pavel grunted again.

'Are they asleep?' Ruzsky asked.

'You can hear them.'

'I think they're still watching us.'

'Here on the train?'

'Yes.' Ruzsky turned over. 'We'll talk about it in the morning.'

Ruzsky woke late. By his watch it was almost ten and there was no sign of Pavel in the compartment. His bunk had been folded away. Only two of the soldiers were still there, smoking in silence with their legs resting on the seats. They didn't acknowledge him.

Ruzsky lifted his head to look out of the window. It was a poor day, snow driving across the wooded landscape reducing visibility to no more than twenty feet. He rolled off his bunk and landed with a thump by the door. He adjusted his coat, and made a point of trying to establish eye-contact with the soldiers. They avoided it.

Ruzsky found Pavel at the far end of the carriage, looking out at the snow. There were fewer soldiers here now, so they could converse in relative privacy.

'You should have woken me,' Ruzsky said.

'So that you could join me in staring out of the window?'

Ruzsky pulled out his silver cigarette case and lit up. Pavel refused his offer.

'Where did you get to?' Pavel asked.

Ruzsky sucked deeply on his cigarette, then blew

the smoke against the glass. 'Nothing interesting.'

'That's for me to judge.'

'I saw someone getting on to the train.'

'Or knew she was going to be on it.'

Ruzsky raised an eyebrow.

'I could get quite insulted sometimes, by you treating me like a simpleton.'

'Do you mind if I don't tell you?' Ruzsky said apologetically. 'Not yet, anyway?'

'I had a feeling this trip wasn't entirely straightforward.'

'We're going to Yalta because we need to.'

'A happy coincidence, then?'

Ruzsky didn't answer. 'There are two of them in our compartment.' He glanced over his shoulder. 'Last night, I went right to the other end of the train and one followed me all the way. They're not soldiers.'

Pavel's head swivelled round to him. 'What did he think you were going to do? Jump off?'

'Seriously.'

'They're following us all the way to Yalta?'

'That's what it looks like.'

'What do you want to do?'

'Nothing. I'm just telling you.'

Pavel glanced down the corridor. A group of soldiers was sitting on the floor, playing cards.

'I have a favour to ask you,' Ruzsky said quietly. 'Beyond Moscow.'

'What is it?'

'My family home. Petrovo. It's on the way – more or less.'

'I thought this was a murder investigation,' Pavel said curtly.

'It will take a day, that's all.'

'Why now?'

Ruzsky could see in his friend's eyes that he knew the answer, just as Maria had understood his state of mind better than he had himself. Everyone was experiencing the unsettling effect of the winds of change. 'I was thinking about Ella last night,' Pavel said. 'She didn't deserve to die like that.'

'No one does.'

'You saw the grief in her mother's face.'

'That's why we're going to Yalta.'

'Some of us in our own time.'

Ruzsky frowned.

'Who's to say who will be next?' Pavel went on. 'The man at the Lion Bridge . . . Are we any closer to understanding why these three people have been killed?'

Ruzsky wrestled with himself as he was assailed by the image of Ella's body on the slab in Sarlov's laboratory. Pavel was right, but he knew it would not dissuade him.

'You can be very stubborn, Sandro.'

'I'm sorry.'

'You don't need to apologize. It's a virtue as well as a vice.'

'I'll be a day behind you. Two at most.'

'I'll come with you. I'd like—'

'No.' Ruzsky looked at his partner. 'I need to go alone.'

Pavel was hurt. 'How long will you really be?'

Ruzsky leant back against the window. 'It takes twenty-four hours in a *troika*, but I can make it in twelve with a good horse. I'll be two days behind you, at the outside.'

Pavel's expression softened. 'I understand. But be quick.'

'Will you be all right?'

'I'll be fine. But I'm worried about you. What if there are bandits or deserters? You're too weak to defend yourself without me.'

'I'll just have to stay out of trouble then.'

CHAPTER TWENTY-SEVEN

The train pulled into Mtsensk just before dawn. Ruzsky lay on his bunk, listening to the hiss of steam and the subdued voices on the platform. He checked his watch. It was just before six. The blinds in their compartment had been drawn, but the station lights penetrated the interior sufficiently to allow Ruzsky to see Pavel's face. He looked at his watch again. Most station halts lasted ten minutes, rarely more, never less. They had been standing here for two, so far.

There was a shout from further down the platform. Ruzsky wondered if Maria would change her mind. He glanced at his watch once more, then nodded at Pavel and jumped off the bunk. As he emerged into the corridor, Pavel was half a step behind him, as they'd agreed. Ruzsky walked into the toilet, looked back and saw his partner leaning against the door to prevent anyone leaving.

Ruzsky closed the door. Now that he had committed himself, he was having second thoughts. He smoothed the ends of his moustache and splashed water on to his face.

The soldiers had been relieved in Moscow and this group appeared less vigilant. Pavel was convinced they were from the Moscow Okhrana; Ruzsky thought they were a replacement team from Petersburg. Either way, they must have been told that the two of them were bound for the Crimea, and they appeared to be fast asleep.

Ruzsky heard the guard's low whistle and opened the toilet door. Pavel was still there. He shrugged as Ruzsky came out. Ruzsky stepped down on to the snow-covered platform, then shut the carriage door quietly. He walked swiftly through the drifting snow towards a darkened side-entrance to the station.

As soon as he was out of sight, he looked back. The train was pulling away and there was no sign of anyone scrambling to get off.

Once it had gone, he stepped out into the dim light. He watched the station-master disappear into the warmth, leaving the platform deserted. Ruzsky went to the waiting room, then to the station entrance, but could see no sign of her. He returned to the centre of the platform, let the drifting snow gather on his face and around the edges of his moustache.

She had changed her mind. The disappointment was crushing.

He glanced around once more. There was little doubt that he was the only passenger who had disembarked.

The station-master caught sight of him through the office window. He replaced his hat and came out into the cold. 'You got off the express?' the man asked. He was assessing Ruzsky, trying to marry his demeanour, which indicated noble birth, with his tatty overcoat and boots, which did not.

'Yes.'

'I'm sorry, I didn't see you. Are you expecting someone? Because there is no one here.'

'I'll need a good horse.'

'You're with the lady?'

Ruzsky turned, and saw her emerging from the shadows at the far end of the platform, carrying a single suitcase and shrouded in the swirling snow.

It was two hours before the horses arrived, but when they did Ruzsky acknowledged that the stationmaster had been right: they were worth the wait.

The road was passable until they reached the start of the pinewoods about fifteen *versts* from the station. Here, they led their horses through a thick snowdrift as the sun peeked above the horizon amid the tall thin pine trees. The sky was clear now, and their breath hung on the still morning air.

Beyond the snowdrift, the road down to the river was clearer and they cantered towards it. 'It's hard to believe,' Ruzsky shouted, as he splashed through what was now little more than a stream, 'that this is sometimes difficult to pass in summer.' He remembered hanging off the back of the *troika* with his brothers.

'I can believe it.' Maria took off her hat and shook out her hair. She was smiling, her cheeks flushed. 'You look as if you were born in the saddle. I thought you were a city boy.'

'Our stable-boy taught us all bareback. At one point I wanted to run away and join the circus.'

The road on the far side of the river was steep and winding, but at the top there was a long stretch across high ground between peasant fields. Up here, the wind had blown the deep snow off the road and Ruzsky and Maria let the horses go, the icy air cutting through their coats and whipping their cheeks, the snow flying up into their eyes and mouths. The freedom was exhilarating, and by the time they reached the end they were both out of breath.

'There's an inn not far from here,' Ruzsky said. 'We can stop for breakfast.'

'Let's press on. The horses are fit. We can stop later.'

Ruzsky turned his mare so that they were alongside each other. Then, without warning, and without letting go of his own reins, he jumped horses, landing behind her. Her mare started briefly, but he had performed the manoeuvre so expertly that the shock to the horse was minimal. He curled one arm round Maria's waist and laid his face against her neck. Her hair tickled his cheek. She reached back and laced the fingers of one hand in his. They were moving with the rhythm of the mare's progress, both at ease in the saddle. The rising sun was a bright orange disc that shimmered through the narrow pines.

Ruzsky listened to the steady thump of the horses' hoofs in the snow. He began to hum quietly.

'What is it?' she asked him.

'I've no idea. Mother used to sing it to us.' He could see that Maria was smiling. 'What's so funny?' he asked.

'Not funny, joyful. Memories.'

'Of what?'

She sighed. 'Of our summers. "Of the azure blue sea and skies bright like joy . . ." '

'Pushkin.'

'So your tutors did not neglect you, Sandro. We had

293

a big white house overlooking the bay, with a long, sloping lawn. My father was the governor and my mother renowned for her beauty and her voice. In the summer she would sing after dinner in the garden. Natalya and I would listen from the upstairs window when we were supposed to be asleep.'

'Your father was the governor? I didn't know that.' Ruzsky waited for her to continue, and when she did not, he asked, 'What do you remember of your mother?'

'Of my mother?'

'Yes.'

'Why do you ask?'

'Piecing together the jigsaw, just as you are,' Ruzsky told her.

Maria thought for a minute or two. 'Everything. Every little detail. Every expression, every act of kindness. If I believed in God, perhaps I could believe it was his doing, but I don't and it wasn't.'

'How long was your father the governor?'

'Some time.'

'You were close?'

'Who were you travelling with?' she asked. 'Another detective?'

'Yes. My deputy, Pavel.'

'Also the son of a noble family?'

'No. He used to be a constable.'

'What did you tell him?'

'To wait until I got there. We were being followed.'

'Why?'

'I don't know.' Ruzsky thought of the night he had arrived at the ballet. 'Who invited Vasilyev to that performance? He was with my family.'

'Your father, I imagine.'

'Did Dmitri say so?'

'Does it matter? I have no idea.'

Ruzsky pulled her closer and eased her head on to his shoulder. 'No, it doesn't matter.'

They were silent again. How quickly she had shied away from discussion of anything personal, and how rapidly she moved from fragile melancholy to prickly defensiveness, he thought.

'How long did you tell Pavel you would be?' she asked.

It was nightfall by the time they neared Petrovo. Maria was fit and a natural horsewoman, but both she and her horse were tiring. They'd rested and fed themselves and the mares at an inn just after lunch, but as it had grown darker, their progress had become slower. Ruzsky had expected to be there by eight, but as they stopped at the crest of the hill he checked his pocket watch to discover that it was past nine.

Her skin was pale in the moonlight. 'Are you all right?' he said, reaching out to touch her arm.

'I'm fine.'

'Only another few minutes. We'll soon be able to see the lights through the trees.' Ruzsky pressed his heels to his horse's flanks. The path was gentler now, but there were no lights. To begin with he thought he must have misjudged the point at which he would be able to see the house, but the further he went, the more unsettled he grew. For a terrible moment, he wondered if the house was no longer there, if it had been burned down or destroyed in one of the peasant rebellions, and his father had not known how to tell them.

Then he saw a light, and made out its shape, nestled in the corner of the valley. Of course, on every previous occasion he'd arrived there, a welcome had been prepared, every light on, torches burning around the gardens and along the driveway.

CHAPTER TWENTY-EIGHT

Petrovo loomed out of the darkness. as Ruzsky reached the driveway, a bank of cloud cleared overhead, and the white façade glimmered in the moonlight. The house hadn't changed, though it seemed smaller than he remembered.

Maria came up alongside him. 'It's beautiful.'

For a moment, and to his surprise, Ruzsky felt a twinge of bitterness. All this should have been his.

The drive and hedgerows had been well maintained, but as he dismounted by the big front door, Ruzsky saw, even in the darkness, the results of his family's neglect. The brass had not been polished, and paint was peeling off the door and windows beside it. Inside, the shutters had been closed and there was no sign of light.

Ruzsky took the knocker and hammered it hard three times.

They waited.

He began to walk round the edge of the house. He stood on the veranda, under the sloping glass roof, looking at the lake. Then he went ten paces backwards down the slope so that he could look up at the house.

The shutters on the first floor were closed too, but he could see a light on in the attic. He ran back to the front of the house and hammered again. 'Hello,' he shouted. 'It's me, Sandro!' He felt like a child, his excitement tinged with fear. He wanted everything to be the same. 'Hello!' He hammered again.

A light came on, glinting through the shutters. 'What is it?' a voice demanded.

Ruzsky's spirits surged. 'Oleg, it's me, Sandro!'

'Sandro?'

'Yes!'

Ruzsky waited impatiently as the bolts were pulled back. He heard the big lock turn. It seemed to take an interminable time and then Oleg stood before him, in his nightgown, a candle in his hand. 'Master Sandro?' He took a step closer. 'Is it really you?'

There was a moment of hesitation, even awkwardness, and then Ruzsky walked forward into Oleg's arms, the candle tumbled to the floor and the hall was plunged once more into darkness.

For a former sergeant in the Preobrazhenskys, Oleg was surprisingly slight, but when he stepped back, Ruzsky saw that the steel was still in his eyes. He bent down, picked up the candle, lit it again and handed it back. 'This is Maria,' he said.

Oleg raised his candle to get a better look at her. His face, Ruzsky thought, was thinner, more lined. 'Maria?'

'Popova.'

If Oleg knew of her relationship with Dmitri, he gave no sign. 'Welcome,' he said.

Ruzsky moved through into the central hallway, and looked up into the shadows of the dome. A wooden staircase gave access to the first-floor gallery from where he and his brothers had spied through the balustrade on his parents' guests. Three tattered military banners on long poles hung down from the balcony where an orchestra had sometimes played. All around him, lurking in the darkness, were Ruzsky's ancestors, grim-faced in military uniform. 'Do you think they ever had fun?' Ilya had asked when they were standing here.

Ruzsky went into the drawing room, which ran the length of the veranda. Oleg and Maria followed him, the light from the candle casting flickering shadows across his father's prized collection of rare and ancient texts. Ruzsky ran his finger along them, disturbing a thick layer of dust. He touched the leather chair by the door and turned the globe beside his father's writing desk. Next to it was a bust of Ruzsky's great-grandfather, who had become ADC to Alexander I and travelled to Paris with him after Waterloo.

He reached the window and pulled back the shutters, allowing the moonlight to stream across the bare floorboards. He turned the key, shoved open the glass door ahead of him, and stepped out on to the snow-covered balcony. He slipped his hands into his pockets and thought of those long summer evenings: Father at his desk, Mother at the piano, the three boys playing on the grass or lying on the veranda.

He found that he was staring at the tree on the hillock by the lake. It was impossible, in the darkness, to make out the tiny gravestone.

'We didn't know you were coming, sir.'

Ruzsky turned to see compassion and concern in Maria's eyes. 'I didn't know I was coming.'

'How is Father?' Oleg gave him a toothless smile.

'He's fine.'

'And Dmitri?'

'Dmitri survived the front – that's the main thing. He's back in Petersburg now.' Ruzsky caught Maria's eye. 'He's fine. Where is the good Mrs Prenkova?'

Oleg looked down. 'She passed away, Sandro, some years ago now.'

'I'm sorry. They didn't tell me.'

Oleg's eyes were hollow. 'You must be ravenous. Come downstairs.'

As they walked through the hallway, Ruzsky guessed that the house's decline had begun in earnest with the death of Oleg's wife. She and Katya were sisters from Petrovo who had married local boys and seen them go on, under the Ruzsky family patronage, to become non-commissioned officers in the Preobrazhensky before entering his father's service. It was the way things had always worked.

As they descended the back stairs to the kitchen, the light from Oleg's candle flickered across the lattice of cobwebs that hung from the ceiling. Since he was taller than Oleg, one caught in Ruzsky's hair. 'You should have warned me,' Oleg said. 'You should have warned me.'

There was no electric light in the kitchen – there never had been – but in the winter darkness, the cavernous room had always been brightly lit by huge torches. Oleg hurriedly lit two more candles as Ruzsky peered through the gloom. More cobwebs tethered the line of enormous copper pots and pans to the shelf beside the range.

He pulled back the wooden bench from the long table for Maria to sit down.

'You should have warned me,' Oleg said again, as he disappeared into the larder. He returned with some bread – old and stale – a hunk of ham and some cheese. He placed the food in front of them. In the awkward silence that followed, the truth of Oleg's life here dawned on Ruzsky. The old man was alone, scraping a marginal existence among the cobweb-shrouded ghosts of their past. He had been forgotten by the family.

'It must be lonely here on your own,' Maria said.

'A boy from the village comes to help with the garden.' He pushed the bread across to them. 'Your father sometimes sends word,' he said to Ruzsky.

It was a lie and Ruzsky knew it, but voiced for Oleg's benefit, he knew, rather than his own. To accept poverty and neglect was one thing, to lose respect for the family you'd served for more than half a century quite another. 'Has he been down to visit?' Ruzsky asked.

'Not for a time.'

'Not since before the war?'

Oleg pretended to think hard. 'A few years, maybe. It's the war, of course.'

Ruzsky knew his father had been here since Ilya's death, but he thought that his visits had been nothing more than an attempt to prove something to himself, and so had petered out. Dmitri had once told him that in the year before their mother's death both parents had eradicated the house and its memories from their minds, but the old man still refused him the chance to take it over and restore it. 'It's like a living tomb,' Dmitri had told him, 'and I think that's the way he wants it to remain.'

Ruzsky thought of his mother. He remembered the cold accusation in her eyes on the morning after Ilya's death. He took a piece of bread. Maria cut some ham.

Oleg was trying to assess her with a subtlety he had never possessed. 'You've come far together?' he asked.

'We were on our way to Yalta,' Ruzsky said. 'We found we were travelling companions.' Ruzsky wondered if Oleg would tell his father about his visitors, but he doubted it.

'All the boys in the village have gone,' Oleg said. 'You remember Kirill?'

'Of course – he rode bareback, like a maniac,' Ruzsky told Maria. 'He was the son of the foreman at the glassworks, and he loved to taunt us with his superior ability. Ah, Kirill . . .'

'Killed. And two of his sons. And many more. What's the news from Petersburg? Will we win?'

'All the talk is of revolution.'

Oleg did not seem to know whether or not to disapprove of Maria. His own personal code considered infidelity – even a hint of it – an abomination, yet he could hardly fail to be affected by her beauty. Even in the dull light of this basement, she seemed to sparkle. Ruzsky watched as the old man sought a way of tactfully framing the questions to which he wished answers.

Oleg waved his hand. 'It was bad enough last time. They know if they come to the house I'll shoot 'em. What have I got to live for?'

'Have you had trouble?'

'Once or twice. When did it start before? 1905? I can't remember. She was alive then. Tanya, I mean. There were some at the door. She stayed in her room. Shouted at me not to go down. I said I'd blow their heads off if they took another pace forward.'

'Who were they?'

'Thugs.'

'From the village?'

'No.' Oleg shook his head vigorously. 'No, no. One of them was – a bad boy. He was dismissed from the factory for stealing. This house belonged to the people – that's what he said. He must have led the others here. I heard some of them were from Tula, but I don't know how they got this far.'

'What happened?'

'They left us alone, but I heard they burnt the Shuvalov house to the ground.'

Ruzsky was shocked. He'd heard of such things, of course, but had not expected them here.

'And assaulted the servants. Killed the butler!' Oleg was obviously proud of his success in defending their property. His face softened. 'I'll leave you, Master Sandro. I know you will want to look round. There are sheets on the bed in your parents' room on the first floor.' His expression remained suitably opaque. 'And in the guest room.' He lit a candle for them, then walked slowly to the door. 'I've done my best, sir,' he said.

'Of course, Oleg.'

'I'm sorry for . . .' He thought better of it. 'Good night, sir.'

'Good night.'

CHAPTER TWENTY-NINE

Ruzsky walked slowly round the ground floor, the candle in his hand and Maria beside him. There were cobwebs in each nook and cranny and dust on every surface. In the dining room, the silver candlesticks and salt and pepper cellars were still on the table, as if waiting for the family to sit down to dinner. Ruzsky opened the shutters, allowing the moonlight to spill into the room. 'We used to eat as a family in the summer, all of us together, with these doors open and the sun streaming in.'

He pushed open the double doors to the library and pulled back the shutters there too. 'The rest of my father's collection of books. And his father's. If you want a rare or unusual text, it's probably here.' He patted the dust off a leather armchair.

A shaft of moonlight fell upon the giant portrait that hung above the fireplace and Ruzsky stood in front of it. 'Your father?' Maria asked.

'My grandfather. They looked very alike.'

'All three of you do.'

Ruzsky studied the face above him. 'They were both tyrants, in their own way.'

'Did you know your grandfather?'

'He died when I was five. We had come here to see him and he passed away in the room upstairs.' Ruzsky's brow creased. 'It was as if a giant weight had been lifted from my father's shoulders. That night I heard him laugh for the first time.'

Ruzsky continued to study the dour, imperious face of his grandfather. 'For a few years, he was a different man.'

'Is he buried here?'

'There is a graveyard beyond the walled garden. My father has never been there, but I have.'

'Is your mother buried here also?' she asked.

'No. In Petersburg.'

'Dmitri never talks of her.'

Ruzsky tried not to react to his brother's name. 'No, well . . .'

'He says your father believes she died of a broken heart.'

'It was a claim he once made.'

'Is it true?'

'No.'

'Why is it that you do not talk of her?'

Ruzsky stared at the portrait of his grandfather. 'I don't know.'

Maria waited for him to continue. After a long silence, he did so. 'She was afflicted with a deep melancholia, even before Ilusha's . . . Sometimes she stayed in her room all day.' He put his hand to his forehead. 'She suffered from terrible headaches. Perhaps my memory plays tricks, but after we left here that last time, she never embraced me again.'

'Where should I sleep, Sandro?'

Ruzsky did not respond.

'I'm tired,' she said softly, 'and this is your home.'

'Of course.' He cleared his throat. 'Of course.'

Ruzsky led her through the hallway and up the stairs. He walked swiftly down the landing, past the orchestra gallery and his parents' bedroom to those reserved for guests. Oleg had lit a candle and placed a bowl of warm water in the first room. He'd also pulled back the covers. Ruzsky patted the bed with his fist and a cloud of dust rose into the air. 'I'm sorry,' he said, glancing up at the ceiling, where the wallpaper had begun to peel, the spreading damp visible even in the dim light. 'Will you be all right?'

Maria moved slowly towards him. She took his face in her hands, her eyes searching his. She kissed him once, with soft, warm lips, then wrapped her arms round him and pressed him to her. 'Thank you for bringing me here, Sandro.' She released him and stepped back.

Ruzsky saw regret in her eyes. Was that all?

'Good night, Sandro,' she said.

'Good night.'

He stepped out of the room, pulled the door shut and took two or three paces down the corridor. He stood in the darkness, his mind clouded and his heart pounding. He waited.

He walked a few more paces, then stopped again. This corridor stripped away time. He felt a tightness in his chest. He was back in the night of Ilya's death, when Dmitri had clung to him by the door of his room, here, just before he had been summoned to his father's study.

Ruzsky remembered every inch of that journey.

He remembered the warmth of the fire, the look on his father's face, and his own terror as the reality of his emotional exile dawned upon him.

He could hear his mother's cries, and Dmitri's shock as he had tried to recount his father's words.

Ruzsky shivered. He found himself at Dmitri and Ilya's door.

The room was empty. The two beds were still there and the old chest of drawers, but everything personal had been removed: Ilya's elephant, which had occupied half the bed, Dmitri's sword, which had hung on the wall, the regimental flag above the door.

Ruzsky was as still as stone. He realized that he had wished to bathe in these memories, and even this had been denied him. He moved towards the shutters and pulled them back. The lake was white in the moonlight. Ruzsky's eyes were drawn along the ice towards the top of the slope on the far side, to the place where a small black stone stood in a clearing beneath the trees. He turned and looked across the corridor towards his own room. The door was shut. After a moment he went to open it. If his father – or perhaps even his mother when she had been alive – had stripped his brothers' room, he was certain they would have done the same to his own. He was right, but disappointment still tugged at something within him.

There was a blanket at the end of the bed where his toy bear had once slept, and Ruzsky lay down and covered himself with it, his boots hanging over the end of the mattress.

He closed his eyes.

* * *

All Ruzsky could see and feel was the ice-cold water against his clammy skin, his arms and legs swirling helplessly. He was drowning, eyes bulging and lungs empty. He was trying to breathe, but could not. They were watching him. His father, his mother, Dmitri ... They were standing there impassively, watching him die. Ruzsky felt the searing, wrenching pain in his chest. This was his punishment, and would be for all eternity.

'Sandro!' The slap awoke him, but seconds passed before his surroundings coalesced. She was above him: it *was* her. It was Maria, her face soft and beautiful, etched with anxiety, Oleg behind her, a candle above his head.

'Sandro?'

He felt paralysed, and he was soaked in sweat.

'Sandro?'

'Yes . . .'

'You were screaming.'

'I was drowning.'

'Screaming and screaming. We couldn't wake you.'

'I'm sorry.' He looked into her eyes. 'I'm sorry.'

Maria turned towards Oleg. 'It's all right, Oleg. I'll look after him now.'

Oleg looked at Maria with understanding, then handed her the candle. They listened to his footsteps recede.

Maria put the candle on the side table, then put a warm hand on his frozen cheek. Ruzsky thought it might be love that he saw in her eyes. She blew out the candle, then slipped on to the bed and pulled him to her, cradling his head on her breast.

They lay still in the darkness.

'Everything's going to be all right, Sandro,' she whispered.

'It will never be all right.'

'It will, believe me.' She tightened her hold on him. 'My sister cried out,' Maria said, 'but I could not stop her. I could never cry out.'

CHAPTER THIRTY

As the cold fingers of dawn crept through the shutters, Ruzsky slipped out of bed, crossed to his brothers' room and looked out over the gardens. Little had changed. The hedgerows appeared overgrown, but everything was covered with a thick layer of snow so it was hard to tell. Nothing moved by the lake. The ice seemed intent on squeezing the life out of the island at its centre. The rowing boat that they had used as children had been tied up by the jetty. The mist cleared grudgingly, making way for the hazy outline of the sun. At length, he went back to his own room, squatted and watched her sleeping. She lay on her front, her face to the side, lips slightly parted, hair fanned across the pillow. He watched the rise and fall of her back, reached forward and brushed a few strands of hair from her cheek. She did not stir.

Ruzsky slipped along the landing and down the wide stairs.

Oleg was dusting the busts in the hallway. 'You weren't made for this, old man,' Ruzsky said.

'Someone has to do it.' Oleg looked up at him. 'When the war is over you'll all be back, and your father will want to know why I've let the place go.'

Ruzsky was moved by the old man's stubborn hope that the old days would return.

'I'm sorry,' he said. 'The horses. I didn't—'

'It's all right.' Oleg snorted. 'I've not taken leave of my senses.'

'I'll ... If she wakes, I've gone out ... just for a walk.'

'As you wish.'

Ruzsky opened the big front door and strolled out on to the driveway. It was much lighter now. He could see the decay in the woodwork of the windows.

Ruzsky made his way slowly to the stables. The roof here was in much better condition and he recalled Dmitri telling him once that it was the last money his father had agreed to spend on the place. He checked the horses, then moved down the corridor between the stalls and unlocked the double doors.

The family's *troika* and sled stood before him, exactly as he remembered them. He ran his hand slowly along the solid wood front of the sled, then leant over to feel the leather of the forward seat. The woodwork was painted red and gold. The bells they had attached to it at Christmas hung on the wall, alongside a couple of spare wheels for the *troika* and an array of leather harnesses. Ruzsky gave one a tug. The leather was still supple.

He turned. Oleg was watching him.

'Still the same,' Ruzsky said.

'Still the same.'

'Do you remember how Dmitri liked to drive it?' Ruzsky thought of them all in the back as the horses charged down the hill towards the gates.

'He's a fine horseman, your brother,' Oleg said.

'Always was, even as a boy. No discipline for learning, but a natural.'

'We should hitch it up and go down to the village.'

'We could do that,' Oleg said, but Ruzsky heard the doubt in his voice.

'Well, perhaps we should ride down, anyway.'

Oleg didn't answer.

'You don't want to go?'

Oleg wouldn't meet his eye.

'What is it? We're not welcome? Is that it?'

'There are a few bad . . . One or two of the young ones. Some of those who used to be employed at the works.'

'Used to be?'

'Didn't get on with the new owner.'

Ruzsky stepped away from the sled. 'What new owner?'

'Your father sold the glassworks, Sandro.'

'When?'

'Before the war.'

Ruzsky could scarcely credit it. The employment provided by the factory – and the benevolent way in which the family ran it – had provided the bedrock of the social fabric of the area.

'I'm told the man was offered the house as well, but did not want it.'

'He was offered the house?'

Oleg was still embarrassed. 'So they say.'

'Who was it?'

'Someone from Moscow. It's all changed, Sandro.'

Ruzsky glanced up at the old muskets along the wall above him. 'Have you still got a working rifle?'

'No good to me. My eyes.'

'But you've got one?'

312

'In the house. You never know when the swine will come back.'

'Come on, then, let's see if we can find ourselves some lunch.'

They walked out into the sunshine and Ruzsky waited by the side of the house for Oleg to get his rifle. When he returned with his old blue hunting coat, they walked down to the end of the drive and turned on to the path that led up the hill. Oleg did not ask why they avoided the quicker route beside the lake.

They climbed up through the silent pine forest, the snow on the path so thick in some places that they were almost stopped in their tracks. They reached a fork, where the path to their left led directly to the lake and the garden. Ruzsky stopped, took the rifle from the old man and the three bullets he offered. 'Better shoot straight,' Oleg said.

'Why change the habit of a lifetime?' Ruzsky grinned.

'Mmm. Always a fine shot.' Oleg raised a bony finger to the sky. He had taught both him and Dmitri to hunt. 'The best. You'd have made a fine soldier, better than your brother.'

The sun was glinting through the trees and it was warmer today. They walked on and stopped in a clearing a hundred yards further up. Ruzsky pushed a bullet into the breech and closed the bolt. They waited. The forest was silent. 'A hare would do,' Ruzsky said. He walked on, cresting the hill and emerging into the larger clearing where his father had helped the estate workers build the tree-house. He had hoped secretly that this remnant of their childhood, at least, had survived, and his disappointment was bitter when he saw that it had gone. There were a few fallen pieces of rotting wood, but nothing more.

He rested the rifle on his shoulder. 'What happened to the dogs, Oleg?'

The old man shook his head.

Ruzsky saw movement on the other side of the clearing. 'Deer,' he whispered.

Ruzsky and Oleg stalked the deer for an hour before they got a clear shot. Ruzsky took it through the heart, then Oleg went back to get one of the horses to drag it home. Ruzsky hunted on alone, roaming through the silent forest, the sun on his face. An hour or more later, he returned to the tree-house clearing, sweating with exertion. The only sound was the drip of melting snow falling from the pines. He walked to the far side of the clearing, then back down the path. He stopped a few yards short of the point at which he knew he would get his first glimpse of the house. Past and present merged, just as they had in the corridor last night. It was not memory that overpowered him, but the pervasive sense that he was rooted in a place and time he had never left.

He began to walk, then broke into a run, the sun still bright above him, the house dancing through the trees. He took the right-hand fork, running hard through the thick snow.

He reached the garden, panting. Maria stood on the veranda on the far side, but he branched off towards the lake. Ten yards from the jetty, he stopped. He could see the boat. He could see the island.

Ruzsky took another step, his feet leaden. He looked at the ice, then turned and walked up the slope, towards the line of trees. He found himself slowing down again, as if he were trying to force his way against an invisible wind. He could see the stone. He pushed his legs forward until he was standing in front of it, his head bent. He read the name, in gold, and saw the small mound of snow and the dead flowers in the vase.

Ilya Nicholaevich Ruzsky
7.6.1882–3.4.1889
Beloved son

Ruzsky knelt and prayed. He saw his brother's impish smile and recalled how they had indulged him and fought for the right to be his protector in any battle. He remembered Ilya at Christmas, the thoughtful way in which he had constructed his presents for his brothers with the help of Oleg or one of the other servants. Ruzsky fumbled in his pocket and pulled out the tiny and crude wooden snuff box that his little brother had made for him that last winter. He kissed it once, rubbed his thumb across its smooth ebony top, then slipped it away again. He stood up and stepped back, then bent and touched the gravestone. 'I miss you.' Ruzsky began to weep. 'Oh, God, how I miss you.'

He waited until the tears had stopped, then walked back to the house. Maria was watching him, but he did not acknowledge her. He crossed the veranda, stepped into the drawing room, then walked up to Ilya's room on the floor above. He climbed on to the bed by the window and curled into a ball.

CHAPTER THIRTY-ONE

Maria stood in the doorway. Ruzsky would have found anyone else's presence intrusive, but he straightened himself and sat up against the wall. She sat down on the bed beside him. 'What happened?' she asked.

'It was spring,' he said. He had never recounted or explained any part of this before, not even to Irina. 'Father told us not to play on the ice. We used to skate all the time in winter, but we had never been here in spring and he told us that once the weather was warm the ice became thin, even if the lake still appeared to be frozen. He told all of us, but especially me. I was the oldest and he believed that carried a special responsibility. "Make sure that your brothers don't go on the ice, Sandro."'

He stared at the opposite wall. 'My father and some of the estate workers had built us a camp on top of the hill. We'd been there all morning – the three of us – and we were coming back for lunch. We reached the lake. I realized I had forgotten my jacket, so I told them to go on home and I would catch them up.'

He stood up and went to the window.

'I returned to the tree-house and got my jacket. The air was quite warm and I was running down the hill when I noticed that wild strawberries were emerging from the melting snow. The forest was silent. And then I heard his cry. Just a startled yell. For a moment, I was unable to move. Then I ran, tearing through the trees as I heard Dmitri's shout for help.'

Ruzsky could almost see Dmitri now, standing there beside the lake.

'I came into the clearing and I saw it all. I didn't pause. I ran out on to the jetty. Dmitri was paralysed. I crawled on to the ice on my belly. I was shouting at Dmitri to get help. And then Ilusha slipped away and I stood and ran towards him and the ice gave way and it was still so cold and somehow I knew that . . .' Ruzsky couldn't go on. He took a deep breath. 'Ilusha couldn't swim, you see. The lake is deep and I dived. It was dark and I held my breath and held it and held it.' He looked over at his brother's gravestone. 'I was tired and cold. So cold.'

'And there was a moment when you wanted to go with him . . .'

'I could see Father's hand stretched towards me,' he said, 'and I knew that by taking it I would never escape.'

She stood behind him, her arms round his waist, lips soft on the nape of his neck. 'Ilusha would not have wanted an older brother who was a coward.'

'But that is what I am.'

'No. No, you're not.'

Ruzsky tried to control his breathing.

'Why did Ilusha go on to the ice?' she asked.

317

He remained silent.

'And why didn't Dmitri stop him?'

Ruzsky still did not turn round. 'What does it matter?'

'Because you hold yourself responsible.'

'Because I *am* responsible.' He stared at the side of the lake where Dmitri had been standing. 'Perhaps Dmitri was doing something else.'

'What?'

Ruzsky cast his eye across the garden to the clearing. 'Perhaps he did not think that the ice would break.'

'But why did Ilusha go on to it if your father had told you not to?'

Ruzsky's mind was numb. 'I don't know.'

'Did he often disobey your father?'

'No. Not about something like that. As good as gold, we always used to say.' Ruzsky turned to her. 'Why could you not cry out? Last night you said you were not able to grieve.'

'For the same reason that you can't, except in your sleep.'

'Your parents?'

'My father was killed in an accident and my mother died of a broken heart. I saw her face in the doorway of my room and I knew. I promised myself I would never allow myself to be hurt again.'

They were standing inches apart. Her breast rose and fell, her breath warm upon his face. 'And I hurt you?' he breathed. He touched her face, a cold hand against warm cheeks. She pressed it to her, resting her head on his chest.

They rode hard against the setting sun that afternoon, weaving through the woods before they picked up the road to the house from the village in the gathering darkness. Ruzsky brought his horse alongside hers and jumped across again.

Maria rested against him, one hand cupping the back of his head, the skin of her neck soft against his lips. Ruzsky curled his arm tighter round her waist.

'Hello, my wounded soldier,' she said. She turned and placed her moist, warm mouth against his. She arched her back, a palm against his cheek. 'No one has ever loved you before, have they, Sandro?'

He did not answer.

Maria turned round, and they rocked with the motion of the horse all the way back to the house, the sunset washing the horizon a blazing red.

Oleg was waiting at the front door to take the horses. Ruzsky could tell from his eyes that he knew, but there was no hint of censure. 'A fire is laid in the drawing room, Master Sandro, the venison cooked. I shall leave it to you,' he said.

Inside, they discovered that Oleg had lit a fire in both the drawing room and the dining room, where the table was laid as it always had been, groaning with silver, a leg of venison – which he must have procured from the village – arranged on a giant salver at the centre.

Ruzsky shut the door behind them and then she was in his arms, with sudden, passionate urgency. He lifted her against the door as her lips sought his. She tugged at his belt, one hand on his back, the other seeking him, pulling at his trousers until he was free, then melting into him, her face against his shoulder. 'God, Sandro,' she said. She traced his neck with her fingertips, her mouth warm as he

319

held her, their bodies fused together. He walked with her to the great bear rug in front of the roaring hearth and, without parting from her, he sank to his knees and placed her carefully on the ground. He moved over her, his face inches from hers. Then he reached down and ran a hand across the top of one of her silk stockings, feeling the smoothness of her skin.

Maria pushed him gently on to his back. Ruzsky began to unbutton her dress, and she helped him, then pulled it off, raising herself up, her knees to either side of his waist, her hair brushing his face as she bent over him. Never taking her eyes from his, she lowered herself against him, straightening her legs. She kissed him, as his hands reached for the curve at the top of her thighs. He pushed gently against her clenching muscles and lay back.

She sat up, her back arched, her hair dusting his knees, her breasts high and proud. In the firelight, her skin seemed luminous.

Ruzsky ran his hands gently up her thighs, over her hips and across her flat, muscular belly. She lifted herself up, waiting as she looked into his eyes. She was smiling at him.

Then she lowered herself again, slowly, almost agonizingly. Ruzsky shut his eyes as the pleasure threatened to burst within him.

They lay that night in front of the fire, wrapped in the bearskin rug. Ruzsky did not sleep, reluctant to concede a moment to the dawn. He was as content as he had ever been.

Fatigue stalked him and slowly he succumbed,

until the sleep of a few hours gave way to the day of their leaving.

He listened to the birds as the light crept into the room and the shadows shortened. He would not move until she stirred.

CHAPTER THIRTY-TWO

Ruzsky stood before Ilya's stone one last time. He thought of his brother's smile. 'Rest in peace,' he said, and even as he spoke a tear rolled down his cheek. He turned away and walked towards the house. On the veranda, he glanced back and raised his hand, then stepped into the drawing room. 'Goodbye,' he whispered. 'I'm not sure we will see each other again.'

Then he composed himself, and strode into the hall-way. Through the window, he could see Maria and Oleg with the horses. He glanced up at the banners and balustrades above him, his breath visible on the air even here, and tried to recapture something of the happier memories of those past summers, but they proved elusive. He walsked out of the front door without looking back.

He put his foot into a stirrup and swung himself on to his horse. 'You'll look after him, won't you, Oleg?'

'Always, sir.'

'Perhaps the rest of my family will be down this summer.'

'Perhaps. Your father will let me know well in

advance, I'm sure. There's work to be done. You've seen that.'

Ruzsky reached down to shake the old man's hand and saw that there were tears in his eyes, too. 'They'll be down before too long, whatever happens,' he said.

'Of course, Master Sandro. As soon as the war ends.'

Ruzsky nudged the horse forward. 'Good luck, Oleg.'

'And to you, sir. And your lady-friend.'

Ruzsky set his horse down the snow-covered drive. He rode her hard up the hill beside the house and only stopped as he reached the top of the path. He turned for one last look. Oleg stood on the veranda, a tiny figure against the grand façade. Ruzsky thought he saw the old man raise his hand once and responded, only to wonder if he had imagined it.

He twisted his head round. Maria was looking at him with an intensity that seemed to him to be something like love. She smiled faintly. 'To a new beginning,' he said, 'for both of us. You agree?' Then he fired his horse up the hill with a shout. He reached the crest and slowed the horse to a walk on the icy descent, only glancing over his shoulder when he was sure that the house was out of view.

Maria was behind him, deep in thought, her long hair and much of her face concealed under a wide fur hat. As he headed down the hill, he tried to keep the past at bay. Sandro the protector, Dmitri had always called him. The guilt, when it returned, was like lead in the pit of his stomach.

CHAPTER THIRTY-THREE

Throughout the journey, Ruzsky had watched excitement build in Maria's eyes, and as they crossed the Crimean isthmus under a clear blue sky, she seemed more than ever like a little girl on the final leg of a long journey home. Her bag was packed and she gazed endlessly out of the open window, the warm breeze of Russia's sub-tropical paradise on both their faces.

The night had transported them to another world. The previous evening they had pulled down the blinds on sleeting rain and mile upon mile of bare brown fields, fringed by straggling birch trees. This morning, they had opened them to a flood of sunshine, fruit trees in full blossom and a bay as blue as aquamarine.

Below, the town of Sevastopol stood perched on a barren rock, narrow streets leading down to a wide harbour. Overhead, black and white gulls circled. Out in the still waters of the bay two grey battleships lay at anchor, the Russian national flag flapping lazily from their sterns. Ruzsky had his own memories of holidays here. They'd come twice to see an aunt who had a modest palace not far from the Tsar's own in

Yalta, but his recollections, though warm, were vague.

The guard knocked and poked his head round the door. 'Everything all right, Mademoiselle?' He looked suspiciously at Ruzsky, as he had throughout the journey.

'Yes.'

'A couple more minutes. You'll arrange your own transport to Yalta?'

'Yes, thank you.'

The guard eyed Ruzsky again. 'You don't wish me to arrange it for you?'

'No, thank you.'

The man retreated.

The train wound slowly down the last hill. Ruzsky glanced at Maria. If her excitement had grown as the journey progressed, so too had the distance between them. Her manner was still warm, but the further south they had travelled, the more she'd retreated into herself. He told himself it was the natural melancholy of a return to her own past.

'You will go straight to the sanatorium?' Ruzsky asked.

She continued to stare out of the window.

'What is it called?'

Maria looked at him. The distance between them was solidifying, but he could not tell why. Once again, he suppressed a sense of alarm. 'The Tatyana Committee Convalescent Home.' She turned back to the window.

The train jerked twice as the brakes were applied, then pulled slowly into the station, the porters on the platform disappearing into a cloud of steam. Maria was instantly on her feet, her small leather case in her hand until Ruzsky wrested it from her. He followed her down on to the platform, a warm breeze on their faces. She disappeared into the steam, too, and he hurried after her.

The platform was busier and bigger than he remembered. A large group swarmed forward in front of him to greet a friend or relative disembarking from the train and Ruzsky lost sight of her again. He halted. He could not see her ahead, so he looked back and, just for a second, as the steam floated down the length of the platform he saw a man at the far end who he could have sworn was Ivan Prokopiev. Ruzsky took a step towards him, but the man slipped from view into the crowd. Then Ruzsky saw Maria emerge into the sunlight by the exit.

When he caught up with her, she looked startled and, for a split second, examined him strangely, as if she had no idea who he was, just as she had outside the theatre in Petersburg. 'Sandro,' she said.

'Are you all right?'

'I'm fine. Why?'

'Can you wait a moment?'

She was squinting into the sun.

'There's something I need to check,' he said. He retraced his steps back to the platform. It was still crowded with passengers and porters, escaping steam and the hubbub of voices. He wove his way through the crowd. An elderly man selling lemonade in old bottles sat next to a group of train guards talking in a small circle. There were a couple of soldiers, but the atmosphere was different from that in the big cities further north. The air was warm, sunlight filtering through the glass roof on to the platform. Some of the men around him were in shirt-sleeves.

Ruzsky reached the point at which he thought he'd

seen Prokopiev, but there was no sign of him. He walked through the exit, squinting, too, as he stepped out into the sunshine. A fly landed on his cheek and he brushed it away. A group of small boys knelt against the station wall, playing with old musket balls instead of marbles. He asked if they had seen a tall man with short hair leaving the station by this exit, but they looked at him uncomprehendingly. Perhaps it was his accent.

Ruzsky went back on to the platform and returned to the relative shade of its central section. Shafts of sunlight illuminated the dust in the hazy air. He gave a brief description of Prokopiev, but although the men there at least appeared to understand him, they all shook their heads.

Ruzsky gave up. He scoured the platform as he returned to where he'd left Maria.

But when he reached the road, she wasn't there. He waited a few minutes, and concluded she had probably gone to the lavatory. He took out his cigarette case, then returned it to his pocket. He closed his eyes and enjoyed the sunlight on his face. Time stretched out. He waited ten minutes or more, then checked his pocket watch. Confusion gave way to mild irritation.

He returned to survey the platform once more, then came back out into the sunshine. Almost all of the passengers had gone. He tried to relax, but a kernel of doubt had entered his mind.

On the far side of the road, a lone *troika* driver was still waiting for his passengers. Ruzsky wandered over and asked him whether he had seen a tall, beautiful, dark-haired woman carrying a simple leather case. Although the man's accent was thick, Ruzsky understood that he had. She'd climbed into a car with

two men and driven up the hill, in the direction of
Yalta. Ruzsky argued with him, but the man was
emphatic. Two more automobiles were waiting at a
rank outside the station – no doubt to ferry rich
bankers from Moscow to their homes on the coast. He
reached into his pocket, pulled out a wad of money
and counted it.

The driver said the journey would take three hours in
a car – much quicker than the last time Ruzsky was
here – and the first hour consisted, as he recalled, of a
comfortable journey across the dusty plain past
occasional monuments to ancient battlefields. After
that, they wound up through valleys and golden hills
to the grey gateway of Aie Petri miles above the sea.
As they passed it, Ruzsky began to feel sick and grew
tired of the interminable twists of the descent, past
crowded Tartar villages and great white villas with
stone-walled gardens and baby cypress trees.

Their journey was slowed by the many simple
Tartar pony-carriages, but eventually Ruzsky caught
sight of the bay of Ghurzuf and the white town
huddled untidily along the shore, brilliant in the mid-
day sunshine. He pulled himself upright as the cab
drove slowly towards the bay. It was just as he
remembered it: an azure sea beneath cloudless skies.
In more than just a geographical sense, this elegant
town was a long way from the empire's frozen capital.
A two-day journey transported one to a different
world. Ruzsky asked to be dropped off at the top of
the hill and, with his bag on his shoulder, he strolled
briskly down narrow alleys, past colourful Tartar
houses, to the seafront.

The Oreanda Hotel, with its giant blue awning,

faced the promenade and Ruzsky had fondly imagined that they would be able to claim they were on police business and insist on staying here for nothing, but he doubted the wisdom of this plan as he walked through the hotel's cool, airy hallway to the reception desk.

In front of him, a swarthy man in a dark green and gold uniform was talking to a colleague next to a potted palm tree. A fan turned on the desk. The man ambled forward, smiling. 'Can I help you, sir?'

'I'm here to check in. Chief Investigator Ruzsky from Petrograd.'

'Yes, sir.' Ruzsky had wanted the attendant to be impressed, but he wasn't. 'Your colleague told us you would be arriving.'

'Is he here?'

'I do not believe so. I have not seen him this morning.' The man examined the rack behind him for Pavel's key. 'He must have taken his key with him, sir.'

'Is there a message?'

The attendant shook his head.

'Which room is he in?'

'Number eleven. Next to your own.'

Ruzsky filled in the form he was given and took possession of his key. He waved away the offer of assistance from the porter and climbed the wide stone steps to the first floor. He knocked on the door of number eleven. There was no answer so he slipped into his own room. It was large and airy with a small balcony overlooking the sea. It had dark wooden floors and a large, four- poster bed. Ruzsky stepped on to the balcony. Even though it was only one floor up, the breeze seemed stronger here. He put his hands into his pockets. Below lay the shimmering water, and above, craggy mountains rose majestically towards the sky. It was the most romantic place in the world, and the thought left a dull ache in the pit of his stomach.

Ruzsky went back inside and tried to turn his mind to the job he had come here to do. He shut the windows, then sat at the desk and wrote Pavel a note on the headed paper the hotel provided, the sun streaming on to his face.

Outside, he knocked once more on Pavel's door to be sure he was not there, then slipped the note beneath it.

CHAPTER THIRTY-FOUR

The chief of police in Yalta's tiny station held a more important post than this leafy, sun-kissed town might otherwise have merited, on account of the proximity of the Tsar's summer palace at Livadia, a car or *troika* journey up the hill. Godorkin was older than Ruzsky had expected. He was tall and lean, with wavy brown hair and a cleanshaven, narrow but pleasant face. He had steady eyes and a relaxed air, and held himself like the former military officer that Ruzsky soon learnt he was. He'd come here for the weather, he said. His family was from outside Odessa. There were sketches on the wall depicting officers of the Ataman Cossacks regiment on horseback, and photographs of five children on his desk. Godorkin was not, Ruzsky was relieved to conclude, Vasilyev's man. He sat, legs crossed, behind a wide teak desk, lit a cigarette and offered Ruzsky one.

As he sucked in the smoke, Ruzsky tried to imagine Vasilyev sitting in that chair and wondered what kind of ambition could drive a man from such serene and peaceful surroundings to the frozen back alleys of the nation's capital. 'Did you know Vasilyev?' Ruzsky asked.

'Met him once. Years ago. There have been two other chiefs between us, and three governors.' He smiled and blew a plume of smoke towards the ceiling. 'The weather didn't agree with them.' There was a quiet knock and Godorkin's plump secretary bustled in with a tray and two cups of tea. She smiled shyly and withdrew.

Ruzsky considered asking about Maria's father, but thought better of it. Perhaps later.

Godorkin pushed a sheet of paper across the desk towards him. 'Your colleague left this list with us, in case we could come up with something else, but I'm afraid we haven't.' It was a note of the victims in Petersburg in Pavel's handwriting: Ella Kovyil. Robert White/Whitewater. Boris Markov.

'As I told your colleague,' Godorkin said, 'Whitewater is on our wanted list. That's why I responded to your telegram.'

'Wanted for what?'

'Armed robbery. He is suspected of having held up the train from Simferopol to Kharkov.'

'Recently?'

'1910.'

Ruzsky frowned. 'Not on his own?'

'He had accomplices, of course.'

Perhaps he imagined it, but Ruzsky sensed that the genial detective was embarrassed. 'It was before your time?'

'Yes, I'm glad to say.' Godorkin leant forward on his desk, suddenly every inch the army officer. 'There was no excuse for it. Just because a case is old, it doesn't mean that it should be forgotten.' He sat back again, waving his arm. This was clearly not the first time he had been over this subject. 'It's damned difficult getting to grips with old cases when there are no files.'

'Why are there no files?'

'Lost. Missing. No paperwork written up. Who knows?'

'So there is no file on this armed robbery?'

'A file exists, but the paperwork within it has been lost.'

'Shouldn't the case have been handled in either Simferopol or Kharkov?'

'They say it was dealt with here.'

'Why?'

Godorkin shrugged. 'I don't know.'

'I'm sorry, but I'm confused,' Ruzsky said. He sat up straight. 'How did you know about Robert White's involvement if there is nothing in the file?'

Godorkin's expression told Ruzsky that the same things had been explained to Pavel. 'White's name was on our wanted list. The details I gave you are all we have. The case notes from the file are missing.'

'What was stolen?'

'A sum of money, I believe. Several thousand roubles. The case has been inactive for some time. I only took over in September last year so it was well before my tenure. I went in search of the file when I received your telegram.'

'Vasilyev was the chief of police at the time of the robbery?'

Godorkin's gaze was steady, but wary. He appeared to assess whether he was being led into a trap, but whatever he saw in Ruzsky's eyes, it won his approval. He relaxed. 'That is correct,' he said.

'His investigation?'

Godorkin grimaced.

'His file?'

'I've no idea.'

Ruzsky turned to the window. He watched a sail being hoisted on a white racing yacht. 'Strange,' he said. 'Vasilyev has a reputation for efficiency.' He turned back to Godorkin. 'You said that you knew of both of them, White and the girl, Ella?'

'She was a sweet little thing. I knew her father.'

'Were you aware that Ella began an affair with this American, White, in the summer of 1910?'

'I was with the military liaison department at the embassy in France at that time. I hadn't seen Kovyil for some years when he died.'

'He wouldn't have approved. Or so his wife said.'

'Of an American criminal? Hardly.'

The yacht tacked across the centre of the bay. The wind had slackened and the craft brought itself round slowly. 'What brings a man like that halfway across the world?' Ruzsky asked.

'Yalta is famous, Chief Investigator. Perhaps you shouldn't underestimate its appeal.'

'Perhaps not.' Ruzsky sat on the sill. His cigarette had gone out – he'd barely smoked it – and he threw it out of the window.

'What is the connection between this office and Livadia?'

'That I can't discuss.'

'You vet staff?'

'We have in the past, if they're local. Sometimes they come from further afield.'

'Who do you deal with there?'

Godorkin smiled. 'Your friend has beaten you to it. He left here yesterday to go straight up to the palace.'

'You must have a list of political suspects. The Okhrana supplies you with information?'

'A certain amount is disclosed to enable us to ascertain that any local individual has no inappropriate political involvement, but normally we know them well enough to be sure.'

Ruzsky faced him. 'Would you mind if I spent some time in your file room?'

Godorkin looked astonished, but not insulted. An honest man, Ruzsky thought.

If Godorkin's intention was to regularize the station's affairs, he hadn't begun with the filing system.

Indeed, there was no system to speak of. The filing cases were kept in a gloomy, dust-laden room in the basement. There wasn't even an electric light. Ruzsky shuddered. This place reminded him uncomfortably of the station in Tobolsk.

'Help yourself,' Godorkin said, with heavy humour, lighting a candle and thrusting it into his hand. 'What are you looking for?'

'I don't know precisely. Other cases around that time. Names familiar to me from somewhere else.'

Ruzsky hoped he would not be offered assistance. He wanted to be alone. 'Broadly,' Godorkin said, 'cases are filed by year, starting at the beginning of the century on the left. Any personal files are at the far end of the room in alphabetical order. I've achieved that much. Shout if I can help.' He coughed once, then slowly climbed the stairs.

Ruzsky went to the far end of the room where there was a small grille for ventilation, which let in a thin stream of light. Beneath it stood a desk. He brushed the dust from its surface, then retraced his steps and found a ledge on which to place the candle.

Godorkin was right. The files had been sorted recently: the layer of dust on some of the cases was thinner than it was around the rest of the room. He found 1910 and took all the files for that year to the desk under the grille. There were about five large piles. Quite a lot, he thought, for a small provincial town, however important.

All of the files had the nature of the crime to which they related inscribed on the front, along with the date on which it had been committed. The date the crime had been reported was also recorded. Most, though not all, files were annotated in the same flowing hand. Ruzsky had seen only one detective upstairs in the main room on the ground floor but he had looked about seventeen – much too young to have been working here seven years ago.

The crimes were mostly incidental: petty theft, vandalism, affray, some domestic violence. It took Ruzsky about an hour to work through them and he reached the end with a sense of disappointment. He supposed that he'd hoped White's name, or Markov's – even Ella's – might have cropped up in some other context.

He began on the files relating to political suspects or criminals. They were not strictly in alphabetical order, so he ended up going through the whole shelf. There was no reference to any of them.

Ruzsky sat down again at the desk. He watched the dust dancing in the shaft of light from the grille. He checked his watch. He had arrived at Sevastopol station shortly after breakfast and it was now almost three o'clock. He was hungry.

He began to sift through the files for 1909. The task

now seemed pointless, but instinct told him that these people could not have passed through Yalta without coming to the attention of the authorities.

And if White had robbed a train, he had certainly not acted alone.

There were fewer files for 1909, but they were no more illuminating. Ruzsky was close to giving up when he saw a small, discarded pile on the top shelf. He brought the chair from the other end of the room. There were ten files, covered in dust. He carried them back to the desk. The top file had the words 'Black Terror' written in the same flowing hand on the front. He opened the buff cover and sifted through the loosely bound, yellowing pages within.

A feeling of unease crept slowly through him.

One name appeared three times. The last entry was for 11 August 1910.

The Black Terror was one of many revolutionary groups that had sprung up at the end of the last century to concentrate on assassinating luminaries of the regime. This small and, by the look of the notes, loosely affiliated cell had been formed on 12 January of that same year by a Michael Borodin, according to the statement of a well-known Bolshevik from St Petersburg. The police had had an informant inside the group because the date and venue of each meeting were recorded alongside a paragraph or two describing what had transpired.

Ruzsky ran his eye over one of the entries again. The reports must have been written by the informant's police contact: '12 July: Dumskaya Hotel. Present: Borodin, the American White, Ella Kovyil, Boris Markov, Olga Legarina, Maria Popova.'

Ruzsky stared at her name, struggling to take it in. *Maria Popova.*

Meeting called to order by Borodin. Further discussion of possible assassination of governor of Odessa. Markov agreed to travel to Odessa to research governor's movements. Popova expressed view that chief of police in Odessa perhaps better target. White spoke of the need for money to carry out revolutionary tasks. Raised possibility of robbing a bank in Odessa, Sevastopol or Simferopol in order to raise funds. All agreed on necessity of this type of action.

Ruzsky's mind swam. *Popova expressed view that chief of police in Odessa perhaps better target.*

He stared at the grille, his vision blurred. There was bile in the back of his throat. A revolutionary? A murderer? He thought of the softness of her skin and the gentle sadness in her eyes. It wasn't possible.

But who were the men she had left the station with this morning?

Had she been watching *him*? Is that why she had come to Yalta?

No, it had been her suggestion. She had told him she was returning before they'd discovered Markov's body under the Lion Bridge.

Ruzsky read through the entries again. Half of him still did not believe the evidence before his eyes. He tapped his fingers against the pages. Why did the reports stop on 11 August? He toyed with the idea of keeping what he'd found to himself, but he decided that it would do no harm to discuss it with Godorkin.

The chief of police sat at his desk, a cigarette burning

in the solid silver ashtray, a blind flapping idly against the window. Ruzsky placed the file in front of him. 'Have you got the folder for the train robbery, even if it's empty?'

Godorkin was already reading. He opened the cupboard beneath him, took out an empty folder and handed it to Ruzsky. 'Simferopol–Kharkov train robbery', it read. '31 August 1910'.

'The entries cease,' Ruzsky said, 'roughly two weeks before the robbery, of which they make no mention.'

'Yes.'

'I assume it takes longer than two weeks to plan a crime of that kind.'

'I should imagine so.'

They were silent. Out of the window, there were two yachts in the bay now, and they crossed each other, their sails a startling white against the sea.

'Ella Kovyil got a job in the Imperial Household up at Livadia,' Ruzsky said. 'How did she manage that, if the department here was doing the vetting?'

Godorkin did not reply. The answer was obvious to both of them. 'Someone must have called a halt to the surveillance,' Ruzsky said, forcing the point home. 'After the robbery, Vasilyev makes sure the case is handled here but goes nowhere. Eventually the notes are removed and disposed of. If there was an investigation, that is.'

Godorkin still did not reply.

'Did you know the Popov family?' Ruzsky asked. 'Wasn't Maria Popova's father the governor?' He tried to keep his tone and expression neutral.

Godorkin shrugged.

'I think the Popov girl must have been the agent. Nothing else would make sense. Her father died some years before?'

The policeman didn't respond.

'You didn't know him?'

'No.'

Ruzsky felt profoundly uneasy.

CHAPTER THIRTY-FIVE

Ruzsky strolled back down the winding alley to the promenade. He had established from Godorkin that the Tatyana Committee Convalescent Home was on the other side of the hill, overlooking the next bay, but even if Maria had gone there to see her sister, neither the prevailing atmosphere nor Ruzsky's state of mind encouraged haste.

He needed time to think.

He stopped beside the wrought-iron railings. On the shingle beach below a group of small boys were throwing stones at a pool of water they'd dug in the sand. Further down, a man was selling cold drinks from a cheerful red and white stall. Ruzsky crossed the road and walked into the hotel lobby. He climbed the stairs to the first floor and knocked on Pavel's door. There was no answer. He cursed under his breath. It *was* unlike Pavel not to leave a note. Beside him, in the corridor, a potted palm fluttered in the breeze from an open window.

Perhaps his departure from the train had upset his old friend more than he'd imagined. Ruzsky rubbed his hand hard across his face and groaned inwardly.

He supposed it had been a typically selfish gesture. He walked towards the stairs again. He needed that cheery, gregarious face now.

The Moorish palace at Livadia was cut from almost translucent white stone. Ruzsky was admitted to the grounds by the security guards at the gate and told to wait in the sunshine beside the front steps. He shaded his eyes as he watched a gardener clipping a hedge while another scrubbed the stonework around the fountain. The garden, like so much of Yalta, was green even at this time of year, packed with the distinctive narrow firs and tall palm trees.

The man who came to meet him was exceptionally tall and lugubrious, but without the military bearing Ruzsky had grown to expect in palace officials. He stooped, as if weighed down by his long, drooping nose. He was thin almost to the point of emaciation, and superior to the point of being irritating. A much lesser individual, Ruzsky judged, than Shulgin at Tsarskoe Selo. 'You are the investigator?' the man said, his voice so soft that it was hard to hear.

Ruzsky nodded expectantly as he listened to the clip-clip-clip of the shears behind him.

'How can I help you?' He had not bothered to introduce himself.

'And you are?' Ruzsky asked.

'I am the chief officer of the Household.'

'You have, I'm sure, already spoken to my colleague.'

The man inclined his head. 'I do not believe so.'

'He came here yesterday, direct from the police station. A big man, with a generous beard. Investigator Miliutin. Pavel Miliutin.'

The man's confusion was genuine.

'Perhaps he spoke to someone else?' Ruzsky asked.

'That's not possible. I was here all day. If he had called, the guards would have sent for me.'

Ruzsky was silent. He turned to face the sea and watched the gardeners at work again. He wanted to leave now, but had no idea where to go. Pavel must have been on to something. He must have followed a lead.

'How can I help you?' the man asked, and now his supercilious manner annoyed Ruzsky.

'Ella Kovyil.'

The official frowned.

'She used to work here. Her father was a non-commissioned officer in the Preobrazhenskys. She was taken on as nanny to the Tsarevich in the summer of 1910.'

'It may be.'

'It may be, or it was?'

Perhaps the man sensed Ruzsky's unease. His patronizing manner melted away and his face grew more serious. 'It was.'

'You were here?'

'I recall the girl, if that is what you mean.'

'Tell me about her.'

The man appraised his interlocutor properly for the first time. 'You have come a long way, Chief Investigator. What is the nature of your enquiry?'

'Ella was found stabbed in the chest in front of the Winter Palace on New Year's morning. Her companion was cut to bits.'

The man did not react. His expression was sober, but neutral.

'Did you know when you employed her that she was a member of a revolutionary organization?'

343

Now the bureaucrat looked as if he had seen a ghost.

'She belonged to a cell of the Black Terror that met regularly through the spring and summer of 1910 at different venues in Yalta.'

'I don't believe it.'

'It's true.' Ruzsky was enjoying his power to shock, even if he wasn't enjoying much else. 'The question that I have is a simple one. Who was responsible for vetting her before she took up her post in the nursery here?'

'She was only here a short time. I could never have—'

'Who was responsible for ensuring she had the correct security clearance to take a job working in close daily contact with the heir to the throne? The chief of police in the town, isn't that so?'

'She was from Yalta,' the man answered defensively. 'She'd lived here all her life. We naturally assumed that if there was anything amiss it would have come to the attention of the chief of police. And, of course, Mr Vasilyev is now . . .' He trailed off, not wishing to offer a criticism.

'The information that I have just given you,' Ruzsky said, 'was gleaned from Mr Vasilyev's files here in Yalta.'

The official pressed a forefinger to the skin above his lip, as if smoothing an imaginary moustache.

Ruzsky left him. He wanted to find Pavel. He wanted to find Pavel *now*.

On the journey down the hill, Ruzsky rested his head on the seatback of the horse-drawn cab and gazed up at the unblemished sky. The path was dusty and the cab threw up a cloud behind it, which was blown gently across the rocky scrubland. He considered the possibility that Ella had once been a police agent, but could not see it. The girl of his imagination, and of her mother's description, was too timid for such a thing. And yet she'd continued in her doomed love affair against the wishes of her family, had stolen something intensely personal from the most powerful woman in Russia – or had tried to.

The cab stopped in front of the hotel and Ruzsky climbed down into the street. He paid the driver and noticed that a different man sat behind the red and white stall on the promenade. He seemed to be avoiding Ruzsky's eye, even though the street was almost deserted.

Ruzsky put the change into his pocket. He watched the group of boys he'd seen earlier climb the steps from the beach and walk off in the direction he'd just come. He patted the cabbie's horse, then moved slowly into the hotel lobby.

He knew people were watching – everyone seemed suddenly too busy and the air of indolence had been replaced by one of unnatural industry. Only the palm trees still swaying in the gentle breeze bore witness to the hotel's normally relaxed atmosphere.

Ruzsky approached the desk. The clerk gave him a frozen smile.

He heard himself ask if his colleague had returned, but now, when the man shook his head, Ruzsky could see that he was lying.

The world seemed to turn more slowly. Ruzsky felt the screeching in his ears that he remembered from the day of Ilya's death – and had the sense that everything around him was disintegrating.

He watched his boots as he climbed the stone steps.

The first-floor landing was deserted, the window still open, another palm swaying in the breeze. A fan turned on the ceiling above him.

He crossed the wooden floor towards Pavel's room. He heard his own knock on the green door, although he could barely feel the impact on his knuckles.

There was no reply.

He knocked again, then harder. 'Pavel.' He waited. 'Pavel!' he shouted. He reached inside his jacket for his revolver. 'Pavel!' he bellowed. The corridor and the room within remained silent. No one had come to investigate the shouting. Ruzsky put his shoulder to the door and shoved. He stepped back and kicked it. He tried again with his shoulder and suddenly it gave.

The room was dark: the thick embroidered curtains were drawn. Pavel Miliutin lay face down on the bed, an arm trailing to the floor.

Ruzsky did not move. The silent breeze cooled his face. His head spun and he pushed himself forward. He opened his mouth to shout, but no sound came out.

He reached his friend and heaved him over roughly, pitching him on to the floor.

The sunlight spilled on to his face. Pavel opened his eyes. 'Sandro?' His breath reeked of vodka.

Ruzsky stood up, gave him a kick, then slumped on to the bed. He saw the bottle on the floor beside him. 'You idiot,' he said.

Pavel hauled himself up, frowning. He rubbed his eyes. 'Why didn't you answer the door?' Ruzsky snapped.

'What time is it?'

'Time I got a new deputy.'

346

'What happened to the door?'

'You didn't answer when I knocked. Everyone in the lobby was behaving as if they knew something I didn't.'

'They've been like that for days.' Pavel yawned. 'They know we're being watched.'

Ruzsky strode forward and tore back the curtain from the window. He picked up his revolver from where he had dropped it and went out on to the balcony. The red and white stall on the promenade had disappeared. The street was deserted, the light fading. There was no sign of life. Even the waves seemed quieter.

He came back into the room. The last of the sunlight illuminated Pavel's creased face.

They both heard the footsteps of someone running in the street and Ruzsky looked down to see a man in a dark suit – young, with long hair – sprinting with his arm stretched back behind his shoulder.

For a moment, he was paralysed, his eyes on the black cylinder as it left the man's hand.

Ruzsky took two quick paces and hit Pavel, knocking him to the floor as the bomb thumped against the wooden frame of the balcony door, then fell to the ground.

There was a moment's silence.

The explosion sucked the air from the room, filling it instead with a deafening roar.

Ruzsky moved his arms first and was relieved to find he could feel the broken glass around him. He tried to push himself to his feet and was able to do so without pain. He could find no injuries, except some blood on his face. He put his hand to the wall to steady himself.

Pavel was staring at him, his face white. 'All right?' Ruzsky asked, but his ears were ringing.

The curtain still twisted in the breeze, but the windows had been shattered, along with the wood-work of the door. Pavel pushed himself to his feet. It was clear to both men that they had been saved by the way the bomb had bounced back off the window-frame before it exploded, the force of the blast twisting the balcony's iron balustrade.

Ruzsky picked up his revolver and walked towards the door across the broken glass, but Pavel moved swiftly to intercept him, a giant hand upon his shoulder. 'Where in the hell do you think you're going?' he bellowed. He had specks of broken glass in his beard.

'Let's find him.'

'No. They'll be waiting for us.' It was clear to Ruzsky that Pavel was not going to let go of him.

'If we catch the boy, we can find who sent him.'

'We know who did.' Pavel prised Ruzsky's gun from his hand and shoved it into his pocket, then wedged the door shut as best he could. He man-handled Ruzsky across the room, pushed him into the chair and sat on the bed.

They watched the red sun sink towards the bay. The wind was still fresh, the world around them quiet. There were hushed voices in the road outside.

'No one is coming,' Ruzsky said.

Pavel did not answer.

The voices died away and only the sound of the waves disturbed the peace.

'No one from the hotel has been up,' Ruzsky said.

Pavel still didn't respond.

'Nor Godorkin.'

Pavel stood. He took out his own revolver and handed Ruzsky's back to him, then brushed the glass from his clothes and beard.

'What should we do?' Ruzsky felt disoriented. He was conscious of how rarely he had looked to Pavel for a lead.

'They're waiting for us,' Pavel said, 'so we're not going to give them the satisfaction of wandering out.' He moved to the door. 'I'll have a look round. You stay here.'

He pulled back the broken door and his footsteps receded in the corridor. After he'd gone, Ruzsky took out a cigarette and smoked it. The night brought a chill to the air, but he didn't move. Moonlight crept through the shadow, the smoke melting into it. He wondered where she was.

He heard more footsteps in the corridor and forced himself to concentrate. He moved as quietly as he could into the darkest corner, facing the door.

The man was moving fast, with steady, straight-forward steps. The door was pushed back and Pavel's bulky figure was silhouetted against the light. 'I can't see anyone,' he said. 'There's an alley we can reach from the balcony on the first floor of the far wing.'

A shot rang out, the bullet thumping against what was left of the woodwork around the window, then ricocheting inside. Pavel slammed himself back against the wall.

Ruzsky stood up. Without a word, he tugged at his partner's coat and dragged him to the door. 'We'll gain nothing by staying.'

Pavel led the way down the corridor outside, into the darkness of the opposite wing. One of the long windows at the far end was creaking in the breeze.

Pavel reached it and looked down at the alley below. 'Swing from the balcony, drop and then run. I'll go first.'

'No.' Ruzsky pulled him back roughly. 'You watch.' He glanced up and down the lane. On the far side, a tobacconist's sign swung from a long wooden pole.

He stepped out on to the balcony, jumped off and landed quietly in the dust. The sea glinted in the moonlight and the only sound was the gentle roll of waves on the shore. He crossed to the other side and watched as Pavel jumped.

Ruzsky pointed down the alley to indicate the direction they should go, then led the way, trying to keep to the shadows. He glanced round the corner. Light spilled from the back of the hotel in a wide arc. He left the shelter of the wall and began to walk away. He heard a shout, then a shot. He ducked his head and ran, turning to check that Pavel was still with him. He pounded over the river, swung left on to Yalta's fashionable Pushkinskaya Street, then right into a narrow alley that led off it. He slowed as he ran up the hill into the warren of Tartar houses. They rounded another corner and Ruzsky pulled Pavel to the ground beside him. They looked back down the slope, breathing heavily.

Two men in dark suits and fedoras dashed into the light. Ruzsky aimed carefully at the first. He fired once and watched the man fold. The other ducked into the shadows and shouted for assistance.

Ruzsky pulled Pavel to his feet. They ran again, the alleys getting narrower and steeper, criss-crossed by lines of washing.

There were more shouts behind them. Pavel hissed, 'Stop,' his voice low, but hoarse. Ruzsky waited while his partner regained his breath.

A window opened above and the alley was bathed in light. A woman looked out and saw them standing in the darkness opposite, heard the shouts of their pursuers. She stared at them, then pulled the shutters closed again.

'Come on,' Ruzsky said.

They moved at a slower pace, but the warren of alleys gave them the advantage. At the top of the hill, Ruzsky led them across the road and into the shelter of a cypress tree.

They sat against its trunk, trying to catch their breath. Pavel's forehead glistened with sweat. Ruzsky watched the road. They heard a horse whinny, then saw a cab race up the hill to the crossroads. In the moonlight, they could see the figure of Ivan Prokopiev climbing out of the cab, the sea shimmering behind him. He was wearing a long black cloak and stood with his hands on his hips, facing the alley up which they had just run. The horse breathed heavily from the exertion, snorting into the night air.

Two of their pursuers emerged.

'No sign,' one said, in response to Prokopiev's barked question.

'Impossible,' Prokopiev said. 'Go back.'

The men began to jog down the hill. Prokopiev waited for a few minutes, then turned round. Ruzsky wondered whether he had sensed their presence, but they were well hidden.

They listened to the sound of the cicadas.

The secret policeman got back into the cab, standing tall as he looked over the town. Then he sat down, barked at the driver to continue along the straight road ahead and disappeared in a cloud of dust.

Neither Pavel nor Ruzsky moved until he was out

of sight. Then they stood up. Ruzsky considered lighting a cigarette, but thought better of it.

'Which way?' Pavel asked.

'Hold on a minute.'

'What's the point in waiting? They'll be back.'

'We're well hidden.' Ruzsky tried to gather his thoughts. The peace of the night was beguiling. 'There is something I need to do,' he said eventually. 'We can walk over the hill and get transport from there in the morning. Or you can stay here, and I'll come back for you.'

'What is it you need to do?'

'Find someone.'

'Why?'

'I'll explain when we get there.'

'Explain now. Don't tell me it's to do with the girl.'

Ruzsky didn't answer.

'Sometimes—'

'I found the names of our victims in Godorkin's files,' Ruzsky said. 'I looked through all the paperwork for 1910 and found nothing. I tried by name and still drew a blank. Then I found the political files. All three of our corpses were in a cell of the Black Terror here in Yalta.'

'The assassins?'

'Yes. The files detail meetings through the spring and summer of 1910. There are six names in the reports: Ella, the American White, Markov—'

'The one we found by the Lion Bridge?'

'Yes. Then a man called Borodin, another woman and Maria Popova.'

'Your Maria?'

'Maria Popova, yes.'

Pavel was silent. They stared at the crossroads. A

crude sign had the word 'Yalta' in one direction and 'Sevastopol' in the other.

'She is a revolutionary? An assassin?'

Ruzsky did not reply.

'So, what did they do, this group?' Pavel asked.

'In the file I saw they were engaged in planning robberies. All surveillance was called off two or three weeks before it happened and there are no further references to that or anything else in the file. Then the records end.'

'So where is Maria Popova now?'

Ruzsky had an overwhelming desire to strike out on his own, but knew Pavel would never accept it. 'She said she was going to a sanatorium to see her sister.' He leant against the tree-trunk.

'Did she say which one?'

'Yes.'

'Did you know she was going to be on that train?'

Ruzsky hesitated. 'Yes.'

'Did she ask you to join her?'

'No.'

'Did she know that you would be coming to Yalta?'

'No.'

Pavel looked at him. 'If this sanatorium exists, what makes you think she'll still be there?'

Ruzsky shrugged.

'Sandro,' Pavel said, 'come on.'

'What do you mean?'

'She's one of them. She has lured you here into a trap. If she gave you the name of this sanatorium, who is to say that they won't be waiting for us when we get there?'

'I'll go alone.'

'That's not the point.' Pavel's voice was gentle. 'I

understand how you feel, but please face the facts as they are.'

'I know how it might look,' Ruzsky said softly, 'but it's not like that.'

'Love is blind.'

'I understand what you say and why, but it's—'

'It's about faith.'

'Yes.'

'Well . . . I trust your judgement. More than anyone's,' Pavel said.

'Why don't you stay here? I'll—'

'From now on, we stick together. What was Borodin doing in Yalta?'

'I don't know,' Ruzsky replied.

'This is the same man – the Bolshevik?'

'I assume so.'

'Well, what about the American? What was he doing here?'

Ruzsky shook his head.

CHAPTER THIRTY-SIX

The sanatorium stood high on the hill overlooking the bay, and Ruzsky and Pavel watched its entrance closely as the red dawn stole through the trees around them.

A nurse in a starched white apron with a cross on her chest wheeled an officer in uniform out of the wide doorway and slowly down the gravel drive. On the still morning air, Ruzsky heard a terrible, hacking cough from inside the hospital.

They could discern no sign of Prokopiev's men, but Ruzsky found it difficult to concentrate on the possibility of danger. If Maria had no sister here, as Pavel suspected, she was a liar and he'd been played for a fool.

Ruzsky nodded at Pavel and walked down the grassy bank to the curved stone porch. The sign next to the entrance announced that this was the 'Yalta Convalescent Home', but a newly painted one above the reception desk read 'The Tatyana Committee Convalescent Home'. A large icon hung on the wall next to it. The charitable initiatives of the Tsar's second daughter still had a long reach.

The elderly porter summoned a nurse. She was a stiff, formal woman in her fifties or sixties with silver hair pulled back from her forehead and tied at her neck. Ruzsky realized that he must look dishevelled and scruffy. He had not shaved and could feel the fatigue behind his eyes.

'Popova?' she said, in response to his enquiry. 'No. We have no one of that name.' She frowned in response to the desolation he could not keep from his face. An intense blanket of loneliness enveloped him. 'Who are you, may I ask?' she went on.

Ruzsky pulled out his papers. 'Chief Investigator Alexander Ruzsky,' he said quietly. 'Petrograd city police, criminal-investigation division.'

The nurse looked at his papers, examined the photograph, then checked his face. She handed them back. 'You are a long way from home, Chief Investigator.' Her voice and expression were sympathetic, as though she appreciated something of the scale of his anguish, if not its cause.

It was not possible, he told himself, that the emotion of their time at Petrovo had been an illusion. It still felt utterly real.

'What is it that you seek?'

Suddenly Ruzsky felt crushingly tired. He wondered if he should leave immediately. Was this another trap? He scanned the lobby and looked over his shoulder towards the bank where Pavel was hiding. He could make out nothing amiss.

'What is it that you want?' the nurse repeated.

'I was looking for a woman called Maria Popova,' Ruzsky said, 'but it is no matter.'

'Why do you seek her?'

Ruzsky saw that she was curious. 'I'm conducting a

356

murder investigation.'

'Is she a suspect?'

It was an odd question. 'No.'

The nurse looked at him steadily. 'I don't know a Maria Popova,' she said. 'Did you expect her to be a patient?'

'No.'

'A nurse, then?'

'No, not a nurse. She came down to Yalta from Petrograd to see her sister. She told me the girl was a patient here.'

Ruzsky saw a flicker of recognition and his pulse quickened.

'We have no one called Popova.'

'But the name is familiar to you?'

'No.'

Ruzsky waited. Then, 'The woman I seek,' he said, 'is tall, with long dark hair. She is strikingly beautiful. She—'

'We have a Catherine Bulyatina. She has a sister named Maria who came to visit her from Petrograd yesterday.'

Ruzsky's spirits rose. 'Bulyatina?'

'Yes.'

'Catherine Andreevna?' Ruzsky asked. Maria's patronymic was also Andreevna. It was too much of a coincidence. They must share the same father. One or other had changed her surname. 'The girl here is Catherine Andreevna?'

'That is correct, yes. Kitty.'

'Is she here now? Might I see her?'

'No. I'm afraid that will not be possible.'

The woman's eyes were steely. Despite his fatigue, Ruzsky tried to summon up the energy to be

357

charming. 'We have come a long way . . .' He sought her name.

'Eugenia Sergeevna.'

'Eugenia Sergeevna,' he repeated, smiling. 'It is a sad case. A young woman and her lover stabbed on the frozen river Neva.'

'I'm sorry for it.'

'It would help—'

'You said the woman is not a suspect.'

'No.' He inclined his head. 'No, she is not. But she may be at risk.'

Eugenia Sergeevna hesitated. 'You would not come all this way for such a reason.'

'She has information that may place her at risk.'

'Information that you want?'

Ruzsky did not know what answer to give. His relief that Maria had been telling the truth was clouding his mind. 'Yes.'

She seemed satisfied that he had conceded. 'It is a long journey,' she said to herself. 'Difficult in these times.' What she meant was that the reason for such a trip must be compelling. 'Why could she be at risk?'

'The victims were colleagues of hers . . . friends.'

'Friends?'

'Yes.'

'Maria Bulyatina returned to Petrograd last night.'

'Are you sure?' Ruzsky tried to keep the disappointment from his voice. But it did not matter, he assured himself. She had come here to see her sister, just as she had told him.

'I'm certain.'

'Would it really not be possible to speak to Kitty? Under your supervision, of course.'

'No, I'm afraid not. Her health is . . . fragile.'

'Miss Bulyatina must love her sister a great deal,' Ruzsky said quietly, 'to come such a long way for only one day.'

The nurse appraised him carefully. 'The war has changed many things, Detective, but not love.'

'Perhaps especially not that.'

'To make such a journey . . . yes, it is a mark of love. Sadly, it was not . . .' She checked herself. 'I must be getting back to my work. I'm sorry we cannot be of more assistance.'

Ruzsky was taken aback by the sudden change in her mood. 'Would you ask Kitty if she would speak to me?'

'No. I'm afraid that would not be appropriate.'

'Have you known the family long?'

'No,' she said.

Eugenia Sergeevna had half turned away. She stopped. 'Maria Bulyatina is truly at risk?' she asked.

'Yes.'

'Why?'

Ruzsky thought carefully. This was not a woman to be fobbed off with half-truths. 'A group of people she was once involved with . . . some time ago, here in Yalta, have become the targets of a killer. Three have been murdered already, in Petrograd. So far as we can tell, the group had only three other members. Maria was one of them.'

'What kind of group?'

'A . . . political group.'

'Revolutionaries?'

He hesitated once more. 'Yes.'

'Bolsheviks?'

'It is not clear.'

359

Eugenia considered this. 'She did not strike me as that type of girl.'

'No.'

'You know her?'

'A little.'

'It's not possible.'

It was heartening to hear someone so formidable echoing his own judgement, Ruzsky thought.

'You wish to arrest her?'

'No.'

'You are a policeman, however.'

'But not an agent of the Okhrana.'

Eugenia's nose wrinkled, and Ruzsky thought it a revealing gesture. If you wanted to know the depths of opprobrium to which the Imperial Crown had fallen even in the eyes of ordinary, decent, middle-class Russians, it was only necessary to mention the name of the Emperor's secret police. It was more respectable to be a revolutionary, no matter how violent.

The woman assessed him for a moment more. 'Very well, Chief Investigator. Kitty may tell you what she wishes. It is a decision for her. I will say no more than that.'

She led him out of the door and past a neatly tended lawn. Ruzsky tried to keep pace with her. 'The sanatorium has been renamed,' he said.

'Funds were provided.'

'By the Tatyana Committee?'

'There are some officers here.'

As Ruzsky rounded the corner of the terrace, the sight of her stopped him in his tracks.

Maria stood in front of the steps down to the lower part of the garden by a long line of tall palm trees. She was dressed in white, fringed by the rich dawn light, long, dark hair tumbling down her back.

Eugenia Sergeevna was still walking towards her. 'Kitty?' she said.

The woman turned. It was not Maria, but the likeness was striking: the same eyes, the same hair and cheeks – the same soft skin delicately lit by the dawn sky.

Ruzsky opened his mouth to introduce himself, but no sound came out.

The look in her eyes was different – it was distant, almost ethereal – but in all other respects she was so like Maria that they might have been twins. 'Kitty,' Eugenia said softly, 'this is Chief Investigator Ruzsky from Petrograd.'

The girl offered her hand, tilted her head to one side, smiled, then sat down on the wicker chair behind. 'Hello,' she said, her response delayed, as if her mind worked only slowly. Ruzsky sat on an adjoining chair.

Eugenia's face radiated concern. 'The chief investigator was asking after your sister, Maria.'

Kitty looked at him for what seemed like an age, her guileless stare as unselfconscious as that of a child.

'He has come from Petrograd,' Eugenia went on. 'He is trying to help your sister.'

'My sister?'

'Yes, my dear.'

Kitty shook her head very slowly. 'No . . . that is not possible.'

Eugenia's face was gentle, but commanding. 'He is trying to assist her, Kitty.'

'No . . . That is not possible, Eugenia Sergeevna.'

'My dear . . .'

Without warning, Kitty crumpled into a ball, clutching her knees and resting her head on the side of the chair, tears in her eyes. Ruzsky forced himself to remain seated.

Eugenia touched her hand. Ruzsky noticed the scars on the girl's wrists.

The only sound was the distant murmur of the sea.

'My dear, she came to see you yesterday,' the nurse whispered again.

'No . . .'

'She travelled all the way from Petrograd.'

'Did she?' Kitty sounded as if she wanted to believe it.

Eugenia glanced at Ruzsky.

'But I do not have a sister, you know that, don't you?'

Kitty turned towards Ruzsky, and he saw now that she was the victim Maria had fought to prevent herself becoming. 'I understand,' he said.

'Do you?'

'I believe so.'

Kitty scrutinized his face with greater interest. 'Who is it that you seek?'

'Maria Andreevna.'

'It's a common patronymic.'

'Yes. Of course.'

'What has she done, this Maria Andreevna?'

'Nothing.'

'Then why do you seek her?'

'Because I fear for her safety.' Ruzsky waited patiently.

'I have no family,' she said. 'Ask anyone here.'

'How long have you been in this hospital, Kitty?'

She did not answer.

'Your sister or . . .' Ruzsky stopped as her lips tightened. 'This Maria Andreevna came a long way to see you.'

Kitty's face was still.

'Do you know why she came?'

Ruzsky watched Kitty struggle with herself.

'What did she say to you?'

'I have no sister,' she repeated.

'What did Maria Andreevna say to you?'

'I don't remember.'

Ruzsky waited for her to expand, but she remained silent, her eyes on the line of palm trees that fringed the sea. 'You came here after your parents died?'

A tear formed in the corner of her eye.

'You lived in a white house overlooking the sea,' Ruzsky said softly. 'Isn't that so? With neatly tended lawns, open windows and a mother with the voice of an angel.'

Tears fell down Kitty's cheeks. She bowed her head. Ruzsky had an overwhelming desire to comfort her, but he remained seated.

Eugenia pulled Kitty to her feet and laid the girl's head on her shoulder, her face concealed by the long dark hair. She stroked Kitty's head until the sobbing eased. 'It's all right,' she said. 'It's all right.'

Ruzsky stared at the ground. 'I apologize, madam.'

Eugenia glanced at him, her expression sympathetic, then took Kitty's hand and led her slowly across the terrace.

At the doorway, Kitty stopped and looked back, strands of hair blown across her face. Then she followed Eugenia inside.

Ruzsky waited. It was a few minutes before the

nurse returned. She sat down and straightened her uniform again. 'Would you like some tea, Chief Investigator?'

Ruzsky felt as though he had damaged something priceless. 'I'm sorry,' he said. 'I did not fully understand.'

'She has blocked the past from her mind. The last twenty-four hours have been . . .' Eugenia's voice trailed off.

'She is here because she harms herself?'

'Yes, and because she is too fragile to live in normal society.'

'And she has never acknowledged her family?'

'I cannot say that Kitty has never acknowledged her family, only that she does not do so any longer. Maria's visit was . . . difficult. She stayed only a short time.'

'Were you privy to what they discussed?'

'No. Maria asked to be left alone with her sister. Afterwards, they were both . . . well, I do not think it was easy for either of them.'

'Did Kitty talk about it?'

'No.'

Ruzsky took out his silver cigarette case and offered it to her. She hesitated for a moment, then reached forward to take one. Ruzsky lit it and watched as she sucked the smoke into her lungs and relaxed. 'You have worked here long?' he asked.

'Eight months.'

'You're from Yalta?'

'No. I worked in field hospitals before.'

'Whereabouts?'

'In different places. Galicia, close to the front line.' She looked at him with pain in her eyes.

'How long will you stay?'

'I leave at the end of the month to return to the front.' Her face showed anxiety now: Kitty would lose a protector.

'Kitty will stay here?'

'She will be well looked after,' Eugenia said, but seemed unconvinced of it.

'You discussed her situation with Maria?'

'Yes, of course.' She drew heavily on the cigarette again.

Ruzsky tried to ascertain the cause of her apprehension. 'Maria was concerned? That is why she came all this way?'

Eugenia looked at him. 'She came to say goodbye.'

Ruzsky felt the colour drain from his face.

'She did not say as much to Kitty, of course, but that is what she told me. She promised to wire money, but what can we do?' Eugenia shrugged hopelessly. 'I did my best to reassure her, but could not make the promise that she asked for. I cannot stay any longer. All of the staff move on – it is the way of things. How can we know who will be here in five months, let alone five years? Kitty is still young. God willing, her life will be long.'

'I don't understand. Why did she come to say goodbye? Where did she say she was going?'

'She did not explain. Maria said only that she wanted to settle things, to be sure that Kitty would always be all right. She was very sad. She was crying. "But if there is a revolution," she kept saying, taking my hand, "what then? Can't you stay? Who can I find who will always be here?"'

'Why did she say that?'

'I don't know.'

'What did she mean about wiring the money?'

'This is a private sanatorium, Chief Investigator. The Tatyana Committee pays for the officers who are recovering here, but other patients' fees have to be met from personal funds. Kitty was only moved here a short time ago and Maria came to see that she was well cared-for. She wanted to give us enough money in one transfer to ensure that her sister would always be looked after here but . . .'

'It would be a sizeable sum. Kitty's parents are dead?'

'Yes.'

'They were—'

'I don't know the details.'

'Would it be possible, do you think, to see Kitty's personal file? It would be most—'

'No. We could not do that.' Another nurse had come on to the terrace and was waving at Eugenia to indicate that her presence was required. She stubbed out the cigarette beneath her foot, then brushed the ash from her white blouse.

'It would be helpful to ascertain whether she has other relatives.'

'Maria said she had no other family here.'

'So Kitty never talks about her past, her family . . .'

'Chief Investigator, I would like to help, but there is nothing I can tell you.' Eugenia stood up. 'I'm sorry.' She offered her hand. 'Good luck.'

As they shook hands, Ruzsky saw, once again, in her eyes the strain caused by too great an acquaintance with tragedy. The nurse who had appeared so strong and calm in the hallway was agitated now. She hurried away.

* * *

Pavel was waiting at the top of the bank beneath the shelter of a tall fir tree. Ruzsky crouched beside him.

'She wasn't there?' Pavel asked.

'No, but she had been.' Ruzsky looked back towards the entrance to the sanatorium and saw Kitty's face in the window above the doorway. She was watching him, her nose pressed to the glass. Pavel saw her too.

'I need to go back into the town,' Ruzsky said.

'Sandro—'

'Just for a few more hours.'

'Sandro, come on.' Pavel stood up, his bulk imposing. 'Maybe Maria was telling you the truth, but she's still a revolutionary. Groups like the Black Terror used to blow officials like your father to the four winds.'

'I know but—'

'Please. Think about it. Prokopiev's men will be crawling all over the town. We have found what we came in search of. All of the victims were revolutionaries. The question is, what were they doing in Petersburg? What had they gathered for? If the murders are the key to something bigger, the answer is not here. This is a trap. Don't you see it?'

'But why were they killed?'

'I don't know, but the answer is in Petersburg.'

'Why do you assume that?'

Pavel frowned. 'Well, why did they come back? The American, the man we found at the Lion Bridge . . .'

Ruzsky was still staring at Kitty. He thought of the nurse's assertion that Maria had come to say goodbye. He clung to the fact that Maria had been telling him the truth about her sister. Had she wanted him to come here? Had she wished him to meet Kitty?

Pavel put his arm round Ruzsky's shoulders and pulled him away.

As they walked down on to the drive, Ruzsky looked back once more at the entrance to the sanatorium. Kitty was still there, her hand resting against the glass, as if waving goodbye.

CHAPTER THIRTY-SEVEN

Pavel and Ruzsky stood side by side looking out of the dirty barred window at the spires of Russia's capital, which were indistinct against a pale, lifeless sky. They did not converse, because, even at this speed, their carriage, a goods wagon, proved an almost total bar to audible forms of communication. They had assumed that the station at Sevastopol would be watched and had gone to Simferopol instead. They had waited several hours before boarding a train bound for Moscow. From there, only troop trains had been moving. In all, it had taken a full two days to get home. They'd passed the last section of the journey to Petrograd in extreme cold and discomfort.

It was instructive, Ruzsky thought, that this carriage was empty. Why wasn't the government using it to bring food into the city?

They jumped down from the wagon as it rolled into the Nicholas station and clambered over to the edge of the track. Ahead of them, amid clouds of steam rising to the glass and iron roof of the station concourse, a lone guard furled and unfurled his flag. An engine's hooter boomed, but the train on the platform did not move.

Ruzsky and Pavel slipped through a narrow passage between two wooden warehouses, the pungent aroma of engine soot and rye bread carried on the breeze. As they passed the low entrance to one of the warehouses, Ruzsky stopped. Every inch of his body ached. The rye bread was in a tin bucket just by the door, but the air was now thick with the smell of cheap tobacco and putrefaction. There was a cough, quickly answered by another. Ruzsky peered into the gloom. Inside, hundreds of wounded soldiers were lying on makeshift pallets on the freezing mud. The men stared at him. There was more coughing.

Outside, a railway worker was walking in their direction, a giant metal mallet over his shoulder. He wore a quilted winter coat, with a sheepskin hat pushed back from his forehead. A cigarette hung from his lip.

Perhaps Ruzsky's face framed an unspoken query, because the man answered: 'They said they were moving them to Moscow.' He spat out his cigarette and continued past them towards the tracks. 'Prisoners of war,' he shouted. 'Escaped from the Germans and treated no better than animals.'

Ruzsky and Pavel tipped themselves over the edge of a low iron fence and trudged down the snowy embankment to the road beyond. The country was falling apart. Ruzsky couldn't help recalling again the ecstasy in those faces in Palace Square as the Tsar read out the declaration of war. War was not an instrument of foreign policy. It was a national disease.

Icy winds cut through their overcoats as they mingled with the crowds moving down Ligovskaya. Ruzsky waved at a *droshky* driver waiting outside the station. Eventually, the man saw them and snapped his reins to bring his horse to attention. 'Ofitserskaya Ulitsa, twenty-eight,' Pavel instructed him, as they climbed into the back.

'Forty-five copecks.'

The *vanka* had a thick, black beard and the hollow eyes of an alcoholic addicted to the worst kind of moonshine.

'You're not serious?' Pavel asked. *Vankas* always haggled, but the quoted price was at least double the going rate. This wasn't the game.

'It's far.'

'It's a mile at most.'

The man was still looking at them. 'I know the building. I don't carry *pharaon* in my cab.'

Ruzsky and Pavel stared at him. *Pharaon* was an insulting street-slang name for policemen, usually reserved for members of the Okhrana. They were shocked by the man's audacity and that he had included them in the same bracket.

Ruzsky leant forward. 'Twenty copecks says you'll take us.'

The man spat noisily into the snow beside them. They set off down the Nevsky in silence.

Ruzsky thought the capital surpassed itself in bleak greyness, snow and sky melting into each other. The city's inhabitants were mere bundles of rags hurrying to be out of the wind. One of the single-deck buses pulled by a team of horses had veered into the course of a tram and there had been a minor collision, which they had to work their way round. The passengers of both vehicles were shouting at the bus driver.

As they came close to the wooden pavement, Ruzsky saw a small group of students coming out of

Filippov's bakery. There were three girls dressed in the distinctive wide green robes of seniors at the Smolny Institute and two boys in the uniforms of cadets at the Corps des Pages. The sight of them brought back vivid memories. For some reason, Ruzsky recalled rounding the corner of the washroom to see Dmitri suspended naked from a chain, upside down, while some of the senior cadets beat him with leather whips. He had been thinking of his brother on the journey home, nagged by lingering guilt about his liaison with Maria. On that winter day at the Corps des Pages Ruzsky had fought to free his brother. The cadets had been seniors and the fight had proved the final nail in the coffin of his military career.

Ruzsky noticed that Pavel was watching him. His expression was quizzical, but when Ruzsky frowned he looked away.

The sled swung past the Kazan cathedral and slithered along the banks of the frozen canal. Ruzsky buried his face in the collar of his jacket and pulled his sheepskin hat down over his eyes. He could feel the stubble on his chin scratching against his neck and his bones ached from the relentless rattle of the goods wagon.

He found himself fantasizing about vodka. He glanced at Pavel. His partner's eyes carried the same message as they had throughout the journey: *How in hell did you get us into this?*

As Pavel paid off the cabbie outside their office, Ruzsky hurried into a lobby so silent they could have heard a pin drop.

The entire department had gathered to hear Anton address them and Ruzsky was confronted by a sea of solemn faces. They stood loosely in groups; cooks, transport boys from the stables, secretaries and typists, even the cleaners. There was tension in every face.

Maretsky stood next to Anton. Clearly he had seen Ruzsky come in, but avoided his eye as he played with his pocket watch. Vladimir and his assistant stood a few feet away. Only Stanislav was absent.

'Thank you all for coming,' Anton said. His fingers were in his waistcoat pockets, his jacket pulled back, a confident stance that failed to conceal his nerves. 'First a piece of unwelcome administrative news, which most of you will already be aware of and will certainly not surprise you. All leave has been cancelled for the foreseeable future. This applies to every member of the department and is by direct order of the minister of the interior.' His face softened a little as he shifted his weight on to one leg, then back again. 'I know it is some years since many of you had any leave and quite a number have made requests in the past few weeks.' He lowered his voice. 'We will ensure leave entitlements are taken once the war is won and the current uncertainty brought to an end.'

He surveyed the room. 'On a more positive note, I have approved an order to allow all members of staff to pick up one loaf of bread every second day from the canteen here after six in the morning. I hope this will do something to alleviate the circumstances that I know many of your families have found themselves in.'

He cleared his throat. 'As to the reason for calling you together like this, I am instructed to inform you that this afternoon approximately ten thousand workers from five armaments factories in Vyborg will come out on strike. Shortly after dark they will gather outside the gates of the Symnov factory. There will be

373

an inflammatory speech and then, most workers imagine, they will disperse.

'In fact, they will be led over the Alexandrovsky Bridge and towards the Winter Palace, where the leaders will attempt to incite the crowd to the point where bloodshed is inevitable. It is the intention of the Okhrana that they will be intercepted long before they reach Palace Square and strongly discouraged from attempting such action again.'

They all knew exactly what he meant.

'I have been asked by the ministry to *draw* this to your attention, and to be on the lookout for any peripheral troublemakers. We all know there are those who try to take advantage of any disorder, however well controlled, to engage in everyday criminality. Second, the ministry, or rather the Okhrana, believes that some of the most notorious agitators have slipped back over the border and returned to Petrograd. I am asked that you all check the suspect bulletins and sharpen your eyes. Report any sightings, at any time, anywhere, direct to me.'

Anton took a pace forward. 'Are there any questions?'

The speech had not invited questions and there were none. Anton walked towards the stairs, the crowd ahead of Ruzsky parting to allow him through. It was only as Anton stopped next to him that Ruzsky realized Pavel was beside him. 'I'd like to see you two, please.'

They followed him.

Anton passed the secretaries outside his office without acknowledgement and turned to shut the door behind them. He ran his hands through his hair. 'An explanation, please.'

Maretsky slipped into the room and shut the door. Pavel leant back against the wall, Anton the desk. Ruzsky did not move.

'I know exactly where you've been, by the way.' Anton went round to the other side of the desk and slumped into his chair. He threw down his glasses and pressed his hands into his eyes. 'What have you got us involved in? Do you have any idea how many times the palace has rung me? Colonel Shulgin has called twice, every day, without fail. The *Empress* would like to know, Anton Antipovich, how the investigation into the death of the girl Ella Kovyil is progressing? Where are the two detectives who came out to Tsarskoe Selo? They are in *Yalta*? What are they doing in Yalta?' Anton picked up his glasses. 'Then Vasilyev telephones. He'd like to speak to the chief investigator, please. That isn't possible? Why is it not possible? He has taken a few days' leave? But all leave is cancelled by direct order of the minister of the interior. Why have they disobeyed regulations?'

'Vasilyev knew exactly where we were.'

Anton flicked his glasses with his hand, sending them flying on to the floor. Pavel picked them up and put them back on the desk.

'He tried to have us killed,' Ruzsky added.

Now Anton seemed lost in the depiction of Napoleon's retreat from Moscow.

Ruzsky took out and lit a cigarette. When offered the case Pavel refused, as did Anton. 'We found a file in Yalta,' Ruzsky said. 'It contained details of the activities of a small cell of the Black Terror. Six individuals in all, three of whom are the corpses we have here. Vasilyev kept the group under surveillance until three weeks before an armed robbery, then nothing.'

'I don't understand. What are you saying? The implication is . . . you think Vasilyev . . . What?'

'It's possible he was involved with the group in some way, or became involved. I cannot say exactly.'

'And the three corpses we have here were all members of this group?'

'Yes.'

'So what happened to them?' Anton asked. 'What were they doing in Petrograd?'

'It appears they had gathered here for some purpose. We don't yet know what it was.'

'Who are the other three?'

'A man named Borodin. Michael Borodin.'

'He's a Bolshevik.'

'Yes. A woman named Olga Legarina.'

They were silent.

'And who is the sixth?' Anton asked.

'We don't know.'

Pavel looked at Ruzsky sharply. He instantly regretted the lie, but found himself unable, or unwilling, to correct it.

'You don't know?'

'The name was impossible to read.'

'Did you bring the documents with you?'

'No.'

Anton rubbed his forehead. Ruzsky could see the tiredness in his eyes.

'We have three bodies,' Ruzsky said. 'Before long, we may have more.'

'What evidence do you have for that claim?'

'The American was stabbed seventeen times. Markov's head was almost severed. Three of the group have been murdered, but three remain.'

'They're revolutionaries,' Anton said.

Ruzsky imagined Maria's body sprawled on the ice as Ella's had been, a knife wound to her chest. He recalled the fear in her face on the night he had followed her outside the Mariinskiy.

Anton pulled his seat to the edge of his desk and reached for the telephone. 'We have to go and see Vasilyev.'

'Vasilyev?' Ruzsky asked.

'Shulgin is with him. They telephoned me about an hour ago. They want all of us to go over. Maretsky and Sarlov, too.'

'I can't,' Ruzsky said, standing. 'I have—'

'Sit down, Sandro,' Anton said. 'You're not going anywhere.'

Pavel and Ruzsky waited with Maretsky in their office for Sarlov to arrive. Maretsky stood by the door, smoking, while Ruzsky and Pavel sorted through the paperwork that had accumulated in their absence. Ruzsky found a thick wad of internal memoranda, a few more, belated, responses to the all-stations missing-persons bulletin he had posted, but nothing that related directly to the case. He opened the drawer and took out the roll of banknotes they had found on the dead American. He sifted through them again, carefully examining the numbers that had been marked.

'Did you come up with a translation of that inscription?' Ruzsky asked Maretsky.

The little professor frowned.

'I gave you the knife. It had an inscription on the side.'

'Oh, yes. I . . . er, I gave it to a former colleague at the university.'

377

'Who?'

'Professor . . . Egorov.'

'What did he say?'

'He's out of town today. He promised to telephone me tomorrow.'

There was an unusual degree of hesitation in the professor's voice. Ruzsky leant back in his chair. 'You know Borodin?'

'Of course.'

'He's a Bolshevik or a Menshevik?'

'Oh, a Bolshevik. A colleague of Ulyanov's over the years.'

'You've discussed him with the Okhrana?'

'No, no.' Maretsky shook his head. 'Too sensitive.'

'So in their definition he's a revolutionary, not a criminal.'

Maretsky shrugged. 'It has never been discussed, Sandro.'

Ruzsky held up the roll of banknotes. 'Do the Bolsheviks use ciphers?'

'What do you mean?'

'These numbers on the banknotes.'

Maretsky looked mystified.

'I think these numbers could represent some kind of code. Have the Bolsheviks used ciphers to communicate in the past?

'I don't know . . . yes, I'm sure.'

'Would the money have been sent to him by mail? Would it have been left for him somewhere? How is it done?'

Maretsky shook his head.

'What about the reference book? He would have carried it with him in his luggage?'

'They will almost certainly go into a library to

decode anything they receive. It's safer.'

As Ruzsky had thought, Maretsky knew more about this subject than he wanted to let on. Most revolutionaries, as far as he knew, used a cipher to communicate. Since the Okhrana intercepted and checked most letters, it was the only reliable means of relaying a message in secret.

'If Borodin is the leader, he would have chosen the code reference book?'

'Perhaps. I don't know.'

'The American must therefore be able to go into a library and decode a message sent by his leader. Correct?'

Maretsky shrugged.

'Are you sure he could not have kept the reference work on him?'

'There would be no security in that.'

'So he might have received a new message anywhere. He would have had to go to a library to decode it.'

'I suppose so.'

'He might have picked up a new message here. When he arrived, perhaps.'

'Perhaps.'

'An English text in a Russian library?' Ruzsky asked.

'Who is to say it was an English text? White must have spoken Russian.' Maretsky seemed not to understand what his colleague was driving at.

'You would commonly find English texts in a Russian library, but not Russian texts in an American or European one.'

Maretsky thought about this. Despite himself, he was being drawn into the conversation. He stared at the floor, deep in thought.

'Major works of English fiction,' Ruzsky suggested.

'Perhaps,' Maretsky mused. 'The Bible's too complicated – too many different editions and they wouldn't
have an English Bible in Germany or France.
Academic books . . . hard to think of many that you
could guarantee you'd find everywhere.'

'So, which author would he choose?' Ruzsky said.

'I see your train of thought, but it's an impossible
task.'

Sarlov put his head round the door. 'Come on. He
wants to go.'

CHAPTER THIRTY-EIGHT

On the top floor of the Okhrana's headquarters, the dull afternoon sun fringed Vasilyev's cropped head. The chief of the secret police stood with his hands clasped behind his back, his shoulders hunched, his squat, round body blocking light from the window.

'Good day, gentlemen,' he said.

Ahead, about eight or nine chairs had been assembled in a circle. Colonel Shulgin was already seated and, next to him, the assistant minister of finance in a dark morning suit. Prokopiev stood behind them and Ruzsky knew that he and Vasilyev were gauging his reaction to his father's presence.

Ruzsky nodded towards Shulgin, then his father. 'Your High Excellency,' he said. He sat as the other members of the city police took their places at either side of him. Shulgin shuffled his papers, glancing through them as if to refresh his memory.

Vasilyev and Prokopiev followed suit. As they did so, Ruzsky caught his father's eye: deep unease lurked in it.

Ruzsky adjusted his overcoat. He had his revolver in one pocket and the police-department crime-scene photographs in the other. Both were digging into his ribs.

'Gentlemen,' Vasilyev said, surveying them carefully, 'we know why we are here. Perhaps the chief investigator would like to tell us what he has discovered.' He took a white handkerchief from his pocket and dabbed his face. Ruzsky detected the scent of cologne. Vasilyev ran a finger across his forehead, along the line of his scar.

'We have continued to investigate the case,' Ruzsky said carefully, 'by express order of Her Imperial Majesty.'

The room was hushed, but Ruzsky saw a muscle flex in Vasilyev's cheek. 'You have been to Yalta?' he asked.

'Yes.'

'And what took you there?'

Ruzsky looked at the pale blue eyes, as steady and inanimate as crystal. 'We had reason to believe that there was a connection between all three murder victims.'

'And did that prove to be correct?'

Ruzsky looked at Prokopiev, then Pavel. 'Yes,' he said, 'it did.'

'Perhaps you would like to give us a few more details?'

Prokopiev, Ruzsky calculated, would have spoken to Godorkin in Yalta. They must know exactly what he'd discovered. 'The victims were all members of a cell of the Black Terror.'

Vasilyev glanced at Shulgin, then at his father, and Ruzsky sensed that this was all for their benefit. 'You once kept them under surveillance,' he added.

No one spoke. Ruzsky realized that Shulgin and his

382

father were already aware of this. 'The American,' Shulgin said, turning towards Vasilyev, 'from . . .'

'Chicago,' Vasilyev replied.

'Yes. How did he first meet the girl Ella? How did he come to be in Yalta?'

'White's mother bore the maiden name Kovyil.'

Ruzsky frowned. Was it the case that even Mrs Kovyil had lied to him? She had given the impression that the American had been a stranger to her.

'So, White's mother was originally from Yalta?' Shulgin asked.

Vasilyev nodded.

'How did she end up in Chicago?'

'She met a sailor.'

'White and the girl Ella were *not* lovers, then?'

'They were cousins. That doesn't stop them being lovers.'

Shulgin considered this. He looked at the papers in front of him.

'We were told by the Americans,' Vasilyev went on, 'that some influential people in the USA would have liked to talk to White, had they been given the opportunity. Executives of a large steel company for one.'

'What did he do to them?'

'He kidnapped one of the men's sons,' Prokopiev interjected, 'a boy of six, then cut him into small pieces and delivered him to his home in a canvas sack.' He turned towards Ruzsky. Had that been intended as a threat? Ruzsky wondered.

They were silent again. Ruzsky's father stared at the table.

'This Friday,' Shulgin said. 'In three days. That is . . .'

Vasilyev nodded gravely. 'That is what our intelligence would suggest.'

Ruzsky wanted to ask a question, but held his tongue.

'We expect it to begin on Friday?'

'Yes.'

'What to begin?' Ruzsky asked.

Shulgin faced him. 'It is of no import to the investigation.'

'But how can we—'

'It is not.' Shulgin's tone was emphatic. 'There is intelligence to suggest that antisocial elements will try to stir up trouble on Friday. At this moment it is not your concern.' Shulgin turned back to Vasilyev, indicating he would brook no further discussion. Ruzsky wondered why he had chosen to bring the subject up. Was Shulgin trying to make him aware of something? 'And this man . . .' Shulgin went on.

'Borodin,' Vasilyev said.

'Yes, still no sign?'

'No.'

Shulgin sighed. 'The murders.' He turned towards Ruzsky 'Were all three committed by the same man?' His tone was impatient now.

Ruzsky deflected the question to Sarlov. The pathologist sniffed and pushed his glasses up to the bridge of his nose. 'Yes,' he said, 'I would say so.'

'Could you expand, Sarlov?' Anton asked. Ruzsky formed the impression, as he glanced at him, that his superior had been aware of the exact direction this conversation would take.

'I cannot say for certain.' Sarlov took off his glasses. 'I did not see the body from the Lion Bridge, but from a conversation with my colleague I should say it is

384

likely that all three victims were stabbed by a man of a similar height. More than six feet tall. The nature of the wounds,' Sarlov waved his glasses, 'is the same in each case.'

'The murderer was a man?'

'Without doubt.'

Ruzsky's father leant forward. 'If the dead are revolutionaries, as you say, then the question as to who is killing them is immaterial, isn't it? Their deaths can hardly be considered a matter of the gravest concern.'

'We do not wish to give the impression that the state is indifferent to murder,' Vasilyev said, with heavy irony. It was a reference to Rasputin's aristocratic killers and the Tsar's lenient treatment of them.

'The savagery of these murders makes them a cause for public concern,' Shulgin responded evenly.

They all looked at Ruzsky.

'What do you think lies behind these murders, Alexander Nicholaevich?' Vasilyev asked.

The chief of the Okhrana stared at him, but Ruzsky refused to look away. Had the murders been the work of this man? A settling of old scores?

'Thank you for your time, gentlemen,' Vasilyev said. 'Naturally we will need to continue to work together.'

It was a moment before Ruzsky understood that they were expected to leave. As they did so, Shulgin and his father remained seated.

Outside, Ruzsky walked away swiftly, but Pavel caught up with him. 'Sandro,' he said, out of breath, 'I know what you're going to do.'

Ruzsky did not answer.

'If these murders are about what happened in Yalta, then you think she will be next.'

Ruzsky stopped.

'In any case, what was all that about?' Pavel's face was earnest and well meaning, and Ruzsky's affection for him swelled. He took out his cigarettes and offered his friend one. They smoked together, side by side, moving their feet against the cold and watching the group of their colleagues fifty yards away. Anton, Maretsky and Sarlov were waiting for their sled outside the gloomy entrance to the Okhrana's headquarters. They, too, were huddled together and Ruzsky had the impression they were ignoring Pavel and him.

'Why have they changed their tune?' Pavel asked. 'The Okhrana, I mean.'

'They haven't.'

'Then why do they want us to co-operate?'

'They don't.'

'So, what was it all about?'

Ruzsky watched Anton, Maretsky and Sarlov get into the sled. 'I'm not certain.'

'Do you think Shulgin has forced them to co-operate?'

'No.'

'Why not?'

'Because that's not how Vasilyev works. He's the spider. He spins the webs.'

Pavel seemed disheartened by this. Perhaps he had believed the investigation might be entering less stormy waters.

'I think we were there for Shulgin's benefit, all right,' Ruzsky said, 'so I would guess the Empress told him to call the meeting.'

386

'Why was your father present?' Pavel asked.

'I'm not certain. It may be that Vasilyev asked him to be there.' Ruzsky stared after the departing sled. 'Perhaps it was an attempt to intimidate me. If you recall, my father did nothing to prevent me being exiled to Siberia. Vasilyev knows we don't get on.' Ruzsky glanced over his shoulder. 'No one watching us. If Prokopiev and his thugs didn't manage to eliminate us in Yalta, will they try again?'

Pavel did not answer. He was staring at his feet.

'Should we be frightened, Pavel?'

'I don't know, Sandro.'

Ruzsky took a long drag on his cigarette, then exhaled violently. 'Christ,' he said.

CHAPTER THIRTY-NINE

Fokin was on stage at the Mariinskiy, his voice echoing around the empty auditorium. Ruzsky and Pavel stood beneath the golden splendour of the royal box, the double-headed eagle of Imperial Russia looking down upon them.

Fokin ignored them pointedly for a few minutes. Ruzsky kept his temper.

'*Yes*,' Fokin said, at length.

'I need to speak to you.'

'I'm busy.'

'So am I.'

'You're the detective?' Fokin asked, knowing perfectly well who he was. The other dancers were looking at him with ill-disguised contempt.

Ruzsky breathed evenly in a bid to remain calm.

'Can't it wait?' Fokin asked, a hand upon his waist.

'No.'

'I know what it is about.'

'Then it will not take much of your time.'

Fokin turned around. 'I'll be down in a minute—'

'Get down here. *Now*,' Ruzsky snapped, and the

tone of his voice made Fokin swing round sharply, then move across the stage. One of the younger dancers sniggered.

Ruzsky took hold of Fokin's arm and moved him through a door beside the orchestra pit. Pavel, who had been standing behind him, followed quietly. The corridor was dark, the man's ghostly face dimly lit by the lights from the stage. He had a big nose and red lips, which he pursed when frightened. 'Where is she?' Ruzsky asked.

'Where is who?'

Ruzsky stared into his eyes. 'Do you want a spell in the Lithuanian Castle?'

'Don't be absurd.'

Ruzsky squeezed his arm tighter. 'Do you have any idea what they would do to a man like you?'

'Let go of me.'

Ruzsky dug his thumb and forefinger into Fokin's arm until he squeaked. Pavel took a step closer, as if preparing to intercede.

The choreographer wriggled, so Ruzsky released him, took out his heavy revolver, cocked it and placed it against the bridge of Fokin's nose. 'I'm afraid I don't have time to be polite.'

'I have no idea where she is.'

'I think differently.'

'Why should I?'

'I think you know.'

Ruzsky pressed harder.

'All right.' Fokin pushed away the gun. A thin sheen of sweat clung to his forehead. 'You'll find her at the Symnov factory today.'

'The Symnov factory?'

'Yes.' Fokin wiped the sweat from his forehead with

the sleeve of his velvet jacket. 'There is a strike. That is where you will find her.'

The Symnov factory loomed like a giant in the half-darkness, its tall brick chimneys towering above them. Ruzsky was jammed inside a tram, the air warm from the heat of bodies despite the cold outside. Pavel was two feet away and they eyed each other warily. The trolley bell rang and they joined the crowd getting off opposite the factory.

It was not yet five, but it was already dark, the moon bright as the crowd flowed towards the gates and the mass of people gathered beyond them. There appeared to be an equal number of men and women – solemn, unyielding faces staring at them as they pushed through.

Ruzsky and Pavel were shoulder to shoulder. 'Why don't you go home?' Ruzsky hissed into his ear, but his friend ignored him.

A group of strike organizers stood at the gates, controlling the flow of people, and Ruzsky forged his way towards a tall man with short hair and round glasses – a student, Ruzsky thought, rather than a worker. 'Identification,' the man demanded.

Ruzsky was a couple of feet ahead of Pavel now. 'I left it behind,' he said.

'Then you'd better take care the Okhrana don't get their hands on you.'

Ruzsky was allowed through into the factory yard, where perhaps as many as a thousand people had gathered. He was acutely conscious of the police photographs and revolver digging into his ribs. He cursed himself for not disposing of them. He surveyed the crowd, trying to get his bearings, and saw

Pavel showing some papers to the man at the gate. Perhaps he had a set that did not list his occupation.

A group of men had gathered round a brazier. Ahead, light flickered on the stone steps leading to the factory entrance. Pavel joined him, and Ruzsky found his concern eased by his friend's grim determination. They slipped through the crowd, scrutinizing faces in the distance while avoiding those close by. Wherever they went, they attracted hostile, suspicious glances.

After ten minutes, Ruzsky stopped in a corner of the yard. He took out and lit a cigarette, then offered one to Pavel. They smoked in silence, listening to the murmur of conversation. At length Ruzsky saw her emerge on to the steps. She looked about her, then disappeared again. He threw his cigarette to the ground and walked towards where she had been. He glanced back to check that Pavel had not followed him and saw a warning in his friend's eyes.

The light on the steps came from flaming torches bolted to the walls. Ruzsky went into the half-darkness of the central hall.

A man stepped forward, his demeanour more aggressive than that of the guard at the gate. 'Yes?'

Ruzsky pointed at the stairwell ahead of him. 'I was with the woman who just came through.'

'Who?'

'The woman who just passed.'

'What is her name?'

Ruzsky frowned. 'Maria Popova.'

The guard relaxed a little. Ruzsky saw that he had a revolver in his right hand. 'Papers.'

'I don't have any. I told the man at the gate.'

'You have no papers?'

'No.'

The man was confused. 'You're with Popova?' he asked again.

'Yes.'

The guard nodded for him to continue on his way, then slipped back into the shadows.

Ruzsky walked up the staircase to the landing on the first floor. A small group stood in an alcove, gathered round a man who leant against the wall with his hands in his pockets. He was tall, good-looking and well groomed, his dark hair short and his features neat, lean and angular. Torchlight bathed his face as he listened to the woman beside him. Ruzsky was certain that this was Michael Borodin.

The man's eyes flicked to the right. He stared at Ruzsky.

Maria swung round. Her expression did not alter. She was a stranger to him.

'Yes?' Borodin asked.

Their eyes bored into him. Ruzsky thought of the guard at the bottom of the stairs and the thousand hostile faces in the courtyard below. 'I . . .' He could feel the muscles in his face twitching, and a pain in the pit of his stomach.

'Who are you?' Borodin did not move, but he did not need to.

Maria offered no acknowledgement. Ruzsky did not move. He could not think.

'Who are you?' Borodin asked again, with greater force.

'I am Alexander . . .' Ruzsky's voice was weak. He could think of no plausible explanation for his presence, or any means of escape. He had told the guard he knew Maria Popova, but if he made the same mistake here she would denounce him.

He took an involuntary step backwards. The hallway was silent, but for the hissing of the torches.

Ruzsky watched, helpless, as Michael Borodin reached inside his coat.

'Alexander is a friend,' Maria said.

Borodin lowered his hand.

Her eyes on his, Maria approached Ruzsky, took his arm and led him to the edge of the group.

Borodin stared at Ruzsky. He had a fierce, unblinking gaze. 'Who is he?'

'He's in the Ministry of War. Sandro. Sandro Khabarin.'

'What is he doing here?'

'I invited him.'

'Why did you invite him?'

'He wished to become one of us.'

'Why does he wish to become one of us?'

Maria looked at Ruzsky. Her eyes carried the most potent warning. Now they were bound together in danger and his heart swelled in gratitude. 'We cannot wait any longer,' Ruzsky said. 'Everyone must play their part.'

'We cannot wait any longer?' Borodin's eyes flicked to the hallway, then back again. 'Why can we wait no longer?'

'Things cannot go on as they are. Even the Tsar's servants know it.'

'And you *are* a servant of the Tsar?'

'We all are.'

Borodin tilted his head fractionally, his scrutiny unbroken. He took his right hand from his pocket and scratched his cheek. Ruzsky could see the bulge in his overcoat and was certain that he was armed. 'What does the servant of the Tsar wish to do about it?'

'It is too late for anything but revolution.'

Borodin smiled. 'But that has always been so.'

'Perhaps.'

'I question whether an official of the Tsar, with soft hands and a softer mind, is prepared to sacrifice himself for our cause. Why not join the liberals, with their many lunatic schemes?'

Ruzsky did not answer.

'Do you question that, Maria?'

'No.'

'No?' Borodin turned to him again. 'She is confident. We trust Maria – perhaps above all people. But should we trust you?' Borodin looked into his eyes. 'Should we trust the man with soft hands? What would you do for the revolution, Khabarin?' He smiled. 'Would you kill a man?'

'Of course.'

'Would you kill a friend at your Ministry of War, another enemy of the state?'

'Yes.'

Borodin turned to the others. 'A man who will kill his own comrades?'

Ruzsky stared at him.

'But you wish to impress us. And not too much. I like that.' Borodin's eyes searched Ruzsky's. 'Very well. A friend of the ballerina is a friend to us all.' He turned back to the group. The man next to him was thin and, like the student at the gate, wore tiny round glasses. The woman on the other side of him could have been his older sister: they both looked as if they had seen neither soap nor water for some time. Her lank hair hung down to her waist, and she held a cloth cap in her hand. Once, she might have been almost pretty, but her face was lined and careworn, her teeth rotten. The pair were resentful, Ruzsky could see, not of him but of Maria and the way their leader responded to her.

There was a fifth member of the group and when he stepped forward into the light, Ruzsky could see that he was just a boy, sixteen at most.

'As soon as Michael has finished speaking,' the older woman went on, 'he will make the announcement. Then we will go.'

'Come,' Borodin said, with sudden urgency. He marched away down the corridor, the torch above his head. They climbed another stone staircase on to an iron gangway, which ran the length of the factory. Borodin walked quickly, the torch splashing light over the machines standing idle beneath them. Their footsteps echoed in the cavernous space.

Ruzsky was at the rear of the group, Maria just ahead of him.

Borodin led them into a room on the far side of the building. There was a clock on the wall and four desks, all facing tall windows with views across the factory floor. A shelf in front of them was laden with boxes of tools – wrenches, hammers, spanners. It was cold in there, too. Borodin spoke. 'Let's talk about your friend a little more, Maria.'

'He looks like a police agent,' the older woman said, her mouth tight.

Ruzsky tried to keep his breathing even, his face blank.

'An official inside the Ministry of War? It was too good an opportunity to miss.' Maria smiled at him. 'I—'

'What is his name again?'

'Khabarin. Alexander Khabarin.'

'How senior is he?'

Borodin had addressed Maria, but Ruzsky answered him: 'Grade seven.'

'How did you meet him, Maria?'

'I was given his name and address by a friend in Moscow. I was told he was loyal and decent and—' she looked at him significantly '—I have not been disappointed.'

'Why have you not mentioned him before?'

'He needed to be convinced.'

'No revolutionary should need to be convinced.'

Maria did not flinch. 'He can provide details of the movements of soldiers and other information that might prove useful. He's strong and brave.' This last remark was in apparent admonishment of other members of the group. Ruzsky understood that she was using her personal standing with Borodin to appeal over the heads of the others.

Borodin's face was dark and unyielding and his every movement suggested barely suppressed violence. 'Why now?' Borodin asked.

'I told you already,' Ruzsky replied.

'Where were you educated?'

'My parents were teachers at the Kirochnaya.'

Borodin nodded. It was an officer's school and explained Ruzsky's aristocratic bearing.

'He still looks like a police agent,' the woman said.

'I found him, Olga, not the other way round.' Maria's voice was still controlled. If she shared Ruzsky's fear, the way in which she contained it was extraordinary.

Borodin turned to the others. 'Maria is right. We cannot allow ourselves to be *paralysed* by mistrust, isn't that so, Andrei?'

The boy was startled. 'Of course.'

'But it would be naïve to imagine they don't try to infiltrate us, wouldn't it?'

'Yes, Michael.'

'Do you think they have succeeded?'

'I don't know. I mean, no, they have not.'

'And yet I wonder. This man Maria has brought . . . it appears she sought him out. The ones we have to watch most carefully are those who have sought us, don't you think?'

'Yes.'

'Factory workers might be unreliable, those who approach us to be involved in our work?'

'Yes.'

'Or students.'

Borodin's hands were in his pockets, his black overcoat drawn back. He wore a smart suit beneath it, a silver watch-chain strung across his waistcoat.

'Yes,' the boy said.

'Students worry me especially, Andrei.'

Ruzsky saw the boy's Adam's apple move violently as he swallowed.

'You're a student.'

Andrei didn't answer.

'Tonight, for instance, we have plans. Plans that only people in this room know about. People in this room and, I'm told . . .' he looked Ruzsky straight in the eye '. . . the police.'

They were silent.

Olga glared at Maria. Ruzsky edged closer to her, but she betrayed no fear, her attention on Borodin. Andrei was furthest from the torch and his breath was visible on the cold air.

'The police are expecting us. Do you think it should stop us, Andrei?'

'No. I don't know.'

'The Cossacks are waiting. Aren't you frightened of them?'

Andrei's face was white in the half-light.

'Or are you more afraid of being discovered?'

The only sound was the rasp of the boy's breathing.

'Two more days, Andrei.'

The boy gulped.

'By Friday, our task should be complete. Do you think they know about us? Answer me!'

'I don't know.' Andrei was blinking rapidly.

'What about our friend the American? What about Ella? What about Borya? Who is killing them, Andrei?'

'I don't know, Michael.' The boy was on the edge of tears.

'Did the police kill them? Are they picking us off one by one before we can reach our goal?'

As the boy shook his head, Ruzsky moved a fraction and felt the photographs pressing against his chest. A bead of sweat trickled down his forehead.

Borodin turned towards him, as if sensing his fear. 'Perhaps the police are watching us, Khabarin. Perhaps they are trying to infiltrate us.'

Ruzsky did not answer.

'An official at the Ministry of War befriends a pretty girl. She vouches for his loyalty, perhaps in ignorance of his real purpose.'

The sweat was running into the corner of his eye. Ruzsky tried not to blink.

'They use an agent to try to get close to us. It would be their way, would it not?'

'I don't know.'

'You don't know? Then you appear to be less of an

expert on the workings of your own government than I think you are.'

They were silent again. Borodin's eyes never left his. 'An infiltrator,' he said softly. 'What should we do with such an enemy in our midst?' He turned away, half shielding the torch. Ruzsky listened to the sound of the boy's breathing, hoping it drowned his own.

The eyes of the group flicked from Ruzsky to the boy, and back again. Maria watched Borodin.

The torch hit the ground. The flame flared, casting nightmarish shadows, as Borodin grabbed a wrench from one of the boxes and held it above his head. Ruzsky saw his eyes glint as he walked purposefully towards him. He felt the ice crack beneath his feet and knew that, this time, no one would be able to save him.

Ruzsky saw the terror on Andrei's face, then the wrench struck the centre of the boy's forehead. Blood spurted into the air. Andrei fell, but Borodin was on to him before he hit the ground, his arm rising and falling. They listened to the sound of the wrench pulverizing flesh and bone.

At last, Borodin straightened. The boy's head was half lit, but unrecognizable, almost indistinguishable from the pool of blood and pulp that lay beneath it.

Borodin breathed heavily. He wiped blood from his face with the back of his hand, which smeared it further. He bent to pick up the torch. 'Get me a cloth, some water,' he barked.

Nobody moved.

'Get it,' he snarled.

Maria moved first, and broke the spell. Olga followed her.

Ruzsky stood opposite Borodin, who was still

panting from the exertion. The revolutionary took out a white handkerchief and cleaned his face, then wiped particles of Andrei's skull from his shirt and coat.

Maria returned with a bowl of water and a cloth. She put down the bowl on the shelf and began to attend to Borodin like a maidservant, washing his face and hands, before she tried to remove the stains from his clothes.

The blood was pounding through Ruzsky's brain.

'You still want to be part of this, Khabarin?'

For a moment, Ruzsky forgot his assumed name, but he recovered. 'Now more than ever,' he said.

'You can report the death to the police, if you wish.'

Ruzsky thought that only a man with an intimate relationship with the police would dare to behave like this in front of a stranger, but he held his tongue. 'Change has casualties. It could not be otherwise.'

Maria bent over and wiped the blood from the silver chain of Borodin's pocket watch. Ruzsky tried to hide his revulsion. He tightened his overcoat and felt the tip of his revolver pressing against him. Could he have stopped the boy's murder? Was Borodin the man who had repeatedly stabbed the American and almost severed Markov's head at the Lion Bridge?

'You don't flinch at the sight of blood?' Borodin asked him.

Ruzsky stared at Andrei's corpse. Olga and the other man took an arm each and dragged it to the far corner of the room. Ruzsky heard a thump as they rolled the body against the wall.

'Why aren't you at the front?' Borodin asked. Maria was concentrating on his collar.

'I work in the war ministry.'

'Don't you want to do your patriotic duty?'

'I'd rather not die for the Tsar, if it's all the same to you.'

Borodin smiled, and took Maria's hand.

They followed Borodin out on to the steps, Olga holding the torch aloft beside him so that the crowd could see his face. For a moment, Ruzsky stood behind him, then saw Maria slip away and followed her to a corner where they would be less conspicuous.

As she turned, he expected to see recognition or warmth in her face, but there was only a blank stare. The woman who had saved his life was again a stranger.

'Good evening, comrades,' Borodin's voice boomed. His face shone. Ruzsky realized that Andrei's death had not been a performance for Alexander Khabarin's benefit: Borodin had enjoyed it. He couldn't dispel the image of Maria kneeling before the man, wiping the blood from his coat.

'Which of us here is not hungry?' Borodin demanded of the now silent onlookers. Ruzsky noticed a soldier ahead of him on the far side of the steps, leaning against the factory wall.

'Which of us here does not hunger for enough bread to eat, to feed their family, enough fuel to warm their home, enough . . .' His voice was drowned in the roar of the crowd.

'Bread,' he went on, when the crowd had quietened. 'That's what I promise you, comrades. Bread, and peace.'

There was another roar.

'How many have you lost in our great patriotic war? Papa's war. Mama's war – though who knows which enemy Mama is fighting?' The crowd shouted its approval, but he silenced them with a sharp cut of his hand. 'We have all lost. Fathers, brothers, husbands. Each and every family has lost a soul, and for what have we been forced to make these terrible sacrifices? So that Papa and Mama could sit at the knee of their unmentionable priest.'

He scanned faces in the crowd, his head twisting one way, then the other.

'It is not men and women who go to the front, but a silent army of the damned, forced to their deaths like cattle. Without rifles, without purpose, without hope, while Mama is paid by the enemy to starve our families to death.

'We see train after train of the wounded arriving at the Warsaw station day after day after day. We see the eyes of the hungry in the slums, we see the corrupt officials in their carriages, and the parasitic merchants and aristocrats who wanted this war for the greater glory of the Empire. Well, I say, enough. ENOUGH!'

Borodin paused.

'This is our country too. We want our land back. We want our people back. We want bread, we want PEACE!'

The crowd howled its approval, but Borodin held up a hand.

'Now, we can wait no longer. We the people, the workers, demand change. We demand a government that can deliver peace, that can give us bread so that our children do not starve while we slave to provide the armaments to protect their empire. Tonight we demand a new beginning. This is not simply a strike. This is a message we wish to send to the heart of the government of this country. To Papa, to Mama.'

Borodin waited.

'Tonight we march to the palace, like our brothers and sisters before us. And we will send a message to the government and the world that we will take no more.' He paused once more, then leant forward. 'Do the police and soldiers dare stop us passing, comrades?'

'They do not dare,' chanted hundreds of voices in unison.

'Comrades, it is better for us to die for our freedom than live as we have lived until now.'

'We will die!'

Ruzsky looked at Maria: her face was stony, her lips tight, her eyes fixed on the man at the top of the steps. He took in for the first time the composition of the crowd: railwaymen in uniform and workers from the tramcar depot in knee boots and leather jerkins, better dressed civilians from white-collar jobs in long over-coats, and pockets of schoolboys and girls. 'Do you swear to die?' Borodin demanded.

'We swear!'

'Let the ones who swear raise their hands!'

Borodin swept down the steps and through the crowd, pushing forward towards the gates. Maria followed, Ruzsky half a step behind her.

He half turned to see Pavel making his way towards him, his eyes wide with alarm. 'Slowly,' he seemed to be saying, but as Ruzsky forged ahead through the factory gates, the big detective was swallowed by the crowd.

The moon was bright. Around him, in every face, Ruzsky saw determination and anger as the protesters cascaded into the streets. He brushed past a group of schoolchildren – would they not be siphoned off from the march? And then Borodin was alongside them once again. He had put on a fur hat. 'Do you fear the police, Khabarin?' he asked quietly. 'Do you fear the Cossacks?'

Ruzsky shook his head.

'If blood is shed, it will be to the greater glory of our revolution, isn't that so?'

Ruzsky said nothing.

'People do not care any more, do they? Desperation is the force we need.' Borodin touched his shoulder. 'Can you fire a rifle?'

'Yes.'

'Then I have a use for you. Tomorrow, at two, we will meet in an apartment on the top floor at 173 Kronversky Prospekt. Maria will advise you if there is a change.'

Borodin crossed in front of him, so that he was next to Maria. He whispered in her ear, then dropped back. Ruzsky wanted to know what he had said.

As they passed the barracks of the Lithuanian regiment, a group of soldiers hurried to the iron railings to cheer them on.

'We're with you,' one shouted.

'Show the dogs,' another called.

As they walked along, more soldiers came to the railings. A few started to sing the first bars of the 'Marseillaise' and the song was taken up by the crowd.

There was a shot from inside the compound and a series of barked orders from the officers.

Ruzsky was swept on.

Half a minute later, there was another shot. Ruzsky wondered if this was the beginning of the end. Was this revolution? What plan had Borodin sought to involve him in?

The strikers were silent as they marched over the bridge. Across the river, the city's ornate classical domes were swathed in moonlight. Occasionally someone coughed, but otherwise the only sound was of hundreds of feet crunching on the snow-covered ground.

Maria had been pushing forward and now they were nearing the front of the crowd again. There was more space here and Ruzsky caught up with her. 'What happened—'

Her eyes blazed. 'I did not ask you to get involved,' she hissed.

Ruzsky took her arm, but she shook it free. He glanced around to be sure that others had not witnessed the gesture, but saw only grim concentration: they expected the worst.

As they came to the far side of the bridge, the protesters wheeled right. Ruzsky turned to see if Borodin was still watching them. He heard muffled cries. The snow had shielded the sound of the horses' hoofs and the Cossacks were close, approaching fast, heads low and sabres raised. For a brief moment, it was unreal and almost beautiful: the dark horses against white snow and moonlight glinting off swords held high above the soldiers' heads.

They thundered silently towards the marchers, snow flying up around them.

The protesters were suddenly still. There was a single cry, and then more. The crowd broke up at the back. There was a high-pitched scream as the horses reached them and Ruzsky saw the first lightning flash of a sabre striking down.

The panic spread, like wind on water, and Ruzsky was a prisoner of a chaotic, uncontrolled mass. He was almost knocked down, but used his strength to hold himself upright against the swell. He took hold of Maria and moved forward, pushing through the chaos around him. She did not resist. Fearful white faces flashed past his eyes as he focused on the broad expanse of Liteiny Prospekt, stretching into the distance. Maria gripped him, her face wild. 'You're a fool,' she said.

Instinctively, Ruzsky turned and saw that a horse and rider were almost upon them. In a split second, they would be dead. He could not move.

Then he was pushed violently. As he was tumbling towards the flailing hoofs, he knew that she had propelled him to his death. But as he hit the snow, he rolled over in time to see Maria take the full force of the collision, her body like a rag doll. The rider was thrown forward, the horse whinnying as it skidded to its knees.

Ruzsky heard more gunfire, and screaming all around him. Ahead, a group of infantrymen was kneeling in the snow, firing volley after volley above the crowd. He scrambled to his feet. Maria was lying flat on her back. He bent down and took her in his arms. Her eyes were open, but her face was as lifeless as that of a statue.

Ruzsky picked her up and ran. He careered into the side of a horse and heard a curse, but kept charging down Liteiny Prospekt. He heard another volley of shots and more screams. He ran faster, slipping and crashing on to his back as he reached the corner. As he rolled over, he saw a Cossack lash out with his whip at the head of the woman who had been running alongside him. She collapsed.

Ruzsky lay still. They were encircled by three

horsemen who were eliminating moving figures one by one until they were just so many black stains upon the white earth. He could hear people crying for help. He raised his head and looked back towards the bridge. There was no crowd now.

A young girl had climbed to her feet and was running towards where they lay. A Cossack circled her, shrieking like a banshee, the glint of steel above his head before he slashed down across the girl's face, cutting it open from the eyes to the chin. He yelled again, slicing the air with his sabre.

Ruzsky edged forward and touched Maria's alabaster cheek. He heard the thunder of hoofs and half turned, but the horse passed within inches of him, kicking snow into his face as its rider sought another figure fleeing for the cover of a nearby house.

He stood up again and scrabbled for Maria in the snow. She felt pitifully slight, her head lolling back against his arm. In the distance ahead he saw a private carriage still waiting outside one of the huge houses, a world away from the gunfire and screams. He ran towards it, slipped, almost fell, but regained his footing and ran on, the sounds becoming distant echoes as he focused on his destination.

He heard the thunder of a horse's hoofs again and turned. The rider was close, bent to strike, and Ruzsky swerved towards the iron railings of the houses alongside them.

The Cossack swung down his whip, but missed. He spun the horse, turning on the smallest circle Ruzsky had ever seen, and charged towards them again, his long whip raised high above his head, his sabre bouncing up and down at his side. Ruzsky stood with his legs apart, Maria in his arms, offered up like a sacrifice. He breathed in deeply. 'Police!' he yelled. 'I'm a police officer!'

He saw the shock in the rider's eyes and the sudden uncertainty as he lowered the whip and veered away, almost crashing into the railings. 'You shouldn't be here!' the Cossack shouted. He waved his hand, then wheeled away.

Ruzsky swayed with relief. He tipped himself forward and stumbled into a run, focusing on the carriage ahead. When he reached it, he almost threw Maria on to the floor. 'The Hospital of St George,' he shouted.

The startled driver snapped the reins. 'Quick,' Ruzsky shouted. 'She's badly hurt.' He knelt over Maria. He checked her pulse, then bent his face low over hers to check that she was breathing. He couldn't see any blood, but looked carefully around her scalp, her ears and her neck. He bent down. 'Don't go,' he whispered. 'I've only just found you. Please don't go.' Her face was still and cold to the touch.

CHAPTER FORTY

A crowd thronged the entrance to the hospital. Two orderlies carried a patient on a stretcher out of a motorized ambulance, shouting at the wounded to allow them passage. Ruzsky swept Maria into his arms, jumped down into the snow and tried to push his way through the crowd. 'Let me pass,' he shouted.

'Wait your turn!' a woman hissed. She turned, half illuminated by the gas-lamp high on the wall above the great wooden doors at the hospital's entrance. Blood streamed down her face.

Ruzsky turned round and walked backwards. He shoved hard, using his height, weight and strength to get through the jostling, cursing crowd. Maria hung apparently lifeless in his arms.

There were two soldiers at the entrance to the hospital, trying to keep the people back, but he pushed past them into the hallway. Inside the cavernous reception area, the wounded were lying on the floor in all directions, alongside soldiers from the front for whom no bed had been found. There was no one behind the desk and nurses in dirty blue and white uniforms, with a red cross on the chest, darted through the lobby trying to avoid cries for help.

The orderlies who had been carrying the stretcher lowered it to the floor in the centre of the room and shouted for assistance. The body of the injured woman was covered with a dark blanket, but her head jerked violently from side to side.

Ruzsky looked down at the woman in his arms. 'Maria?' he whispered. But she did not open her eyes. He moved to the far corner and laid her down. 'I'll find a doctor,' he said.

He ran through the wooden and glass doors to the ward beyond. The smell that assaulted him was so foul that he almost gagged. The room was full of the dead and dying, mostly soldiers covered in putrid, leaking bandages. There were many beds, but the injured were laid out on the floor between them and even down the aisle in the middle. This part of the hospital had once been a school and the tall windows and high ceilings ensured that it was freezing cold, despite the crush of bodies. Ruzsky saw that several panes on the window closest to him had been broken. Few of the injured had blankets.

A patient screamed at the far end and Ruzsky caught sight of a doctor bending over a struggling soldier, trying to restrain him. He crossed to him. 'Doctor?'

The man looked up. He was young, a boy even, of no more than twenty or twenty-one, but his face was as haggard and lined as that of someone twice his age. 'Doctor, I need your help.'

'Everyone does.'

'Please could you come this way?'

'I have work to do.'

'It will only take a minute.'

'IT ALWAYS DOES!' Suddenly the doctor looked as if he might cry. He put a hand to his face and rubbed his eyes unsteadily.

'Just one moment of your time, Doctor.'

'One moment, one moment. My life is measured in moments.'

Ruzsky took his arm and led him down the centre of the room.

The doctor rebelled. He pulled his arm free and walked away in the opposite direction. Ruzsky ran after him. 'Please, Doctor.'

'No!'

'Please.'

'NO!'

Ruzsky could see tears in the man's eyes now. 'It's my wife.'

'It's always someone's wife. Or husband. Or child.'

'*Please*, Doctor.'

'No. I will tend the soldiers.'

Ruzsky's patience snapped. He grabbed the man's arm and manhandled him down the centre of the room.

'Let go of me!'

Ruzsky stopped. 'For Christ's sake, don't make me beg.'

'There are hundreds of patients.'

'But none like her.'

A glimmer of humanity flickered in the doctor's exhausted eyes. 'You'll have to wait your turn.' He rocked gently on the balls of his feet. 'Where is she?'

Ruzsky led him to where Maria lay on the floor, her eyes closed. He knelt down and touched her cheek. The doctor knelt beside him.

411

'Doctor!' an old woman shouted, from the other side of the hallway, but he ignored her. Ruzsky noticed that most people around them were waiting with quiet dignity and he felt ashamed, but unrepentant.

'What happened?' the doctor asked, as he took Maria's pulse.

'The full impact of a horse,' Ruzsky said.

The doctor listened to her chest, then checked her body with his hands, starting with her head, neck and shoulders, moving down her chest. She opened her eyes, wincing as he touched her ribs, her face distorted by pain. She did not make a sound. Relief flooded Ruzsky.

'Any blood?' He checked her clothes to answer his own question. 'Were you knocked out?' he asked Maria.

'Yes,' Ruzsky answered for her.

'For how long?'

Ruzsky looked at his watch. 'Twenty minutes,' he answered. 'Perhaps twenty-five.'

The doctor held up three fingers. 'How many?'

'Three,' Maria answered weakly.

'Now?'

'Five.'

There was a haunting shriek from inside the ward, but it had no impact on the doctor. He covered each of Maria's eyes in turn, checking the response of her pupils to light. He straightened. 'Shock,' he said. 'Take her home, keep her quiet. If the pain doesn't lessen, bring her back.'

Before he had finished his sentence, he had mentally moved on. He stood up, oblivious to the cries for help all around him. Ruzsky saw a boy lying

412

on the floor on the opposite side of the hallway, painfully thin, his skin yellow, body wasted. He scooped Maria into his arms. As he walked towards the exit, she rested her head against his shoulder, her breath warm against his face.

Ruzsky put her down by the door to her apartment and supported her as he fumbled for the keys. Once inside, he lowered her on to the *chaise-longue*, then took the sheepskin rug from the floor, laid it over her and set about making and lighting a fire. Then he sat by her feet and they watched the flames in silence. He moved closer, took her pulse, then placed his hand against her forehead. The fire crackled loudly. Her skin glowed a soft, honeyed amber.

'Are you in pain?'

She did not speak, but closed her eyes.

Ruzsky watched the firelight flickering on her face. When she had drifted off to sleep, her chest rising and falling rhythmically and without apparent discomfort, he allowed himself to relax a little. He got up and glanced around the room, from the pot plant in the corner to the theatrical posters and Parisian street scenes that adorned the walls. The richness of the décor had somehow become gloomy. He made his way over to the window. Outside, a cold wind whipped at the snowflakes and rattled the windows in their frames. Ruzsky wiped the condensation from the glass. Below, the street was deserted.

He went over to the dresser, opened it, took out the bottle of bourbon and poured himself a large measure, which he drank in one gulp. He tipped his head back in pleasure and relief. The desire to get blind drunk, so familiar from his time in Tobolsk, was overpowering.

He poured himself another glass and drank that, too.

Maria lay still.

Ruzsky thought about the boy at the factory, and wondered what had happened to his body. He moved to Maria's desk and stood before a bundle of letters, an inkwell, two or three fountain pens and a blotting pad.

He glanced across at her, then untied the gold ribbon round the letters. He sifted through them. Most were notes and instructions from the Mariinskiy, some from Fokin, others from the theatre's administration department, offering her roles and discussing her salary. Ruzsky was surprised to see how little she was paid. He reassembled the pile in the same order and retied the ribbon.

There were three drawers at the back of the desk and he opened each carefully in turn, his eyes on Maria. They were all empty. It was as if they had been recently cleared out.

Ruzsky straightened again. He listened to the clock. He watched the rise and fall of her chest. He bent to touch her face. She did not stir. He sat down beside her and allowed himself to drift back to Petrovo.

Eventually, he stood up again and moved quietly down the corridor to her bedroom. He eyed the brass double bed and switched on the light. The room was bare. There was nothing on the chest of drawers, or beside her bed; no photographs, hairbrushes or ointments. He pulled open the drawers. There were a few clothes in some, but no underwear. No dresses hung in the wardrobe.

He spotted two suitcases beneath the bed, pulled them out and heaved them on to the mattress. Clothes and other possessions had been packed for a hasty departure, including a battered photograph album and several bundles of letters. Ruzsky looked at the album first, but he knew before he opened it what it was going to contain. Maria's mother had looked strikingly like her. In fact, the facial and physical similarity between all three women was remarkable. Her father had been a big man, with a huge beard.

Several pictures had been taken in front of a white house, smaller but not dissimilar in style to the royal palace at Livadia, a string of palm trees in the background. Maria and her sister were dressed in white, a young boy – their brother, perhaps – sandwiched between them.

Ruzsky had not known that she had a brother. He wondered what had become of him. He put down the album and untied the thickest bundle of letters. They were so dog-eared that some had almost fallen apart, and he laid each one carefully on the bed.

Most were in one hand – her mother's – and full of endearments that he could not recall having received in any communication from his own parents. Even the few from her father displayed an easy affection. They had been written when her parents had been away, mostly locally – places like Odessa and Sevastopol – but once from Moscow and twice St Petersburg.

Ruzsky folded away the letters and retied them. With a heavier heart, he sifted through the rest of her suitcase. Hidden in the bottom, he found an envelope filled with roubles and a red leather jewellery case. It was crammed with everything of value that she owned. Among the pieces, he noticed a diamond necklace that had once belonged to his mother. Dmitri must have given it to her.

Ruzsky closed the suitcase, switched off the light and sat on the bed in darkness.

Maria drifted in and out of consciousness. When she woke, she did not speak.

Ruzsky smoked. He listened to the clock and watched the minutes tick past.

There was a bookcase against the far wall and eventually he decided to look for something to keep himself awake. The selection was not extensive, but contained most of the Russian classics. He ran his finger along the leatherbound volumes, took out and glanced through a collection of Pushkin's poetry. Then a volume on the top shelf caught his eye. He reached up and took it down. *Uncle Tom's Cabin*. It was the only book on the shelves in English. An odd choice.

Ruzsky turned it over in his hand. He thought of the claim he had made to Pavel that the marks on the rouble notes amounted to a secret message in code.

The reference book had to have been in English for the benefit of the American. Isn't that what he and Maretsky had agreed? Major works of English fiction, so that the American could get the work out of a library in Chicago, Baltimore or Boston.

Uncle Tom's Cabin was perfect. An American novel that was popular in Russia.

The book was well thumbed and Ruzsky leafed through it. He reached into his pocket, removed the roll of roubles and returned to Maria's desk. He sat down and took out a sheet of paper. As he had in his office, he assembled the notes in order of the numbers written inside the double-headed eagle. He examined the figures underlined in each serial number. The sequence on the first note was 4692. Ruzsky looked at it for a moment. It might refer to page four, line sixty-nine and letter two. Or page four, line six, letters nine and two. Or page forty-six, line nine, letter two. Or page four, line six, word nine, letter two.

He worked through the novel. On page four, there was no line sixty-nine. By a process of elimination, he whittled down the possibilities until there was only one that made sense. If the first numbers – 4692 – meant page forty-six, line nine, letter two, then what he found was K. If he applied the same process to the numbers on the first seven notes, the result was KRESTY.

Kresty. With the second seven, he got *Crossing*.

Kresty Crossing. He had never heard of it. Ruzsky closed the book. If she had packed for departure and this was the code-book – as seemed certain – why had she not planned to take it with her? *Kresty Crossing*. It sounded like a railway junction, or bridge.

He watched the firelight flicker on her beautiful, peaceful face, her chest rising and falling evenly.

'What have you begun?' he whispered.

'It's late,' she said.

Ruzsky woke with a start. He had nodded off. He glanced at the clock. It was four in the morning. He sat up straight, but her expression made his heart sink. 'Are you all right?' he asked.

'Yes.' Her voice was tired and weak, but there was a hint of impatience.

'Do you still feel dizzy?'

'No.'

'But you're in pain?'

'I'd like you to leave,' she said.

Ruzsky continued to stare into the fire.

'I thank you for what you have done, but I ask you to leave and not trouble me again.'

He felt a tightness in his chest. 'You'd like me to leave?'

She gave an almost inaudible sigh.

'Did you know the boy?' he asked.

'Not really.'

'Why did—'

'Not now,' she said.

'Your name is not Popova.'

Maria closed her eyes.

'Your sister does not acknowledge that she has a family. Who are you?'

Maria's face was still.

'Does my brother know about your past?'

'No.'

'He's an officer in the Life Guards.'

'You don't understand.'

'What have you planned, Maria?'

'Nothing.'

'Don't—'

'It is not your affair.'

Ruzsky leant forward. The stony glare in her eyes unnerved him. 'All those years ago in Yalta, Vasilyev had an agent reporting on your meetings.'

She did not answer.

'Three other members of your group have been murdered. The American was stabbed seventeen times. Markov's head was nearly severed—'

'Please go.'

'Why does your sister use a different family name?'

'What do you want of me?' she asked.

Ruzsky was stung by her hostility. 'I could ask the same of you. What purpose have I served? What part of your plan was I needed for?'

Maria did not respond immediately. He listened to

the sound of her breathing. 'I never asked you to get involved.'

'Tell me about the Kresty Crossing.'

She pushed herself upright, grimacing with pain. 'If you're even half the man I once imagined, then you will leave now and never trouble me again.'

'It's not so simple.'

'Then do so for your own sake.'

She lay back, exhausted. Ruzsky was on his feet. 'Borodin thinks someone is closing in on you, doesn't he? Three of your number have been killed.'

'I should imagine more die every second in the Tsar's army.'

'You're not in the Tsar's army.'

'Nor am I dead. Yet.'

Ruzsky stared into her eyes.

'What can I tell you that will make a difference, Sandro? What do you want to know? That Michael Borodin has been my lover, too? That he still is when the fancy takes him? Does that disgust you? Perhaps you would like to imagine the hands of the man who beat that boy to pulp tonight all over my body. Would that convince you?'

'I don't believe a word.'

'Oh, yes, you do. I saw the look in your eyes when I was trying to clean him up. He's violent to me, too. Do you want to know what he does to me when I'm naked?'

'Why are you saying this?'

'You shouldn't have been greedy. You should have taken what was offered and left it at that.'

'I don't believe you. This isn't the woman I know.'

'Perhaps that woman is a figment of your imagination.'

'No.'

She was silent again, for so long that Ruzsky thought she had drifted back to sleep. He went to the window. It was snowing, thick flakes swirling out of the darkness into the pools of light cast by the gas-lamps.

'I'd like you to leave now,' she said quietly.

'A boy was murdered tonight.'

'Then come back in the morning with your constables and arrest me.'

'I think you may be the next victim, and I believe that you think so too.'

Maria was staring at the ceiling. 'Please leave, Sandro. We will not be seeing each other again. And if you're a gentleman, you won't make me repeat that.'

CHAPTER FORTY-ONE

Ruzsky let himself out into the bitter night, the hurt bewildering in its intensity. On the doorstep, he almost walked into a bulky figure huddled against the railings. He mumbled an apology then realized it was Pavel. His partner wore a thick sheepskin cap, but still looked white with cold. Ice crystals had formed in his beard and he was shuffling from one foot to the other.

'What in the—'

'I tried the hospitals. You weren't there, or at your apartment.'

'Christ, man,' Ruzsky said. He gripped Pavel's shoulders, then pushed open the door and forced him inside. 'Why didn't you wait in here?'

'I'm all right.'

Ruzsky glanced towards the hall porter's little box beneath the stairs. The man was eyeing them warily.

'Is she alive?' Pavel asked. 'I saw her go under the horse.'

'She's alive, yes.'

Pavel took off his gloves and blew into his hands.

'You need to get warm,' Ruzsky said.

Pavel knocked the remaining snow from his boots.

The hall porter shouted something incomprehensible at them.

'What happened at the factory?' Pavel asked.

Ruzsky glanced up the curved stairwell at the floors above. 'Are you tired?'

'Why?'

'Because I would like to go back to the factory. I'll explain on the way.'

There were no trams running so early in the morning and they had to walk down to the Mariinskiy before they found a *droshky*.

The *vanka* was a monosyllabic Tartar, who scarcely bothered to haggle over the fare. He was wrapped in at least a dozen layers of clothing and, as they crossed the Alexandrovsky Bridge, Ruzsky could see why. The sky was clear, a bright moon sparkling off golden spires, but it was viciously cold, a north wind sweeping across the ice and biting through their overcoats. They huddled together in the back for warmth.

Pavel paid the driver outside the tall black gates and tried to persuade him to stay for the return journey, but he shook his head and disappeared towards the south side of the river.

Ruzsky led the way into the courtyard. It was deserted now and bathed in moonlight. The braziers that had been burning earlier had been knocked aside. He strode towards the darkened entrance to the vast, red-brick building, the wind roaring in his ears.

It was quieter within, and their footsteps echoed. Pavel put a hand on his arm and drew him to a halt. His eyes questioned the wisdom of continuing. 'Two minutes,' Ruzsky mouthed.

They mounted the stairs. It was dark but for fingers of moonlight feeling their way through tiny slit windows. They reached the landing where Ruzsky had first seen Borodin, but the corridor disappeared into darkness in both directions. Ruzsky followed the route he had taken earlier towards the gangway over the factory floor. They saw light ahead and Pavel pulled him back roughly into a stairwell.

They heard voices. The conversation grew louder, then quieter as the torchlight faded.

They waited until the factory was silent again, then Ruzsky led the way down to the floor below, groping, in the darkness, past giant black machines that smelt of grease and oil.

They stopped again. Above them they could see light from a series of flame torches flickering across the ceiling of the supervisor's office where Andrei had been murdered.

Suddenly the voices were louder again. Two men stood in the doorway, their voices booming across the factory floor. One whispered something and the other laughed.

Ruzsky edged forward, skirting one of the machines, and looked up. One of the men was Ivan Prokopiev, his closely cropped bullet head instantly recognizable. The other was Michael Borodin.

Ruzsky stepped back, colliding with Pavel, who mouthed that they should leave immediately. Ruzsky shrugged. 'How?' he murmured back. Some of Prokopiev's men were still in the foreman's office at the end and Prokopiev and Borodin were now behind them.

The answer presented itself when the two men returned, still in animated conversation. Ruzsky heard Prokopiev say, 'Hurry up,' to his officers at the far end of the walkway. He and Pavel took this as their cue.

They moved silently up the stairs, then retraced their steps to the courtyard. They did not stop until they had reached the high iron fence surrounding the barracks of the Lithuanian regiment.

'There is your answer,' Pavel said, trying to recover his breath.

Ruzsky's heart was pounding, and his palms and forehead were clammy.

'It's as you suspected. Borodin and Vasilyev are allies. They must have been since Yalta. That's what lies behind our murders. Vasilyev must be eliminating everyone who is aware of that association.'

'It's a neat theory,' Ruzsky conceded.

'Don't tell me you're surprised?'

'Whatever one might think of Vasilyev – or his associate – I can't picture either of them following in someone's footsteps then slashing him seventeen times like an amateur for the fun of it.'

'Perhaps the other one does the killing. Borodin . . .'

The way in which the boy had been bludgeoned to death made some sense of this, but still Ruzsky couldn't accept it. 'No,' he said. 'I think Borodin and his allies are angered by these killings. If anything, they have disrupted their plans.' He glanced back down the street to check that they had not been followed.

'What are their plans?' Pavel asked.

Ruzsky turned his back so that he was shielded from the wind.

'At that meeting,' Pavel went on, 'Vasilyev was giving Shulgin and your father the impression that these men were dangerous. Why was he doing that?'

'I don't know.' Ruzsky needed time to think. 'Go home and get some sleep. We'll talk tomorrow.'

'Don't do anything foolish. Remember what happened in Yalta.'

'I will see you in the office at one.'

'What—'

'There is something we need to do.' Ruzsky tapped his colleague's shoulder affectionately, then started walking. After twenty yards, he turned back to watch Pavel melt into the night. He and Tonya lived over in Palyustrovo, beyond the Finland station. It was a walk almost as long as Ruzsky's, but at least a warm bed awaited him.

Ruzsky set his face to the wind and trudged on towards Vasilevsky Island.

He didn't encounter a *droshky*, so had to keep walking, crossing the Birzhovny Bridge to the Strelka alongside a pedlar pushing his cart laboriously up the incline. He helped the man for twenty yards or so – until the downhill section of the bridge – earning himself a toothless grin.

He pulled his cap down further as he slipped through the austere buildings that dominated this end of Vasilevsky Island. He thought of the summer days when he and Dmitri had stood with the servants close to where University and Nicholas Quays merged, listening to the whistling of the winches and the shouts of crewmen from all over the world. The memory of such innocent pleasures troubled him. Would that world ever return? He was worried not for himself but for his son. He would see Michael tomorrow, come what may.

Ruzsky was so lost in thought that he almost walked straight into them. Only the presence of a dark automobile in the region of Line Fourteen – an unusual sight – alerted him. He ducked into the shadows. There were two officers in the car, Prokopiev's men, not the surveillance teams who would have been much less conspicuous. Ruzsky slid further back and moved silently away. Ironically, he knew there was now only one place in the city where he would be safe.

At night, the servants locked and bolted the entrance to the yard at Millionaya Street, but there was a gap above the doors through which Ruzsky had slipped many times in the past. Inside, he climbed the stone steps to the kitchen door. A light was on. He knew that Katya woke early. He checked his watch: it was half past five. He waited. Even out of the wind, it was still bitterly cold.

Katya bustled into the kitchen and he knocked quietly on the window. At first she was startled, then she frowned. She came to the back door and opened it a fraction. 'Master Sandro,' she said.

'Katya.'

She did not move.

'Might I come in?'

'They're all asleep, Master Sandro.'

'I want to see my boy before they wake.'

Reluctantly Katya allowed him entry. In the hallway, she examined him cautiously. Ruzsky realized, from her reaction, what a mess he must look. He hadn't seen himself in a mirror for days and he doubted it would be a pretty sight. 'Thank you,' he said quietly.

'Be careful, Master Sandro,' she replied.

Ruzsky walked up the stairs and drifted silently through the house. He climbed the last steps to the attic.

He found Michael asleep on his front, clutching his worn-out bear. A new train track had been assembled on the floor. Ruzsky touched his son's head, then kissed his ear. 'I love you, my boy.'

Fatigue overwhelmed him and he felt unsteady on his feet. He left the room, slipped back across the hall-way and opened another door. By the light of the moon, he saw Ilya's animals on the shelf above his bunk and moved towards it. He looked at the photograph of his brother, with the two candles at either side. Then he saw that the bed was already occupied.

Dmitri sat up, his hair tousled. 'Sandro? What are you doing here?'

Ruzsky did not answer.

Dmitri lay down again. He was in the full dress uniform of a colonel of the Guards. 'There is room,' he said, and shifted to the side of the bunk.

Ruzsky lay down beside his brother and closed his eyes.

Dmitri took his hand and they lay still, as they had in the days and weeks after Ilusha's death.

Ruzsky wrapped his arm round his brother's chest. After a few moments, sleep took him.

He dreamt of her, but it was more memory than illusion. He watched the image of her crouched in front of Borodin, wiping the blood from his clothes. The others were not there. It was just Maria and the revolutionary. Maria ministered to him slowly, upon her knees, Borodin's dark head lowered, his eyes upon her.

Ruzsky awoke, bathed in sweat – or, at least, so it seemed. It took him a few moments to understand that in fact his brother's skin was clammy with perspiration. Dmitri rolled over. 'Sandro?' He had apparently forgotten that his brother had slept alongside him. 'Is it you?'

'It is I.'

Dmitri slumped down. 'Thank God,' he whispered.

Ruzsky placed his arm over his brother's shoulder and they lay still in the darkness.

Thoughts of Maria crowded in upon him. He wondered if his brother was similarly tortured and tightened his grip. Dmitri took his hand. 'I'm sorry, Sandro,' he said. 'I don't know why I didn't stop him.'

Ruzsky listened to Dmitri's breathing.

'I thought you two were the chosen ones. You and Ilusha. I hated you both, did you know that? I thought Father cared only for you. Why didn't I stop Ilusha going on to the ice? Do *you* know, Sandro? Was I jealous? Did I want him to die?'

Dmitri was babbling, still half asleep. Ruzsky gripped him tighter, until fatigue, once again, overwhelmed him.

CHAPTER FORTY-TWO

'Master Sandro?' Katya's anxious face was close to his. 'Master Sandro?' She shook his shoulder.

'What is it?'

'One of the boys has drawn you a bath.' The unspoken message in her eyes was that she would like him to wash, then leave before his presence was detected.

'All right,' Ruzsky said. 'Where's Michael?'

'He's gone out.'

'With his mother?'

'No. Mistress Ingrid has taken him to the Summer Garden.'

Ruzsky forced himself upright. 'Thank you, Katya,' he said. Then, 'I'm sorry.'

She flushed. She was embarrassed by her reluctance to admit him to the house earlier, Ruzsky thought. Times are hard, her expression suggested. A servant cannot afford to be without employment.

But Ruzsky saw more in her eyes than that. Katya had joined the household staff when he was nine. She had adored Ilya and treated him as her own son. It was not just his parents who had found it impossible to forget, or forgive. Ruzsky might not have been there when his brother stepped on to the ice, but everyone thought he should have been. Hadn't his father asked him to take care of the boy? Hadn't he been told to make sure Ilya never played on the ice? 'I'm sorry,' he said again. 'I will leave now.'

Katya did not move. Her face softened. 'You're not cared for properly.'

'I can care for myself.'

'When did you last eat?'

Ruzsky felt a dull ache in his stomach. He could not recall.

'Bathe and wash yourself, then come to the kitchen.'

'No,' Ruzsky said. 'No,' he repeated, to fortify himself. 'Better not.'

But he felt awake enough now to weaken at the idea of bread and cheese, or even just bread. He thought he could smell fresh coffee.

Katya turned her attention to his feet. 'Your boots . . .'

Ruzsky gazed at them, as if noticing the holes for the first time. His socks were still damp and his toes numb from being repeatedly frozen and thawed.

Katya left the room. She returned a few moments later, clutching a pair of tall black leather boots. 'He has finished with these.'

'No.'

'Don't be so proud.' It was an admonition that carried a resonance beyond the question of boots and, knowing that she had strayed too far, she averted her gaze. 'A bath has been drawn for you. Come to the kitchen when you're dressed,' she muttered.

After she had gone, Ruzsky turned the boots upside

down. Like all his father's footwear, they had been beautifully fashioned by Meulenhoff, a German cobbler whose tiny premises had once been squeezed between much grander shops around the back of Gostivny Dvor. The man had been interned in the first days of the war, then sent home.

Ruzsky dropped the boots, yawned and lay down again. On the other side of the mattress, he could see the indentation that marked his brother's presence alongside him in the night. He covered himself with the blankets.

The house was quiet. He heard the tinkle of bells on a passing sleigh.

Ruzsky reached for Ilya's elephant. Robbed of human affection, it smelt of dust. He held it up, looking into its one eye. 'I see you, Ilusha,' he said.

He pushed himself upright and checked his pocket watch. It was eleven o'clock.

He went down to the bathroom on the floor below, where a hot bath had indeed been drawn for him in the large tin tub. Katya or one of the other servants had placed some shaving tackle and pomades on the shelf beneath the mirror.

Ruzsky turned on the tap and felt the heat of the water. It was hardly more than a dribble, but it was a luxury he had not enjoyed since he'd last stayed in this house on the eve of his marriage. He undressed. The room was dark and cluttered, the walls covered in military prints and photographs of generations of Ruzsky men attending the Corps des Pages and serving in the Guards. The line drawings and photographs closest to him were of his father's younger brother, who had served in Her Majesty's Life Guard Cuirassier Regiment – the Blue Cuirassiers – at

Gatchina, before retiring permanently to Paris with his Belgian mistress.

The only non-military photographs were of the family's yacht, the *Sinitsa*, on which they had once enjoyed holidays in the Gulf of Finland. Ruzsky settled into the bath. He felt uncomfortable to be enjoying the luxury that would once have been his by right.

About forty-five minutes later, shaven and with a full stomach for the first time in days, Ruzsky emerged from the kitchen to find his father by the doorway. The old man's expression softened. 'Good morning, Sandro.'

'Good morning.' Ruzsky was aware, awkwardly so, of the boots Katya had given him.

'Did you sleep well?'

'Yes.' Ruzsky nodded. 'I'm sorry, I should have told you that—'

'Michael is in the Summer Garden with Ingrid.' The old man was gazing into the rectangular pool of light stretching away from the drawing-room window.

Ruzsky watched him. 'Are you quite all right, Father?'

'Yes.' He turned to his son. 'Of course, yes.'

'You look tired.'

The old man attempted a smile. 'Yes.'

They heard the sound of horses' hoofs on the cobbles and stepped into the drawing room to watch them pass. It was another detachment of the Chevalier-Guard in white and red dress uniforms and blue overcoats, upright in their saddles. Their mounts were finely groomed, the men's uniforms spotless.

After they had gone, a private sled passed. They

heard the crack of the driver's whip. The old man was about to turn away when he caught sight of another group of soldiers, this time on foot. They wore khaki overcoats, rather than dress uniform, but their epaulettes identified them as members of the Izmailovsky regiment, and their demeanour as reservists. 'Dmitri says there are few regulars left in the capital,' Ruzsky said.

His father kept his eyes upon the soldiers until they had disappeared from view.

The telephone rang in the hall. Neither man moved, although their heads inclined towards it until the call was answered. They heard the quiet murmur of one of the servants, then a final tinkle as the receiver was replaced. The young man who had welcomed Ruzsky to the house on his first visit appeared in the doorway. He glanced at him, as if unsure whether to impart information of any significance in his presence. 'It was Mr Vasilyev's office, sir,' he told Ruzsky's father. 'He will be here at any moment. He sends his apologies for the delay.'

'Thank you, Peter.'

After the servant had gone, the old man frowned. 'Mr Vasilyev will be late for his own entry to hell.'

Ruzsky was about to speak, but found he did not know how to begin. In forty years, he could not recall a conversation with his father upon matters of the world, let alone affairs of state. 'I imagined you would be at the ministry,' Ruzsky said.

'Not today.'

'Does Vasilyev often come to see you here?'

'No.' An intense weariness seemed to suck the life from his face. 'No,' he said again.

'What does he want?'

'That is the question, Sandro.' He sighed. 'He says, to protect the assets of the state. That is the pass he would have us believe we have come to. To protect the wealth of the Tsar from the mob.'

'He tells you there will be trouble?'

'Yes.'

'When?'

'Soon.'

'On Friday?' Ruzsky asked.

His father smiled. 'Go and find your son.'

They held each other's eyes. The old man's sparkled with affection.

'Last night, Father, I saw Vasilyev's men—'

'Find your boy first.' The old man placed a hand upon his son's shoulder. 'He is so looking forward to seeing you.'

Ruzsky pulled on his overcoat and took the sheepskin hat from its pocket.

'It's a little warmer today,' his father said. 'You'll not need that.'

Ruzsky thrust the hat back into his pocket. 'I'd like to talk to you, Father. It's just about—'

'Your case. I know. After this meeting, when you come back. There is much we should have talked about.'

'Yes.' Ruzsky opened the door, but hesitated on the threshold.

'You'll come and stay whenever you want, won't you, Sandro?' Now the old man's eyes radiated warmth and sadness in equal measure.

'Yes, Father.'

'It is your home.'

'Yes.'

'You know that, don't you? You're a grown man,

you have your own life, of course, I realize that, but this will always be your home, whenever you wish it to be.'

'I understand.'

'Do you?'

'Yes.'

'You could even . . .' He ignored his son's unspoken question. 'But I'll see you in a few minutes.'

'Are you all right, Father?'

'Yes.' The old man gestured for him to leave. 'Please go to him. He is waiting.'

Ruzsky returned his father's smile and turned away. As he walked down Millionaya Street, he could not contain the spring in his step.

Entering the Summer Garden a few minutes later, Ruzsky glanced at the sign attached to the heavy iron railings: 'Dogs, Beggars, all Lower Ranks of the Army and Navy Prohibited from Entry.' Inside the railings, a group of soldiers in long greatcoats stood around a coal brazier. They were laughing and smoking – also forbidden in public to the lower ranks – and as Ruzsky passed them he saw they were drunk. Like those he had seen passing through Millionaya Street earlier, they were dressed in khaki, but this group was from the Pavlovsky regiment, whose barracks overlooked the Field of Mars. One had a crude tin drum in his hand, filled with illegal moonshine.

Ruzsky wandered along the line of lime trees, scanning the gardens for a tall blonde woman and a small dark-haired boy. Behind him, the soldiers hummed the national anthem with heavy irony.

He wondered if they were taunting him, but resisted the urge to look over his shoulder.

He stopped in the clearing, fringed by firs, known as Children's Corner. The marble statues in the gardens were enclosed by wooden boxes in winter, but the bronze of an old man sitting in a chair was still exposed to the elements. It was surrounded by high wrought-iron railings and Ruzsky stared through them, thinking of the old men who used to build snow mountains here in winter, and charge the children of the rich a few copecks to sled down them.

Ruzsky heard a cry and swung round. Michael was standing next to Ingrid, clutching the dog's lead. For a moment, they examined each other, then Ruzsky bounded across the frozen ground and swept his boy into his arms. 'Hello, Father.'

Ruzsky put him down and knelt before him. He touched his face, then his shoulders. 'Hello, my boy. How are you?'

'Very well, Father.'

Ruzsky clasped his son's face between cold palms. 'Pleased to see me?'

Michael nodded. He pulled the great hunting dog closer and stroked its head.

Ruzsky thought his son was avoiding his eye. He glanced at Ingrid.

'You went to Yalta, didn't you?' Michael asked.

'Yes.'

'Grandpapa said he thought you would go to the house at Petrovo.'

'Why did he say that?'

'He said you would go to the house on the way. Is Petrovo far from here?'

'Quite far, yes.'

'It's where Uncle Ilusha died.'

'Yes.'

436

'Is that why you went there?'

'Part of the reason, yes.'

'Can we go there together?'

'One day.'

Ruzsky stood up slowly. He put an arm round his son and glanced at Ingrid. Something in her expression prevented him looking away. She rewarded him with a smile, wry, amused, betraying undisguised pleasure.

He studied her face. It sprang to life as the smile widened. 'Mistress Ingrid,' he said, mock-formal.

'Master Sandro,' she replied, in the same vein.

'The winter treats you well?'

'Tolerably so.'

The soldiers were singing more loudly behind them, their manner boorish and designed to provoke. Ruzsky led his son away. The soldiers sang still louder.

'They're always in here now,' Ingrid told him.

'The servants say there will be a revolution,' Michael said.

Ruzsky and Ingrid exchanged another glance.

'Why will there be a revolution?' Michael asked.

Ruzsky was about to utter something reassuring, but found he could not bring himself to lie. 'The Tsar is not popular. He is blamed for the war.' The soldiers' voices were dying away now.

'If you are a policeman, is it your job to stop it?'

'No.'

'Will the revolutionaries attack the police?'

'No.' Ruzsky pulled his son close. 'Don't worry. It will be all right.'

'Why will it be all right?'

'It just will.'

'The servants call the police *shemishniki*.'

'Well—'

'What do they mean by that?'

'Nothing of importance.'

'They say it is because they get two copecks for every man they arrest.'

Ruzsky looked into his son's intelligent eyes. 'That's the secret police, Michael.'

'You're not the secret police, are you, Father?'

'No.'

'You're a detective and you investigate murders, isn't that so?'

'It's true.'

'But Uncle Dmitri says the rioters hate *all* policemen.'

'I'll be fine, my boy.'

'I don't want them to hurt you, Papa.'

'No one is going to hurt me.'

They had reached the edge of the Field of Mars. Michael was still clutching his father's hand. 'I'll race you,' Ruzsky said, but his son shook his head.

'I don't want to run, Father.'

Ruzsky squeezed the boy's hand and looked into Ingrid's vivid blue eyes. They seemed to offer warmth and support, and uncomplicated affection, but were also tinged with sadness. He saw in them an echo of his own corrosive loneliness, which made him want to offer his unqualified friendship in return. 'I'm sorry,' he said.

'Sorry for what, Sandro?' she asked, but he could see she knew all too well what he meant.

'You deserve better,' he said.

'So do you.' She looked at Michael. 'But in one respect you're as lucky as a man can be.'

Her childlessness was not a subject Ruzsky felt he could broach.

Then, in the distance, he noticed a man running in their direction. Ruzsky's heart lurched. It was Peter, his father's valet.

CHAPTER FORTY-THREE

The house was silent. The servants were gathered in the hallway, facing the study door. Inside, the old man's body lay in the middle of the rug, his head, or what remained of it, twisted to one side. He had a revolver in his hand. There was a pool of blood on the desk, and smears on the chair and across the rug where Dmitri must have dragged the body in his vain attempt to find some sign of life. His brother sat on the floor in the corner, pushed up against one of the bookcases, his face and shirt also covered with blood. On the mantelpiece, a clock still marked the time of their father's ordered, certain world.

The old man stared up at the ceiling with lifeless grey eyes, his skin a ghostly white.

Ruzsky knelt beside him. 'Father . . .'

His face was almost untouched, but his brains spilled from the back of his skull.

'Oh, Father . . .' Ruzsky put his arm beneath his father's neck and lifted his head to his chest. He tightened his grip, as tears burned his cheeks. The smell of blood and gunpowder caught in his throat. 'Oh, Papa, Papa . . .' He wept. 'Papa, I'm sorry.' He had used the same words on the night of Ilya's death. It was the last time he had called his father 'Papa'. 'I'm sorry . . .' He half turned to see Michael in the doorway.

'Is Grandpapa all right?'

Ruzsky could not speak.

'Is he all right?' the child repeated.

He screwed his eyes tight shut.

'Papa, is he all right? Is Grandpapa all right?'

The fear in Michael's voice dragged Ruzsky back to reality. He lowered his father's head, his face and hands covered with the old man's blood, and went to his son. 'He's had an accident,' he said, and nudged Michael towards Ingrid. 'Grandpapa has had an accident.' Ruzsky wiped his nose, smearing his face with his father's blood as he tried to compose himself in front of his son. 'Your uncle Dmitri and I will try to wake him. Will you go with Aunt Ingrid while we do that?'

'*Is* he going to wake up, Father?'

'I don't know.' Ruzsky said. His voice shook. 'Perhaps it is time for him to go to another place.'

'The same place they sent Uncle Ilusha?'

Ingrid took his hand and led him away before Ruzsky could reply.

As he watched them go, Ruzsky realized that the servants were staring at him. He tried to wipe the blood from his face and found that his hand was shaking uncontrollably. 'Go to the city police head-quarters in Ofitserskaya Ulitsa,' he snapped at Peter. 'Ask for Deputy Chief Investigator Pavel Miliutin and tell him to come here with Dr Sarlov. Do not speak to anyone else.'

The man was almost hopping from one foot to the other.

'Is that clear?'

'Yes, sir.'

Ruzsky returned to the study and closed the door. He knelt before his father, hands clasped in front of him like those of a supplicant in prayer. Then he straightened the old man's black tie, brushed the thick white hair off his forehead. He looked across at Dmitri, whose head was bent, his face obscured. His arm rested upon the leather chair where they had once sat to discuss their reports from the Corps des Pages, or to which they had been sent by their mother to await punishment.

Ruzsky listened to the clock. It had always seemed to him that the rhythm of the pendulum altered to fit the mood of the occasion: quick, suspenseful beats in his childhood, lingering, leaden strokes now, marking his guilt. He placed his palm on his father's still warm cheek. The skin hung from the cheekbones, leaving no sign of the smile he had witnessed in the hallway that morning. Had he known he was saying goodbye? Had he been hoping his son would stay?

He remembered his father coming up to the attic to help with the train track. The old man had been reaching out to him, and he had given nothing of substance in return. Ruzsky kissed his forehead. He was overcome by a sense of profound hopelessness, of death's finality, and the futility of regret.

'Don't blame yourself,' Dmitri said.

Voices rose and fell outside. Once or twice, they heard the sound of a sled or an automobile in the street.

Dmitri got up and came to him. They hugged each other. When they parted, they sat together, side by side, before the old man. 'It's the two of us now,' Dmitri said. His face was puffy, his eyes red.

Ruzsky's eyes had been drawn to a group of photographs on the wall by his father's desk. There were four: his mother, Ilya, Dmitri and himself.

Ruzsky stared at his own image. In his mind's eye, this picture had been removed – stored or destroyed – a blank space on the wall where the eldest son had once gazed down on his father.

But he was there.

They heard a knock, but they did not answer it. This was the last time the three would be alone together, and neither man wanted to bring it to a close.

CHAPTER FORTY-FOUR

Pavel slipped quietly into the room. He looked at Ruzsky only long enough to confirm that there was no need for words. He carried out his work discreetly, without asking questions. He examined the body, removed the revolver from the old man's grip and slipped it into his overcoat. He checked the desk and the area beside it.

Sarlov entered, and both he and Pavel came and went in silence for half an hour or more. When they had completed their tasks, they stood in front of him. Pavel crouched down with his notebook open. 'He had visitors, you know that?'

Ruzsky nodded.

'Vasilyev and two of his men. The meeting lasted ten to fifteen minutes. Your father saw them out and returned to his study. The valet said he seemed subdued. Approximately two minutes later, the servants heard the shot.'

Ruzsky stared at Pavel. His partner was waiting for a response, but he had none to give.

'With your permission,' Pavel went on, 'we will . . .' He glanced at Sarlov. 'If we could take your father's body down to Ofitserskaya Ulitsa . . .'

Ruzsky looked at his brother, but received no lead from him. He turned back to his colleagues and nodded. 'We'll . . . arrange it,' Pavel said. 'Is there anything else you would like us to do?'

Ruzsky shook his head.

'Is there anyone you wish us to notify?'

'No.'

Pavel stood up, but both he and Sarlov lingered. 'I'm sorry, Sandro. If there is anything else . . . anything at all . . .'

'I will see you in the office later today.'

Pavel said no more. His compassion was the more moving for remaining unspoken. He and Sarlov slipped out and pulled the door shut.

Ruzsky opened the window a fraction. In the garden he could see a snowman Michael had built earlier. He wondered if the old man had helped him. 'When did you last see him?'

'Last night,' Dmitri said.

The morning sun disappeared behind a bank of heavy cloud.

Dmitri left the room, and returned quickly with a yellow carnation. He tucked it into the buttonhole of their father's jacket. Ever since their mother's death, the old man had ordered fresh flowers for her bedside table every week, just as she had when she was alive.

'Do you think they will be happy together,' Dmitri asked, 'wherever they are?'

'Content, perhaps.'

'Is that the best we can hope for? To be content?'

'We were born to a different age.'

Ruzsky tugged the wing of his father's collar back inside his morning coat.

There was a soft knock at the door. Pavel and Sarlov came in, and Ruzsky saw from their faces that it was time for them to take the body away. He straightened his father's coat once more and stepped back, then, with his brother, watched his father carried away.

As the door was pulled shut, Dmitri moved to the desk and picked up the paperweight their father had always used – a rock Ruzsky had given him during a family holiday at their aunt's estate in the Crimea. He put it down and pushed it to and fro.

Despite the blood, the removal of the body made the old man's death seem almost an illusion. The voices outside died away as the servants drifted back to their work. Pavel and Sarlov left with the ambulance.

The telephone in the hall was silent. Even the wind had faded to a whisper.

Ruzsky thought of the loneliness that must precede suicide. Was it for want of another's support that his father had reached such an impasse? He'd assumed the old man would be too proud to share a dilemma with his eldest son – yet hadn't he tried?

As Ruzsky looked out of the window at the lifeless skies, he grew more certain. A liar or cheat could always dream of escape, because he did not fear his conscience, but for an honourable man, sometimes there was only one way out. The old man's responsibility was to protect the assets of the state – what mistake or threat could have demanded such a sacrifice?

'Did you know he was going to meet Vasilyev this morning?' Ruzsky asked. He was surprised by the strength in his own voice.

'No.'

'Do you have any idea what they would have talked about?'

'No.' A moment later Dmitri continued, 'I sometimes think that you believe Father talked to me in a way he never did to you, but it wasn't so. He never confided in me.'

Ruzsky knew that he was right. 'You were an officer in his regiment . . .'

'But not like he was. Not like you would have been.'

Ruzsky saw the distress in his brother's eyes. As it had once before, grief diminished him. 'Let us not quarrel,' he said.

The tension on Dmitri's face eased. 'Yes. Let us not quarrel.'

Ruzsky found Michael playing with Ingrid in the attic. The pair were side by side on the floor, putting together the train track. The boy looked up at him with naïve but brittle optimism. 'Is Grandpapa awake now?'

Ruzsky sat down. He put the station at Mtsensk by the edge of the track, then assembled the house and village at Petrovo a short distance away. 'I think Grandpapa has gone to be with Uncle Ilusha.'

'Does that mean we won't see him again?' Michael asked, as he fitted the first locomotive on to the track and hitched carriages behind it.

'Not in the way we are used to.'

Michael concentrated on putting together his train.

'I'm sorry, my boy.'

'Will you come and live here, now, Father?'

'Yes.'

'With Mama?'

'I will talk to her.'

'I will miss Grandpapa. Will you miss him also?'

'Very much.'

'Some of the servants said you didn't like each other, but you did, didn't you?'

Ruzsky swallowed. 'I loved him. And I think, in his way, he loved me.' He pieced together two stretches of track. 'He was my father, just as I am yours. It is an unbreakable bond.'

There was a long silence.

'How did he have an accident?' Michael asked.

'I don't know.'

'Was he sad?'

'No.'

'Then why did he have an accident?'

Ruzsky did not offer an answer: he had none to give.

Michael put the last carriage on his train and pushed it round to the station at Mtsensk. He unloaded the little wooden passengers and assembled them on the platform with their luggage. One family had been modelled on Ruzsky's own: two parents with three boys and a small group of servants. There was even a *troika* waiting for them. 'Can we speak to Grandpapa?' Michael asked.

'In our dreams,' Ingrid said.

Michael seemed encouraged. His frown eased. He loaded the passengers back on to the train, sorting each group into its compartment, then stored their luggage.

CHAPTER FORTY-FIVE

In the hallway of the Okhrana's Headquarters, they had clearly been expecting him. Ruzsky neither had to explain who he was, nor offer identification. He was led down the corridor to the lift, almost colliding with a man bringing a box of papers out of the print room.

As the lift began its ascent, Ruzsky reflected upon the bomb that had been thrown at him in Yalta. Had not the intention been to kill the pair of them? If so, why had the Okhrana's many trained assassins not been instructed to try again? Perhaps they were waiting for the right moment. Had it arrived?

Vasilyev was standing by the door to his dark, wood-panelled office, and offered his hand as Ruzsky entered. 'I'm sorry, Sandro,' he said, in his low, smoke-roughened voice. 'Please have a seat.' He pointed to the table around which their last meeting had been conducted. 'Please.'

Vasilyev retreated behind his desk, silhouetted against the light. Ruzsky noticed an oil of the bay at Yalta above the mantelpiece. It looked as if it had been painted from the window of Godorkin's office.

'You have been told of my father's death?'

'Your office informed the government and Colonel Shulgin telephoned me directly. It must have been a great shock.'

Vasilyev's insincerity brought a flush of anger to Ruzsky's cheeks. Beneath the table, he clenched one of his fists. But he vowed that he would not allow himself to be provoked.

'Some tea?' Vasilyev leant forward to tap a service bell on his desk.

A young boy in a starched linen jacket appeared through a side door. 'Tea,' Vasilyev instructed him. 'Would you like something stronger?'

'No.'

Vasilyev slipped his hands into his pockets, waiting for the servant to withdraw.

Out of the window Ruzsky watched the fading light that shrouded the city's rooftops. For the first time, he felt like a stranger in the land of his birth.

Vasilyev smiled. It was as if he could read Ruzsky's mind. He picked up a silver case from his desk. 'Cigarette?'

Ruzsky declined. Vasilyev lit one for himself.

'You came to a meeting at Millionaya Street,' Ruzsky said.

'Yes. Tragically, it appears that I was the last—'

'What was it about?'

Vasilyev gave another tight smile. Only good manners, his expression suggested, required him to continue the conversation. 'I'm afraid, Sandro, that I am not at liberty to—'

'Did you arrange the meeting?'

Vasilyev scratched his cheek with one manicured fingernail. 'It was your father who requested that I come to the house.'

'Why?'

'He did not say.'

'He must have given some indication.'

'There are many meetings, in many locations.'

'You had frequent contact with him?'

'He helped to run an important ministry.'

'Would it not have been more usual for him to ask you to go there?'

Vasilyev shrugged. 'His request was not *un*usual.'

'But you knew what the meeting would be about?'

'I had some idea.'

'But you are unwilling to tell me?'

'I am not at liberty to do so.'

'The meeting was arranged to discuss the assets of the state.' Ruzsky tried to recall the precise words his father had used that morning. He had spoken of Vasilyev's desire to protect the wealth of the Tsar – but to what, precisely, had he been referring? Not, surely, palaces, jewels and private wealth, which would have been neither man's concern. 'You were discussing how to protect the liquid assets of the state in the event of revolutionary threat?'

As Vasilyev exhaled a thick plume of smoke, the picture began to come into focus. All paper money would be worthless in a time of severe unrest. But there was one asset that would be crucial to the Imperial Government's future financial viability. 'You were discussing what to do with the gold reserves,' Ruzsky said.

Vasilyev's head sank further on to his chest. His face hardened. 'What we were discussing was no concern of yours.'

'It was of concern to my father. So much so that it killed him.'

'On the contrary. It would be naïve to imagine a connection between a routine business meeting and the sad personal events that transpired thereafter.'

'If the meeting was routine, what prevents you enlightening me as to its details?'

'Routine or not, I draw a distinction between a high official of the Tsar and a mere chief investigator of the Petrograd city police.'

Ruzsky's cheeks burned. 'Why was my father present at the meeting we held here yesterday?'

Vasilyev did not answer.

'What interest could he have had in two bodies found on the Neva?'

'You tell me,' Vasilyev said.

'You invited him?'

Vasilyev said nothing, but Ruzsky saw that he was right. 'A revolutionary group is assembled. Some personal papers are stolen from the Empress of All the Russias. Something is planned for this Friday – strikes, more significant protests or unrest in the capital. A meeting is convened to discuss the gold reserves, and how best to ensure their safety in the event of law and order breaking down.' Ruzsky stopped. 'My father had served this state for a lifetime, yet within five minutes of that meeting he was dead. It does not take an investigator to make a connection.'

'A *connection*?' Vasilyev enunciated the word slowly and with the utmost precision. 'I am not certain you understand, Sandro, as your father most certainly did, the true nature of our predicament.'

'*Our* predicament?'

The young man came back with a silver tray. Vasilyev poured a cup of tea and offered it to Ruzsky, who waved it away. 'These are challenging times,' Vasilyev went on. He looked out at the dull afternoon light as he sipped his tea. 'When our home catches fire, we must look to see what we can save. Is that not so, Sandro?'

Ruzsky was stilled by Vasilyev's change in tone.

'The bigger the fire, the greater the danger. But each man has a different notion of what is precious. For one it is a painting, or some symbol of great wealth. But for another . . . a son, perhaps a grandson.'

The words hung in the air. 'For a third, it is the woman he loves.'

The chief of the Okhrana smiled. 'Always choices to be made, Sandro. Isn't that so?'

'You think we'll disappear?'

Vasilyev sipped his tea, then put down the cup on the edge of his desk. 'My advice to you is to save what you can before the house burns down.'

'Did you make the same threat to him?'

Vasilyev shook his head. It was not a denial, but an expression of surprise at Ruzsky's naïvety.

'My father's opposition to you sealed his fate.'

'Goodbye, Sandro.'

'You told him what you would do to us if he did not agree?'

'I have a feeling we will not meet again.'

Outside, Ruzsky leant against the stone wall and breathed in the cold night air. He was not ten yards from the entrance to the Okhrana's headquarters and yet all was quiet. A tram had stopped, its dull yellow light a hazy beacon against the black trees behind. A man got off and disappeared down the street, then the bell rang and it continued on its way.

Ruzsky took out and lit a cigarette. His hand shook violently. He could see the dome of St Isaac's in the distance and, closer, the spire of the St Peter and St Paul Cathedral, but this was no longer his city: it was alien, remote.

The old man's love had sealed his own fate and, if it had not done so already, old Russia was dying with him.

Ruzsky thought of Michael, sitting alone in his room in Millionaya Street, and began to run. 'Hey!' he yelled at a *droshky* driver on the far side of the street. 'Hey!'

CHAPTER FORTY-SIX

Ruzsky burst through the front door of Millionaya Street. Ingrid was in the hallway. 'Sandro,' she said, alarm on her face.

'Where is he?'

'In his room, but—'

Ruzsky had already reached the stairs.

'*She* is up there,' Ingrid hissed.

Ruzsky pounded up towards the attic.

Michael sat on his bed, looking at a book. Irina was in the centre of the room, packing his clothes into a leather case. Ruzsky steadied himself against the door.

Irina stopped what she was doing. Her narrow face softened – the first time it had in his presence for many years. 'I'm so very sorry, Sandro,' she said. She remained where she was, awkwardly folding one of Michael's white cotton shirts.

Irina was wearing an overcoat, her long, slender hands in black leather gloves. A new jewel sparkled at her throat in the dull light of the single electric lamp. Her hair was glossy and her fox-like face made up with meticulous care. She was a far cry from the radical student he had married. 'What are you doing?' Ruzsky asked. He received no answer. He kissed his son's forehead, sat by his side and draped an arm round his shoulder. 'Where did you find this?' he asked, turning to the book's hand-drawn front cover.

'Uncle Dmitri gave it to me.'

Ruzsky looked at the pictures and the neatly inscribed verse. The story recounted the preparations for the fictional wedding of Tsar Dmitri I. Dmitri had drawn and written it in the era before their parents had discouraged his precocious artistic talents.

'I'm sorry I was not here,' Irina said.

Ruzsky pulled his son closer to him.

'He was a strong man.' *Strong* rode high in Irina's lexicon of approval. It was everything. But she failed to draw any distinction between the strength of the hero and that of the villain. 'What are you doing?' he asked again.

'Sandro . . .'

'Where are you going?'

Irina inclined her head towards the room opposite. She wished to talk to him out of Michael's earshot.

Ruzsky hugged his son. 'I'll be back in a minute,' he whispered. He followed his wife through to Ilya and Dmitri's room, their footsteps echoing on the wooden floorboards. Irina shut the door and stood close to him in the half-darkness. Ruzsky wondered if she would take him in her arms and what his own response would be. 'I'm sorry,' she whispered, her voice hoarse. 'Truly sorry. You know how he felt, don't you? Whatever may have been said?'

Ruzsky wanted her to put her arms round him now and wondered if it was too late for them. He thought of Michael sitting alone on his bunk next door. 'Irina—'

'It is not healthy for him here, Sandro, don't you see that?

'I can't be without him.'

'I cannot leave him here, Sandro.'

Ruzsky looked at his wife. Even in the twilight, he could tell that she was keeping something from him. 'You're going away,' he whispered.

'No—'

'You were going to take Michael away from me.'

'This is no place for him, Sandro.'

'This is his home.'

'It would not be for long. Just for a few months. Until the situation here—'

'You plan to take him from Russia?' Ruzsky was incredulous. 'To Nice? To the grand duke's promenade?'

'Sandro—'

'My father's body is barely cold and you would rob me of our son?'

'Be reasonable. What is left for him here?'

'This is his home.'

'But who will care for him?'

'I—'

'You're never here. You're always at work.'

'Ingrid is—'

'Ingrid is not his mother,' she said crisply. 'I am. And think of what happened to your father.'

'What do you mean?'

'Do you think he was alone in feeling like that? Look about you. The tension is in every face. Look in the mirror. You will see it in your own. Old Russia – *our* Russia – is on the brink of catastrophe. The dogs in the streets know it.'

Ruzsky could not think straight. She was right, but

if he let her go, he was certain it was the last he would see of his son. 'It's out of the question.'

'I'm his mother, Sandro. It's not your right to decide—'

'I won't countenance it.'

'I'm his *mother*.'

'You're an adulteress and, unless I am mistaken, society will grant you no rights whatsoever.' He had uttered the harsh words more violently than he meant to, but he hadn't finished. 'Please leave this house,' he said.

Irina did not move. Her silence admonished him.

'Please leave.'

Irina hesitated for a moment, then retreated rapidly down the stairs. Ruzsky walked across to the far side of the attic. He saw that Michael had heard every word of their exchange. 'Will I be staying with you now?' his son asked.

Ruzsky could see on the boy's face the answer he wished to hear. 'Yes,' he said.

As soon as Irina had gone, Ruzsky lifted the receiver in the hall and placed a call to Maria's apartment. It rang and rang, but there was no answer.

He tried the Mariinskiy Theatre. 'I would like to speak to Maria Popova.'

'Not performing tonight.'

'Is she there nevertheless?'

'No.'

'Would you mind going to look for her? It's important.'

'She's not here.'

'Could you take a message?'

'Call again in the morning. She will not be in the theatre before then.'

The line was cut.

Darkness crept silently through Millionaya Street. Ruzsky worked alone in his father's study. In the central drawer of the secretaire, he found a single envelope, addressed to their cousin in England but not yet consigned to the mail. He slit it open. The letter had been written the previous evening.

My dear William,

I fear it is now almost a year since my last missive, for which please accept my most profound apologies. This war continues to take its toll upon us all.

There has been some good news. Dmitri survived frontline duty in the Brusilov offensive with nothing worse than a relatively minor injury to his arm, and is back at the barracks in Petrograd. Sandro has, to my great relief, now returned from Tobolsk, and taken up his former post. He is gloriously unchanged, and my grandson a constant source of joy. In other circumstances, there would be much to celebrate.

But, as I'm sure you will have read in your own newspapers, the conduct of the government, and of the war, remains scandalous. The murder of Rasputin has been greeted with universal celebration, but upon sober reflection, has changed nothing. The Empress, already domineering, neurotic and hysterical, has become quite unhinged. All men of competence in the government have been dismissed, and we have been left with men of the calibre of Sturmer and Protopopov, who are universally detested and beneath contempt.

I pause, my dear cousin, in the hope that I must be exaggerating, but I fear it is not so. Such things – and much worse – are said upon every street corner. The list of those who have beseeched the Emperor to form a government led by men respected in the country at large continues to lengthen: the Dowager Empress has pleaded with him, as has his brother Michael Alexandrovich, and more grand dukes, senior members of the Duma and foreign ambassadors than one cares to count. The Emperor listens to all of them, but says nothing, smoking incessantly and drinking tea prescribed by a quack doctor, which those around him at Mogilev believe to be a mixture of henbane and hashish, which reduces him to a state of almost complete inertia.

So, what then, dear cousin, is to become of us? I fear the worst. As each day lengthens, the few remaining officials of any honour and competence try to prevent the inevitable catastrophe. All around is panic, greed, mistrust and fear. We are increasingly in the hands of our own secret police, a group of men as un-scrupulous as any enemy. A Guards officer attempted to assassinate the Empress two weeks ago, but was caught and hanged. However, it is only a matter of time before someone succeeds. There are plans to remove the Emperor and make his brother regent to his son before the revolution on the streets begins, but I fear it is already too late. It is now only a question of when and in what form change will occur. Everyone knows it.

Forgive me, my old friend, but I find it impossible to convince myself any longer that my fears are unfounded. While I have no right to do so, I hope you will forgive me if I request that you offer those members of my family who may find their way to England all possible assistance. I will, of course, never leave my post, and the same is true, I'm sure, of Sandro. I have grave fears, however, for Dmitri's wife Ingrid, and am attempting to persuade her to travel abroad. It may become necessary for her to take my grandson with her. I am transferring adequate funds.

It is late and I must try to sleep. Pray for us, please.
Your ever loving cousin,
Nicholas

Ruzsky folded the letter and put it back into the envelope. His father had expected disaster, but there was no sign here that he was about to give up. Ruzsky thought of the way the old man had revered the Emperor's father, the giant Alexander III, who had appeared to them, when they were children, as nothing short of God-like. Then he recalled the Tsarina's haunted face at Tsarskoe Selo not two weeks ago.

He continued with his work. He sifted through the rest of the desk drawers and made piles on the floor around him of papers that he should discuss with Dmitri. The biggest contained those relating to the family's financial situation. Most pressing was a letter from the manager of the Moscow Bank on the Nevsky, asking for firm confirmation of the order to press ahead with the transfer of a significant part of the family's cash reserves to the bank in London. It was dated yesterday and had been delivered by hand. A statement revealed that the balance of their father's account stood at more than a million roubles. The old man had clearly been liquidating assets for a considerable period of time.

Other papers detailed the rest of the family's wealth. There were shares in three private banks and numerous companies, including several involved in arms production. But the paperwork was not assembled in order. The old man had not been intending to take his leave so suddenly.

Ruzsky worked alone in his father's study by the light of a desk lamp, looking for documents or letters relating to what he had been told that morning. He found nothing. He remembered his father's precise words now: 'To protect the Tsar's wealth from the mob.'

Ruzsky moved his chair, and knocked over a pile of letters that he and his brother had written from the Corps des Pages. He bundled them together again, then sank to his knees and dragged his hand along the ledge beneath the desk where his father had always kept the key to the safe.

There was no sign of it. He stood up and went into the hall where he placed another call to Maria's apartment. There was still no response. He asked the exchange to put him through to the theatre.

'Mariinskiy.'

He had reached the same operator, but in the background he could hear people gathering for the evening performance. 'I would like to speak to Maria Popova, please.'

'Not dancing tonight.'

'Could you get a message to her? It's important.'

'Call again in the morning.'

As the line was again abruptly cut, Ruzsky swore violently under his breath. He stood in the silence of the dark hallway, thinking, then moved through to the drawing room.

A sled was parked on the opposite side of the street, in a dark corner beyond the gas-lamp, its driver huddled on the front seat in swathes of blanket, as if expecting a long wait. Vasilyev's men were making little attempt to conceal that they were watching him.

Ruzsky returned to the hall. He placed a call to Tsarskoe Selo. A woman answered. 'May I speak to Colonel Shulgin, please.'

'Who is calling?'

'Chief Investigator Ruzsky of the Petrograd city police. Please tell him it is urgent.'

Ruzsky waited. It seemed an interminable time before he heard footsteps cross the hallway at the other end of the line. 'Colonel Shulgin is engaged. May I take a message?'

'Could you ask him to telephone me? Chief Investigator Ruzsky in Millionaya Street.' He gave the number. 'At once. Please tell him it is urgent.'

'Call again in the morning.'

'Will you tell him it is urgent?'

'I already have. He says to telephone again in the morning.'

Ruzsky walked back slowly to his father's desk. He pulled out his silver cigarette case and lit up, then watched the smoke curl towards the ceiling and imagined his father sitting here alone. He turned over the case to look at the family crest. It had once belonged to his great-grandfather and had been passed to each eldest son on his eighteenth birthday.

There was a knock at the front door. Ruzsky stood up and moved to the doorway as he heard a servant's footsteps. He reached into the pocket of his jacket and checked that his revolver was loaded.

CHAPTER FORTY-SEVEN

He relaxed as he heard Pavel's voice. Seconds later, the big detective slipped into the study. Ruzsky put the revolver back into his pocket. 'Expecting company?' Pavel asked.

Ruzsky pointed at the leather seat opposite his desk. Pavel took it. Ruzsky wondered if he had noticed the Okhrana agent outside and, if so, why he had not mentioned it. 'That was where we used to sit,' he remarked, 'while Father read out our school reports.'

'I'm sorry, Sandro.'

'Don't tell me, you've found that all is as it appeared. Sarlov says there was no sign of a struggle, the cause of death is suicide and the only fingerprints on the revolver belong to my father.'

Pavel did not speak.

'He'd been a different person since I came back from Tobolsk,' Ruzsky said. 'He'd changed, and I had barely begun to appreciate it, let alone respond.'

'Don't punish yourself.'

'It is inevitable. If I'd taken the hand of friendship, then who knows—'

'Who knows indeed? He was a strong man. Honourable, as you have said yourself on many an occasion. He knew exactly what he was doing.'

Ruzsky looked at the rock on the corner of the desk. It was the most unattractive paperweight imaginable.

'Have you seen the man outside?' Pavel asked.

'Yes.'

'They're not making any attempt to hide themselves.'

'Whatever Vasilyev is doing, he wanted my father out of the way.'

'In case you've forgotten, he wants you out of the way too.'

'This morning's meeting was about how to protect the wealth of the Tsar from a revolutionary mob,' Ruzsky said.

'Your father told you that?'

'Not in so many words.'

Pavel's expression was wary.

'I've started going through his papers. He feared there would come a point when paper money would cease to have any value. He would not have concerned himself with the Tsar's private possessions. This must have been to do with the gold. The Imperial reserves.'

'But how could that have led to his death?'

'I think Vasilyev has robbery in mind. My father stood in the way.'

There was a lengthy silence. 'But how would that have led to—'

Ruzsky thought of what Vasilyev had implied that afternoon. 'I think he was threatened.'

'But your father was . . . He was a minister of the

Imperial Court. He had many connections. Have you called Colonel Shulgin?'

'I left an urgent message. He did not come to the telephone.'

Pavel stared at the light on the desk. 'What do you want me to do?'

'I would ask a favour.'

The big detective waited.

'There is no answer at her apartment or at the Mariinskiy. Could you find her, try to speak to her alone?' Ruzsky ignored the despair in his friend's eyes. 'Tell her what has happened to my father. Try to convince her to leave the city. Just for a few days.'

Pavel contemplated his friend. 'I suppose it is too late to persuade you to reconsider?'

'Reconsider what?'

Pavel sighed. 'I will do what I can, Sandro. Will I find you here tomorrow?'

'No. I will come to the office.'

'Very well, then.'

As Ruzsky listened to his friend's receding foot-steps, he thought of the things he had chosen not to share.

What had Borodin planned for the Kresty Crossing?

He needed time alone to think.

Ruzsky sat in the kitchen. He had said good night to Michael long since, and the servants had withdrawn. The house was quiet down here, and it was where he had always felt most comfortable as a child: here he could avoid the constrictions of his parents' world.

He heard Ingrid's soft footsteps before she came in. She had bathed and changed. She wore a high-necked rich blue dress that matched the colour of her eyes. 'Is he still asleep?' Ruzsky asked.

She nodded.

'He has fared well, better than I might have expected.'

'Perhaps he is blessed with only partial under-standing. For now, at least. Have you had something to eat?' she asked.

He shook his head.

'Do you mind if I join you?'

Ruzsky gestured to the far side of the wooden table and she took a seat opposite him. She shook out her hair and ran her hands through it. 'If there is anything I can do, Sandro, any way in which I can help, please just tell me how.'

'When did Dmitri go out?'

'Shortly before you returned.' Ingrid examined the texture of the table, brushing her palm across its surface. 'He often seeks comfort with her now.' It was said without rancour or bitterness. 'She can offer him that, at least.'

Ruzsky felt himself flush and tried to conceal the pang of jealousy that pierced him. He wondered if Ingrid had any inkling that the same woman tormented them both.

'She plans to take him away,' she said quietly, 'by the end of this week. Do you know that?'

For a moment, Ruzsky thought she was talking about Maria and Dmitri.

'Irina,' Ingrid went on, 'and her grand duke.'

'Yes. To Nice.'

Ingrid reached forward and put her hand on his. 'I'm truly sorry, Sandro.'

Ruzsky gazed into her deep blue eyes. He did

not know whether he should withdraw his hand.

'He was an extraordinary man,' she said.

'He was extremely fond of you.'

'And he adored you.'

Now Ruzsky pulled away his hand gently. 'We had our . . . difficulties.'

'But he was always so very proud of you. Of who you are. He could not conceal it.'

Despite himself, Ruzsky was pleased. 'He concealed it for many years.'

'He talked about you almost constantly over the past few months. He could not hide his excitement at the prospect of your return.'

Ruzsky tried to imagine this. If Ingrid's face had not radiated such sincerity, he'd have suspected her of humouring him. 'He had changed. I failed to see it,' he said, and thought again of that last conversation in the drawing room. 'I failed to respond,' he added.

'Don't blame yourself. It is the last thing he would have wanted.'

The great gaping void of the suicide hung between them.

'Did you see any sign that he would do that?' Ruzsky whispered.

'No.'

'Was his behaviour in any way out of the ordinary over these last few days?'

'He was subdued, gentle. But then, that is how I shall remember him.'

'Did you speak to him this morning?'

'I saw him in the hall after breakfast. I asked if he was going to the ministry and he said, no, not today. I thought that was odd, in such times, but he did not appear to wish to converse, so I took Michael upstairs

468

until we went to the Summer Garden.' Ingrid tried to smile. 'I think Michael hoped we would wake you. One of the servants had told him you were here.'

'And when you came down again?'

'The study door was ajar, and I could see a light on. I assumed he was at his desk. As you know, he did not like to be disturbed.'

'Had he received any callers the previous night?'

'No.'

'Telephone calls?'

'Several, but I did not answer them. Dmitri was dining at his mess. Your father took his meal in the study. But he worked late. I needed a glass of water in the middle of the night – at one or two in the morning – and did not wish to trouble the servants so I came to get it myself. When I passed his study, the light was still on.'

'You did not look in?'

Ingrid shook her head.

'He never made any comment about the work of the ministry?'

'Never. Nor about the government, except in the most general terms, and then only to discuss the progress of the war.'

'And to Dmitri?'

'I . . . I do not believe so. It was Dmitri's great frustration. He said they never talked about anything in depth, merely exchanged platitudes.'

Ruzsky wondered again where his brother was. 'Did anything about the past few days strike you as out of the ordinary? Any visitors? Any chance remark?'

'The city is tense, Sandro. It has affected us all. The servants . . . everyone.'

'And you saw signs of tension in my father?'

'He spoke of his concern.'

'What did he say?'

'He asked me at breakfast yesterday, or the day before, if I would like to consider going to Sweden, perhaps, or England, until things were calmer. Funds would be made available in London, he said, for as long a stay as I wished.'

'And what did you reply?'

'I said that I wanted to stay with my husband at this difficult time, and to help look after Michael.'

'Had he suggested you go abroad before?'

'No.'

'Did he give any particular indication as to why he raised the matter then?'

'No. He said we should discuss it again, perhaps tomorrow.'

'Did he mention a deadline? Did he mention this Friday, for example, as a time that concerned him?'

'No.'

'Did he ever talk about Vasilyev with either you or Dmitri?'

'No.'

'Had you ever seen them together before that night at the ballet?'

'No.'

'Did Dmitri mention it? They made ... odd companions.'

'Your father was a member of the government, Sandro. Even Dmitri understands that that requires one to deal with a wider circle than the Guards' mess.'

Ruzsky took out a cigarette and tapped it against the silver case before putting it into his mouth and lighting it. He offered the case to Ingrid, but she declined.

'Will there be a revolution?' she asked.

'Few seem to doubt it.'

'When he is sober, Dmitri says many of the soldiers would relish killing their officers.'

'Not if they're hanged for it.'

Ingrid leant forward. 'A German in Millionaya Street,' she whispered. 'I suppose I must fear the mob.'

'We should all fear the mob.'

'It is so long since I have seen someone smile. In the street, I mean.'

'They never do in the winter.'

It was an evasive response, and they both knew it. Ruzsky saw the fear in her eyes. He realized that she had long since stopped looking to Dmitri for protection.

Ruzsky got up. He failed to find either vodka or wine in the kitchen, so opened the hatch into the cellar. It was dark, but he located a bottle on the rack. Back in the kitchen he saw that it was champagne. He looked at Ingrid. 'It hardly seems appropriate, but . . .'

Ingrid watched as he went to get two glasses from the cupboard and opened the bottle. 'I was never an expert on vintages,' he said. 'Father tried to explain, but gave up.'

'I'm glad you reached some kind of understanding, Sandro.'

Ruzsky lifted his glass. 'To the future.'

Ingrid raised hers and they drank. The temperature in the cellar had ensured that the champagne was chilled.

'Michael asked me tonight why your father had an accident.'

'And what did you say?'

'That I did not know, but that you would find out.'

Ruzsky contemplated his champagne, then downed it. He refilled both glasses.

'Would you ever leave the city, Sandro?'

'Why do you ask?'

'It is just that your father was someone whose opinion I trusted.'

'And his question frightened you?'

She looked at him, seeking reassurance. 'Was that foolish?'

'No.'

'Does it frighten you, too?'

Ruzsky looked out of the low kitchen window to the darkness of the garden. 'It is hard to turn your back,' he said.

'On a life,' she answered. 'Of course.'

And on a love, he thought, though he did not say it.

Ingrid put her hand over his again. Ruzsky felt drunk. He realized he hadn't eaten since that morning, which already seemed a lifetime away. He turned his palm upwards so that their fingers interlocked. 'We'll be all right,' he said.

'I hope so.'

Ingrid withdrew her hand and they drained their glasses. 'I . . . will see you tomorrow,' she said.

'Yes.'

'Good night, Sandro.'

'I have a favour to ask,' he said. 'I need a day, perhaps two. I need to know that Michael is going to be safe.'

'Just tell me what you wish me to do.'

'There is a man outside. I . . . I am being watched now. I cannot leave the house unless I know you have found somewhere safe.'

'Where do you wish us to go?'

'The Hôtel de l'Europe, perhaps. Anywhere but here. Not tonight, but in the morning. So far as I can tell, only one is with me, and he will not wish to risk losing sight of his target. If you hide some spare clothes beneath your coat and do not return, it will take them some time to locate you.'

'Of course, Sandro.'

'Good night,' he said.

Ruzsky listened to her progress through the house.

He refilled his champagne glass and lit another cigarette.

Five minutes later, he climbed the stairs from the kitchen. The desk lamp was still on in the study and he switched it off. He had intended not to linger, but that proved impossible. He sat down in his father's chair. The air was still thick with the pungent aroma of the cleaning fluid he had used to scrub the rug clean.

He thought of his brother in the apartment off Sadovaya Ulitsa, and the comfort he must have found there. He wondered what his father would have done in such circumstances, and realized, with trepidation, that the answer lay in that small patch of scrubbed carpet. Though he had often fought against his father's certainties, they were many times more attractive than the vacuum he was faced with now.

Ruzsky stood up and went through the shadows to the telephone. He paused, then picked up the earpiece and rang Maria's number. Once again there was no answer.

He hung up the earpiece and headed upstairs. He

473

halted on the landing outside his parents' bedroom. On a small table beside their bed stood a vase of fresh yellow carnations. He went through to his father's dressing room and opened the cupboards to the rows and rows of suits, morning suits, full-dress uniforms, frock coats, mess jackets and tunics. At the bottom of the cabinet there was a line of field boots, hand-made walking shoes, dress shoes and dancing shoes. He took out one of his father's dress uniforms and held it up to the moonlight. It had been made by Nordenshtrem, the country's most prestigious military tailor. He replaced it, shut the cupboard and moved to the window.

The sled still stood there.

He looked up and down the street, then stepped back and made his way to the top of the house. He found sheets and blankets, checked that Michael was sleeping, bent to kiss his head, and lay down on the floor beside him.

The shouts at first seemed distant, but the sound of breaking glass woke Ruzsky. Michael was sitting up in bed.

The voices were suddenly closer.

Ruzsky rolled on to his feet and put on his trousers. 'Don't be afraid,' he told his son, and picked up his revolver. He ran down the stairs, checking that there was ammunition in the chamber. He reached the first floor and his father's bedroom.

Another window smashed.

Ruzsky looked out. 'Jew-lover!' one man yelled, though none of them could have seen him at the window.

There were about twenty in all, a rag-tag collection

474

of Black Band thugs. One or two carried banners emblazoned with images of the Tsar. Ruzsky could still see the Okhrana agent wrapped up in his sled, though he had moved fifty yards down the street so that he would not be directly associated with the assault. The road was darker; someone had knocked out the gas-lamp.

'Jew-lover!' they bawled again. Several of the group held rocks, which they were throwing at the windows on the ground floor.

Ruzsky turned to see Michael in the doorway, his face pale. 'What are they doing, Papa?' Ingrid was behind him.

'Stay here,' Ruzsky instructed. He walked down the last flight of stairs to the hall. He was dressed only in trousers and a loose white shirt, the holster slung over his shoulder. He pulled out his revolver as another missile crashed through the drawing-room window. The valet, Peter, was in the hall. 'Have you got a gun?' Ruzsky demanded.

'No, sir.'

'Have any of the servants?'

'I don't believe so.' Peter's face betrayed no fear.

'Did my father keep any other guns in the house?'

'Only his revolver, sir, so far as I'm aware.'

The shouting from the street grew louder. Ruzsky saw his son's face poking through the banisters. 'If anything happens to me – if any of them are armed – bolt the door behind me and telephone Pavel Miliutin, my deputy in the city police. Do you understand?'

'Yes, sir.'

Ruzsky strode forward, pulled back the door and charged down the steps. His sudden appearance brought a hush to the crowd. 'You have ten seconds to

leave the street, by official order, and I will shoot anyone who remains a moment longer.'

Ruzsky looked from face to face. He saw in them
the hunger for violence, the desire to storm into the
world of wealth and privilege that lay behind him. For
a few seconds, he feared that his ultimatum would not
be enough, that he would have to carry out his threat.
Then one man turned away, and the others followed
slowly.

He saw a curtain twitch in the house opposite, but
none of the neighbours – friends and colleagues of his
father for many years – came to offer help.

CHAPTER FORTY-EIGHT

The following morning, Ingrid and Michael left. Ruzsky had helped Ingrid conceal a few spare clothes inside her coat and now, from his father's bedroom window, he kept his eye on their receding figures until they disappeared at the end of the street.

He saw with satisfaction that the man in the sled did not follow them. He gave them barely a second glance.

At the city-police headquarters, Ruzsky found his colleagues gathered at the window. Beside Pavel, Maretsky looked like a dwarf. As they turned to see who had entered, the professor mumbled his condolences.

Ruzsky joined them at their vantage-point. The man who had tailed him from Millionaya Street had parked alongside another *droshky* on the far side of Ofitserskaya Ulitsa. Ruzsky could tell from Pavel's expression that the second driver was also Okhrana.

He heard chanting and craned his neck to identify its source. About a hundred or more protesters were walking in their direction, carrying a tawdry red banner bearing the slogan 'Fair pay for a fair day's work'. He watched the faces of the Okhrana men as the protest passed. 'You were followed here too?' he asked Pavel.

'Yes.'

'How long have you had a tail?'

'Since first thing this morning.'

Ruzsky glanced at Maretsky, then tugged Pavel to the other side of the office. 'Did you manage to—'

'I could not find her. I searched half the night.'

Ruzsky's chest tightened. 'Where did you look?'

'She was not at her apartment. The neighbours had not seen her.'

'Perhaps she came back later.'

'I checked for the last time at past one in the morning.'

'Did you—'

'She wasn't at the Mariinskiy. They had been expecting her for a rehearsal in the afternoon, but she did not arrive. When I impressed upon them the urgency of my enquiry, they gave me the name of a Guards officer ... your brother.' Pavel's tone was neutral. 'I went over to the barracks. The officer on duty said that Major Ruzsky had been expected at dinner in the mess, but had not been present. Then I went to the Symnov factory, but could find no sign of anyone. When I got back to her apartment at one, your brother answered the door.'

'You spoke to him?'

'He was in uniform – as if he had been intending to go to the dinner. He looked tired and worried, so I introduced myself and said I wished to speak to her in connection with a case. He replied that he did not know where she was.'

'And you believed him? It was not possible she was inside the apartment?'

'Sandro, I could see the concern in his face. He said he had been due to meet her at seven that evening, but she had not appeared.'

Ruzsky retreated to his desk. What was she doing? 'Have you ever heard of the Kresty Crossing?' he asked.

'No. Why?'

'Maretsky?'

The professor was startled. 'What?'

'Have you ever heard of somewhere called the Kresty Crossing?'

'Er . . . no. What is it?'

'It's a place. At least, I assume it is.'

'Should I be aware of it?'

'I don't know.'

'Why?' Pavel asked again.

'You remember the numbers on the money we found on the American? Well, the message spells, "Kresty Crossing".'

'How do you know that?' Pavel asked.

'I found the code book.' He did not say where, but when he looked at his partner he saw that Pavel had understood. He moved over to the map of the city on the wall above Pavel's desk.

'Are you sure it's a place?' Pavel asked.

'It sounds to me like a railway junction.'

All three were silent as they studied the map. Ruzsky traced the line of each route out of the capital, but no crossings were marked.

'What makes you think it's a railway junction?' Maretsky asked.

'Because the last thing we know that the group in Yalta did was rob a train.'

Ruzsky stared at the telephone in front of him. He picked up the earpiece and asked the operator for a connection. As the call was put through, he imagined the bell ringing in Maria's empty hallway. There was no answer. He broke the connection.

Pavel was watching him. Ruzsky knew he was testing the limits of his friend's loyalty.

He sifted mechanically through the paperwork that had accumulated on his desk. There was a note from Sarlov, but as he picked it up he saw Maretsky slip out of the door. 'Have you heard from Professor Egorov?' he asked.

Maretsky stopped.

'You said he was going to return to Petrograd today. You showed him the inscription on the knife.'

'Of course. I'll call him.' Maretsky shut the door behind him.

Pavel had returned to the window and was looking at their watchers on the street with the fascinated air of a small child following a military parade. Ruzsky sat down and glanced over Sarlov's note, then unhooked the telephone again. 'Sarlov? It's Ruzsky.'

'Sandro, yes. I'm . . . well, we're all sorry. I'm sure – well, I hope you know that.'

'Thank you, yes.' Ruzsky cleared his throat. 'You wanted to speak to me.'

'Yes . . .' Sarlov seemed hesitant.

'Your note referred to the boy at the Lion Bridge.'

'Yes.' Sarlov blew his nose. 'Of course. Do you recall the brand on the American's shoulder?'

'Yes.'

'Well, the boy at the Lion Bridge had something similar.'

'On his shoulder also?'

480

'I can't say for certain. I didn't see it. The Okhrana performed the autopsy, if you recall.'

'You discussed it with a colleague?'

'It came to my attention, yes. The marks sounded alike. I thought you'd like to know.'

'So, both men had the mark, but not the girl.' Ruzsky was referring to Ella, but thinking of Maria. He had seen nothing like it on her shoulder either. 'If anything else springs to mind, would you telephone me, Sarlov?'

'Of course.'

Ruzsky terminated the call. He tried to work out what reason there might be for the men in the group to have the mark, but not the women. He grasped the telephone once more. 'Would you put me through to the Ministry for the Railways,' he told the operator.

Pavel was still facing the street. The shouts outside were louder.

Ruzsky asked to be connected with the assistant secretary to the minister. A man in that office listened patiently to his explanation, but said that he had no idea where the Kresty Crossing was or what it might be. He suggested that Ruzsky call the Bureau for Railway Building and Maintenance and gave a number, which turned out to be for the administration department at the headquarters of the North Russia Maritime and Customs police. Ruzsky called the operator and was eventually put through to the correct department at the bureau, but the wrong individual. The man said the office he required was on the floor below, but he could not recall the number.

More than ten minutes later, Ruzsky spoke to someone in the railway maintenance department. Despite it having been impressed upon him that this was a criminal investigation, the man said he was too busy to check the detailed maps that were kept on the top floor. He conceded, when Ruzsky would not let the matter drop, that he believed it was a road crossing on the line out to Tsarskoe Selo, but he could not be certain. Everyone in the department was stretched to breaking point, he said, ensuring the lines were in working order for the war effort, and he did not have time to pursue the matter further. He terminated the call.

They heard rapid footsteps on the stairs and along the corridor. A constable appeared in the doorway, a sheepskin cap in his hands, his hair damp with sweat.

They waited while he caught his breath.

'Another body, sir,' he gasped. 'A woman.'

CHAPTER FORTY-NINE

Ruzsky flew down the stairs, the constable alongside him. 'A woman?' he demanded.

'Yes, sir.'

'How old?'

'I don't know, sir.'

'Young?'

'I—'

'Twenty? Thirty? Older?'

'Something like that, sir, yes.'

Ruzsky ran out into the street towards the *droshky* waiting opposite. They had lost Pavel, but he did not wait. 'Where?' he demanded of the constable, as the young man got in beside him.

'Vyborg side,' the man shouted at the driver. 'By the Finland station.'

The driver cracked his whip and the sled moved. 'Go via the quay,' Ruzsky instructed him.

The man did not look round, nor did he query the instruction. Only *likachy* drivers were allowed to take their vehicles along the palace embankment. Ruzsky glanced back over his shoulder and saw Pavel run out of the building. The big detective hailed another sled. He had two more constables with him.

Ruzsky turned back to his companion. 'She was dark?' he demanded. 'Dark hair? Long dark hair?'

'Yes, sir. I believe so.'

'You're sure?'

'Yes . . . yes.' He did not seem certain. 'She had a knife through her . . .' He pointed at his eye.

It could not be her. Ruzsky's heart threatened to break out of his chest and his forehead prickled with sweat.

The sled hurtled past the Admiralty and the façade of the Winter Palace. They swung on to the Alexandrovsky Bridge.

'Whereabouts?' Ruzsky heard himself shout. 'Tell me where exactly.'

'I'll show you, sir.' The constable seemed equally agitated.

They were over the bridge now and hurtling down the broad, tree-lined avenue towards the spire of the Finland station.

'Here,' the constable shouted at the driver, pointing towards a narrow side-street between the tenements.

The man slowed the horses, then wheeled them into the alley and down towards a tall, dark building surrounded by armed men.

Ruzsky leapt from the sled before it had ground to a halt.

Ten or more Okhrana agents, armed with rifles, stood in a semi-circle around the entrance. The queue outside the bakery opposite stared at the scene in awed silence.

Ruzsky strode towards the officer in charge. 'Chief Investigator Ruzsky,' he said, 'city police.'

The man's broad, bearded face was unyielding. 'We've instructions to let no one through.'

'A murder has been reported by my constables,' Ruzsky said.

The other sled drew up and Pavel came over. He produced his identification papers. 'Deputy Chief Investigator Miliutin,' he said. The man remained unmoved.

The two groups faced each other. Ruzsky slipped his hand into his jacket, grasping the handle of his revolver. The silence was broken by the screech of an engine, then a loud clank as a train shunted inside the Finland station.

Ruzsky seized his moment.

'You – *stop!*' the officer shouted, but Ruzsky had already broken into a run, darting through the entrance, past a mound of garbage.

'Wait!' he heard Pavel shout. He half expected a shot.

Ruzsky pounded up the stairs. The stench of urine and decay brought tears to his eyes. The walls glistened with water. He tried to focus only on the steps ahead of him. He turned the last corner.

A man was bent over the body.

Ruzsky saw one slim leg twisted at an impossible angle; a long leather boot.

The man straightened and turned. Prokopiev. A knife protruded from the dead woman's cheek.

'Sandro, I—'

It was not her. It was Olga.

Christ, it was not her.

Ruzsky leant against the wall as he tried to recover his breath. He was soaked in sweat, his throat dry and palms clammy. The Okhrana officer caught up with him and bellowed in his ear, but Ruzsky was oblivious to what he said.

'All right, all right,' Prokopiev shouted, as he came down the steps. He waved the man away, and Pavel, who stood behind. 'I'll deal with him.'

Prokopiev faced Ruzsky, his hands thrust into his pockets, waiting for the others to withdraw. Ruzsky was still trying to control his breathing. He wiped the sweat from his forehead.

Prokopiev examined him as a gamekeeper might a cornered animal, but, as Ruzsky came to his senses, he realized that something had changed in the man. Ivan Prokopiev appeared tired, and there was a hint in those dark, intense eyes, if not of humanity then at least of irony, or weary disillusion. 'Are you all right, Chief Investigator?' he asked. 'You do not look well.'

When the others had retreated out of earshot, Prokopiev took out a cigarette case and offered it to Ruzsky. 'Did you think it was someone else?' he asked, as the match flared.

Prokopiev glanced at his boots. They had been newly polished. 'I heard about your father,' he said. 'I'm sorry for that.'

Ruzsky took a pace towards the body, but Prokopiev raised his hand. 'Don't go any closer,' he said.

Ruzsky gazed at the dead woman from where he stood. The hilt of the knife bore a striking resemblance to the one they had discovered on the Neva. 'You know who she is?' he asked.

Prokopiev shrugged.

'Might I take a look?' He inched forward, and this time Prokopiev made no move to stop him.

Olga had fallen awkwardly, her body twisted. Her assailant had been waiting in the shadows of the doorway and her face, never beautiful, was savagely distorted.

Ruzsky squatted, an arm resting upon his knee. He reached forward to touch the skin of what remained of her cheek. She had been dead for some time. He examined the knife. It was an ancient weapon with an iron handle, but no inscription that he could see.

There were three stab wounds: one in the left cheek, another in the mouth and a third directly through the centre of the eye. He didn't need Sarlov to tell him that the killer had been tall. The wounds were deep. A pool of congealed blood had frozen on the stone floor around her head. Her remaining eye was fixed upon him. It appeared to be as filled with hatred for Ruzsky and his kind as it had been when she was alive.

Prokopiev climbed slowly up the steps and leant on the iron balcony. 'So, who did you think it was, Chief Investigator?'

'There are no witnesses?' Ruzsky asked, ignoring the question. He reached for the pocket of Olga's overcoat.

'There's nothing in it.'

Olga's clothes were ill-fitting and loose, so he started to ease the overcoat away from her right shoulder.

'What are you doing?'

Ruzsky did not reply.

'Step back, Sandro. Please.'

But Ruzsky was now pulling off the shirt to allow himself a glimpse of her shoulder.

She had the mark: a dark star branded on white skin.

'Move back,' Prokopiev said.

'You see this brand? The American had one and so did the man we found at the Lion Bridge.'

Prokopiev bent down to take a closer look. Ruzsky

could see that he knew exactly what it meant.

'The mark of the assassin.' Prokopiev sighed, almost inaudibly. He straightened, and his eyes bored into Ruzsky's. 'Do not mourn them, Sandro.'

'You knew the woman?'

'Few will regret her passing.'

'You knew her from Yalta?'

'An anarchist.'

'How did she come to be here?'

'No tears will be shed for her. But for *your* girl . . .' He paused. 'Now, she is a very different matter.'

Ruzsky searched for some sign that this was another threat, but Prokopiev's expression was concerned – almost imploring. 'Did you know her in Yalta?'

'No.'

'You were on the train with us?'

'When you disappeared? Yes.'

Ruzsky gestured at the body. 'Vasilyev has been behind these killings, hasn't he? He wishes to remove all traces of the connections that date from Yalta?'

'You're smarter than that. No general kills his own soldiers before the battle begins.'

'What battle?'

'Your time is short.'

They heard laboured footsteps on the stairs below. 'Back,' Prokopiev instructed. He fixed Ruzsky with an intense stare. Your time *is* short, his eyes blazed.

Vasilyev turned the corner, his dark cape fastened at the throat by a gold chain. He mounted the steps with his head thrust forward, his face glacial. He bent over the body. 'Thank you, Chief Investigator. That will be all.'

As Prokopiev led him away, Ruzsky glanced back at

the dark figure stooped over the body. At the foot of the stairs, he noticed a pool of blood and stopped.

Prokopiev propelled him onwards. Ruzsky tried to turn back, but the door of the apartment building was slammed in his face.

Pavel was waiting on the far side of the road, to one side of the queue. 'Who was it?' His eyes told Ruzsky that he knew who it was not.

'Olga Legarina.'

'She's also from Yalta?'

'She's one of the group, yes.'

'Did you get a look at the body?'

'It's the same killer, with a similar knife. She had an identical mark on her right shoulder.'

'The same as the American?'

'Prokopiev called it the mark of the assassin.'

'If we don't reach her, she's going to die, isn't she?' Pavel said, without emotion, as if he was considering the possibility for the first time. 'We had better find her.'

Ruzsky was staring at the doorway opposite. They weren't robbed. They were assassinated. He thought of what he had uncovered in the records in Yalta. 'Popova expressed the view chief of police in Odessa better target.'

He ran back to the sled. 'Hurry up,' he called.

CHAPTER FIFTY

The records division of the Petrograd city police was housed in the vast cellar that ran all the way under Ofitserskaya Ulitsa. It was cold, the documents it contained damp and frayed at the edges.

The duty clerk led them to the far wall and pointed at a section of buff-coloured files that stretched for thirty yards or more. No one had ever counted how many servants of the regime had been murdered in the past twenty years, but it clearly ran into thousands. For each assassination, the local police office telegraphed notification and a request for information to every major city department in the country. Every crime against the regime was recorded here.

The only desk in the cellar belonged to the clerk, so Pavel and Ruzsky sat on the floor. Pavel began on the shelf for 1910, Ruzsky for the year before. Each folder contained the telegraph traffic for one week.

'What are we looking for?' Pavel turned the tattered sheets in the first file. 'An assassination in the Crimea?'

'And the surrounding area, unless something else leaps out at you.'

The ceiling shook as an automobile passed on the street above. Ruzsky thought again of the brief description of the group's activities in the records in Yalta and its references to the chief of police and the governor of Odessa. 'I think they concentrated on the peninsula, and possibly Odessa.'

Pavel did not look convinced.

Ruzsky riffled through the telegraphs in his hand. They provided a window on an empire in which it was all too easy for criminals to evade capture.

After half an hour, Ruzsky found a string of correspondence relating to the murder of an Imperial official – the principal private secretary to the governor in Kazan. No group was mentioned and the two suspects were 'believed to have travelled to Moscow'. He replaced the file and began to work through the next, but he was finding it hard to concentrate. 'It's age that divides them,' he said.

'Divides who?' Pavel asked, without looking up.

'The victims. Olga, the American and Markov from the Lion Bridge are all considerably older than Ella. And it is they who have the mark.'

'So?'

'The mark of the assassin predates . . .' Ruzsky stopped.

'What?'

'Hold on.' Ruzsky shut the folder on his lap, stood up and put it back. He moved down the line of shelves, examining the dates. 'I'm going to start earlier.' He found the section for 1905. He had recalled not Ella's history but Maria's. He took down the file for the first week of that year. It contained a seamless record of similar, mostly anonymous crimes from across the Empire. They merged into each other, but

491

he flicked through the pages methodically, before he replaced the file and started on the next.

The telegraph traffic for the year was endless, as the revolution that had begun in St Petersburg slowly consumed the whole of Russia. It was particularly heavy from Odessa during the summer, as revolutionary fervour spread to the Black Sea fleet, sparking a mutiny on the battleship *Potemkin*. Members of the local police department had recorded the string of ordinary crimes that occurred during the period of anarchy, even as the fabric of their world teetered on the brink of extinction. Ruzsky gave a wry smile.

He looked up at his partner, who sat with his head bent, absorbed in his task.

He returned to his own file and began to leaf through the pages once more.

'What are we looking for, Sandro?'

'You know what we're looking for.'

Pavel had not raised his head. 'If you say so.'

They worked on without a break. As the light began to fade Stanislav appeared. 'I'm surprised you're here,' he said. 'I heard—' The look on Ruzsky's face told him not to continue. 'I'm sorry, anyhow.' He shrugged, and fiddled nervously with his moustache. 'There's an alert for Friday.'

'What do you mean?'

'The entire Petrograd garrison. I heard that Shulgin and Count Fredericks want the reserve battalions brought in from Peterhof and Gatchina, but the Tsar won't hear of it.'

'I thought the Tsar was at the front.'

'Apparently not. There are delegations on their way. Italians, French . . .'

'Why is there an alert?' Ruzsky asked, although he thought he knew the answer.

'I don't know, but the city is being divided up by military district and they are to patrol the streets before dawn. The Finland regiment on Vasilevsky, the Preobrazhenskys on South Quay and along Horseguards, the Volynsky from the Nevsky down to Nicholas station.'

Ruzsky put down his folder and stood up.

'What are you doing down here?' Stanislav asked, looking about him.

'Why is there an alert?' Ruzsky asked again. 'You must have heard speculation.'

'I heard you found another body. The newspapers are going to love that.'

'Well, you'd better ask Vasilyev before you get them to print it.'

Stanislav tugged harder at the ends of his moustache. 'What are you doing down here?' He glanced at Pavel.

'Some research,' Ruzsky answered.

'Into what?'

'Never mind.'

'It is still your case?'

Ruzsky took a pace forward. 'I'd like you to do something. I want to know what all the murder victims were doing in Petersburg, especially the American. He was staying at the Astoria, so go there. Talk to the bell-boys and the chambermaids. See what you can find out. What did the American do with his time here? What visitors did he receive? Where did he go when he went out? Did the girl, Ella, ever go there?'

'The Astoria?'

'Yes.'

'He was staying at the Astoria?'

'Yes.'

Stanislav raised an eyebrow. 'What else?'

'Just find that out, and get back to me. I want to know exactly what the American's movements were from the moment he arrived until the moment someone stuck a knife in his chest out on the ice.'

A few minutes later, Ruzsky tramped up the stairs to the deserted offices of the criminal-investigation division. The secretaries had tidied their desks, and all the doors around the central room were shut. He picked up his telephone and asked the operator to put him through to Colonel Shulgin at Tsarskoe Selo.

It took a long time to make the connection, and when it was achieved a woman answered, her voice distant. 'Yes?' she demanded.

'Might I speak to Colonel Shulgin?'

'Who is it?'

'Chief Investigator Ruzsky, Petrograd city police, criminal-investigation division.'

'Oh, yes.'

He heard her footsteps receding.

Ruzsky drummed his fingers as he waited.

'Yes?' another voice answered. 'Shulgin here.'

'It's Ruzsky, sir.'

'Oh . . . yes, Ruzsky.' There was a long pause. 'I was sorry to hear about your father.'

'I rang you last night, sir.'

'Yes, you said it was urgent. My apologies.'

Ruzsky could tell someone else was listening, or standing close. 'I'd be grateful if I could speak to you in person at the earliest opportunity.'

'Yes.' Shulgin's tone was noncommittal.

'Preferably tonight.'

'That is not possible, Chief Investigator.'

'My father's death was no accident, sir.'

Shulgin was silent.

'It occurred within minutes of an unscheduled meeting with Mr Vasilyev. I'm sure you will agree that it was quite out of character.'

'The meeting was not unscheduled. And Mr Vasilyev is privy, I'm afraid, to a great deal of information that disturbs the minds of the sanest of men.'

'That is hard to accept,' Ruzsky said quietly.

'So are many things, at this time.'

'You were close to my father.'

'We were colleagues.'

'Close colleagues.'

'I was aware of your father's concerns.'

'Would you share them with me?'

Shulgin sighed. 'No. I'm sorry. I cannot.'

'Am I not to be permitted to know why my father took his own life?'

There was a longer pause. 'Nicholas Nicholaevich was a senior government official. Our hands are bound in ways we might not wish.'

'So he placed a revolver in his mouth and pulled the trigger purely as a result of the situation in which Russia finds herself at this time?'

Shulgin's silence suggested that he, too, did not believe this was an adequate explanation.

'In the meeting we attended you made reference to events you expected to take place this Friday. You spoke with Mr Vasilyev about intelligence connected to the day after tomorrow, sir.'

'Yes.'

'We have been informed that the Petrograd garrison has received specific orders relating to that day.'

'Yes.'

'Would you mind telling me why?'

'You know the answer perfectly well.'

'You fear unrest?'

'Yes.'

'It is more than a routine matter?'

'We would not issue an alert without specific intelligence. But what bearing does this have on your investigation?'

'I thought it might shed light on the victims. It is possible that they have been murdered as a result of activities they planned to conduct in the capital.'

Shulgin was silent again.

'There has been another body, sir. A fourth victim. A woman.'

'I see.'

He could tell that Shulgin already knew. Ruzsky pictured him standing alone in the hallway of the Alexander Palace, the Tsar and his wife secluded in the rooms behind him, their children asleep. It seemed not just incongruous but suddenly quite mad that the government of an empire should rest upon such foundations.

'I appreciate the burdens of office,' Ruzsky said, 'especially at this time. But it is not just blind faith that prevents me believing in my father's suicide.'

'I understand that.'

Ruzsky waited for Shulgin to continue.

'Do you know who she was?' Shulgin asked. 'This new victim.'

'She was another of the revolutionaries from Yalta. Olga Legarina was her name.'

'Have you spoken to Mr Vasilyev about this?'

'Briefly.'

'I see. If you . . . hear of anything, you will let me know, won't you, Sandro?'

The sudden intimacy surprised Ruzsky, and touched him. 'Yes. Of course. '

As he replaced the earpiece, he had a strong mental image of Colonel Shulgin walking slowly away across the hallway of the Alexander Palace.

Ruzsky rested his elbows on his desk and his face in his hands. He thought of his father. He wanted to place a call to the study at Millionaya Street and for the old man to answer. He was about to push himself to his feet when the telephone rang. He picked it up.

'Chief Investigator?'

'Yes.'

'Colonel Shulgin.'

'Yes.'

'We . . .' There was a long pause. 'We would like you to present yourself here at first light.'

'Yes, sir.'

'Come alone.'

'Yes, sir.'

A few minutes later, Ruzsky walked back along the corridor and returned to the cellar.

CHAPTER FIFTY-ONE

The clerk had gone home, and Ruzsky persuaded Pavel that he must do likewise. He sat in the basement, alone in his task. The work was laborious, but it was how he liked it. He flicked through the files covering the period from 1905 to 1908 but, with the exception of the era of quasi-revolution in the first of those years, little serious crime had been reported from the Crimean peninsula and its immediate surroundings. There had been assassinations in other parts of the country, but not in Yalta, Sevastopol or Odessa.

Pavel had checked through the records for the latter half of 1908 and the two following years, which left Ruzsky with nowhere to go but backwards.

He began on the files for 1904.

He had reached July before he found what he was looking for. His eyes had begun to droop, but the sight of the name on the telegraph snapped him awake:

GOVERNOR BULYATIN MURDERED STOP BOMB THROWN IN CARRIAGE STOP WIFE AND SON ALSO FATALITIES STOP TWO DAUGHTERS UNHARMED STOP FURTHER INFORMATION SOONEST STOP YALTA

Ruzsky stared at the telegraph, then turned the pages. A period of intense traffic had followed, culminating in the identification of a suspect.

SUSPECT IN BULYATIN CASE IDENTIFIED AS MICHAEL
BORODIN STOP AWAIT FURTHER INFORMATION STOP

But if the office in Yalta had uncovered further information, none came. The Bulyatin case was referred to with diminishing vigour for the remainder of the year, the suspect Borodin not at all.

Ruzsky took the original telegraph from the file, folded it up and slipped it into his pocket.

The wind had strengthened again, and it was snowing heavily, drifts gathering against the houses and around the bases of the gas-lamps. The streets were deserted.

Ruzsky crossed the canal and turned off Sadovaya Ulitsa. The light was on in her window and there was no sign of a cab or sled outside. A dark shape emerged from the shadows, hurrying towards him: a woman – old or young he could not tell – cloaked in the robes of mourning, her face covered with a veil.

Outside Maria's building, Ruzsky looked up through the swirling snow. He saw her at her window, silhouetted against the light. He pushed open the door and climbed the stairs.

At the top, he leant back against the wall. He thought of the document in his pocket, and the reason for her exile. Did she think of the white house she had told him about in Yalta, with its high ceilings, airy rooms and views of the bay?

He imagined a young girl leaning out of the

window to listen to her mother sing on a warm summer's evening, her sister beside her.

Ruzsky knocked. He heard footsteps, then nothing. He thought of her beyond the door, in the darkness. A minute passed, perhaps more. A key was turned and the door opened. She wore a long red dress, a black velvet bow in her hair. She was painfully beautiful: her lips were slightly parted and her eyes shone with a potent blend of love, loneliness and loss. She had been waiting for him. She had known he would be searching for her. She took him into her arms, and he breathed in the scent of her. 'I'm sorry,' she said. 'Sandro, I'm so sorry.'

Ruzsky closed his eyes, transported for a moment to the place he most wished to be.

'I wanted to come to you,' she whispered.

Maria let him go, but only so that she could look into his eyes, her long fingers resting on his jaw. Her expression was intense: she was trying to offer reassurance and support in the dark hours she knew all too well. 'I met him once,' she said, 'before you came back, after a performance. Despite everything, he was charming and kind. He reminded me of you.' She came closer, her face almost touching his. 'I'm sorry, Sandro, if I'd known . . . I would have told you. You understand that, don't you?' The look in her eyes was that of a little girl desperate to be believed.

'He was as good as murdered.' Ruzsky slid down the wall to the floor. She joined him there.

'Your group was gathered here by Vasilyev,' Ruzsky said, 'for a robbery. He plans to steal some of the Tsar's gold. He duped my father.'

Maria looked down at her hands. In the riot of emotions that crossed her face, Ruzsky found the final pieces of his jigsaw. 'It's going to be moved,' he said suddenly. 'Vasilyev would have needed someone to sign the papers, so he must have convinced my father and Shulgin that the gold had to be moved out of the city to Tsarskoe Selo.'

Ruzsky took Maria's chin and forced her to meet his eye. 'Talk to me,' he said. 'Please.'

But Maria looked down, her hair covering her tortured face.

He reached into his pocket, took out the piece of paper and handed it to her.

He watched her expression as she read it.

'Have you come to arrest me?'

'I've come because I fear I'm going to lose you.'

Maria laid her head against the wall with a sigh. Then she raised her knees and put her head on them. The desire to reach out and touch her was almost more than he could resist.

'Less than a second,' she said, 'to destroy so much. How can it be possible?' She lifted her head and tipped it back against the wall.

Ruzsky waited.

'Sometimes, even now,' she said, 'when I am asleep, I can see the clear sky and the sea. I can hear the sound of the cicadas and feel the sun on my face. I was smiling. I was my father's assistant's favourite, and he was making me laugh. Father and Mother, my sister and brother were all in the carriage in front of us. I could hear Papa's laughter.'

Maria put her hands to her cheeks. Ruzsky could not tell if she was crying.

There was a long silence.

'We had been to Livadia. It was the summer, and they had had a function in the gardens for local

501

officials and their families. My sister and brother and I had hidden beneath the tables and gorged ourselves on cake. We had played with the older girls, the Tsar's daughters, and everything was perfect. All the adults drank champagne and talked in small groups.

'On the way home, Father laughed and Mother started to sing. He joined in. I think they were drunk.' She smiled, her face the image of her sister's. 'We were rounding the corner. It was very hot. I could see my mother's parasol. Kitty was looking round, waving to me, and so was Peter, my brother. A man stepped out. He wore a black suit and a fedora – a dark shadow on a bright day. I saw the bomb leave his hand and then there was silence. I knew something terrible was about to happen. We had heard of assassinations, of course, but never in Yalta.

'The taste of my father's flesh and the sight of it on the front of my white dress, the smell, these things have stayed with me every moment of my life.

'Nobody screamed. It was still such a perfect day. Our driver stopped and his assistant, Kemtsov, stood up. He had blood on his face, too, and pieces of flesh clung to his dark suit and hat. I saw the shock on his face. He climbed down from the carriage. He walked slowly and I think he called out. But there was no answer.

'The man in the fedora was no longer there. The cicadas screeched. The sun shone. It seemed to take an age for Kemtsov to reach my parents' carriage.

'I did not want to call to him.

'I stood up and squinted at the sun. I stepped down on to the dusty road and stumbled. I could not feel my legs. When my balance returned, I walked slowly to where Kemtsov stood. Kitty was alive. My father's great body had shielded her. She didn't have a scratch on her, but I knew from the expression on her face that we had lost her. She held my brother's hand. She, too, had been dressed in white. There was a tiny breeze. I remember a strand of hair blowing across her face.

'Kemtsov fainted, but we did not help him. I held Kitty's hand and we stared into each other's eyes. It was as if the world around us had ceased to exist.' Maria's head dropped to one side. 'And it was strange, because *then* I could not hear anything.'

Her face was wet with tears. Ruzsky enfolded her in his arms and she clung to him tightly.

'It's all right,' he whispered.

Her fingers dug into his back. 'No,' she cried, 'it's not all right. It will never be all right.'

Ruzsky held her until the convulsions ceased and her breathing slowed. He released her and she tried to compose herself, wiping tears from her cheeks and removing the hair from her eyes.

'Michael Borodin. *Michael Borodin*. Such an ordinary name,' she said, as if in a trance. 'I was at the piano when my uncle first mentioned him. It was in the big hall of his house. The window was open and the evening was cool. "The police have no doubts," he said, "but the man has fled." They would put out an All-Russias bulletin, but I knew even then that it would be up to me to find him.'

She was silent.

'And you did?'

'It has not been easy.'

'You infiltrated the group.'

Maria did not answer.

'You infiltrated the group alone, or at Vasilyev's urging?'

'Alone.'

'You have never been his agent?'

'The suggestion is obscene.'

'But you did not kill them.' It was a statement, shielding a question. He hoped merely that she would confirm it.

She shook her head slowly. 'For many years, I had lived for their deaths,' she said wearily, 'but no, I could not kill them.'

'Does Dmitri know about this?'

'No! He knows nothing.'

Ruzsky looked out at the glow of the gas-lamps in the street. He thought of Ella's pretty face on the ice, then of the knife in Olga's eye, then of Maria risking her life to push him away from the Cossack's thundering hoofs. And he knew that, whatever she had done, his love for her was as fundamental and unyielding as his love for his son. He was bound to her. For the moment he did not wish to know more. 'What shall we do?' he asked. His heart ached for her. 'If I have found out the truth, then so will they. And when they do, they will kill you.'

'Yes.'

'Borodin still lives. Why have you not already—'

'I have tried, but he is unpredictable and suspicious. There was a meeting last night, and he was supposed to arrive with Olga, but he never came.'

'But you are certain he will be at the Kresty Crossing?' Ruzsky saw the flicker of recognition in her eyes. 'I will help you.'

'No.'

'I will do anything you ask of me.'

'You are your father's son. You are the chief investigator, and you believe in the old certainties, the old

Russia. You could never be an accomplice to murder.'

Ruzsky felt a knot in his stomach. He was desperate to deflect her. 'They must suspect you.'

'How could they? I was no more than a girl at the time of my parents' death. Soon after, I fled the unhappiness of my uncle's house and took another name. For all that anyone knows the young Maria Bulyatina might as well have been blown apart in that carriage.'

'Borodin will kill you. He must suspect—'

'But he does not. You have seen how he is with me.'

'And you will risk everything for this final act of revenge?'

'What is it that I risk, Sandro? What is it that I have?'

He smarted at her rebuke. 'I would do—'

'It is too, too late. It was too late a long time ago.'

'So you came to Petrovo to say goodbye?'

Maria did not answer.

'If I had not been married. If I had not turned away . . .'

'It was already too late for me, even then.'

Ruzsky pulled her gently towards him until her head rested upon his shoulder, and her legs were entwined with his. He held her face as the tears rolled down her cheeks. 'What can I do?' he asked.

Maria did not answer. He cradled her head on his shoulder and rocked her. 'It will be all right,' he whispered, but knew she did not believe him, and he wasn't sure he believed himself.

He was tortured by the image of Borodin covered in the young man's blood on that night at the factory, and of Maria bending before him to clean it from his clothes. Could she really defeat this man? 'This will consume you,' he murmured.

'Sandro . . . This is my fate. It has chosen me, but it is also the one I have chosen.'

'This man has dragged you into his world. He will extinguish all the light your family once created. Is this what your father would have wished for you?'

'Do not speak of my father.'

'To abandon your sister . . .'

'Do not speak of them, Sandro.'

'Don't leave Kitty to her fate.'

'Sandro, I beg you.'

'No, Maria. I beg *you*.' But he knew he had lost her. Maria's sacrifice was not wild and hasty, but considered. This was her fate. The passion they had shared at Petrovo had been fuelled by the urgency of the condemned. 'Please,' he whispered, his voice hoarse.

'You must let it run its course.'

'I cannot.'

'Nothing can change this, Sandro.'

She reached for him, her legs wrapped round his waist now, her cheek pressed to his. They touched each other with urgent desperation. Ruzsky kissed her cheeks, forehead, nose and eyes.

'Sandro,' she whispered, 'my Sandro. I'm so sorry.'

Ruzsky crushed her to him.

'I'm so sorry,' she said again. 'I would do anything for you, anything except this.'

Later, they stared at each other in the darkness of the hallway. Ruzsky knew he must leave, but could not. 'I will try to stop you,' he said.

'Then we may both pay a terrible price.'

'For my father's sake, for the sake of all that he

506

stood for, I cannot allow their plans to continue uninterrupted.'

Ruzsky could not take his eyes off her. He was hardly able to breathe.

'Goodbye, Sandro.'

Ruzsky walked out into the stairwell.

He faced her. He could not bring himself to say goodbye.

Slowly, without taking her eyes from his, Maria Bulyatina shut the door.

CHAPTER FIFTY-TWO

Ruzsky slept fully clothed in Michael's bed, and was awake long before dawn. He pulled back the tiny curtain. It was still snowing heavily, the gas-lamps dull orbs in a sea of swirling darkness. But Ruzsky could see the sled. Its occupant was still there, wrapped in blankets.

He checked his watch. It was almost six, Thursday, but he could not be certain of the date.

He walked across the hall. Dmitri had not returned. He searched the bedrooms on the lower floors for good measure, then took a few minutes to shave.

When he had finished, he climbed back to the top floor and walked slowly through the rooms. He wished to take leave of his childhood home today. He looked at his own room, then Ilya and Dmitri's. He went to his father's bedroom on the first floor.

Ruzsky stared at the carnations, which had begun to wilt, and surveyed his father's silver hairbrushes, neatly set out on the dresser. He felt like a ghost, drifting silently through a former life.

Then he went down to the telephone and asked the

508

operator to connect him to the Hôtel de l'Europe. 'Madame Ruzsky,' he said.

'What room number, sir?'

'I'm not certain.'

After a momentary delay, he was connected and a sleepy voice answered.

'Ingrid?'

'Sandro.'

'I'm sorry to wake you.'

'What is it, Sandro?'

'I just . . . wanted to check you were all right.'

'We're fine. Michael is still asleep.'

'Will you stay in the hotel today? I know it is hard, but if it is possible . . .'

'I'll do my best.'

'Just stay inside if you can.'

'Have you seen Dmitri?'

'No,' Ruzsky tried to sound untroubled, 'but I'm going to look for him now. There's something I need to talk to him about. He's probably staying in the barracks, or perhaps he's taken a room at the yacht club.'

'Of course.'

'Go back to sleep.'

'Goodbye, Sandro.'

Ruzsky went to fetch one of his father's thick woollen overcoats from the cloakroom and took a new sheepskin hat from the shelf. As he put them on, he glanced once more around the darkened hallway. His gaze rested on the scabbard that hung on the wall just inside the drawing-room door.

He hesitated only a moment more, then walked forward and out into the street, the front door slamming behind him.

It was snowing harder than ever. An Arctic wind chafed his ears as it whistled down from Palace Square. Ruzsky pulled down the flaps of his hat and began to walk, his eyes half closed against the driving snow. At this time and in this weather, the city was deserted; his only company was his pursuer.

Ruzsky deliberately walked through the Summer Garden, forcing the Okhrana man to leave the sled and follow him on foot.

At the iron gates to the main Preobrazhensky barracks opposite the Tavrichesky Garden, a sergeant in the guard box eyed him suspiciously. 'Yes?'

'I'm looking for Major Ruzsky.'

'At this time in the morning?' He was one of the old school. On his top lip, he sported a long, elegant moustache with fine waxed curls at its tips. He consulted his list. 'Not present.'

'Has he been here at all during the night?'

'Who is asking?'

'His brother, Alexander Ruzsky.'

'No.'

'Thank you, Sergeant.'

Ruzsky retraced his steps past the Summer Garden, along Millionaya Street and across the lonely expanse of Palace Square to St Isaac's, the Astoria, and finally the yacht club. It was the same story there. The doorman knew Dmitri well – they all did – but he had not seen him for several days.

Ruzsky checked his watch then continued on his cold, lonely walk down Morskaya, past the gilded window of the jeweller Fabergé, and the dusty premises of Watkins, the old English bookseller.

As he turned towards the Tsarskoe Selo station, he had almost forgotten that the man from the Okhrana was behind him, but when he looked round, he was only about twenty yards away. He had abandoned all pretence of concealment.

Outside the ornate gates of the Alexander Palace at Tsarskoe Selo little more than an hour later, Ruzsky pulled his coat tight around him. He was cold now, through to his core.

The palace grounds were deserted. The sentry had retreated to his box. In the building overlooking the gate, an officer of the palace police watched him.

Ruzsky had lost all feeling in his feet, and stamped hard in an effort to restore it. His welcoming committee was taking a damned long time.

At length, the guard instructed him to proceed. He pointed to the near corner of the palace. 'They are waiting,' he said.

Ruzsky began to walk, his head low against the wind.

Another uniformed guard was standing outside the large wooden doors to the family's private wing. He ushered Ruzsky up the steps and into the hall where he took off his hat, coat and gloves and tried unsuccessfully to prevent the snow falling on to the polished wooden floor. A footman removed them from his arm.

Colonel Shulgin strode down the corridor towards him. His face was like granite, but his eyes communicated a different message, Ruzsky thought, comradeship or compassion. 'Come this way, please,' he said, and led him to the antechamber. They sat down in a pair of upholstered chairs beneath the portrait of Marie Antoinette. Ruzsky had once been told that it hung over the Empress's desk.

Shulgin examined his hands. 'I'm sorry about your father,' he said, beneath his breath, staring dead ahead. 'I had not imagined . . .'

'I must speak with you.'

They heard footsteps from the direction of the Empress's private apartments. She swept into the room in a dark dress with a cream brooch. Shulgin and Ruzsky both stood up and bowed low.

The Empress waved them back to their seats, and took one opposite. She was about to speak when they heard a child's cry in the distance. She got up, then chose to ignore it and sat down again, smoothing the front of her dress.

There was another scream, a boy's, high-pitched and heartfelt. This time the Empress stood up and departed without a word.

Ruzsky listened to her rapid footsteps. 'Colonel Shulgin, I very much need to—'

'Later, Chief Investigator. Please bear in mind where you are.'

At length, the Empress returned. She offered neither explanation nor apology, and after they had repeated their bows and seated themselves once more, she stared at the floor. Ruzsky wondered if she was having difficulty remembering why he was there, or even who he was. A phrase from his father's letter echoed in his mind: *she has become quite unhinged . . .*

What struck him most was how tired she looked – in fact, more than tired. He himself was exhausted, and so, by the look of it, was Shulgin, but the Tsarina's fatigue was of a different nature. Her face and mouth were pinched, her eyes hollow. She gave the impression of having to exert a gigantic effort of will simply to articulate a question.

'You have not recovered . . .' she placed her head in her hand, as if having to steel herself to think straight '. . . you have not recovered the girl's possessions?'

Ruzsky did not answer. He could not imagine what he was supposed to say.

'The Chief Investigator is primarily conducting a murder investigation,' Shulgin said. Ruzsky noticed the tension in his voice and face. He wondered whether any of them had had any sleep.

The Empress did not appear to understand. She frowned heavily at Shulgin.

'This is the chief investigator, ma'am. Chief Investigator Ruzsky. He was assigned to investigate Ella's murder. Since then there have been two more victims.'

'But you have still not recovered her . . . possessions?'

Ruzsky stared at the Empress. He wondered if she was under the influence of a sedative. 'No, Your Majesty.'

'Then why have you come here?'

There was silence.

'You instructed me to summon him, ma'am,' Shulgin said. The strain in his voice was barely hidden now.

'He has not got to the bottom of it.'

'No, ma'am. He has not.'

They heard a soft patter of feet. Ruzsky caught his breath. For a moment he thought he'd seen a ghost. A girl with a shaven head, dressed in white, hovered in the doorway. It was the Grand Duchess Anastasia.

Ruzsky could not take his eyes off her. She looked pale and unwell. There were deep shadows under her eyes. It had been little more than ten days ago that he had seen her playing in front of the Alexander Palace with her brother and sisters, her long dark hair framing a face of exceptional beauty.

'Mama?' Anastasia came to her mother and whispered something to her.

The Empress hugged her. Then she released her daughter reluctantly. Anastasia smiled shyly at Ruzsky and Shulgin, then withdrew.

The Empress stood up and followed her.

'Measles?' Ruzsky whispered, pointing at his hair.

Shulgin nodded.

The minutes ticked by, but Shulgin did not meet Ruzsky's eye. 'Why am I here?' he asked.

'Because the Empress summoned you.'

'But why—'

'No reason is required, Chief Investigator.'

'May I be assured that you will speak to me when this audience is at an end?'

Shulgin sighed. 'Your father's death will be discussed at the Imperial Council tomorrow morning. In the meantime, I am empowered to offer my most profound condolences.'

They heard the Empress's footsteps. As she entered the room again, she appeared to be in pain.

She sat awkwardly, and looked at him. 'You have not found the girl's possessions?'

'I was not aware, Your Majesty, that we were looking—'

'So, you have not found them?'

Shulgin's eyes flashed a warning.

'No, Your Majesty,' Ruzsky said.

They endured another lengthy silence.

'Have you spoken to Mr Vasilyev?'

'On a number of occasions, Your Majesty.'

'You are working together on the case?'

'Together . . . yes.'

Shulgin leant forward. 'The chief investigator's father was the assistant minister of finance, ma'am, if you recall . . .'

'Yes,' she said.

Ruzsky waited for condolences to be offered, but the Empress continued to look straight through him.

'Very reliable family,' Shulgin added.

'Is that reliable in the general or specific sense?' she asked. 'As reliable as most of our reliable families?' The Empress glared at Shulgin, then turned her attention back to Ruzsky. She seemed more alert now. 'Your father met with an accident?'

Ruzsky hesitated. 'Yes.'

'I'm sorry for it.'

'That's kind of you, Your Majesty.'

'Does this mean you will give up on the case?'

'Of course not.'

Her expression became opaque once more. 'But you have not yet recovered any of the girl's possessions,' she said again.

'No, Your Majesty. We were not aware that any were missing.'

'Has he spoken to that filthy newspaper?' she snapped at Shulgin.

'No, ma'am. Vasilyev has taken care of that.'

'But they will not be publishing what the American took to them? We have a guarantee of that?'

'Yes.'

They heard another cry, fainter, but Ruzsky could see the son's pain mirrored in the mother. 'Yes,' she said, distracted. 'Well . . .'

Shulgin lowered his head and stared at the floor,

but not before Ruzsky had recognized the desperation in his eyes.

'I wish to be informed immediately you have recovered the girl's possessions. I wish this matter to be given the most urgent priority. I don't want to have to go through this again.' The Empress came to her feet.

Anastasia and one of her elder sisters were at the doorway. They stared silently, round-eyed, at the two men. As the Empress reached them, she placed her arms round their shoulders and ushered them gently from the room.

Shulgin sighed and got up. He muttered something under his breath, then led Ruzsky back down the corridor. All the doors were shut, but Ruzsky could still hear the boy's whimpering.

In the hallway, he accepted his coat.

'I'm sorry,' Shulgin said.

'The American took the material Ella stole to a newspaper?'

Shulgin glanced around to be sure they were alone. 'The *Bourse Gazette*. I'm sorry I brought you here, but she insisted.'

'I always had the impression that you and my father were old friends.'

Shulgin stared at him with hollow eyes. 'Your father knew too much, Sandro, and so do I.'

'As the minister responsible for the State Bank, he had to sign papers authorizing any movement of the gold reserves from the central vault?'

'If he told you that, he should not have done so.'

'He was reluctant to sign the papers?'

'I simply cannot discuss this. But he had his reservations.'

'Vasilyev persuaded you all that this was necessary?'

'Mr Vasilyev is in possession of much intimidating and unpleasant information. I needed little persuading of the seriousness of our predicament.' Shulgin glanced over his shoulder again, aware that he had raised his voice.

'So my father signed the papers?'

Shulgin avoided Ruzsky's eye, but he did not deny it.

'But he wanted to countermand his order? That was why he called the meeting with Vasilyev?'

'He did not telephone me before the meeting.'

'You must know that Vasilyev's intention was – is – robbery. He had assembled the group, of which Ella was a part, for precisely that purpose.'

'The group to which you refer has dedicated itself to creating great difficulties for the government and its servants, and in that, I may say, it has been successful, thanks largely to the activities of that misguided girl.'

'Vasilyev knew all of these people in Yalta. Borodin may appear to be their leader, but Vasilyev—'

'He has infiltrated the group most successfully, for which we should all be grateful.'

'He controls them.'

'He is able to provide substantial reports on their activities, which the Emperor, in particular, appreciates.'

'They're Vasilyev's creatures. I have seen the evidence with my own eyes.'

'Well, then, *present* it. I am not at liberty to *mistrust* a government colleague upon whose advice so much now rests.'

'He has convinced you that tomorrow will bring

517

revolutionary activity on such a scale that the regime's wealth must be put beyond the reach of the mob?'

'That is a matter upon which I cannot and must not comment.' There was a stubborn determination in Shulgin now.

'My father didn't trust him,' Ruzsky said.

'That's not a matter for me.'

'And neither do you.'

'I have no *choice*,' Shulgin hissed, his face close to Ruzsky's now, his eyes blazing. 'Publication of the material stolen from the Empress's private quarters would have the most damaging consequences.'

'What was stolen?'

'I cannot say. And do not press me. As the Empress has indicated, the details are not a matter for the city police.'

'She brought me here *only* to ask about her stolen possessions.'

'She is naturally concerned and, at times, confused, about to whom she has spoken, and to whom she has not.'

Ruzsky could see the futility of his task. 'Whatever Ella stole could be the final nail in the Romanov coffin,' he said. 'Or so Vasilyev has claimed. But my father realized what he really had in mind.'

'Good day, Chief Investigator.'

Ruzsky turned away, but as he did so, he glimpsed Shulgin's unguarded expression. He looked like a man who has felt someone walking across his grave.

CHAPTER FIFTY-THREE

The offices of the *Bourse Gazette* were close to Sennaya
Ploschad, in a nondescript grey building in a narrow
side-street. As the *droshky* driver dropped Ruzsky and
Pavel at the entrance, a black automobile drew to a
halt twenty yards away, on the opposite side of the
road. The surveillance had been stepped up.

A porter ushered them through the ground floor,
past a series of giant black printing presses to a steel
staircase that led up to the editor's office. As they
passed through the newsroom, the noise and bustle
fell away, and they were greeted with looks of
hostility. Ruzsky was glad of Pavel's robust company.

The editor was much younger than he had
expected, in his twenties or early thirties, with dark
hair that hung to his shoulders and a long, narrow
nose. He had bony hands, which he kept clasped
together in front of his face, and did not move as the
porter introduced them.

'How can we help you, gentlemen?'

There was a man behind him, standing in front of
a series of framed pages of the newspaper and a
photograph of a man Ruzsky took to be the proprietor.

Both wore the expression of carefully cultivated disdain he had come to expect from the Petrograd intelligentsia. Another slipped into the room behind them, a notebook and pen in his hand. He was even younger, and slouched in the corner, his manner deliberately disrespectful. 'I don't think we'll need the office-boy,' Ruzsky said.

'I demand that you do not threaten us.' The editor got to his feet.

'You *demand*?' Ruzsky said.

Pavel stepped forward, his manner conciliatory. 'We are conducting a criminal investigation.'

'And we are a newspaper,' the editor countered.

For a moment, nobody moved, then Pavel took a pace towards the young man, picked him up and threw him out of the room, then slammed the door. An overcoat hanging on the back fell to the floor.

'How dare—'

'Sit down,' Pavel ordered. The man did as he was told and glowered at them.

'I apologize for our ill-humour,' Ruzsky said, then seated himself. 'I am Chief Investigator Ruzsky,' he said. 'This is my deputy, Pavel Miliutin.'

The men stared at them.

'We are investigating a series of murders. You may recall that two bodies were found on the Neva on the first of January.'

'A series of murders?' the editor asked, his curiosity aroused.

'Yes.'

'The two bodies on the Neva?'

'And two more since.'

The men frowned.

'A man at the Lion Bridge with his head almost

severed about ten days ago, and a woman close to the Finland station yesterday.'

Ruzsky could see he had their attention now. 'An American came to see you,' Ruzsky went on, 'just before the first murders. His name was Robert White, although he may have used an alias.'

'Anyone who visits this office with information does so on a guarantee of anonymity.'

'He's dead.'

Pavel took the photographs from a folder under his arm and spread them out on the desk.

'This is the man who came to see you?' Ruzsky pointed at the American's corpse.

Neither man answered. They were transfixed by the photographs, which appeared to be having the desired effect.

'Whitewater,' the editor said quietly. 'That was the name he gave.'

'What did he want?' Pavel asked.

'He said he had some material that would be of interest to us.'

'What kind of material?'

'He didn't say.'

Ruzsky stared at them. 'Explosive is what I imagine he told you.'

'We have done nothing wrong,' the editor said.

'No one has suggested you have.'

The man looked at the photographs again. He pulled over the picture of the bodies on the Neva. 'Who is the girl?' he asked.

'You don't know her?'

He shook his head. He glanced at the photograph of the body at the Lion Bridge. 'Who was he?'

'His name was Markov. He was from Yalta.'

'From Yalta?'

'Yes. Both men and the woman at the Finland station were stabbed repeatedly. It's possible the murders had something to do with the material you were offered.'

Neither man met his eye.

'What was it?' Ruzsky asked.

Ruzsky could see that White had told them exactly what he had in his possession. 'It was revealing,' he went on. 'That's what he told you. Something revealing that related to the personal lives of the Imperial Family.'

The editor piled up the photographs and moved them to the other side of the desk, as if trying to distance himself from them. 'He said it was evidence we would wish to print.'

'Evidence?'

'Yes.'

'Of what?'

The editor shrugged. 'Of the corruption of the Romanovs.'

'What kind of evidence?'

'He was . . . vague about the detail.'

'Where did he say he had got this material?' Ruzsky asked.

'He didn't.'

'An American walks in alone, off the street, and promises you material such as this and you believe him?'

'He did not come in off the street. Nor was he alone.'

'He was with the girl?' Ruzsky pointed at the top photograph. 'With Ella?'

'Not with her.'

'Who, then?'

'I do not feel inclined to tell you.'

'Someone you knew?'

'Someone whose sympathies we know of.' The editor smiled. He had recovered his confidence. 'We wished to examine the material,' he said smugly. 'That was all.'

'What proof did they offer that it was genuine?'

'We did not get that far.'

'You were told that the material had been stolen?'

'It was intimated. But as you will understand, we did not wish to investigate that too closely until at least we had had sight of it.'

'You were told you could meet the woman who had acquired it?' Ruzsky asked. He leant forward and pointed at the picture of Ella's bloodied body on the ice. 'They told you this girl worked at Tsarskoe Selo from where the material you were promised was stolen?'

'Naturally we would have handed any stolen property to the police.'

'Naturally. You planned a private printing?'

Neither man answered.

'Why did they offer you this material?' Pavel said.

'They did not say.' The editor held his gaze.

'The American came with a man?'

'No.'

'A woman then. Did she give you her name?'

'I cannot disclose her identity.'

'The material was never delivered?' Ruzsky asked.

The editor shook his head.

'But you were expecting it?'

'The agreement was that it would be delivered today before eight.' The editor looked at the clock on the wall beside him. It had just gone three. 'And, upon verification, we'd print for tomorrow morning. I imagine your presence means it is unlikely we will receive it.'

'It was supposed to be delivered today?'

'That is correct.'

'You set a deadline?'

'No. The American was specific. He wanted the material on the streets late this evening or early tomorrow morning. Not before, not after.'

'Why?'

'No reason was given.'

Pavel and Ruzsky looked at each other. 'They must have given you some indication?'

The editor shook his head again.

'But you accepted their demand?'

'We accepted nothing.' The man leant forward. 'We promised what we needed to in order to gain access to the material. Naturally, once it was in our hands, the question of its distribution was for us.'

Ruzsky got to his feet. 'Thank you for your time,' he said.

They stopped in the lobby to light cigarettes. 'Vasilyev has been behind this from the start,' Ruzsky said. 'He put Ella up to the theft. Then he must have claimed that his intelligence was that a group of revolutionaries wished to publish it.' He began to walk out of the building. 'Let's go back to the office,' he said.

CHAPTER FIFTY-FOUR

Another crowd of protesters was streaming past the entrance to the city-police headquarters. To Ruzsky the demonstrations seemed to be getting bigger, but quieter. This one was led by a group of Tartar waiters carrying a banner demanding, 'Fair tips', and he might have laughed, but there was nothing amusing about the hunger he saw in every face. He glanced over his shoulder at the automobile that had pulled up behind them. Vasilyev's men were also distracted by the protest.

The last stragglers passed them and Ruzsky and Pavel crossed the road. Inside the building a constable stood between two men in handcuffs in front of the incident desk.

Ruzsky climbed the stairs fast, pulling away from Pavel. In the central area of the criminal-investigation division, he passed Maretsky, who stood at his own window, watching the march.

Another pile of papers had accumulated upon Ruzsky's desk, on top of which was a note from Veresov, headed 'Bodies on the Neva'.

Veresov had found no match for the fingerprints on

the dagger in their files so whoever the killer was he did not have a criminal record. It seemed to Ruzsky that the present uncertainty was seeping into every corner of the city.

He poked his head round Maretsky's door, ignoring the sporadic shouts from below. 'What about the knife?'

The little man's porcine eyes examined Ruzsky as though he was a stranger. 'I'm sorry?'

'The knife. The murder weapon.'

'Oh. Professor Egorov will be back tomorrow,' he said.

'I thought you said he was due to return today?'

'He has been delayed.' Maretsky faced the street again, and Ruzsky returned to his cubicle. Pavel was already there. He closed the door quietly and picked up the telephone. 'Could you put me through to the university?' he asked.

There was a long wait.

'Porter's lodge,' a voice answered.

'Might I speak to or leave a message for Professor Egorov.'

'Professor Egorov?'

'Yes.'

'We have no Professor Egorov.'

Ruzsky stared at Pavel, who stopped riffling through his own paperwork.

'Are you there?' the voice asked.

'Yes. You're sure?'

'Of course.'

'Thank you,' Ruzsky said.

The professor was sitting behind his desk, staring at his hands. He looked up at Ruzsky and closed his eyes. Ruzsky took a seat opposite and waited for an explanation.

'I admire you, Ruzsky,' Maretsky said quietly, opening his eyes again. 'You're honest, and you don't judge people.'

'That's not true.'

'You don't judge me.'

'Who am I to judge anyone?'

'Anton is a good man.'

Ruzsky did not see what he was getting at.

'He has tried to protect us. But they know everything that we do so it is hard for him.'

'I don't see—'

'We have to be careful what information we bring into the building, don't you see that?'

Ruzsky inclined his head.

'I gave the knife to a colleague. His name is not Egorov. I will take you to see him.' Maretsky put on his coat.

They crossed the bridge from Palace Embankment to Vasilevsky Island, where the cab turned left and slithered down towards the twelve colleges at the far end of the street. Ruzsky made a point of not checking whether they were being followed, but Maretsky could not restrain himself. 'It's all right, old man,' Pavel told him jovially, but Ruzsky heard the tension in his voice.

There were two black automobiles on their tail now.

They were not far from Ruzsky's dilapidated room here, but their surroundings could not have been more different. Built to house the government of Peter the Great at the foundation of St Petersburg, the beautiful red and white buildings of the twelve colleges had been taken over long ago by the university. Like so much of the landscape of the city, they had been designed to project the power and majesty of the Russian empire.

As the three climbed down from the *droshky*, the Okhrana's vehicles pulled up on the other side of the street. The still falling snow blurred the day's journey into night.

Maretsky led them through the stone archway and up to a long, cavernous corridor. They passed a handful of students wrapped up against the cold. He stopped, knocked once on a door to their right and opened it to usher them in.

Professor Egorov's *alter ego* was a tub of a man, with a drooping white moustache and steady, pale blue eyes. His dusty rooms gave the impression of someone rarely troubled by a world beyond its four walls, and Ruzsky envied him the tranquillity of his environment.

His question drew the response he'd expected: a heavy frown and a doleful glance at Maretsky. The professor knew immediately who he was. He emerged from behind his desk and produced the murder weapon from a drawer. He handed it to Ruzsky. 'It's Persian. The date suggests it was inscribed during a period of conflict over northern Azerbaijan, which lasted through 1812 and 1813.'

'What does it say?' Ruzsky asked.

'It bears the name of a Russian general.'

'Which one?'

The professor did not relish the question. 'Nicholas Nicholaevich Ruzsky. Your great-grandfather, I assume. Or a generation before?' He shook his head. 'It belongs to your father?'

Ruzsky returned to the corridor.

528

'Sandro,' Pavel said.

But Ruzsky walked rapidly away, eager for the cold night air to clear his head.

'Sandro, wait,' Pavel called after him, his voice echoing in the hallway. But Ruzsky did not stop.

CHAPTER FIFTY-FIVE

Snow swirled around the entrance to the house in Millionaya Street. Ruzsky had to knock three times before the door was answered. He was swept into the hall by a gust of air that scattered snow half-way up the stairs.

'It's a terrible night,' Peter told him.

'Is my brother here?'

'I believe so, yes, sir.'

Ruzsky removed his sheepskin hat and overcoat, dusted off the snow and handed them to the young servant. He began to climb the stairs. The upper part of the house was in darkness. He moved slowly through the shadows. He tried the room on the first floor where Ingrid and his brother were officially quartered, but it was empty.

He checked all the other bedrooms on the same level, including his father's, but there was no sign of anyone.

He returned to the centre of the landing. 'Dmitri?' He walked up the stairs to the second floor. 'Dmitri?'

He moved to the wooden steps that led to the attic and climbed them.

'Dmitri?'

He checked his own room – now Michael's – but it was empty, as was the one opposite. Ruzsky glanced at the toy soldier at the end of Ilya's bed and the elephant on the shelf above it.

As he emerged, he saw movement from the corner of his eye and spun round. Peter was at the bottom of the stairs. 'Your brother has just gone out, sir. He said you would know where to find him. "Where this began," he said.' The servant held up a small key. 'He asked me to give it to you.'

Downstairs, Ruzsky went to the far wall of his father's study, took down the painting and slipped the key into the lock of the safe. Alongside his mother's jewellery, he found large bundles of banknotes, some in roubles, some sterling, some American dollars. At the back of the safe was an envelope marked with the Imperial seal, his father's name and the instruction 'By hand'.

He went to the desk, opened the envelope and pulled out a thin sheaf of papers. Wrapped around them was a note with the Imperial eagle at its head.

Nicholasha, I enclose just some of what they have to offer. Vasilyev says he has been unable to recover the rest and may not be able to do so before Friday. The possibility of their publication on that day is still significant. I feel, therefore, that we must do as he suggests; perhaps not all of the gold reserves, but a significant proportion should be moved to the vault out here. He will need you to sign the order. We are considering all other options, but His Majesty will not consider recalling any further battalions.

Vasilyev says the movement of the gold should begin on Thursday night, before this information is broadcast in the city. The atmosphere here alternates between panic and denial, so I suggest, my old friend, that we act upon our own initiative – S.

Inside was a series of neat, handwritten notes that each began with the same instruction in the left-hand corner: 'For immediate transfer'.

2 December 1916. Povroskoe from Tsarskoe Selo for Novy. You have not written anything. I have missed you terribly. Come soon. Pray for Nicholas. Kisses – Darling.

Ruzsky put the first down on the desk. Povroskoe was a remote village in the Russian interior. It had been home to the peasant priest, Grigory Rasputin, who also went by the name Novy. Tsarskoe Selo meant the Alexander Palace and, by implication, the Empress.

They were messages for transcription by the tele-graph office from the Empress of All the Russias to a peasant priest.

9 April 1916. Povroskoe from Tsarskoe Selo for Novy. I am with you with all my heart, all my thoughts. Pray for me and Nicholas on the bright day. Love and kisses – Darling.

Ruzsky stared at the neat, careful hand.

He turned to the last note. This was an actual telegram, complete with the stamp of the Povroskoe office.

7 DECEMBER 1914 STOP FROM PETROGRAD FOR NOVY STOP
TODAY I SHALL BE BACK IN EIGHT DAYS STOP I SACRIFICE MY
HUSBAND AND MY HEART TO YOU STOP PRAY AND BLESS
STOP LOVE AND KISSES STOP DARLING

Ruzsky sat back in his father's chair.

He understood all too well the tension he had seen
in Shulgin's face. The rule of the Romanovs could not
possibly survive the publication of such material.

He put the documents back into the safe, locked it
and put the key into his pocket.

Lights from the upper floors of the Winter Palace
blazed defiantly into the gloom as Ruzsky stared out
at the frozen Neva. He saw a dark figure in the centre
of the ice. He hesitated for only a moment, then
stepped out and walked purposefully towards his
brother, blocking the old fear from his mind. The
marine police had placed no warning flags here, or
none that he could see.

Dmitri wore a long, dark blue regimental overcoat
and a sheepskin hat. His hands were thrust deep into
his pockets.

They stared at each other through the falling
snow.

'Don't try to stop me, Sandro.'

Ruzsky did not speak.

'Father is dead. You are absolved of your
responsibilities.'

'It's not about responsibility. It's about love.'

The word hung between them. Dmitri took off his
hat. 'Did you open the safe?'

'Yes.'

'You understand, then?'

'I do now.' Ruzsky wiped the snow from his eyes and face.

Dmitri lowered his head. He stared at his hat as the flakes gathered on his hair. Ruzsky thought he looked handsome in the darkness, and young – like the boy he remembered.

'I could have warned him,' Dmitri said, terrible guilt etched into his face – as it had been in Maria's last night. 'I knew they planned to steal the gold. I knew they had to trick Father to do it.'

'How could you know what threats they would make?' Ruzsky asked him. 'Or how far Vasilyev would go?' Ruzsky could not take his eyes from his brother's. What he saw there was a confused and tortured version of what he had seen in Maria's eyes the previous night: a swirling mixture of love, loss and regret. But it was guilt, above all, that swam to the surface. He had put his love for Maria and his desire to become the man he thought she wanted him to be above everything. Dmitri had watched his father walk into a trap and done nothing to prevent it closing around him, and it was tearing him apart.

Ruzsky thought of his brother's fear on the evening of Ilya's death as they awaited the summons to their father's study. He thought of the way they had held each other for comfort and strength. 'Dmitri,' he said quietly, 'let us go home.'

'I know how they must have threatened him,' Dmitri said. 'I know what happened at that meeting. Father wanted to countermand the order and cancel the movement of the gold and I know how Vasilyev threatened him. You saw the way Father looked at Michael. You know what was in his mind every time he glanced in his direction.'

'Michael is not Ilya.'

'But which one of us can look at him without—'

'That's not his fault.'

'It's no one's fault, Sandro! It never was.' Dmitri stared at the ice by his feet. 'But Father would have moved every mountain in Russia before he'd let anyone hurt a hair on the boy's head. He wasn't going to lose him twice.' His voice quivered. 'I didn't know what they would do. How could I have guessed?' The question was rhetorical and Ruzsky remained silent. 'Do you understand why, Sandro?'

'Do I understand?'

'Do you understand why?' Dmitri was pleading with him. 'She makes me feel as if I have come home at last. But the past hangs heavily upon her, and I can soothe her pain.'

'I understand.'

'I'm not a coward.'

'You don't have to prove anything to me.'

'She needs me. In this, at least, she needs me.'

'Did she ask you to kill them?'

'Once I knew what had happened, she did not need to.'

'She told you about her father?'

'What I am doing is only just, Sandro.'

'She has told you each name and where they can be found?'

'She is entitled to justice. She will not find it in any other way.'

'The couple on the ice were expecting you. The American and the girl, Ella. You had met them before?'

'Maria hated the American almost as much as she hates Borodin. She was sure the pair planned the murder of her father together. She convinced him the girl Ella was an informer for the city police and the army, and that their plan here was in danger of being discovered. He led the girl out on to the ice. He was expecting her to be despatched by an assassin on the far side, in the shadows of the fortress – that's what he'd been told. Maria begged me not to harm the girl, but I could hardly have left a living witness.'

'But you left your footsteps. Those last three paces up to the embankment were designed to taunt me.'

Dmitri stared at him. 'I knew you would find me, Sandro.'

'And you wanted me to.'

Dmitri did not answer.

'That's why you didn't go to the Strelka,' Ruzsky said, almost to himself. 'You left the ice to go home.' He looked at his brother. 'If he was here, Father would beg you to stop.'

'But he's not. He's dead, and that house is an empty shell, full of ghosts at every turn. I've had enough of ghosts. If I survive, we will leave Russia, begin again . . .'

'He would still beg you—'

'He would do no such thing. I was never you, Sandro. I was never Ilusha. I was the son he didn't understand. I was the one for whom he could never conceal his disdain.'

'Dmitri—'

'Though you will deny it, it is true. But he can't reach me now. I have found a purpose that I have long searched for.'

'Then it is I who must beg you,' Ruzsky said. 'And I plead with you on my knees.'

Dmitri looked at him, his anger melting into sorrow and regret. 'I'm sorry, Sandro. This is all I have to give her.'

'I cannot lose you.' Ruzsky's voice was unsteady. 'Don't you see that?' He took a step towards his brother.

'I understand.' Dmitri shook his head, as if to rid himself of his dilemma. 'I understand, Sandro, but I must go.'

'Dmitri, I beg you . . .'

'Don't try to stop me.'

'In God's name—' Ruzsky's cry was taken by the wind.

'Stay there, Sandro!' Dmitri turned away and began to run.

'Dmitri!'

Ruzsky lunged forward, lost his footing, and crashed straight through the ice into the darkness below. The cold was savage, expelling the air from his lungs.

He bobbed up against a solid wall. He gasped, but took in only water and choked. He kicked down, searching for a sign of light, the blood roaring in his ears.

For a moment, these brutal surroundings were familiar. He recognized this place. He remembered welcoming its oblivion once before. But in his mind's eye he could see his brother walking across the ice to his fate. He could not let him die alone. He began to kick, his lungs stretched, the cold numbing every fibre of him. He saw ripples on the surface of the water.

Lungs exploding, he pushed upwards until he burst through the hole.

A hand grasped his.

A man was stooped over him and it took Ruzsky a few moments to recognize who it was. 'Pavel?' he asked.

'Be quiet,' the voice hissed. 'Save your energy.'

CHAPTER FIFTY-SIX

When Ruzsky opened his eyes again, Pavel was bending over him, and he could see Katya and Peter looking anxiously over his shoulder. He was in dry clothes, but he was chilled to the marrow. He was lying on the floor of the drawing room in Millionaya Street, next to a roaring fire, the side lamps lit.

Ruzsky heard Katya whisper something to Peter and they left him alone with his deputy. Pavel moved back to the long white sofa.

Ruzsky looked up at the ornate cornices of the ceiling and the low chandelier, then across to the oil of the mountains of the Hindu Kush and the curved sabre that hung alongside it. He grasped for the familiar in a world that was growing ever more remote. 'You've been following me,' he whispered quietly. 'You've been watching me from the start.' He did not want to look at Pavel: he didn't want to see the guilt and regret he would find there. He had experienced too much of both. 'They must have threatened Tonya, or your boy.'

They were silent. Ruzsky listened to the crackle of the fire.

'They didn't have to,' Pavel said. 'It's been clear how the land lies for a long time. Only you refused to see it.'

Ruzsky closed his eyes again. Pavel's face merged in his mind with Dmitri's. He thought of his brother's solitary progress across the ice, and of the guilt that haunted his every waking moment. He thought of his father's body sprawled across the floor of the study. They could have anyone. They could destroy everything. 'I understand, Pavel.'

'No, you would never understand.'

There was a long silence.

'You work for Vasilyev alone? Not Borodin and his group?'

'We all work for Vasilyev.'

'In Yalta they tried to kill us both.'

'It was a warning. You were to be allowed to pursue the murder case – after all, Vasilyev, more than anyone, wished to know who was killing his men – but you were not to uncover the link between him and the revolutionaries. And in Yalta you did. The bomb was an attempt to warn you off, but the young fool was incompetent and that's why he nearly killed us.'

Pavel stared at him mournfully.

'In your own way, you were trying to protect me,' Ruzsky said. 'You thought that if you watched me and reported back all that we were doing, they'd have no need to dispose of me. Isn't that so?'

'Even if it was, it would not exonerate me.'

Ruzsky looked at his friend. 'For Christ's sake, you do not have to seek *my* forgiveness. What have *I* done that is of any benefit to anyone?'

'You have caused Vasilyev some discomfort.' Pavel examined his hands. 'He wanted to find out who was

539

killing his creatures, but he did not want you to know what they were doing.' He looked up. 'He could not decide what to do with you.'

Ruzsky heard the regret in Pavel's voice and saw it in his eyes. His heart sank. Their friendship was destroyed and they both knew it. The consequences of this betrayal outran even a complete understanding of the motives for it. 'I'm sorry,' Ruzsky said.

'I deserve no pity.'

'And should feel no shame. There is no one left to serve. Each of us must find his own way through. I didn't understand that before. I do now.' Ruzsky pulled back the blankets and forced himself upright. His head exploded with pain.

'If you go out there, they will kill you.'

'I have no choice.'

'It is too late. The gold is already being loaded at the Tsarskoe Selo station. There is nothing you can do.'

'I cannot leave him. He is my brother.'

'If that is his destination, then all you will achieve is to die together.'

'But I cannot abandon him to his fate.' Ruzsky looked at his partner. 'Do they know he is coming?'

Pavel shook his head.

'Will Maretsky tell them about the knife?'

'He would not help them.'

'I ask only for a chance, Pavel.'

The big detective straightened, his eyes never leaving Ruzsky's. 'Of course, my friend. I will ask them to prepare a sled.'

A few minutes later, Ruzsky opened the door and stepped out into the night. A plain sled had been prepared, without the family's livery. A servant was wrapped up in the driving seat and the horses shifted quietly in the wind. Pavel was waiting for him in the darkness.

Ruzsky climbed into the back, and looked into the face of his deputy. 'You are too late to reach the crossing,' Pavel said. 'Try to get on to the train.'

Ruzsky offered him his hand. Pavel took it cautiously. 'Good luck, my friend,' he whispered. 'There will be many of them.'

The sled pulled away.

As Ruzsky looked back, he saw that Pavel was still watching him, his big body framed by the light of the doorway.

CHAPTER FIFTY-SEVEN

Okhrana men in long black overcoats had sealed off the Tsarskoe Selo station and were standing in a ring around its entrance in the darkness. It was still snowing heavily, and Ruzsky ducked his head and walked past them towards Sadovaya Ulitsa.

He had left the sled some distance away and told the servant to return home.

Fifty yards on, he stopped and looked back to check that he was out of sight. He reached up for the wooden fence next to the road. It took all his strength to lever himself over it and into a snowdrift three or four feet deep that had gathered on the far side. For a moment, he was lost in the powder, crystals of ice in his eyes, mouth and ears.

He fought his way through it until he stumbled and fell on to an icy pathway. He picked himself up and brushed the snow weakly from his clothes. There were no lights on in the two sheds ahead, but he could see sparks from a brazier spitting into the night sky. The coal fire stood in a small clearing. Ruzsky moved forward to warm himself, standing so close that sparks gathered on his clothes.

He heard voices and slipped into the nearest shed. It was dark and smelt of oil. Bits of machinery – winches, old signal posts, hammers and wrenches – hung from the ceiling alongside rows of guards' flags. Ruzsky shut the door and waited until the men had passed. They were talking quietly among themselves, and he could smell the pungent aroma of their tobacco.

He took the Sauvage revolver from inside his jacket and checked that there was ammunition in its chambers. He wasn't certain if it would still fire after being bathed in the frozen waters of the Neva, but he replaced it and stepped outside. He walked to the far end of the shed, crouched down and looked towards the station.

The snout of an armoured train, of the kind used to transport heavy fighting equipment to the front, poked out beyond the shelter of the glass and iron roof above the concourse. Across the track, through the snowstorm, Ruzsky could see a group of men standing guard. Above the engine, the Tsar's personal flag flapped in the wind.

To Ruzsky's left, there was a large mound of discarded equipment covered with snow. He waded through another thick drift to reach it. He felt his body temperature plunge once more, his hands icy as he touched an old piece of track and clawed his way up it so that he had a view of the station concourse. He was close to the platform where he and Pavel had boarded the train to Tsarskoe Selo.

Behind the huge black engine were four or five goods wagons with their doors open. Through a cloud of steam, Ruzsky could discern figures on the platform. Four men wheeled a trolley down towards one of the wagons and unloaded its contents. The gold bars shimmered in the light of the gas-lamps.

Ruzsky could make out Prokopiev, who was several inches taller than the group of agents around him. The Okhrana deputy threw his cigarette into the night, then he and two colleagues strolled towards the engine and climbed in.

Ruzsky watched the last of the gold being loaded. A man got into the carriage and another slammed its door. The other two wheeled the trolley back towards the station entrance.

The engine wheezed and hissed. A cloud of steam curled round the corner of the roof and was lost in the swirling snow.

Ruzsky stood up and caught sight of two guards right in front of him, not ten yards away. He cursed silently and dropped down, his heart pounding. He raised his head slowly. The men had not seen him. They, too, were watching what was happening on the platform. They walked round to his right, blocking his departure.

There was a series of shouts. The engine let off a loud hiss of steam, then turned its wheels once, shunting the carriages forward.

More men appeared on the platform.

Prokopiev stuck his head out of the side of the engine and looked back at the carriages. 'All right!' he called. 'It's ready!'

The train shunted forward once more, but still did not pull away.

The two guards were still standing between Ruzsky and the train.

The engine blew off another head of steam, shunted forward and this time kept moving, its great iron wheels grinding their way along the track.

The guards watched its departure, then moved away.

Ruzsky edged forward. No one was visible at the rear of the train. The Okhrana men inside were behind closed doors and those in the armoured engine had ducked down to avoid the blizzard.

The train gathered speed. As the last wagon drew level, Ruzsky began to run. He slipped once, picked himself up and waded through to the path. Out on the track, the snow drove hard into his face and mouth.

He heard shouts behind him and what sounded like a shot, but the train was moving at the pace of a run now and his eyes were on the great iron bar at the rear of the last car.

He reached it, took hold of it, but was almost pulled off his feet. He grunted and jumped. He was half up on the ledge, one leg trailing along the ground. He pushed himself forward. Another shot rang out and he looked up to see the two guards down on one knee, their rifles pointing towards him, but the train roared on, and their bullets were lost in the darkness.

When he could no longer see the station, Ruzsky pulled himself upright and climbed the stepladder to the iron roof of the carriage. The snow whipped into his face, and the night groaned and howled around him. Flat on his stomach, almost unable to see, he clawed his way slowly forward. He reached the end of the carriage and slipped down into the gap, then climbed up to the next. He repeated the exercise until he was only a few yards short of the engine.

They were out of the city now, the landscape a brilliant white. Occasionally Ruzsky looked ahead, but all he could see was the Tsar's yellow and black flag snapping in the wind.

CHAPTER FIFTY-EIGHT

The train slowed.

Ruzsky pushed himself on to his knees. The snow had stopped and the moon cut through thinning clouds to leave slivers of light dancing over an indifferent landscape. They were coming down a slight incline, and ahead Ruzsky could see a road that ran through the middle of the wood and up to the edge of the track. It had been recently cleared. A large military truck was parked across the line. The train jolted as the brakes were applied, almost sending him tumbling over the lip of the carriage. It came slowly to a halt less than ten yards from the obstacle. Ruzsky kept low, but the only sound was the wheezing of the engine.

Ahead, he saw two Okhrana men walking towards the truck. He heard a shouted command, but there was no response. The men looked about them.

The engine grew quieter. The forest around it was still.

One of the men moved up to the rear of the truck, a revolver in his hand. He wore a black fedora, which spun high into the air as his body slumped to the ground, the powder lifting around him as the snow cushioned his fall.

For a second, there was no reaction, even from his companion. Then the second man turned, his own hat falling in his haste. He got no more than a yard before the air was filled with the crack and whistle of rifle shots. Dark figures emerged from the woods, charging towards the carriages. There were shouts, doors banging, more shouts, screams, then the dull pop of shots muffled by the wood.

Vasilyev was sacrificing his own men in the interests of staging an authentic robbery.

Then all was still once more.

Ruzsky heard the roar of the truck being started and watched a line of headlights swing through the wood from down the lane. The convoy wound its way down to the crossing.

On the far side of the track, the road ran straight up a hill. Halfway up it, in the moonlight, Ruzsky could make out Borodin and Maria. She was not wearing a hat and her long hair was swept back from her face, as if she wanted to be recognized. Despite her height and slender grace, she seemed frail alongside him.

There was a hiss of steam, then an eerie silence.

Ruzsky listened to the clank and whimper of the engine.

There was a shout. 'I have him!'

All of the men in the clearing moved at once. Figures swarmed from the shadows. There was a shot, then another. Borodin turned in the direction of the confrontation, but Maria continued to stare straight ahead.

Ruzsky heard a distant cry. His heart was pounding. Had they been waiting for him? He saw Dmitri being led over the brow of the hill.

He pushed himself up, fumbling for his revolver, and as he did so, he felt the cold metal of a gun barrel on the back of his neck. 'Good evening, Chief Investigator,' Prokopiev said. 'Time to join us.'

Ruzsky put down his revolver. 'Don't hurt him,' he said.

'We'll see.'

'Don't hurt him.'

He saw the tension in Prokopiev's face. '*Get down.*'

Ruzsky swung round and jumped into the drift beside the crossing. He walked forward.

Dmitri turned, his face white. He was ringed by men in long overcoats, their rifles and revolvers pointed unerringly at him. There was fear in his eyes, such as Ruzsky had only ever seen in the eyes of condemned prisoners before they were led to execution. He took his brother's hand.

Dmitri fell into his arms and Ruzsky held him tightly. For a moment they were thousands of miles away, far from the harsh-faced men who surrounded them, clutching each other on the top floor of the house at Petrovo.

Ruzsky looked up to see Michael Borodin striding towards them. He saw no shred of humanity in the man's eyes.

Borodin pulled them apart. He kicked Ruzsky and forced him to his knees. 'Mr Khabarin,' he said.

Ruzsky stared at Maria.

'Your Russia is dead, Prince Ruzsky,' Borodin said. He cocked his revolver. 'And your kind will soon be finished. You understand that, don't you?'

Ruzsky listened to the last gasps of the steam engine. Maria's expression was one of infinite sadness, as if she was reaching out to him but could never touch him again.

He felt the cold metal of Borodin's revolver at the back of his skull, but did not flinch. He mumbled a prayer. He thought of his father's smile in the hallway of the house on Millionaya Street and Michael pounding through the snow into his arms.

The world around him was out of focus. All he could hear was his own breathing. He kept his eyes on Maria.

Dmitri moved, a blur on the periphery of Ruzsky's vision. He got only a yard towards Borodin before the revolutionary fired a single shot through his forehead. His body crumpled and fell.

The clearing was still. Maria had taken a pace towards them.

Ruzsky crossed himself. He waited. He closed his eyes.

'There was no need for him to die,' Borodin whispered, his mouth close to Ruzsky's ear. 'She wanted you both to live. That was the trade.'

Ruzsky looked up at Maria. Her sadness was not for him, but for herself, he saw. She had come to say goodbye. He heard the snort of a horse and the bells on a sleigh.

'Start walking, get in and go away,' Borodin said. 'Turn and you'll regret it.'

Ruzsky did not move.

'She has paid for your freedom. Better take it before I change my mind.'

Ruzsky stared, transfixed, at Michael's tiny figure beyond the crossing. Ingrid sat next to him, two Okhrana agents on either side of them, their guns pointed towards him. He looked down at the body of his brother sprawled in the snow.

'Don't you want to know what she thinks you're worth?'

Ruzsky kept his eyes on his son.

'She has offered what only a woman can give. She sent your brother to kill me, but when she understood that she could not stop you trying to save him, she traded her own freedom in order to keep *you* alive. How about that?'

Ruzsky could not think.

'I would start walking, Prince Ruzsky.' Borodin leant closer, his breath warm against Ruzsky's ear. 'Or perhaps you think she can escape.

'We had a telegram from the local police in Yalta. They found out that a very clever chief investigator went to see a girl in a sanatorium. So I think I will have them both.'

Ruzsky's head pounded. His mind screamed at him to turn round.

'Start walking, Mr Khabarin, and don't look at her again or none of you will leave this clearing.'

Ruzsky looked at the guards towering over his son. He began to walk, concentrating on the sound of his boots in the snow.

The Okhrana men watched him approach.

He walked through the quiet of the Russian forest.

He could feel her eyes upon his back. Ahead, he saw that Michael was crying, and his son's tears triggered his own. 'It will be all right, my boy,' he said.

As he crossed the tracks, Ruzsky whispered, 'I'm sorry.'

He climbed into the sled and took his son into his arms. The driver cracked his whip and the sled jerked forward.

As it climbed the hill, Ruzsky could resist no longer. He turned and saw her standing alone in the clearing, watching him.

She did not move. Her eyes were fixed upon him until she disappeared from view.

THE END

AUTHOR'S NOTE

The February revolution in Russia broke out little more than a month after the end of this novel. It began with protests over food shortages and escalated rapidly as it became clear that the regime could no longer rely upon the loyalty of large sections of the armed forces. The fictional Dmitri had many real-life counterparts who were well aware of the dangers of having the capital's barracks full of reservists. Had the Tsar kept some of his better soldiers in Petrograd, revolution might have been averted.

After the revolution, the Tsar was forced to abdicate. He tried to do so in favour of his young son, but soon realized this would mean that they would be separated. For all his many faults, there is little doubt Nicholas II adored his family. Instead he handed the throne to his brother, Michael. However, Michael was soon forced to concede that there was no place in the new Russia for a Romanov tsar.

Lenin and many other revolutionaries returned from exile immediately after Nicholas's abdication, but it seemed for a while as if a liberal, democratic

Russia might emerge. However, a second revolution in October – a coup, in fact – left the Bolsheviks in charge, with drastic consequences. As many contemporaries predicted, the removal of Nicholas II led to a period of great suffering for all Russians. A stubborn man who had resisted all reform ended up pushing his people into a catastrophe.

This novel is not history, but I have striven to recreate the atmosphere of the time and to be accurate in all possible details. The telegrams quoted in the final stages of the book are genuine, though it is most unlikely that the Tsarina had a physical affair with Grigory Rasputin. Lonely, desperate and half mad, Alexandra clung to the peasant priest spiritually, but the idea that the two could have become lovers still seems preposterous, even if it was believed by many contemporaries.

Anyone wishing to explore this extraordinary story further should read Edvard Radzinsky's *Rasputin, The Last Word* or *Alexandra, The Last Tsarina* by Carolly Erickson. The best contemporaneous account of the old regime is *Once a Grand Duke*, by Grand Duke Alexander, and the most complete and scholarly study of the revolution is *A People's Tragedy* by Orlando Figes. I would also recommend *Michael and Natasha* by Rosemary and Donald Crawford, the story of the doomed love affair between Grand Duke Michael, brother of Nicholas II, and a divorcee.

Those wishing to take their research a stage further should go to a library and try to get hold of a copy of the memoirs of the French ambassador to Petrograd, Maurice Paleologue, which provide a fascinating day-by-day account of the onset of revolution.

The Imperial Family and many other members of Russia's former élite were, of course, executed by the Bolsheviks. The St Petersburg of today is still full of reminders of a world that disappeared with them.

THE MASTER OF RAIN
by Tom Bradby

'An immensely atmospheric, gripping detective story with just the right mixture of exoticism, violence and romance'
The Times

Shanghai. 1926. Exotic, sexually liberated and pulsing with life, it is a place and a time where anything seems possible. For policeman Richard Field, it represents a brave new world away from the past he is trying to escape. His first moment of active duty is the brutal and sadistic murder of a young White Russian woman, Lena Orlov. The key to the investigation seems to be Lena's neighbour, Natasha Medvedev. But can he really trust someone for whom self-preservation is the only goal?

With the International police force riven with rivalries, it is soon clear that Field must make his own way through the investigation. And in a city where reality is a dangerous luxury, Field is driven into the darkness beyond the dazzle of society to a world where everything has its price and the truth seems certain to be a fatal commodity. . .

'Nigh on impossible to put down . . . this intelligent thriller brings Shanghai to life as *Gorky Park* did for Moscow'
Time Out

'Rich, dark, atmospheric, this fine novel captures time and place perfectly. A great crime story that ends up in a place you won't predict'
Lee Child

'The atmosphere and menace of Twenties Shanghai are brought to vivid life as the backdrop to this gripping tale'
Daily Mail

'*The Master of Rain* is that rare thing: a truly epic crime novel, brilliantly researched and superbly executed'
John Connolly

'Does for Shanghai what Raymond Chandler did for Los Angeles – stylish and cool – debauchery at its most elegant'
TIME magazine

0 552 14746 X

THE SLEEP OF THE DEAD
by Tom Bradby

The brutal murder of Sarah Ford and the disappearance of her six-year-old daughter, Alice, shattered the rural serenity of Julia Havilland's childhood. But these are not the only scars that have resolutely refused to heal. Shortly afterwards, Colonel Mitchell Havilland sacrificed himself on a Falklands hillside in an act of characteristic – but baffling – heroism. When Julia comes home from China fifteen years later, it is to a place of ghosts.

Whilst she awaits the outcome of the enquiry that seems destined to end her short but spectacular career in military intelligence, Julia is drawn back across the landscape of the past, to find that it is not just the tortured image of her much-loved father that returns to haunt her. Everything she has ever believed in and lived for has suddenly been called into question, and unless she confronts her demons, she will not survive. For there have been other deaths, and the dead will not sleep. . .

'Lives up to the promise of its remarkable predecessor, *Shadow Dancer* . . . confirms Bradby's considerable promise as a thriller writer'
Daily Mail

'A race-against-the-clock thriller and a complex psychological drama'
Irish Independent

'Every bit as assured as its predecessor . . . an exemplary psychological thriller and a novel of character'
Crime Time

'Intriguing and emotive, this is a slow builder that proves to be well worth the wait'
The Mirror

0 552 14587 4

SHADOW DANCER
by Tom Bradby

'Taut, purposeful and above all else human . . . a compelling story of love and torn loyalties . . . Exceptional'
Daily Telegraph

Colette McVeigh: widow . . . mother . . . terrorist. A woman who has lived the Republican cause for all of her 29 years. A woman whose bothers are both heavily involved at senior levels in the IRA, whose husband was killed by the British security forces. A woman who is now an informer for MI5.

Apprehended by the police in an aborted bombing attempt in London, Colette is given two choices: talk and see her children again or stay silent and spend the rest of her life watching them grow up from behind the bars of a prison cell.

Unwillingly she is led to betray her past by her young MI5 handler, David Ryan, who always knew where his loyalties lay. But when he follows Colette across the Irish Sea to Belfast, the values are quickly sacrificed on the pyre of the province's history. And, as he watches Colette put herself in increasing danger to keep her side of the bargain, he realises that his professional integrity is irrevocably and fatally compromised. . .

'A remarkable first novel . . . Bradby handles the tension with skill to produce a gripping tale'
The Times

'The best book on the northern conflict since *Harry's Game* . . . An excellent read on any level'
Irish Independent

0 552 14586 6

DAYS WITHOUT NUMBER
by Robert Goddard

Michael Paleologus, retired archaeologist and supposed descendant of the last Emperors of Byzantium, lives alone in a remote and rambling house in Cornwall. His son, Nicholas, is summoned to resolve a dispute which threatens to set his brothers and sisters against their aged and irascible father. An overly generous offer has been made for the house, but Michael refuses to sell.

Only after the stalemate is tragically broken do Nick and his siblings discover why their father was bound at all costs to reject the offer. Their desperate efforts to conceal the truth drag them into a deadly conflict with an unseen enemy, who seems as determined to force them into a confrontation with their family's past as he is to conceal his own identity.

Nick realizes that the only way to escape from the trap their persecutor has set for them is to hunt him down, wherever – and whoever – he may be. But the hunt involves excavating a terrible secret from their father's past. And, once that secret is known, nothing will ever be the same again.

0 552 14878 4

A SELECTED LIST OF FINE WRITING AVAILABLE FROM CORGI BOOKS

14783 4	CRY OF THE PANTHER	Adam Armstrong	£5.99
14812 1	SONG OF THE SOUND	Adam Armstrong	£5.99
14667 6	DEADLINE	Campbell Armstrong	£5.99
14586 6	SHADOW DANCER	Tom Bradby	£5.99
14587 4	THE SLEEP OF THE DEAD	Tom Bradby	£5.99
14746 X	THE MASTER OF RAIN	Tom Bradby	£6.99
14919 5	DECEPTION POINT	Dan Brown	£6.99
15073 8	ANGELS AND DEMONS	Dan Brown	£6.99
14578 5	THE MIRACLE STRAIN	Michael Cordy	£5.99
14604 8	CRIME ZERO	Michael Cordy	£5.99
14738 9	THE SMOKE JUMPER	Nicholas Evans	£6.99
13991 2	ICON	Frederick Forsyth	£6.99
14923 3	THE VETERAN	Frederick Forsyth	£6.99
14877 6	DYING TO TELL	Robert Goddard	£6.99
14878 4	DAYS WITHOUT NUMBER	Robert Goddard	£6.99
13678 6	THE EVENING NEWS	Arthur Hailey	£5.99
14376 6	DETECTIVE	Arthur Hailey	£5.99
14901 2	WALLS OF SILENCE	Philip Jolowicz	£6.99
15021 5	THE ANALYST	John Katzenbach	£6.99
14970 5	THE BUSINESS OF DYING	Simon Kernick	£6.99
14584 X	THE COLD CALLING	Will Kingdom	£5.99
14585 8	MEAN SPIRIT	Will Kingdom	£5.99
14870 9	DANGEROUS DATA	Adam Lury & Simon Gibson	£6.99
14966 7	BLOOD DATA	Adam Lury & Simon Gibson	£6.99
07583 3	NO MEAN CITY	A. McArthur & H. Kingsley Long	£5.99
14798 2	LAST LIGHT	Andy McNab	£6.99
14799 0	LIBERATION DAY	Andy McNab	£6.99
14666 8	HOLDING THE ZERO	Gerald Seymour	£6.99
14816 4	THE UNTOUCHABLE	Gerald Seymour	£6.99
14391 X	A SIMPLE PLAN	Scott Smith	£5.99
10565 1	TRINITY	Leon Uris	£6.99